THE WARD

S.L. Grey is a collaboration between Sarah Lotz and
Louis Greenberg. Based in Cape Town, Sarah writes
crime novels under her own name, and as Lily Herne
she and her daughter Savannah Lotz write the
Deadlands series of zombie novels for young adults.
Louis is a Johannesburg-based fiction writer and editor
who worked in the book trade for many years. He has
a Master's degree in vampire fiction and a doctorate in
post-religious apocalyptic fiction.

THE WARD

S.L. GREY

CORVUS

First published in trade paperback in Great Britain
in 2012 by Corvus, an imprint of Atlantic Books Ltd.

10 9 8 7 6 5 4 3

A CIP catalogue record for this book is available
from the British Library.

Paperback ISBN: 978 0 85789 586 8
E-book ISBN: 978 0 85789 587 5

Printed and bound by CPI Group (UK) Ltd, Croydon, CR0 4YY

Corvus
An imprint of Atlantic Books Ltd
Ormond House
26-27 Boswell Street
London WC1N 3JZ

www.corvus-books.co.uk

S.L. Grey thanks: Lauren Beukes, Rina Gill, Mike Grant, Adam Greenberg, Sam Greenberg, Bronwyn Harris, Sarah Holtshausen, Savannah Lotz, Charlie Martins, Helen Moffett, Oliver Munson, Sara O'Keeffe, Laura Palmer, Lucy Ridout, Becci Sharpe, Alan and Carol Walters, Maddie West, Naomi Wicks and Sam Wilson.

PART 1 >>

chapter 1

FARRELL

I can't see.

I try again. Open my eyes.

Nothing.

Or rather, when I open my eyes there's a shear of pain which might be light if I could see. But I can't see and the light goes straight into my cortex and becomes pain.

This can't be happening to me. I turn my head away from the doorway, and try to make the rest of my body follow, but it's heavy and it takes all my effort to budge. When I do manage to twist my legs and arms over, there's a rip in my right arm and a pinch and pull on my dick. I stay where I am, squeezing my eyelids closed, panting, head pressed against something hard and cold.

Someone grabs my sore arm and shoves it off my side with an impatient tut, and pulls at something embedded in the soft skin in the crook of my elbow. I try to move my fingers but my hand is bandaged. I smell sweat, bad breath, something medicinal, the reek of burned stew. Something's clamped onto my finger, then there's a liquid slosh and a rustle of cardboard or plastic. Finally the pain in my eyes recedes with a flash. Now I recognise it: somebody's turned off the light.

Where am I? I open my eyes again, but I only see darkness for a second before the acid burn returns. I close my eyes and feel around with my left hand. Sheets, narrow mattress with a metal rail. Tape in the crook of my right arm, a narrow tube leading upwards. Muffled rattling sounds and beeps from outside, loud conversation, crying, a resigned moaning.

I'm in a hospital.

Where's my iPhone? It's an effort to pat down my body to check my pockets but I realise I'm wearing a short gown, tied loosely at the back. Where did I leave my camera? Where the fuck's my stuff?

Hospital beds have call buttons, right? I feel along the cold edges of the bed – nothing – then probe my unbandaged left hand into the space beyond it. On my left, some sort of cabinet. On my right, nothing until the drip tube stretches and tugs at my vein. I try not to imagine a void, but the vertigo makes me want to vomit. I clutch my hands over my chest for a few minutes until the panic subsides. I feel behind me. Blank wall, then a plastic plate of some sort. I finger it for the call button until I realise it's an electrical socket.

Fuck. What kind of a moron built this place?

Christ, I need my phone. How did I get here? What happened to me? I don't feel like I've broken anything. I don't feel any serious pain, except for my eyes when I try to open them. But I'm weak, and moving hurts. 'Hello?' I call. 'Hello?' My voice is too feeble. I try to knock my knuckles on the bed's railing. Nobody comes.

I close my eyes. I draft a MindRead post in my head. 140 characters or less. **MRers, help. Pls check my FindMe app and report back. Don't know where I am.**

I'm sure if I crowdsourced this problem one of my followers would help me out in minutes. But then again, if I could get online to post the problem I wouldn't need to crowdsource the fucking solution in the first place.

I could just call Katya. She'd take my call, even after what happened. I could use the hospital's phone. But I don't even have the strength to turn over, let alone walk around looking for a phone. Oh yeah, and I can't see to look for a phone. And nobody can hear me fucking calling. Jesus Christ!

This would be funny if it wasn't happening to me.

'Hello? Hello?'

Come to think of it, what *did* happen with Katya? I know *something* happened, but, when I try to think about it directly, it's like I've got a blind spot. All I have in my head is this still of her leaving, crying. That doesn't help. She's done that a few times before.

But I didn't do anything to hurt her, not that I can remember. What the fuck *happened*? Did Glenn do this? Where am I? And what's wrong with me?

Maybe Glenn thought I cheated on Katya or something. That would give him the excuse he needed. Maybe Katya told him that. But she'd never do that if it wasn't true. She loves me.

Oh Jesus. Glenn's going to find me and kill me. He's going to find me lying here, wherever the fuck I am, blind and half naked, and he's going to kill me. Christ. Oh Jesus. Oh Jesus.

'Hello? Help!' At last I'm shouting loud enough.

'Yes? What?' A woman's voice barks at me.

'Where am I?'

The woman sighs. 'New Hope Hospital. Green Section,' she finally says, like a prisoner of war giving up his name and rank.

Oh shit. 'New Hope? Why am I here? I've got medical aid.'

'No. Medical aid had no record of you. They brought you here.'

'What do you mean no record?'

I can just imagine her smirking at me. Rich man lying helpless in a state hospital, finding out how the other half lives.

'Expired, actually.'

I'm going to fucking *kill* Lizzie. She's supposed to handle my medical aid and bullshit like that. Jesus. I've heard horror stories about this dump. Everyone calls it 'No Hope'. I can't believe I've landed up in here.

'You need to call Da Bomb Studios. Speak to Lizzie Gebhart, my assistant. She'll sort it out.'

'I'm not phoning for you. It's your problem.'

'Okay, then. Tell me where my phone is. I'll call myself.'

'Your personal belongings are in your cubby.'

5

'Do you mind? Could you—' But she's gone.

I say, 'Hello? Hello?' a bit but I know I'm wasting my breath. I try to feel around the bed for my cubby – wherever that is – but I'm really tired. I curl up and imagine what I'd say if I could get online.

MR alert: &JoshFarrell has found self. In fucking No Hope, can you believe!?

&LizzieGstring you're in deep shit. Prepare for a month's mail duty.

At least that brings a smile to my face as I fall asleep.

I struggle to wake up. Someone's talking to me. A man.

'... so apologies for the cramped conditions. I'm afraid New Hope doesn't have any private wards.' He pauses, no doubt sharing a joke at my expense with the grumpy nurse. 'But, after last year, nobody's keen on a measles epidemic again.'

'Measles?'

'That's what you've got, Mr Farrell.'

Measles?

'As you can tell, it's a serious disease. Especially in adults. It's notifiable. Any idea where you caught it?'

'No. How—'

'Could be anywhere. I keep telling the board that it's only going to end when mandatory immunisation kicks in. Eventually it's going to kill everyone who doesn't get vaccinated.'

'Can measles make me... make me not able to see?' I can't even say the word 'blind'. I can't go blind. I'm a photographer, for God's sake. Seeing is my work. Seeing is my fucking *life*. 'I'll get better, right, Doctor?' I say in as deferent a tone as I can manage, as if he's personally in charge of whether I will see again or not.

He breathes out a long pause. 'Uh, there are rare cases of permanent eye damage. At the onset of the measles we typically advise that you take twenty thousand units of vitamin A and that will usually protect you. Your GP should have prescribed—'

'I didn't go to a GP. I don't know how I got here. Or when.'

'There is a good chance your sight will recover,' the doctor says. 'But it's crucial that the ophthalmologist sees you and prescribes an antibiotic suspension. It's a shame we missed him yesterday. He'll be doing his rounds in this section again tomorrow.'

'But... if I need the medicine now to prevent—'

'We'll see what we can do. The best thing to do is get the virus out of your system and recover. You need to rest and replenish. You have severe liver damage and bronchitis and your kidneys are in distress. All you need to do is lie still and let the drip do its work.'

The doctor leaves and I start to probe the space around my bed for the cubby.

'Can I help you with that, Mr Farrell?'

I jerk with fright and then pretend I didn't.

'I'm Nomsa,' the woman says in a comfortable, attractive voice. She's standing near me, and she smells of quality soap and hand lotion. 'I'm a supply nurse here. I've just come on shift.' She presses something into my left hand. Her hands are leathery, but smooth. 'Here's a call button. We rigged up a remote one for you. I bet you don't know you're bedded in a supply closet. Closest we get to an isolation ward in Green Section.' She laughs.

She makes me feel at ease for the first time in... since I came here. 'Thanks. That other nurse...'

'Sister Elizabeth?'

'She's not very helpful.'

'No. But she's good at her job. She's here all the time. Almost runs the section. It's thankless work and terrible conditions. At least I get a chance to work in the private clinics half the time. Get a break from all this.'

'I suppose.'

'You were looking for...?'

'My stuff. She said it was in a cubby.'

Nomsa rustles next to my bed, and pushes a plastic bag into my hands. The bag's handles are tied together at the top and I can't open them with my right hand bandaged. Under the dressing, my palm hurts like hell. Nomsa takes over and opens the bags. 'We should get that to the laundry, probably,' she says as the stench hits me.

I dig around inside. I can feel my jeans by the oversized Batman belt buckle. They're damp with what smells like rotten vomit and ammonia. I grit back the urge to puke as I rifle around for the pockets. Thank God. I drop the bag over the edge of the cot and wipe my iPhone and wallet on the edge of the sheet.

'Is there a camera bag in there?' I ask Nomsa.

I put my hands over my eyes while she shuffles through the cubby next to me. 'No. Sorry.' Jesus. Where could I have left it? I can't even remember how I got here, where I was.

'Nomsa, do you mind dialling a number for me?' I hold out the phone in Nomsa's direction.

She takes it. 'Looks like it's off.'

'You can just turn it on. Little button on the top.'

A minute. 'No. Nothing. Maybe the battery's dead.'

Fuck. 'You don't have an iPhone charger, do you?'

She just laughs. 'May I take your valuables for safekeeping at the nurses' station? Safer than leaving them in here.'

I hesitate.

'To be honest, patients' valuables go missing all the time. It's much safer to lock them up at the nurses' station.'

What am I going to do with a dead phone anyway? 'Okay. Thanks.' She lifts the handset and wallet off my chest and I can actually feel my phone getting further away from me. It's fucking ridiculous. I think about asking her to give me the photo of Katya from my wallet. But what would be the point? I can't fucking see it.

'Just press the call button if you need anything.'

'Nomsa?'

'Mr Farrell?'

'What day is it?'

'The sixteenth.'

'What day of the week?'

'Wednesday.'

It was Monday morning when Katya left. I must have been here two days. I can't remember anything. What did I do?

Shit. Maybe Katya caught the measles too. I've got to get hold of her.

'I need to…' I try to sit up and a slump of blood pressure makes me woozy and nauseous. 'Ugh.'

'You just need to rest. That's the most important thing, Mr Farrell.'

'Nomsa?'

'Yes, Mr Farrell.'

'You've been really helpful. Can I ask you one more favour?'

'Ask away.'

'I need to get hold of my girlfriend, and someone at work. Could you call them for me?'

'Of course. What are their numbers?'

Jesus. They're in my phone, not in my head. But, with effort, I piece together Katya's cell number and give it to her. 'Work should be in the book, under Da Bomb Studios. Speak to Eduardo da Gama or Lizzie Gebhart.'

'I'll give them a call, let them know you're here. You'll have to pay, though.'

'Sorry?'

'Oh, don't worry, Mr Farrell. Just joking.'

I hear a clink as she hangs another drip. As my nausea settles, I feel sleepy once more.

I wake up screaming. Acid scours along the veins in my right arm. I forget my eyes and open them wide; the pain belts me as I make out the figure of a large man standing by my bedside. Someone's trying to kill me. I feel three drops of something fall onto my face. I give in to unconsciousness.

I dream someone's lifting the sheets, removing my gown. I feel something soft running over my body, like a delicate fingertip. In the dream, I try to open my eyes to see Katya, but my eyes are glued shut. There's a flash like lightning through my eyelids, then the sheet is replaced again.

When I wake, Nomsa is changing the J-loop of my drip. 'I don't know how this happened, Mr Farrell. Someone… did it wrong. Let's replace it. This might…' As she draws the needle out, it feels like she's dragging a fish hook through my veins.

'Hang on, hang on.' She puts my arm down for a second and I hear the snap of rubber gloves and feel the slickness of blood trickling down my arm. 'Eish,' she says under her breath and squeezes my arm above the entry point. I try to open my eyes to see what's happening. I see the vague shape of Nomsa silhouetted against a shaft of light from the doorway, in the exact same position as the large man in the night, then the pain kicks in and I have to flinch away and squeeze my eyes shut.

I saw! I saw for a second there! My eyes are getting better. They're getting better!

'Orderly!' Nomsa calls into the corridor. 'Orderly!' Trying to disguise the panic in her voice. Someone else runs into the room.

'Shit,' he says.

'Hold this,' says Nomsa.

The fingers on my upper arm change owners. There's a tug and a rub and another couple of tugs at the wound in my arm, then a dressing is pressed over it. Another scrub and a dressing is finally taped in position.

'That... that was...' Nomsa starts, but stops again. 'We'll need to put the drip in your left arm, okay, Mr Farrell?'

'Mm,' I mumble, worrying about the numbness in my right arm and wanting to sleep again.

Soon I'm hooked up again and my head tilts comfortably to the darker side of the closet, the side away from the door. I test my eyes. Open one-two-three burn. **MR alert: &JoshFarrell can see.** Open one-two-three-four burn. Open one-two-three-four-five burn. Then my eyes are too heavy to try again.

Chapter 2

LISA

'Now, Ms Cassavetes,' the doctor says, yawning and scanning my chart. 'You haven't been entirely truthful with us, have you?'

I've never seen her before. She's a spindly woman with cheap hair extensions and late-onset acne, and she doesn't seem to be bothered that I've lied about my medical history. The doctor I saw yesterday just before the op was an ancient man with a paunch, and to be honest I hadn't actually *had* to lie to him. The consultation took less than ten minutes. He'd peered at my face, asked me if I was allergic to anything, outlined the procedure, and the next thing I knew I was being prepped for theatre.

I should have known then that I wasn't going to get away with it. It had been way too easy, and it's *never* that easy.

'Ms Cassavetes?' The doctor runs a hand through her plastic hair. 'Do you understand what I'm saying?'

I flutter my eyelids, pretending that I'm still woozy from the anaesthetic.

'Before we can let you go, I'm going to insist that a CAT scan is done. Just to be on the safe side.'

Oh God. That's not good. How much will that cost? If they charge me extra, I won't have the money to pay for a motel to hole up in while the bruising fades. If I'm forced to go home early, Dad will have a conniption when he sees the bruises. And Dr Meka will totally flip out. She'd flatly refused to condone any more surgery, even though she must know it's the only way. Worst-case scenario I can phone Sharon, ask her to help me out. But after last time she'll probably tell me to get stuffed and grass me up to Dad. I open my mouth to tell the doctor that I don't want a scan; that all I want is to be let out of this hellhole, but I can't get the words out and I end up just nodding meekly. Pathetic.

Shaking her head in exasperation, the doctor chucks the file on the end of the bed and stalks off. The nurse with her – the one Gertie has nick-named Lumpy Legs – glares at me and angrily whips back the curtains shielding me from the rest of the ward.

Gertie looks up from her *You* magazine. 'What was that all about, doll?' she asks.

I shake my head and shrug. Luckily Gertie isn't that interested. I get the idea that she thinks I've had some sort of surgery on my sinuses and there's no way I'm going to put her right.

'Ag shame,' she says. 'Still feeling kak?'

I nod. I'm usually pretty good at keeping myself to myself in hospitals, but my silence hasn't stopped Gertie from going on and on about her 'kak bowels', the trouble she's having with her 'bitch' of a daughter and how many months she's spent in and out of various Joburg hospitals. This one, she insists, is the worst of the lot: 'If you're not at death's door when you get here, doll, you will be when you leave.'

But I don't really mind her constant chatter. Listening to her is better than being alone with my thoughts, and she hasn't tried too hard to pry any personal details out of me, apart from the usual 'Where you from?' and 'What's a chick like you doing in a place like this?' And if she thinks it's weird that I've chosen to have the op in Johannesburg instead of a hospital closer to home in Durban, she hasn't let on.

'At least they're giving you some attention,' she gripes. 'Count yourself lucky, doll. I could die just now and no one would even notice.'

I close my eyes and pretend to sleep.

*

'Check it out, doll. New arrival,' Gertie says, snapping me out of my doze. I have no clue how long I've been out, and for once I don't remember dreaming.

I sit up as a new victim is wheeled into the ward. All I can see of her is a lump under a sheet and a whorl of grey hair. There's something about the way the nurses are uncharacteristically fussing around her that makes me think she isn't going to last much longer. A middle-aged man with a face as round and flat as a plate follows in the gurney's wake, and the nurses swish the curtains around the bed, leaving him stranded. He pulls out a Bible and starts mumbling under his breath.

Gertie watches him carefully. She leans over to me and murmurs, 'Don't be fooled. He's probably already plotting how to spend the inheritance. I know the type.'

I try to smile at her, but the painkillers are wearing off and it hurts when I move my cheek muscles. My nose feels as if it's blown up to the size of a balloon, and I have to keep reminding myself to breathe through my mouth. Did it feel as uncomfortable and painful as this last year? I touch my nose gently, trying to feel if the bump has gone, but unlike last time, when the doctors used a discreet sticking plaster, this dressing is bulky and attached to my cheeks with layers of tape. Still, at least the bandages hide most of my face.

The Bible-toting man glances around the ward, clearly trying to catch someone's eye, but, apart from me and Gertie, the other patients are all comatose, sleeping or attached to rusting oxygen tanks, battling for each breath. His eyes drift to mine and I look away, feeling blood rushing to my cheeks.

'Would you like to pray with me, miss?' he asks.

'Don't bother,' Gertie says to him. 'You won't get a word out of her.'

'Would you—?'

'No thanks,' Gertie says, cutting him off mid-sentence. 'I'll meet my maker soon enough. *Then* we'll talk.'

He swallows and nods at the body behind the curtain. 'It's my mother,' he says.

'Oh ja?' Gertie says, radiating boredom. Leaving the new patient's curtains closed, the two nurses emerge and murmur something to him. He nods his head, bites his lip and sits down on one of the plastic visitors' chairs.

'Hey!' Gertie calls to Lumpy Legs. 'Where's lunch? I'm wasting away here.'

'On its way, Mrs February.' She waddles over and fiddles with Gertie's drip. 'Have you managed a bowel movement yet?'

Gertie snorts. 'You managed to stay off the doughnuts yet?'

Lumpy Legs tuts. 'I know you're uncomfortable, but there's no need for that,' she says in her no-nonsense voice. 'Nothing wrong with being a larger lady, is there?'

'Obesity is the number-one killer in the world,' Gertie says to her, winking at me.

Lumpy Legs glares at me again as if it's me who's just insulted her. I clear my throat and force myself to speak. 'Um. I'm supposed to have a scan. Do you know when it will be?'

'When they're ready for you,' she snaps, before exiting into the corridor. I swallow the lump in my throat. If I start crying, that'll be it. I won't be able to stop.

'Don't mind her, love,' Gertie says to me. 'Miserable bitch. Shouldn't let people like that be nurses. The caring profession, se gat. They're all sadists.'

I've done my best to be as cooperative as I can, but it's obvious that the nurses hate me. I've heard them grumbling in the corridors about the hospital's new policy to attract private patients by providing non-essential procedures. They wouldn't know that I'm here because I don't have a choice. Even if I had the cash to splash out on a private clinic, I'd have to find a doctor willing to perform the operation. And with my history I've run out of options.

An orderly pushes a trolley piled with lunch trays into the ward.

'Finally,' Gertie says, clawing in the grubby water glass on her locker for her teeth.

I'm grateful that I can't smell anything; the sight of the food is enough to turn my stomach. It looks like minced roadkill, the cracked plates slopped with gritty-looking meat and a smattering of lumpy mashed potato. The thought of watching Gertie shovelling that down her gullet makes me feel instantly sick. I kick my blankets away. Even the juice they provide is the colour of bile; the cheap concentrated kind that comes in huge plastic tubs.

'Where are you going, doll?' Gertie asks.

I have no idea where I'm going. All I know is that I have to get out of here. 'Not hungry,' I say.

The religious man looks up from his Bible as I swing my legs off the bed. I can feel his eyes grazing my thighs, hovering over my stomach and my breasts, barely concealed beneath the flimsy hospital gown. I know what he's thinking: 'How can a monster like that show herself in public?' I grab my robe as fast as I can, and wrap it around my body. Ducking my head, I scurry out, slippers squeaking on the linoleum.

'Hey, Lisa!' Gertie calls after me. 'If you're going to the cafeteria bring me back a brandy and Coke.' She roars with laughter which ends up in a coughing fit.

I know she's got a packet of menthols hidden in her bedside cabinet. But her secret is safe with me. If she wants to kill herself slowly that's her business.

God. This place is beyond grim. What would Dad say if he saw me here, shuffling down these crappy corridors, the green paint peeling off the walls, the linoleum on the floor scratched and worn with age and overuse? He'd probably say that it serves me right. That I'm getting what I deserve for lying to him again. At least the corridor is empty, the patients all tucking into their lunches, the nurses doing whatever nurses do when they're not being mean – thinking up ways to torture the patients, or whatever.

I keep my head down to avoid catching a glimpse of myself in the glass that surrounds the nurses' station, concentrating instead on the floor, the walls, the sounds of lunch being trundled into wards and forced down. My gaze is drawn to the sluice room; the door is propped open and the shelves are piled with overflowing bedpans and sputum bowls. I pass an abandoned cleaning trolley parked at an angle next to the shower room, the mop head thick with filth, a muscular cockroach skittering under its wheels. I'm glad I have the dressing over my nose so I don't have to confront what it smells like in here.

I need to find somewhere quiet, somewhere private, so that I can go over my options again. But where? I can't leave the ward – it's blocked by a rusty security gate. The sight of it totally freaked me out when I arrived. I mean, I know that Joburg is a violent city, but this is a hospital, not a prison. When I was still able to convince Dad that the only way I was going to get better was to have another op, he booked me into a series of private clinics which specialised in cosmetic procedures. They were more like hotels, with private rooms, satellite TV and nurses who didn't treat me like crap. A million miles from this dump.

Just past the men's toilets there's a grubby 'Waiting Room' sign tacked next to a door, and I creep towards it. I hesitate, then turn the handle and peer inside. I'm hit with a waft of smoky air. Two wizened patients are sitting puffing away under a huge 'No Smoking' sign, their drips standing behind them like disapproving relatives. They immediately stop speaking and stare at me in disgust, and I scuttle away as if it's me, not them, who's been caught doing something illegal.

Stiff with self-consciousness, I walk on. I'm nearing the end of the corridor, and the snoozing security guard jerks awake, glances at me distrustfully, and then rests his head on the gate again and closes his eyes. I'm about to turn around and head back when I spot a narrow alcove diagonally opposite the security gate. There's an open door leading into what looks to be a small, darkened storage room. Maybe I can hide in here. Gather my thoughts.

I head towards it, the sound of a cough stopping me dead.

No *ways*. There's a man in here, lying on a narrow bed, a drip snaking out of his arm. What the hell is a patient doing in here? The cot he's on barely even fits into the room. He's one of the few people under sixty I've seen in the ward and he's lying there, eyes closed, his face covered in a fine sheen of sweat. I creep closer, careful not to wake him. Even though he looks like he's at death's door I can't tear my eyes away from his stubbly face and his shock of black hair. He reminds me of someone, someone familiar. I edge even closer. That's it. Robert Pattinson. *That's* who he looks like. But not like Robert was in *Breaking Dawn*, more like when he was in—

'Ms Cassavetes!' Lumpy Legs calls.

I jump guiltily and turn to face her.

She's striding towards me, puffing with exertion. 'What do you think you're doing?'

A bored-looking orderly is trailing behind her, pushing a wheelchair. I drop my head, hiding my face behind my hair.

'Are you deliberately trying to make my life difficult?' she says.

'Sorry.'

'They need you in X-ray,' she snaps, gesturing to the wheelchair.

'I can walk.'

'Hospital policy.'

I glance back at the storeroom. 'There's a man in the—'

'Yes, yes, that's none of your concern. Now *please*,' she says, voice heavy with sarcasm, 'if it's not too much trouble.'

I do as she says. The chair is surprisingly comfortable and I lean back and pray that the orderly won't try to chat to me. Thankfully as soon as Lumpy Legs is out of sight he plugs earphones into his ears and pops a strip of gum into his mouth. He mutters something to the snoozing security guard, who yawns, stretches and takes his time unlocking the gate. The orderly wheels me through it and into a lift, its stainless steel walls smudged with fingerprints, a wad of filthy tissues balled in the corner. We rattle down, my empty stomach turning in on itself, the orderly humming along to 'Beautiful' by James Blunt, popping his gum every so often. The lift shudders to a halt and he sweeps me out into another long corridor, this one painted a tired yellow, a stretch of wall scored with deep circular marks that look horribly like bullet holes. The strip lighting crackles and hisses, and we crawl along for what feels like miles, squeaking down corridors lined with foldaway beds containing passive patients, weaving around a woman in a wheelchair stranded outside the open door of a filthy toilet, and trundling past a group of skeletal, yellow-skinned men and women queuing patiently outside a barred dispensing window.

At last we draw to a stop outside the X-ray department. The wooden benches outside it are full of patients in hospital gowns waiting for their turn, but no one looks up as the orderly parks me behind a gurney containing an elderly man with a dried-up face and clawed hands. His mouth is open, revealing stumpy blackened teeth. A middle-aged nurse with bloodshot eyes pushes through the black doors, and for a second or two our eyes lock. Then she flinches and turns away, just like I knew she would.

'You took your time,' Gertie says, as I'm wheeled back into the ward. 'You've been gone for hours. You missed all the excitement.'

She points to the bed opposite. It's empty. The blankets are puddled on the floor, the mattress covered with a yellowing plastic sheet. It had once held a woman with swollen, blue-veined feet, dyed red hair and a hectic cough. 'Another one bites the dust,' Gertie says. 'Off to the great morgue in the sky.' She cackles.

I'm relieved to see that the religious man is gone, although his mother is still hidden behind the curtains. The woman on the other side of Gertie farts loudly and then moans in her sleep.

'Charming,' Gertie says.

Lumpy Legs bustles in. 'Doctor's on his way,' she snaps in my direction.

'Twice in one day, hey, doll?' Gertie says to me. 'I'm lucky if they remember to change my drip.'

'Oh, Mrs February,' Lumpy Legs tuts, whipping the curtains around my bed.

Another doctor appears behind her, this one an Indian man with tired eyes and a worried expression. He glances down at my chart.

'Ms Cassavite,' he says, mispronouncing my name. 'We have your scan results here.' His voice is high and girlish, heavily accented. 'I am sorry to have to inform you that the news is not so good.'

Lumpy Legs looks at him with a mixture of reverence and fake concern. She fiddles with my sheet.

The doctor rattles off a flurry of medical jargon. 'Are we clear?'

I shake my head, doing my best to smother the growing excitement. I understand exactly what he's just said, of course, but I want him to repeat it. I want to be *sure*.

'In the terms of that of a layperson, Ms Cassavite, if we do not operate again, you could have serious complications.' He checks his notes again. 'I see here that this is not the first time that you have been having this procedure. And that you were not informing this hospital of these facts. It is pertinent that you must sign another consent. And we must also be sure that you will be liable for the extra expenditure.'

'When will you operate?'

'In a few days. As soon as a theatre is available.'

'And afterwards? Will I... will I look... different?'

'Different? I am not understanding you fully, Ms Cassavite.'

'Will I still look like the same person?'

'We will not know for sure until the operation is over, Ms Cassavite,' he says. 'But you must prepare yourself for the worst. The shape, it could alter quite radically. The damage is extensive. Much reconstruction might be necessary.'

Okay, a couple more days in this horrible place, but it will all be worth it. The doctor's eyes widen in disbelief as he takes in my expression. I'm not surprised. He wouldn't know why I'm smiling.

Chapter 3

FARRELL

I know it's night because the ward sounds different, more subdued. No ringing phones, no clattering carts or running children.

I listen to the quiet conversations of the nurses, the old women moaning in pain like mourners at a funeral, the building breathing, the stale air circulating, the tick of the drip machine. And underneath it all, a distant thrum, like the hospital is built over a massive beehive, or a full stadium buried hundreds of metres deep.

I've been drifting in and out of sleep all day, my rest more like a series of naps than the dead semi-coma I was in before. I'm more alert now, feeling more, and I scan my body: the ache in my right arm, the jag of the drip in my left, the pinch of the catheter, a sharp pain in the palm of my right hand. My lower back feels bruised and my throat is still acid-burned. My hands and toes are freezing and I can rub them together for a few minutes before I grow tired again. I don't feel hungry or thirsty – the drip has kept me hydrated – but my lips are dry and cracked. My hair is filthy, unwashed for days. I must look and smell like shit.

I test my eyes compulsively, but I can't get past the count of eight before they sting shut again. And while they're open, I can't really see anything, just blurred shapes as if something's grown over the lenses. Christ, I can't go blind. I can't just lie here and lose my sight.

The light floods on and I hear what sounds like a drawer opening. I turn my head and force my eyes open.

One. The distorted outline of a man's huge frame at a cabinet. White jacket.

Two. The shape turns to me. A smudge of dark grey over the hazy white of his coat.

Three. He looks down. Finds what he's looking for in the drawer. Four.

Five. My eyes are burning, screaming. The man comes closer. I open them wide as a headlit deer's.

Six. He looms over me. Takes my arm. Other arm under the pillow. I can't find the fucking call button.

Seven. Two round blurs on his grey face. Massive glasses. Drops of sweat from his face fall onto my cheek.

Eight. He opens his mouth and his breath smells like rotting flesh. I have to close my eyes. He's gripping my arm. Where's the fucking button?

My eyes refuse to open again.

I feel him roughly pull the needle out of the J-loop, and he mutters something in a thick voice that I can't make out. Then silence. As soon as my eyes can stand it, a minute, maybe two, later, I open them again and look. He's gone; left the light on, but there's nothing to see except the fuzzy glare of this storeroom.

It takes me three eight-second bursts of vision to find the remote. Once I have hold of it, I slump back and press the button, not letting go until my thumb stiffens. Minutes later a night-shift nurse stands in the doorway.

'Yes?' Shit. It sounds like Sister Elizabeth, the Ugly Sister.

'Someone… changed my drip.'

'Yes?'

'What's in it? Is it the right thing?'

'Yes,' she says from the doorway. She doesn't come closer, she doesn't check. She has no fucking idea.

I'm crushed by a wave of exhaustion. As I drift off, the panic becomes muffled. Someone – someone who shouldn't be here – is putting something in my blood.

But I'm so tired. I can't do any more.

'Sister? Sister, have a look at this.'

I recognise Nomsa's voice in my sleep haze. I feel her wiping my arm where she's inserted another fresh drip needle.

The sister says something to her that I can't make out.

'But he can't keep getting new needles. His veins are bruised.'

Sister Elizabeth lowers her voice and mutters again.

'And I don't know who put…' I can sense Nomsa looking at me, probably trying to determine if I'm actually awake, although I'm doing my best to pretend I'm still asleep.

'Besides,' says the Ugly Sister, this time loud enough for me to hear, 'the hepatitis is clearing up. The bilirubin counts are coming down. He'll only need a drip for hydration.' She leaves the storeroom.

It's getting worse. I open my eyes and there's no pain. Its absence is unnerving. All I can see are blotches over the doorway's blurred radiance. I can feel the mould eating into my eyes, and, unless eyes spontaneously regenerate, I'm fucked.

'Mr Farrell,' Nomsa says. I hadn't heard her come in. 'How are you feeling?'

'Okay, actually. I feel stronger. More awake… But my eyes…' Suddenly I have an embarrassing urge to cry. I don't want to go blind. And Nomsa is the only person in the world who seems to care. I hold myself together.

I feel her fingers opening my eyelids and she shines a light into them. 'There's much better reaction. And the conjunctivitis is clearing up. The antibiotics have worked well on that. Doctor will say whether we should extend the course. You say you still can't see?'

'Everything's blurred. I can see light and shapes.'

'I'll ask Doctor about the ophthalmologist. But he's only doing rounds this afternoon.'

'But what if it gets worse? If it becomes permanent? If there's something I can do now to avoid…'

'I'm going to ask Doctor, and I'll try to find out.'

'Nomsa?' I ask, not sure if she's still in the room.

'Mr Farrell?'

'Did you manage to get hold of Katya and the studio?'

'No answer. I left messages, so I hope they'll get them. I'll try again later.'

If I could get hold of Katya, she could call an ophthalmologist for me and he could come see me. I don't want to go blind. Jesus... From fucking measles. There must be something simple I can do. If I can just get to the nurses' station, they'll let me use the phone. I'm sure I'm strong enough.

I push myself to a sitting position, and need to take several deep breaths before I have the energy to move again. I have to hoist my legs over the short railing at the side of the bed. Either that or work out how to lower it, which I guess would take more energy. I get my left leg over the side, but with it dangling there I can't find the purchase to hoist my right leg over with it.

Then I make a stupid decision. I assume that, if my torso goes over the edge of the bed, my right leg will follow the rest of me. I'm correct. My body crashes onto the floor, my head hitting the edge of the cabinet. The drip line stretches, still attached to my vein. A jag of pain rips through my arm. At last the drip stand teeters and crashes down on top of me. The hook at the top thumps onto my skull and furious sparks fly through my brain, but at least the pull on my vein is slackened.

The Ugly Sister runs in bellowing something at me. The blurry shape of an orderly follows. As they manhandle me back onto my bed, I shout, 'I need to use the phone. Nomsa? Can I speak to Nomsa?'

'Nomsa is with another patient. Don't do that again.'

When she leaves me, I'm too weak to move but my mind doesn't stop racing. I can't remember what happened that morning before I came here. All I have is this picture of Katya crying, leaving. I have the feeling she was going back to her parents' – she always does. What happened that morning? My hands throb, as if in answer to a question I don't want answered.

D &KatyaModel Please D me now. Please. R u ok?

I'm stuck here, with no way of knowing if Katya's okay. I have to find out. But I can't even get myself out of my fucking bed.

Later, Nomsa says I can try to walk. She reaches down and loosens my catheter. I feel like I've been released from a ball and chain.

She lowers the railing on the bed and this time it's easier for me to flip my legs over and stand. I push myself up against the bed and Nomsa steadies me against the drip stand. I test my weight for a moment. Good to go. I start to shuffle off.

'Keep left and don't go too fast. Don't overdo it.'

'Ja, right.'

'And don't get lost.'

'Thanks, Nomsa.'

'It's a pleasure, Mr Farrell.'

Once out of the storeroom I do as Nomsa suggests. I keep left, trailing the foot of the drip stand along the plastic skirting, stopping every minute or so to close my eyes and catch my breath. My sore hand throbs worse from gripping clumsily onto the drip stand. The top layer of the dressing is starting to come loose. I stick it back down as well as I can and shuffle through the blurscape at ten steps a minute, listening to the keening geriatrics, the rhythmic slap of a physiotherapist beating phlegm out of some old man's lungs. There's a limbo chatter in the wards, the trundle of gurneys, the pained circulation of the air-conditioned air, and always, always, that subterranean thrum, like thousands of excited voices interred in the city's rock. I get the eerie sense that we're locked in, that nobody leaves this place except out the smokestack.

It's just the isolation speaking. I wish I had my phone. Jesus, who knows how many followmobs I'm missing while I'm stuck in here. I'm going to lose serious Kred points.

The effort of my next minute of shuffling pushes the thought out of my mind. I reach the nurses' station, their hustling dark-blue shapes whirling around in a complex dance like bees at a hive. The bustle makes me nauseous and I need to calm my stomach before I even think of asking someone for my phone. I move to a quieter stretch of hallway, press myself to the wall, close my eyes and catch my breath.

In the room next to me, a machine starts making a panicked alarm, but softly, as if it doesn't expect anyone to listen.

'I'm afraid she's passed on, Mr du Plessis,' comes a voice from inside the ward – it's the Ugly Sister, sounding a touch less bitchy than usual. 'I'll call Doctor to prepare the certificate. My condolences for your loss.'

A wail. A man howling. It's deep and overloud, and it annoys me. I can tell he's a fucking rebo phoney. 'Lord, Thy will be done,' he shouts. 'Oh Jesus, please take her into your blessed arms and—'

'Your Lord doesn't have much practice at hip replacements, does he?' says another voice, the harsh croak of an old woman.

'Mrs February!' the Ugly Sister barks

'Well, it's not right, making a scene like that. Disturbing everyone.'

'Muh-muh-mother!' the man wails again.

Something sweet-smelling rushes out of the ward door and almost smacks straight into me. I can make out a blur of long blonde hair, and catch a subtle scent that reminds me of gardens, reminds me of the girls at work. 'I'm... sorry,' she mutters as she slips past me.

'Doll!' the old woman's voice calls. 'Where you going? You're missing the drama!'

'I can't... I can't, Gertie!'

She scurries away, her shape flitting down the main corridor like a mouse making a break across a cat-guarded floor.

There's something about this woman's smell, her voice, some subtlety in her accent that's not exactly normal, but it's familiar. Everyone else here – nurses, doctors, orderlies, caterers and all the old, dying patients – is part of the hospital, they are part of this building; but there's something about the sweet-smelling blonde blur that makes me know she's like me, that she doesn't belong in here. Maybe she's got a phone she can lend me.

I gather myself and follow. It takes minutes for me to shuffle up, dragging the clinking drip stand with me, to where she's standing in a crook of the wall.

'Hi,' I say. Her shape jolts, turns its back to me. Her shoulders are shuddering as if she's crying. Christ, maybe this was a bad idea. But it's worth a shot.

'I wondered if you had a cellphone on you? I—'

'No,' she says, swallowing a sob.

Jesus.

'Sorry,' she says. 'That was rude. I... I did have a phone. The battery's dead.'

Shit. 'Uh. Okay. Thanks anyway.' I close my eyes and prepare to make my way back. I take a few deep breaths then turn, catching my foot in the drip stand and landing up slumped on the floor.

'What's wrong with you?' she says. 'Can't you see?'

'Not much,' I say.

'Oh,' she says. Her hand awkwardly flutters onto mine, trying to help in some way, and eventually I pull myself up on the drip stand.

'Thanks.'

'I th—'

'Muh, muh, mother!' the man's voice echoes through the corridor.

'Ms Cassavetes,' the Ugly Sister calls her in that offensive voice of hers. 'What are you doing out of bed?' Her bulk shoves past me like I'm just another irritating obstacle in her day.

'S-sorry,' the girl says, and scuttles back the way she came.

'It's just one call, come on. You can't be fu— you can't be serious!'

'I told you,' the blurry-faced drone behind the nurses' station says. I hear her yawning. 'It's against hospital policy. No patients are allowed to use the phones.'

'Please. You want me to beg?'

'It's the rules.' She sniffs and her large blue shape drifts away.

Fuck. Now what?

Not knowing what else to do, I walk away, testing myself again to see how far I can go. This time I make it past the blonde girl's ward, past the nook where we spoke, and all the way down to the ward kitchen, where I can smell the coffee and chips the visitors have smuggled in and the stink of meat pies nuked in the communal microwave oven. I feel my way along the green-striped wall towards the next door. It's closed but I can smell cigarette smoke coming from inside it. I find the door handle and let myself in.

I close the door behind me and peer into the blur, squeezing at my bandaged hand to soothe it. It feels like it's been cut. I make out the shapes of a few chairs, a yellowish table and a maroon or brown couch. The blonde girl's sitting on it.

'Hello again,' I say. 'Are you smoking?'

She takes a few seconds to respond. 'No.' She shifts herself so that she's sitting at an angle away from me. Almost turning her back. As far as she can without physically getting up to stand in the corner. 'I don't smoke.'

There's something nasal about her voice. I can't really make out her face, but there's a whiter smudge in the centre of it, probably some kind of dressing or bandage. Nose job? I sit on one of the chairs. The thick plastic which covers the upholstery sticks to my bare thighs and I wonder when last they were wiped down. I make sure my smock is covering my dick.

'What are you in for?' I say, trying to sound chatty, conversational. Her muttering is really annoying me and in ordinary circumstances I'd just leave. But here, blind as a fucking bat, I might need her help to get hold of Katya.

Another long pause, then a sigh. 'My face.'

Jesus. This is like a bad day at work. Interviewing a fifteen-year-old model pre-shoot, trying to get her to ease up. I challenge myself to get more than two words out of her. 'What's wrong with it?'

A pause. 'I had an accident.'

Definitely a nose job. That's what they all say, as if it's some sort of disgrace when who the hell cares? But why the fuck would she get it done in No Hope? Christ, surely nobody's here if they've got another option?

I lean forward in my chair, and she shrinks back into the couch.

'Don't worry,' I say. 'Remember, I can't see much.'

'Are you blind?'

'No. Well... at the moment. I have a problem...' She shifts into an easier position. I want to tell her – convince myself – that it's just temporary, but I can't force out the words. The ophthalmologist will be here this afternoon, and it will all be better. I rub my hand again; the ache's not improving. 'This place is stuffy. I'm thinking of going for a walk outside,' I say to divert the conversation. 'You want to come?'

'You can't leave the section without being discharged.'

'What?'

'They won't let you out without the paperwork... I think they're afraid of criminals.'

I give it some thought. 'Nah, more likely they don't want patients wandering around. Just as well, I suppose. You could have people who are sick with really bad stuff wandering into this section if there's no control.' I don't want to think too hard about the diseases that must breed in this place. 'Locked in for our own protection, huh?'

She doesn't say anything.

'I'm Josh, by the way. Josh Farrell. But everyone calls me Farrell.' Only Katya calls me Josh.

'I'm Lisa,' she says.

By three thirty the eye doctor still hasn't come. I lie on my bed, trying to stay awake; my long walk earlier has really sapped my energy. But I can't trust any of the nurses to remember me when he comes. I feel I should be standing right at the nurses' station, waiting for the doctor.

I dream that there are pigeons in glass jars arrayed on the shelves in this storeroom, flapping silently in their panic, suffocating slowly.

I see a round grey face looming over the entire hospital like a malicious moon, an insane scientist watching his rats dying in their trap. There are people in the jars now, old people scrabbling at the sides, moaning, too weak to scream or kick, suffocating, coughing up mouthfuls of blood-streaked phlegm. The grey-faced moon watches over it all, its soulless eyes staring, sweat pouring down, dripping off its badly shaved chin. Dripping onto my face.

'Mr Farrell, Dr Marx is here.' Nomsa's voice.

I try to rub the sleep out of my eyes, but my vision won't clear. Then I remember.

'Let's have a look.' The dark shape of Dr Marx's face merges some of the dark spots into a shadowy patch. He shines a light into my eyes which glares and radiates. 'Hmm. Yes, the conjunctivitis is clearing, but you do have quite serious ulceration because of the keratitis. We want to avoid this becoming an adherent leucoma. I'll prescribe an antibiotic suspension, but it would have been better if we had seen to this earlier.'

'But I've been waiting for—'

'Nurse, please fill this as soon as possible. Two drops, each eye, twice daily.'

'Thank you, Doctor,' Nomsa says. The doctor bustles out without another word. 'There you are, Mr Farrell. Your eyes will get better now.'

'What does he mean "it would have been better if we had seen to this earlier"? The other doctor already knew what I needed yesterday morning. Why couldn't he have given it to me then?'

'Dr Koopman is not an ophthalmologist. He can't prescribe—'

'Okay!' I snap. 'Fine. Can I just get those drops now?'

Nomsa goes out without a word.

Dammit. I've managed to piss off the only decent nurse here.

Half an hour later, Sister Elizabeth comes in to check my drip.

'Have you got my eye drops?' I ask her.

Once again she barks, 'No medical aid,' as if that's an answer.

'What does that mean? I'm in a public hospital here. Free healthcare for the people and all that.'

'You get generic if you don't have medical aid.'

'Okay, so? Where is it?'

'There's no stock at the dispensary. It's on order.'

Oh God. 'What?' I'm biting my tongue, trying to keep myself calm, trying to keep the bureaucrat on my side. 'How long will it—'

'I don't know.'

'Is there stock of the medicine Dr Marx prescribed?'

'Yes.' She's enjoying this.

'So what do you want from me? What must I give you?'

'You have nothing I want, Mr Farrell.' She walks out.

Chapter 4

LISA

Lumpy Legs pulls at the Micropore tape holding the dressing in place, catching my skin with her fingernails. I try not to wince or let her know she's hurting me, but I can't help crying out when she yanks the cotton wool plugs from my nostrils. I breathe in through my nose for the first time in ages, but all I can smell is a faint tinge of disinfectant and the irony scent of dried blood. She drops the bandages and plugs into a stainless steel kidney bowl. They're gross-looking, caked with black scabs and iodine. I lift my hand to touch the incision and trace the new shape, but she slaps it away.

'Don't touch.'

'Sorry, I was just...'

Using a clump of cotton swabs she starts cleaning the bridge of my nose. It stings, but it's not as painful as I was expecting – more a throbbing ache than anything else. She pushes my head back and wipes around my nostrils. 'Eish,' she says, scowling.

'What does it look like? Is it bad?'

For a second her expression softens. For an instant I'm a real person, not some spoiled chick who's had an unnecessary 'procedure'.

'It's not too bad,' she says.

She's lying. I think about asking for a mirror, but there's not really much point. I know from past experience that it will just make me even more anxious.

The Indian doctor rustles his way in through the curtains. He's harassed and distracted and doesn't even greet me or Lumpy Legs. He barely glances at my face.

'The operation is to be done tomorrow night,' he says. 'So, Nurse, nil by mouth from midnight onwards.'

Lumpy Legs grunts in response.

I force myself to speak up. 'So everything's healing okay? It's fine to operate again?'

He sighs. 'That's when we can fit you in. There are many emergencies.'

That's not really what I wanted to hear. But before I can speak again he bustles out.

Lumpy Legs finishes replacing the dressing, her grumpy expression back on her face, and rips the curtains back.

'Everything all right, doll?' Gertie says innocently, although we both know she's been eavesdropping.

'I think so. They want to operate again tomorrow night.'

'Shame. Sinuses blocked up again, ja? Like I said, my grandson Reuben – Larissa's third – had trouble with his when he was a baby, and after his grommets we...'

I lie back and let her monologue wash over me.

If looks could kill, I'd be dead several times over by now.

Gertie's daughter Kyra – a thirty-something woman with straightened brittle hair and a too-tight T-shirt – has been shooting me dirty looks ever since she arrived five minutes ago. I stare down at my hands and fiddle with the plastic hospital bracelet around my wrist. I'm way out of my depth here, not sure where to look.

I hate visiting time. Even the comatose women who are wheeled in here straight from theatre ('the veggies', Gertie calls them) attract crowds of family members every evening. I'm beginning to recognise some of the regulars. Most of the women look overtired and overworked, and they slump with relief onto the hard plastic chairs. They barely glance at the patients they've come to see, spending the time shouting at their children, who chase each other up and down the corridors, scattering bright-orange Nik Naks across the floor. The men all look bored and resigned. Still, the sight of all these families makes me feel homesick, painfully aware that I'm miles away from home, and that no one even knows I'm in here.

I'm itching to flee to the waiting room, but Gertie has asked me to stay for 'moral support, doll'. And it looks like she's going to need it.

Kyra curls a lock of limp hair around a finger. 'Five hundred rand, Ma. It's not much.'

'Do I look like I've got five hundred rand?' Gertie snaps. 'When was the last time I was able to collect my pension?'

Kyra's boyfriend hovers at the door. Well, I *think* it's her boyfriend. He's got a patchily shaven scalp, ferrety teeth and a lazy eye. His fingernails are dirty.

Kyra's eyes narrow. 'What you looking at, bitch?' she says to me. 'You looking at my man?'

Gertie snorts. 'As if she'd look at that piece of kak! And don't you talk to my friend like that. She's worth two of you.'

'Ma! Don't call Jannie a piece of kak. He's good to me.'

'Good to me se moer. He's a taker. A user. Just like you, my girl.'

'I'm not a taker!'

'What are you then? Coming to the hospital to beg from me! And what did you bring me? Fokkol!'

'Ma!' Kyra whines. 'Don't be like that.'

'Get out. You're making me sicker. You aren't getting any blarry tik money from me.'

Kyra opens her mouth to say something else, changes her mind, shoots me another vicious glance and stalks out.

'Sorry about that, doll,' Gertie says.

'It's okay.'

'It's not okay. Three kids. And all of them blarry useless. Just like their father.'

Gertie heaves her bulk into a sitting position and rummages in her bedside cabinet. 'Think you can help me to that place you were talking about? Need a ciggie.'

She's suddenly hit with a coughing fit, as if just the idea of a cigarette is more than her lungs can take.

'You shouldn't smoke, Gertie.'

'I shouldn't do a lot of things,' she says, struggling to breathe. She sounds defeated. 'And I'll have to face all that kak when I get out of here.'

She attempts to slide off the bed. Her hospital gown rucks up, showing off large mottled thighs riddled with knotty veins. I fetch her robe for her and help her steady the drip stand.

Using my shoulder and the stand for support, she starts edging out of the room.

'Not a nurse in sight, eh, Lisa?' Gertie puffs as we make our slow way down the corridor. 'They always vanish during visiting time.'

She stumbles and I grab onto her upper arm to steady her. She's a large woman, but her skin feels loose and saggy as if all the flesh beneath it has turned to jelly.

Two undernourished children with cheap lollypops stuck in their mouths race past, bashing into my legs. A woman with bloodshot eyes and a torn polyester shirt sits on a plastic chair outside one of the rooms, breastfeeding a baby. Two toddlers sit at her feet playing with a crumpled Coke can. Gertie smiles at the children, but they look at her with wide, empty eyes.

It's a relief to reach the waiting room. Even the dead plants look cheery in comparison to the dull and hopeless green corridors.

I help Gertie settle on the couch. She lights up, and the first drag sets off a barrage of wet-sounding coughs. The second drag seems to dry them up.

'That's better,' she says, jetting twin streams of smoke from her nose.

There's a clattering sound from outside the door, and someone yells, 'Shit!'

'Wait here,' I say to Gertie.

'Does it look like I'm going anywhere, doll?'

I knew it. It's the guy – Farrell. I smooth my hair behind my ears, forgetting that he can't actually see me. He's somehow managed to get his drip stand wedged in the doorframe and is groping at it with his bandaged hand.

'Let me help you.'

His face relaxes. 'Lisa?'

He remembered my name! 'Yes.'

Gertie squints through the smoke and looks him up and down as I lead him in. 'So this is why you keep slipping out of bed,' she says.

Blood rushes into my cheeks – thank God he can't see me clearly – but how could she possibly think someone like Farrell would be interested in me?

'So,' Gertie says to him once I've introduced them. 'What are you in here for?'

'Measles.'

'Hey? That's a kiddies' disease, isn't it? My three all went through that, and the grandkids, too.'

'I had… complications. Problem with my sight.'

'Ah,' Gertie says, nodding wisely. 'Heard of that. Neighbour of mine – real bitch – went blind one night, just like that, in her sleep. Just woke up and said that everything was black. Didn't stop her saying all those things about my Reuben, though.' She leans over and pats Farrell's hand. 'But that won't happen to you. Don't you worry.'

Farrell frowns. But who can blame him? It was hardly a sensitive thing to say. Gertie launches into an account of her bowel problems and drags in another lungful of smoke, before letting it drift out of her mouth.

Farrell coughs and waves his good hand in front of him. 'Christ,' he says, interrupting her. 'Do you mind?'

Gertie stiffens. 'I do mind. My ciggies are the only pleasure I've got in life.'

'You're not supposed to smoke in here.'

'Oh ja? Who are you, the blarry cigarette police?'

This isn't going well. I try to smile to defuse the situation, but Gertie's eyes are narrowing dangerously, and for an instant she looks just like her daughter.

'What are you doing here anyway?' she snaps at him. 'You don't look like the type who'd show up here. Why aren't you in the Sandton Clinic or whatever it's called?'

'Long story,' Farrell says.

'I got time.'

'There's some screw-up with my medical aid. So I ended up here with all the...'

Gertie narrows her eyes. 'All the what, hey? The dregs?'

'That's not what I meant!'

'We can't all be rich whites with back-up plans.'

'Gertie,' I say, 'Farrell didn't mean—'

'Save it,' Gertie says. 'Thinks he's too good for people like me.' She struggles to her feet. 'Got to get back.'

'I'll help you.'

'No. You stay with Frankie here. More your type, isn't he?'

'It's Farrell,' he says.

'What kind of name is that? Sounds like a poof's name.'

'You can't manage on your own,' I say to her.

'Don't you worry about me, Lisa.'

She leans heavily on the drip stand and, dropping her cigarette butt at Farrell's feet, starts shuffling off. Farrell and I sit in silence while she huffs her way out, muttering under her breath. Mind you, she seems to be finding it easier to walk than before.

'Jesus,' Farrell says. 'Thought she'd never stop talking. She a friend of yours?'

'Um... not really. She's in the bed next to mine.'

'Christ. That must be a nightmare. You ever get any sleep?'

He smiles at me and I find myself smiling back, feeling slightly guilty at sharing a joke at Gertie's expense. Still, he's right, she does go on and she didn't need to take offence like that.

'So when do you get out of this shithole, Lisa?'

'I'm not sure. I have to have another op. Tomorrow, they said.'

'Jesus. You think it's a good idea to go under the knife again in a place like this? What are you doing in here, anyway?'

I don't know what to say to this. I fiddle with the bracelet, touch the bandages again. What if I come out of the next operation looking even worse than I do already? A big gaping hole where my nose once was?

'I don't have a choice,' I say. But is that true? Would they let me out if I insisted?

'Your medical aid also screwed up?'

'No... um. Nowhere else could fit me in.' It's as close to the truth as I can manage.

'Seriously? Not even the Park Lane?'

I shrug. 'I'm not from here. From Joburg, I mean. They had a vacancy here and so I just...' I let my voice trail away.

'So where are you from?'

'Port Shepstone. The South Coast.'

He sniffs. 'Oh yeah? Haven't been there since matric. I knew you didn't belong here.'

'Really?'

'Yeah.' He smiles. 'Well, it's nice to meet someone normal in here.'

Normal! Heat rushes into my cheeks again and I'm suddenly hit with the perverse urge to tell him everything. Blurt it all out. About my disorder, the fact that I know I have a problem, that it doesn't help *knowing*. That it doesn't matter how often people tell me I look 'fine', that I look 'normal', that all the kind words in the world don't make up for the truth I see in the mirror. But I don't of course.

He flexes his shoulders and yawns. His teeth are very, very white. He's actually better looking than Robert Pattinson, his jaw isn't as heavy, and his nose is perfectly straight. 'Shit,' he says. 'I miss my phone. My followers will be freaking out by now.'

'Your followers?'

'Yeah. MindRead.'

'Oh.'

'Aren't you on it?'

I shake my head, wanting desperately to lie, but what if I do and he catches me out? 'No,' I say. Who'd want to follow my MindRead messages anyway?

'You should be, Lisa. Trust me. It's the best way to network. Got some of my biggest clients that way.' He pauses as if he's waiting for me to ask him a question.

'Clients?'

'Yeah. I'm a photographer.'

'Really? That's amazing. I've... I've never met a photographer before.'

He shrugs. 'It's not that great. Not really. But I've done some good gigs this year, apart from the commercial stuff. Like really creative. You know, a few shoots for *Dazed & Confused*, and you know Die Werk Kak? Seriously hot up-and-coming band?'

'Of course,' I lie, not wanting to appear stupid.

'I did their publicity shoot. Real cutting-edge stuff, we shot it on location in Newclare, trying to get that raw gangland feel, you know?'

He carries on mentioning names and magazines I've only vaguely heard of and I find myself saying 'wow' and 'that's amazing' and grinning like an idiot, barely able to believe that he's telling me all this stuff. *Me.*

He pauses and leans forward, rubbing unconsciously at his bandaged hand. 'Lisa. Look, this is going to sound batshit. But... have you seen something – someone – strange in the wards?'

'What do you mean?'

'It's just... last night I woke up and it was as if... there was someone there. Someone... I dunno, dangerous maybe.' He runs his hand through his hair. 'Christ. I sound like I've lost my mind.'

'No. You don't sound crazy. This place also creeps me out.'

He looks at me gratefully. 'Yeah. Jesus. I cannot *wait* to be out of here and away from all these fucking *freaks*.'

I feel my face falling and stand up. If he knew what kind of a freak he was talking to, what would he say? 'I'd better see that Gertie's okay,' I blurt. *Why* did I say that?

He raises his eyebrows. 'Fine,' he says. Is he disappointed? For a second all I want to do is sit down next to him again. But that would look stupid. 'See you around,' he says, his voice sounding distant.

Stupid, stupid, stupid.

I slump out of the room. The corridor is empty. There's a dirty nappy dumped under the chair where the breastfeeding woman sat, and again I'm grateful that I can't smell anything.

Gertie's propped up in bed. She sniffs when I enter and carries on flicking through her *People* magazine. 'Boyfriend dumped you, hey?'

'He's not my boyfriend.'

'He's too stuck up for his own good, if you ask me. I know his type.'

'He's not stuck up, Gertie. He's just... Look, I think he's really worried he's not going to get his sight back.'

'Oh ja? We've all got our own problems. Call the fokken Care Bears.'

I lie down and think about what Farrell said about going under the knife in a place like this. What if it *does* make it worse? If there's something wrong, shouldn't I be seeing a specialist or something? A snapshot of the Christian man's mother jumps into my head – Gertie said she only came in here for a hip replacement. I've put a fake name and number in the 'In case of emergencies, contact...' section on the hospital form, and if anything goes wrong tomorrow night...

For a second, all I want to do is call Dad, beg him to come and fetch me. But then what?

Gertie's snoring gently, and the woman in the bed next to her whimpers and smacks her gums. Otherwise the ward is unnaturally silent; even the hissing oxygen machines sound quieter. I can't sleep, and I have no idea of the time. It must be well past midnight though. My mouth feels dry and gummy, and the wound beneath the dressing is aching dully. I'm tempted to reach across and take a sip of Gertie's vile orange juice, but I can't. Not if they're operating this evening.

The air is still and hot. Has the air con broken down or something? The back of my neck is damp and itchy, my hair feels limp and greasy. When did I last have a shower? I loathe using the bathroom, brushing my teeth and showering with other people around. But now would be the perfect opportunity. I'll more than likely have the place to myself. I climb out of bed as quietly as I can, ditching the hospital gown for the single pair of silk pyjamas the nurses have let me keep in my locker, and grab my shampoo, towel and body spray. I creep out into the corridor. It's deserted, the only sound the slap of my footsteps.

Thank God. The toilet stalls and shower cubicles are empty, their doors all slightly ajar. It doesn't look as if they've been cleaned today, and I bet it stinks of urine and worse in here. I avoid the mirrors – they're not real mirrors anyway, just polished squares of stainless steel, as if the hospital staff are worried people will smash the glass and slash their wrists. There's a pile of dirty tissues in the sink and even the floor of the cleanest shower is grimy and slimy, a hank of black hair squirled in the drain. I decide to keep my flip-flops on as I shower, holding my head back so that the water doesn't splash the dressing on my nose. It feels wonderful, and I try not to think about Farrell as I soap my body. As if he'd be interested in me, however clean I am, however made-up, however painstakingly groomed.

Through the hiss of the water I hear the bathroom door creaking open, and the shuffle of footsteps. They sound as if they're heading my way. There's a pause, and then the handle of my shower cubicle moves.

'There's someone in here!' I call. How could they not hear the water running? Then I hear something else – a scratching sound. I quickly rinse the rest of the shampoo out of my hair and grab the towel.

'Hello?' I haven't heard the footsteps again, and with the water turned off I can make out another sound – a raggedly huffing sound, as if whoever's outside is struggling to breathe. My heart starts to thud as I remember what Farrell said about someone weird coming into his room.

Oh God.

'Who's there?' My voice wavers.

No answer. I press my ear to the door. The breathing sound has stopped, and then I hear the scuff of footsteps receding. The bathroom door bangs shut.

Body still damp, I pull on my pyjamas. I count to three, hesitate and, before I lose my nerve, unlock the door and peer out.

The bathroom is empty, but I can't miss the man-sized muddy footprints tracked across the floor, leading right to my shower cubicle.

I run out into the corridor. It appears to be as deserted as before, but then I catch a glimpse of movement. A bulky, malformed shape is shuffling towards the far end. There's something… wrong about the way it's moving, as if the proportions of its body are skewed. It's too far away for me to figure out if it's because its legs are too short, its arms too long or the head too big. It pauses, turns around as if it can feel me staring at it – and then it's gone.

I have to tell someone.

The nurses' station is deserted, but a few doors down from my ward I hear the murmur of voices. I race towards it. An exhausted-looking nurse, one I haven't seen before, bustles out of the room.

She strides past me, fiddling with a beeper on her belt. 'Excuse me!' I whisper, touching her sleeve to get her attention.

'Get back in bed,' she snaps.

'There's someone in the ward! He was in the bathrooms. While I was showering!'

She sighs and rolls her eyes. 'Just the cleaners.'

'What cleaners?' I gesture to the empty corridor. 'Really, there was someone. I saw him!'

She mutters something in Zulu. 'I will come just now. There are other emergencies tonight. You must wait.'

What else can I do but head back to bed? Should I go to Farrell, tell him what I've seen? He'll hardly thank me for waking him up at this time of night. I can always find him in the morning. If he's still talking to me.

Then I realise I've forgotten my shampoo and towel in the shower cubicle. I'm tempted to leave it until the morning, but it's all I've got and I can't risk it being stolen.

I enter the bathroom cautiously. One of the stall doors is shut. A toilet flushes, making me jump, and behind the closed door someone mumbles to themselves. Just another patient.

I head towards the shower cubicle.

Oh God.

This wasn't here before. I'd remember.

Someone's scratched a word into the door's paintwork, the letters six inches high and angrily scored right through to the wood:

RUN

Chapter 5

FARRELL

Now that my mind's working at full pace, and it's just my eyes I'm waiting for, the images are starting to creep back in. Why was Katya crying like that? Why was there blood on her face?

I lie in the storeroom's darkness, willing myself to remember. Monday morning is a blank. I'm not sure whether I can't remember or if I'm choosing not to remember. I can smell my vomitty clothes next to this cot. I can hear that thrum again somewhere below, and I'm sure I can make out screams, or music, or something woven into the whine of the machine, just at the edge of my hearing. I know I'm making it up, finding a pattern in the white noise of the air-con fan, but, once I've heard the sound, there's nothing I can do to loosen its grip.

I swear there's something scratching in the glass-fronted cabinets at my side.

Concentrate. You're just avoiding it again. Think.

Okay, this is what I remember.

Normal Monday morning. We were up about seven. Sunday night, I'd made Katya her favourite linguine and we watched a movie. Christ, what was it? We watched it... Why can't I remember? Did we drink a lot? We had... let's see... we had a bottle of red. Nothing special. That was all; Katya knew how I felt about her getting high at home.

I woke up tired. I took a shower, I think. The usual routine. Then next thing I know she's crying. This is what I see in my mind. She's crying like a toddler, snot dripping out of her nose, eyes red and ringed with black smudges. There's blood on her face. I can't understand the look in her eyes. I've never seen her cry like this before. *Why, Kay?* She backs away from me, as if scared. *Let me go, Josh!* That doesn't sound right. This sounds like someone else's story.

Then I remember I'm sitting on the couch, my head in my hands, elbows on my knees. *Take a good, long look*, she says, although I'm looking at her. *It's the last time you'll see it.* She doesn't bother to wipe the blood off her cheeks. *Take a good look at the face you love so much*, she says again. She picks up a tog bag and leaves.

That picture of her face in my mind is—

'Mr Farrell?'

'Hhhr... Wha...'

'Mr Farrell, I've got something for you.'

'Oh, Nomsa. What time is it?'

'Five thirty. I'm just about to start my shift, but I've got a present for you.' The clatter of a little cardboard box, the crackle of a plastic seal breaking. 'Lie back. Open your eyes.'

I do as she says.

The cleansing flush of cold drops on my eyeballs. Left eye. Right eye. Nomsa puts the little bottle in my palm and closes my fingers around it.

'It's the Maxitrol drops you need. Two drops morning and night for two weeks. Please don't tell anyone; I'd get into trouble.'

'But how will you—?'

'Just don't let them see it. Absurd that they have the medicine you need but won't supply it.'

The thank you is forming on my lips but she's gone already. I imagine the mould in my eyes burning away like mist in the sun, but I worry about what I'll see when it has. Katya's bloodied face. I squeeze my sore hand. It couldn't have been me, could it? And if for some fucked-up reason I hurt her, I'm dead. Glenn will cut me up into little pieces if I've laid a finger on his daughter.

There's no way I would have hurt Katya. Surely? But does Glenn know that?

'Jesus. Did you hear?'

'Yes. I'm going down now.'

'We need all available staff from this floor in casualty. Skeleton staff to remain only.'

'How many do they think?'

'I don't know. More than a hundred. Maybe two.'

'Fuck.'

'At least seventeen dead.'

'We'd better get down there.'

As they hurry past my closet, my fingers itch to check my phone for the news, see what happened. A bomb? A crash? Where?

I get out of bed, pulling myself up by the drip stand. I unplug the tube from my arm. There has to be a TV somewhere on this floor, or a radio, or someone with a web connection. Maybe someone else's visitors will be able to tell me what's happened.

I shamble along the corridor. If it was five thirty a.m. when Nomsa came in, it's about seven now. It should be busy this time of the morning but the section is dead quiet. One of the old women starts groaning again. It goes on and on; there's nobody here to help her.

I stand against the wall across from the nurses' station trying to get my bearings, waiting for someone to come past; waiting to hear something that will explain what's going on. But all I see is quiet, still smudges. Then another two dark-blue nurse shapes run past me towards the Green Section's exit before I can stop them, their soft shoes squeaking on the lino. A patient coughs up a gout of mucus in the ward nearest to me, then subsides into silence again. What the hell is going on?

'Farrell!' Lisa appears in my blur and grips my wrist. She's breathing in heavy gasps as if she's been running. 'Thank God! This place is not... Something's not right and last night I didn't get any sleep and I was thinking about what you said about having another operation in here and then and then—'

'Whoa, slow down.'

She takes another hitching breath. Christ, this is just what I need now. I try to wrangle my arm out of her grasp but she's not letting go.

'I need to get out of here,' she says, and I can hear the tears in her voice. 'There was a man in the bathroom while I was showering and I think... I think he was following me, watching me. I wondered if he... He was creepy, like you said.'

'What do you mean?'

'Big, limpy. Like his legs were different lengths. He had a white coat, like a doctor. But he wasn't.'

Jesus. 'Did he have, like, grey skin? A weird big head, sweaty?'

'Yes, that's him! He was following me. He followed me into the bathroom.'

'Did he hurt you?'

'No... he was... God. I've got to get out of here. I can't stay here anymore.'

'But how? We're locked in.'

'There's nobody here. Even the security guard's gone.'

'I heard there was an accident. Do you know what happened?'

'Yes, the Gautrain, you know, the one they built for the World Cup—'

'I know what the fucking Gautrain is, Lisa!' She whimpers. 'Sorry,' I say quickly. 'What about it?'

'It crashed. More than four hundred people on board. Lumpy Legs – the nurse, you know, the sister, the one that's so mean – well, I overheard her talking to one of the other nurses about it this morning.'

Holy fuck. The fucking Gautrain...

'Anyway, the security guard's not at the gate. We can buzz ourselves out,' she continues. 'He'll be back soon. Now's our only chance to leave. I mean... I can help you if you also want to leave now. I think... I think something bad's going to happen.'

This woman has serious issues, obviously. *Something bad's going to happen*. But fuck. If she's also seen that freak, maybe she's right. I consider my options: wait here till I can see and am officially discharged, or take the gap and get back into the real world. Find Katya, find out what happened. Find out if Glenn is hunting me. Then, when I've done that, go and see a proper fucking doctor.

'*Please*, Farrell. The security guard's coming… We have to go now.'

I'd have to leave my iPhone and my wallet behind at the nurses' station. I can always claim the insurance though, provided that isn't as fucked as my medical aid.

'Okay,' I say. 'Let's do it.'

She sighs with relief and starts hustling. She pulls me along, the cool air whistling through my bare-arse gown as we go. I turn back to see the dark shape of the guard strolling behind us. He's in no hurry.

'Stop, Lisa. Stop! If he sees us running, he'll chase us. We're just going for a walk, okay? Let's go slowly. We're still between him and the door.'

Lisa slows down but I can sense how panicked she is by the increasing pressure of her grip on my arm. That's my fucked-up arm from the drip. I try not to cry out, and instead shift her fingers up to my bicep.

I dart another smudged look over my shoulder. The guard's still some way behind us and we're nearly at the security gate.

Oh shit. 'Oh shit.'

'What?' says Lisa, tugging on my arm.

'The eye drops. I need the eye drops.' No way am I going anywhere without those. 'You go ahead. Don't worry. Good luck, okay.'

'Where are they?'

'They're on a shelf on the far side of my bed.'

'Dammit…' Lisa casts around, indecisive, breathing heavily. 'Oh God. Okay. He's gone into the toilet. I'll be back. Don't go anywhere.'

She sprints off and I stare into space for a minute. I imagine that the blurs I see are getting just a little crisper around the edges. An image of Katya's bloodied face blindsides me and I feel like I've been kicked in the chest. Glenn's fat head looms over it.

Next thing, Lisa's pressing the vial into my hand. Her quiet, shocked voice surprises me. 'Did you see what was on the cabinet by your bed?'

'I didn't see anything. I can't see.'

'Okay.'

'What was it?'

'No, don't worry. It's nothing.'

'Come *on*, Lisa! What the…? Lisa?' She's ducked out of my eyeline and now I can't spot her blur anywhere. Has she gone without me?

'Lisa!' I call, aware that my voice is too loud in the deathly ward. I grope towards the security gate and walk into the guard's patio chair; it clatters across the lino loud enough to wake the dead. 'Lisa,' I hiss. *Fuck it.*

'I'm here. Here. I brought you something to wear.' She shoves a cotton bundle into my hands. 'Just some scrubs. They look clean enough. Better than that, anyway.'

Lisa leads me down a hallway to a lift and presses the button. The air smells different outside the Green Section, both fresher and ranker, as if fresh air from the outside world is mixing with the gasses of seriously diseased and decomposing people in other sections, each washing over us in currents.

The lift door opens with a ding and Lisa presses a button. Soon as the door closes, I struggle to orient the baggy pants, then pull them on, keeping the gown on over them. We descend for a bit, then the door opens again into a poorly lit space.

'Where are we? What's here?'

'I don't know. Two doors. One with a keypad.' Her voice trails away as she goes. She rattles at the door and mutters something.

'What's there? Please keep talking.'

'It's locked. The other door looks like… Oh, Farrell.'

We both hear the lift grinding in the shaft behind us.

Fuck. 'It could be the security guard,' I say. 'What about the other door?'

'Uh…'

'What's the problem?' The lift's grinding closer.

More hesitation. Then she grabs my wrist. 'Okay, come.'

I hear a heavy metallic click and a rubber squeal – somehow a familiar sound – and Lisa pulls me through the door with a squeaking shear, then slams it behind us. Clink. That's it, that's where I know that sound. It's just like the lock on the beer fridge in a bottle store. They don't open from the inside.

A muffled voice from the other side of the door, then it stops. I hear only our breath. When I open my eyes, the light is bright, light green, like underwater. It's cold.

Dead silence. Then what my mind's been trying to ignore. The smell kicks in. Lisa grabs me and hides her face, cowering between me and the door.

'What is this place, Lisa?'

Chapter 6

LISA

'Christ. It stinks in here.' Farrell pulls up the top of his gown to cover his mouth and nose. 'Fuck... Are we in the fucking morgue?'

'Yes.'

'*Fuck.*'

The morgues they show on *CSI* and *Silent Witness* are always clean, brightly lit places, clad in stainless steel and hi-tech fittings, but this area is small and dingy. The floor is covered in that crappy linoleum, and the dented cadaver drawers are grubby and scratched and smeared with dirty fingerprints. Although it's chilly, it's as if there's not enough oxygen in the room, and I'm starting to feel light-headed. Still, as gross as it is in here, there's a part of me that's coldly fascinated by what I'm seeing.

Farrell shuffles to the side of the room and peers myopically at the three gurneys shoved against the drawers. They're piled with lumpy, zippered black plastic bags.

'Jesus,' he says. 'Are those bodies?'

'I think so.' Two of the bodies aren't anywhere near large enough to fill the bags out and I try not to look at them.

'Christ. Why aren't they in the... freezer or wherever they keep them?'

'I don't know. Maybe there's no space.'

Farrell flaps a hand in front of his face. 'Christ... I've never smelled anything like it.'

'Try not to breathe too deeply,' I say. 'You'll get used to the smell soon.'

'How the fuck would you know that?' he snaps. 'Look, let's just go back.'

For a second I want to do just that. The light-headedness is turning into a weird disconnected feeling as if part of me has skipped away for a bit. But then I remember that grey-faced man and what I saw in Farrell's room and the world snaps back into focus. We can't go back.

'Come on,' he says, making for the door behind us.

'Wait! Think about it, Farrell.' I don't recognise my voice. I sound sure of myself, in control. 'There has to be another exit through here. I mean... I mean, it's unlikely that they'd bring the dead bodies through the hospital.'

'Lisa, what the fuck are you talking about?'

'I mean, funeral directors have to fetch the dead people from somewhere, right? There's probably a back entrance or exit.'

He hesitates. 'Lisa, you're creeping me out a bit here. How in the fuck would you know something like that?'

Heat races to my cheeks. 'Um, you know. TV and books and stuff.' A sudden image of my room back home flashes into my mind – the room I sometimes don't leave for days at a time. What would Farrell say if he saw the pink flouncy coverlet, the piles of cheap true-crime paperbacks, my *Grey's Anatomy* DVDs and the Girls Aloud posters that I haven't bothered taking down for years?

'Let's try through here,' he says, heading towards the double doors in front of us.

They're made of thick black rubber and he has to push against them with his shoulder to shove them open wide enough for us to slip through.

'Ah, man,' Farrell says. 'It smells even worse in here. Like rotten meat only... I dunno, sweeter.'

This room is far larger than the last. The walls and floors are covered with cracked porcelain tiles and mildewed grouting; shallow open drains criss-cross the floor. The light winks off a saw and pair of scales that are on a shelf next to the row of sinks at the far side. There are two stainless steel tables in the centre of the room; one is empty, but lying on the other is what looks to be a twisted, charred tree trunk. I don't get it. Why would there be burned wood in a morgue?

But my stomach figures it out before my brain registers what I'm looking at, and I have to swallow convulsively as saliva floods into my mouth.

It isn't wood.

Of course it isn't.

I grab Farrell's arm to steady myself. 'Oh God,' I breathe.

'What?'

'You don't want to know.'

'Christ,' he says. 'Is that what I think it is?'

The thing on the table was once a person, its back twisted into an impossible converse foetal position, its limbs drawn tightly into its sides as if they've shrunk into its body. Its skin is a cracked, hard, blackened mass; its fingers, toes and hair are gone. I can't tell if it was once male or female, young or old. Then the nausea disappears and I find myself taking a step forward and gazing down at the face, nothing but a charcoal rictus mask. It looks fragile, like, if I touched it, it would crumble.

'You think this is someone from the crash?' Farrell asks.

I jump as a door in the far right-hand corner of the room swings open and bashes against the wall. A stocky man wearing thick green gloves and a gore-spattered industrial-looking apron appears. He's mumbling to himself. He starts when he catches sight of us.

'What are you doing in here?' he says in a thick accent. 'You should not be in here.'

Farrell clears his throat. 'Sorry, we—'

'No, no, no. This is not good.' He's foreign – Spanish or Cuban. I can't tell how old he is; his olive skin is unlined, but his hair is wispy and thinning. He stares at the dressing covering my nose and my hand automatically leaps to my face. His gaze slides to Farrell's hospital gown, blue scrub trousers and bare feet. 'How did you get here?'

'We're lost,' Farrell says, trying to grin charmingly. 'We'd really appreciate it if you'd point us towards the exit.'

He remains impassive. 'There is no exit down here. This is a restricted area.'

'Yeah. Sorry about that,' Farrell says. 'Please, we—'

'Which ward are you from? You are patients? You should not be here.'

The black doors smash open, and a porter pushing a gurney containing a sheet-draped body barrels in. 'Incoming,' the porter says. He's a youngish guy with cornrows and bloodshot eyes.

The Cuban man sighs. 'How many more times? Do not bring them in here. They are to go to the viewing room for storage.'

The porter stares at him blankly.

'The viewing room. Now!' the man snaps.

The porter shrugs. 'Don't know it, boss.' He glances at me and Farrell, then at the charred body on the table, but his bored, slightly resentful expression doesn't change.

'Wait here,' the Cuban guy says to us. Muttering under his breath, he herds the porter and the gurney back towards the double doors.

'Now's our chance,' Farrell whispers when they've disappeared.

We head towards the door in the corner of the room. Farrell stumbles into one of the shallow drains in the floor and I grab his arm to steady him, trying not to step into the globs of... matter... and drying blood that haven't been sluiced away.

The door opens into a long, narrow corridor. It ends in a metal roll-down shutter like the doors you see in warehouses and halfway along it there's another door set into the wall. I jiggle its handle and push against it.

'Locked.'

'Fucking great,' Farrell mutters.

'There has to be a way to open that rolling door.' Then I see it. There's a chunky control panel hanging from a thick cord attached to the ceiling. I race up to it and press the single red button.

Nothing happens for a second, and then there's a whir as the metal door's mechanism grinds into life. It starts inching upwards. Light seeps in from underneath. Daylight. I'm sure of it.

'I think we can get out this way,' I say, as Farrell shuffles up behind me.

The door behind us bangs open.

'Hey! No, no! You must not open that!' the Cuban man shouts. He jogs towards us. 'No!'

I turn to face him. 'I'm sorry, but you don't understand. We really need to—'

'What in the hell...?' Farrell says, scrunching up his eyes and leaning forward. He sounds shell-shocked. 'This can't...'

I turn back to the door. It's now halfway open, and my stomach clenches into a sick, hard knot. Even with his blurred vision, there's no way Farrell could have mistaken what's in front of us. I realise I'm looking straight into the back of a huge refrigerated truck that's backed up against the doorway. There's not enough space to slip around it, but, even if there was, I'm not sure I want to get any closer. The truck's floor is piled with more of those black body bags, seemingly chucked randomly one on top of the other. To one side there's a stack of bulbous transparent plastic bags, smaller, sealed with tape. I don't want to think about what they contain.

I wait for the nausea to wash over me, but it doesn't. All I feel is that strange detached calmness, as if my brain has decided that it's not actually going to process what my eyes are seeing.

'What the hell is this?' Farrell says to the Cuban guy. 'What the hell is going on?'

'The accident – it is very bad. There are too many people to deal with. The city morgue is backed up as it is. We have to store them somewhere for now. It is standard procedure.'

'You store them in a truck?'

The man nods. 'Yes.'

'But that's disgusting. That's not right!' Farrell rubs a hand over his eyes. 'How many bodies *are* there?'

'There are many.'

'Christ.'

The man shrugs. 'You should not have been here. I now have no choice but to call security.'

'Please,' I say to him. 'Please. We need to leave.'

'How do I know that you are not thieves? Burglars? *Ladrones*?'

'We're not. You have to trust us.' My cheeks are cold, and I rub my palms over them. Tears have leaked from my eyes without my being aware of them. 'Please.'

He sighs. He looks from me to Farrell again, and seems to come to some sort of decision. 'This way.'

We follow him back to the locked door. He pulls a bunch of keys out of his pocket, inserts one in the lock and opens the door. The hinges scream as if they haven't been oiled in months.

'What's through here?' Farrell asks. He squints his eyes and shakes his head as if he's trying to clear his vision. 'It's too dark for me to see.'

The door opens into a dim, sloping concrete walkway that seems to go on forever. It looks dusty and unused.

'It is the old service corridor. You go up here, yes? Take the elevator to the third floor.'

'Thank you,' I say. 'We're very grateful.'

'You don't tell anybody you were here. Okay?'

We head through the door, and it slams behind us, the lock clicking with finality. Farrell stumbles, bangs heavily into my side.

'Christ,' he says. 'Can't see a thing.'

I hold onto his elbow and guide him forwards. There's something not quite right about the camber of the slope, the angle feels awkward. It's slow going, but I begin to make out the lift doors at the end. They look old-fashioned, purely functional, larger than the kind you see in malls and parking lots. Made specially to accommodate the gurneys containing... But I don't want to think about that. I don't want to think about what we've just seen. I can't. I tentatively touch the bandage on my face.

Farrell sighs, runs a hand through his hair. 'Lisa, you think we're doing the right thing?'

'What do you mean?'

'I mean, don't you think we're blowing this out of proportion?'

I pause and turn to look at him. It's not warm in here, but sweat beads his forehead. 'No. There's something weird going on here, Farrell. What about that freaky guy who was spying on me?'

'I know all that.' He sounds irritable again, pissed off with me and I'm tempted to just agree with him. But I can't. I can't go back. 'Say we get out of here,' he continues. 'What then?'

'What do you mean?'

'You got any money?'

'No.'

'So what are we going to do when we do get out?'

'I don't know. We'll go across to the mall, call someone.'

'Who? You're not even from here.'

'Haven't you got any friends? Someone who'll give us a lift?' He doesn't answer. 'Let's just play it by ear. After what we saw... back there, you really want to stay here any longer?'

He shrugs.

We've reached the lift. I press the button, and the doors slide open with a clank. The interior is clad in stainless steel and I can't avoid catching a glimpse of my reflection. A tall skinny woman with a dressing over her nose and lank blonde hair drooping over her shoulders stares back at me. I don't recognise myself. I look older, haggard, tired. I look like a stranger.

'What floor did he say?'

'Three,' Farrell snaps, folding his arms and moving away from me. I can feel tears pricking my eyes again and I will them not to fall. I know he's worried and probably as freaked out as I am, but... *Please don't hate me.*

I press the button and the lift shudders upwards. My stomach drops and I'm hit with another wave of wooziness.

The lift grumbles to a stop.

I swallow the tears back and do my best to sound normal. 'When we get out we just have to—'

The doors slide open onto pure chaos.

'Where the *fuck* are we?' Farrell asks.

But it's obvious where we are. We're at ground zero. Casualty. After the near silence of the morgue, the noise is overwhelming. Screams, howls, shouting, and above it all someone's yelling, 'I shouldn't be here! I've got medical aid! Listen to me!'

The corridor in front of us is stacked with hospital beds and gurneys and, although I'm trying not to look too closely at the patients lying on them, I can't help it: a half-naked woman, her thighs covered in seeping blisters; a sobbing boy, his knees drawn up to his chest; a nurse frantically trying to jab a drip into the arm of an emaciated teenage girl whose face is a mask of blood. Nurses run up and down the corridor, shouting instructions at each other and a doctor in a bloodstained white coat hurries past us, screaming into a cellphone, 'Don't you understand? There are no more fucking beds!'

I grab Farrell's arm to hold him back as a pair of grim-faced paramedics dressed in soot-smeared overalls speed past us clutching a defibrillator. They disappear into a curtained-off area.

'Which way?' Farrell asks.

I rip my eyes away from the sight of a nurse pulling a shard of glass out of the arm of a screaming boy, a woman with gore-soaked blonde hair bawling next to them, and search for the signs.

The right-hand corridor leads to Maternity, the left to casualty and admissions. There has to be an exit through there.

'Left,' I say. 'Stay close.'

No one tries to stop us as we weave our way through the chaos. We edge past a man lying on a filthy sheet. His right arm ends in a bandaged stump and he stares up at us blankly. A small child sits huddled next to a woman wrapped in a blanket; neither looks up as we pass.

The noise intensifies as we head further into the casualty ward, and I realise that the patients we've already passed are the ones who are going to make it; the ones who aren't going to end up in the black bags, stored in the refrigerated truck.

'Triage,' I mumble. 'That's what they're probably doing.'

'What?' Even though I know he can't see clearly, Farrell's eyes are glassy with horror.

'They're prioritising the injured. Sorting them into the ones that are the most critical.'

'Jesus, Lisa.'

A harried nurse pushes out of a curtained-off area, and for a split second I get a glimpse of a woman whose face is nothing but a mass of raw flesh. We stumble through what was once the waiting-room area. The plastic chairs have been shoved aside to make room for more makeshift beds and drip stands, and another pair of paramedics, their faces scored with exhaustion, race past us, pushing a twitching body on a gurney. Next to the nurses' station a doctor is trying to revive a hugely fat man, his shirt cut away to reveal a fish-belly white stomach. The doctor yells for back-up.

Someone grabs my wrist. At first I think it's Farrell, but it can't be. Head down, he's making his way towards the glass exit doors, the flash of emergency lights blasting into the waiting room, saturating the scene in flickering red light.

I look down and straight into the eyes of a skinny dark-haired woman. She's young, maybe a year or two older than me, and she's lying on the floor next to the admissions desk. Even though her clothes are torn and covered in soot and filth, I can tell that they were once expensive. She tightens her grip on my wrist. I try to loosen it, but she's strong.

'Help me,' she whispers. 'My daughter – I need to find my daughter.'

'I... I...'

'*Please.*' She begs me with her eyes. But what can I do? Farrell is almost at the exit doors now.

Follow him. Run.

'I'm sorry,' I whisper, hating myself. Pulling my wrist free, I skitter away. I don't look back.

Chapter 7

FARRELL

I can still make out the whoops and wails of the ambulances as they negotiate their way through the chaos back there. I can even imagine screaming and crying, but that's probably just reverberations from the hellish soundscape we blundered through. Whether it was the injured people or their desperate relatives I couldn't tell, but all their shouts and cries meant the same thing: pain and fear. And the smell. Burned clothes, burned hair, burned flesh.

I inhale deeply to try to clear the person-ash out of my lungs and get my breath back. Take in air right to the bottom of my lungs, slowly out; deep inhalation, slowly out. As I do, I think of Katya. If Nomsa left a message for her, why hasn't she come to see me? Was what happened on Monday morning that bad? Or maybe it's just that she's on a shoot. Yes. A job. That's much more likely. I'll get home, sort this out.

Next thing, I'm on my arse on the grass.

'Are you okay?' Lisa asks.

My mind comes back into focus. I must have just gone faint from all the heavy breathing. It's the first time I've had some fresh air all week. For a moment I expect my vision to resolve out of the grey like it does after you've passed out, but then I remember that I can't see. Where the hell are my eye drops? Have I lost them?

I fumble around on the grass.

'Here,' Lisa says, pressing the vial into my hand.

'Thanks.' I tip a couple of drops into each eye. Even though Nomsa said twice a day, morning and night, I'm desperate for this shit to clear out of my eyes, and to have my full senses back. Outside, in Johannesburg, you've got to be on your guard.

I concentrate on what I can make out. Greenery, spots of colour, a fresh smell: freshly cut grass and floral scent. I breathe again, careful not to overdo it, stay sitting on the spongy grass, my arse getting wet from the dew. I imagine the clean air replacing every molecule of the death stench we've been through. There's birdsong.

'Where are we?'

Lisa's still standing by my side. 'A garden. Someone's house.'

'How did we get in here?'

'I don't know, we were just running. I went through this gate across the road.'

I can picture the sort of house, those boxy suburban properties around the concrete monolith of New Hope Hospital. But why would anyone leave their gate open to the street? 'We'd better hope there are no dogs.'

'Let's keep going.' Lisa grabs my wrist and tries to help me up, but she crashes down over me when she starts to pull. Her body is warm, tense. She struggles off me, sits on the grass next to me and groans.

'You okay? We both seem to be falling today.'

'Ugh, headrush. I'm starving. I was supposed to have the surgery today so I haven't eaten for ages.'

'Are you sure it's okay for you to be out here? I mean, if you were supposed to have an operation, then shouldn't you—'

'But you said that I shouldn't risk having surgery there again!'

Christ. Is she really that suggestible? What do I know? 'Why were they going to operate again anyway?'

'They said... I had complications after the last one.'

'Shit, Lisa. That doesn't sound good. What kind of complications?' Christ, what if she collapses on me or something? Starts haemorrhaging or whatever.

'I'm not going back there. You didn't see what I saw. I'm not just being paranoid. There's something seriously wrong in that place.'

'Christ, Lisa. Of course it's going to be a bit weird. There's just been a huge accident—'

'*Besides* that!' she snaps. 'I *know* about hospitals, and I'm telling you, there's something wrong there. Normal hospitals don't just let psychos drift around stalking their patients. You saw him too!'

'Okay,' I say. 'Okay.' But now I'm out here, breathing normal air that doesn't stink like puke and death and cheap disinfectant, I'm starting to think maybe I overreacted. What if that grey freak was just some deranged old man with dementia or something? That could be it. The Green Section was full of freaky old people.

'Plus, that woman in my room,' Lisa continues. 'She died after a hip replacement. That doesn't happen. That fre— that man. He was trying to tell me to run... Like he knows something.'

Honestly, I'm trying not to, but all I hear is a hysterical woman. I'm trying to give her the benefit of the doubt, but it sounds to me like she's just got a notion in her head and is making up a whole plot around it. What a Z-type fuck-up.

I say nothing. Birds chatter in the trees around us. I smell a waft of fresh air. I don't want to run around. I'd much rather just sit for a moment. This is the most comfortable I've been for a long time.

'And then there's what they were trying to do to you,' she says.

'What do you mean, do to me?'

'Next to your bed... What they... Oh, hell. Never mind.'

'Jesus, Lisa! What the fuck did you see?'

She's silent for a while, deciding. A bee buzzes around my head, then leaves.

'Pictures,' she says.

I wait. She says nothing more.

'What pictures?' I'm losing my patience.

'I shouldn't have said anything. Never mind.'

'*Don't* fucking tell me to...' Jesus. Her blurred shape flinches away from me again. I have to relax. How can I speak like this to someone I don't even know? To anyone? 'Sorry. I didn't mean to... I'm sorry, okay?'

She doesn't say anything. I look to her, but her shape gives me no clues. Now she's just sitting there.

'Lisa? You okay? I'm sorry.'

'They were pictures of you. Those instant ones – what do you call them?'

'Polaroids?'

'Yes!' Who the fuck uses Polaroids anymore? 'That's it. Like someone had been taking pictures of you as you slept.' Her voice is flat, like she's talking to herself. 'But in them you were marked. You know like how a cosmetic surgeon will mark you with black felt pen before the surgery? Or like one of those diagrams in a butcher shop. You know, a cow, divided up into choice cuts.'

'What the fuck?'

She reaches forward and for a second I think she's going to jump on me, try to kiss me or something. Before I can push her back, she pulls the neck of my hospital gown down, then instantly recoils. 'Oh my God,' she breathes.

'What?'

'On your... on your... chest.'

I rip my gown up and crane down to see my torso. Through the blur I can make out bold black marks across my stomach and chest. *Holy fuck.* I feel like vomiting.

'Jesus, Lisa. What the fuck's going on in there? Some kind of sick joke? You think the nurses are trying to mess with me?'

'I don't know. How would I know?'

That has to be it. Some kind of sick joke they play on the rich people who wash up by accident on their wards.

I need to get some perspective. Calm the fuck down. Calm Lisa down. Take charge. I do my best to sound as rational and focussed as I can. 'All we have to do is get far away from here, report this shit to whoever the authorities are and then I guess you should go to another hospital. There are loads of private clinics in Joburg, there must be a vacancy somewhere.'

'I can't go to a private clinic.'

'You don't have medical aid?'

'It's not that. There are other... complications.'

'Like what?'

She doesn't answer.

'Like *what*, Lisa?'

'Nobody else will do the surgery. It's not safe. I've had too many. I only came here because they didn't ask... because they said they would do it.'

'What do you mean you've had too many?'

'It doesn't matter.' She's quiet, then she's crying.

The air's ripped by a helicopter's blades chopping above us. Its dark shape squats down behind the trees at the hospital.

Lisa gasps and swallows as she stifles her tears. 'Sorry, sorry,' she says. I wish she'd stop apologising.

The helicopter's noise is a wake-up call. Soon as I'm home I'm going to make things right. I get up. First step, find a phone. The hospital is my best bet. 'Can you help me back to the hospital?'

'No!'

'Hang on, hang on. Just to Reception. They don't need to know who I am. I'll just ask to use the phone.'

'No, Farrell, please. I told you, something bad is going to happen there.'

'You don't think your "something bad" has already happened? There are dead bodies piling up outside from a train crash and you think they're planning to carve me up. What else can happen?'

She just shakes her head.

'Besides,' I say. 'You have to have your operation. You should see a doctor straight away. I'll just call someone to come and get us.' Who? If Katya's on a job, she wouldn't be able to. What about Eduardo? I'll just call a taxi, go home, sort it out from there. 'It's our only option.'

'What if there's someone here? Instead of going back to the hospital?'

'Where?'

'Here. In this house.'

'Right. Like some householder's going to let a woman and a blind man wearing a patient's gown in to "use the phone". Across the road from New Hope Hospital, which, if you weren't aware, is where they patch up the crims and hijackers. Not bloody likely.'

Lisa's up and pacing as a helicopter clatters over our heads. I can even see the outlines of her arms as she riffles her hair in agitation. I blink, blink again. It's not a trick. I'm seeing better.

'Farrell. There's a—'

'Freeze!' I duck. CRACK!

'Farrell!'

Holy fuck, someone's shooting at us.

'I said *freeze!*'

I stand still, raise my hands halfway up. The voice is coming from behind me, but I don't know which direction I'm facing now.

'Lisa!' I whisper. 'Lisa!'

The man shouts again, his voice tinged with excitement. 'Shut up. Get down on the ground!'

'Lisa!'

CRACK!

'One more move and the next one's in your back. It's not a good day to test us.'

I crumble to my knees, wondering where Lisa is, why she's not answering. She can't be far. I sink to my belly. All I can hope is that this is a security guard. If it's a burglar, we're fucked. There's no reason for him to keep us alive.

A walkie-talkie sputters. 'Dispatch, come in. Goosen, Patrol 907. Two intruders apprehended at 67 Hospital Road. Request backup.' Thank Jesus. I breathe again. This guy is probably private security, probably less likely than a criminal to kill us. I hear Lisa whimpering a few metres away from me, also from the level of the lawn. She's okay. That's good.

Then I hear the sssh-sssh-sssh of lawn-footsteps coming towards us.

'Hey! Stop there! Identify please.'

'I'm RN Nomsa Makgatho. I work at the... at the hospital. These patients got lost in the chaos there. I'm here to bring them back. Can I show you my ID card?'

The guard's boots thump by us. Nomsa. Thank God. She'll be able to explain what's been happening.

'Okay, Nurse. But you better keep a closer eye on your patients, okay? You're blarry lucky I didn't shoot them.'

'Yes, Officer. I'm really sorry.'

Will Nomsa be able to explain the pictures in my room?

If there *are* any pictures.

The chilling thought hits me: Lisa's the crazy one. Of course she is. It sounds like she's addicted to cosmetic surgery, like Michael Jackson or something. She's just paranoid and for some reason she's making up some lie. What if she's the one who drew the lines on me?

Nomsa will sort things out.

The guard radios back to dispatch. 'Patrol 907 to dispatch. All clear. Situation at 67 Hospital Road resolved.' His boots thud away.

Nomsa bends to help me up.

'No,' Lisa says. 'I'm not going back!'

'Come on, Clien— Ms Cassavetes,' Nomsa says, moving away from me. 'We need to prep you for the surgery, and you really shouldn't be running around out here. You'll need all your str—'

'*No!*' Lisa screams. 'Get your hands *off* me!'

'Apologies, Ms Cassavetes, but you are in my care.'

Lisa half-screams, then she's silent. I hear her flump to the ground.

Christ. 'What did you do?'

'I'm sorry about that, Mr Farrell, but it's vital that we get Ms Cassavetes back to the wards as a matter of urgency. She's quite comfortable now, don't you concern yourself. The orderlies are right behind me to collect her now. Why were you out here with her?'

'I'm sorry. I thought... I don't know. I just got spooked...'

She laughs. 'Spooked, Mr Farrell?'

'With everything going on, the accident...'

'That's understandable,' she says soothingly. 'We've never seen anything like it. But it's all under control now.'

'Lisa – Ms Cassavetes – she said there was something going on in the ward. She says she saw someone, a man stalking her or something.'

I don't mention to Nomsa that I've seen him too; I don't want Nomsa thinking that I'm as fucked up as Lisa.

'Ms Cassavetes is overwrought, Mr Farrell, and I probably shouldn't be telling you this, but she has quite a complex medical and psychological history. Prone to hysteria.'

That makes sense. Fuck it, I even *knew* Lisa was just hysterical, but I still let her drag me out of there. Messed-up chick. I actually feel sorry for her.

'Now, shall we get back?' She takes my arm.

'Wait. She said there were photographs, Polaroids of me in my room.' I pull my gown up, wishing to Christ that I could gauge Nomsa's expression. 'And there's this.'

'Goodness!' Nomsa says. 'How odd.' She laughs a tinkly laugh. 'Why have you been drawing on yourself, Mr Farrell?'

'I didn't do this!'

She tuts. 'Probably one of the interns showing a little bit of disregard, then. Don't you worry, I'll make sure they're disciplined. Now, let's get you back, safe and sound.'

I want to ask her again about Katya – if she tried calling her again – but Nomsa's already leading me briskly through the trees.

'It will all work out, Mr Farrell, you'll see. Ms Cassavetes will have her surgery tonight. And you, Mr Farrell, have an appointment.'

Chapter 8

LISA

Have I been sleeping?

I don't remember passing out, but I feel that same grogginess that comes after waking suddenly from a deep sleep. And for some reason I'm lying flat on my back. I only ever sleep on my side.

I open my eyes, and the light makes them water. I blink frantically and try to turn my head away, but my skull feels like it's been filled with cement. My temples throb.

And it's not just my head that feels strange. I try to lift my left hand, but it doesn't want to move. I attempt to wiggle my fingers. Nothing, maybe a faint tingling, but that's it. It's as if there's a glitch in the wiring between my brain and body and the messages aren't getting through.

Oh God.

The first wisps of panic start snaking through my body – my pulse rate picks up, blood pounds in my ears, and a cold hand starts squeezing my lungs.

I suck air in through my lips. I need to think about something else, divert my mind, stop the panic smothering me.

First things first. Figure out where I am.

I hear the clatter of something metallic. A bedpan? Then a groan, a hacking cough. And the ceiling looks familiar – grubby white paintwork and rows of strip-lighting. There's the rustle of fabric being swished back, and someone nudges my shoulder.

'Where you been, doll?'

Oh thank God! Gertie. So I'm definitely back on my ward. But how the hell did I get here? *Think!*

'You were gone for ages,' she says, 'missed all the fun.' Her voice sounds far away and muffled as if someone's stuck cotton wool in my ears.

I can make my lips twitch, but my tongue feels swollen, stuck to the roof of my mouth, and when I try to speak nothing happens.

Could I have had the operation already? Is that it? That would explain why I'm paralysed. Still feeling the effects of the anaesthesia.

That's it. That must be it. So I just have to wait for it to wear off.

'Doll? You okay? They given you something? I thought you looked a bit spaced out when they wheeled you back in here. Listen, you'll never guess what. You know Lulu next to me? She fell out of bed. And what with all the nurses buggering off it was up to me to help her back in. And, ooooh, my back is killing me now...'

Concentrate. Take a deep breath and try to get the words out.

Help me!

'Lisa? Why are you crying?'

Am I? Now that Gertie mentions it I can feel the wetness on my cheeks, and my sight is getting blurrier.

'I'll get Lumpy Legs for you, doll.'

Yes! Get help! Get someone!

'What's that, Lisa? You trying to speak?'

Another rustle of the curtain around the bed; the squeak of footsteps on linoleum.

'Oh,' Gertie says. 'It's *you*.'

'Yeah. Forgotten your name, sorry.'

The panicky grip loosens. Farrell's here. He'll help me. He'll get me out of here.

'Come to see her before she goes under the knife?' Gertie says. 'Shame, she's been crying. Hasn't said a blarry word though. Out for the count.'

So I'm pre-op, not post. But why can't I move?

'It's okay, Lisa,' Farrell says. 'Everything's going to be fine. Nomsa explained everything.'

No! The pictures, remember the pictures.

The mattress shifts as Farrell sits on the corner of the bed.

Gertie sniffs loudly. 'Phoah. I'm not being funny, Frankie, but you need a shower.'

'It's *Farrell*.'

'No need to get all uppity, it's not me who smells like they've been rolling in streetkid shit.'

'Christ. Ugh. I must've stood in something when we were in the garden. Some dog shit or something.'

'What garden?'

'Some house outside the hospital. Me and Lisa were trying to—'

'Oh, I get it,' Gertie interrupts. 'Wanted some privacy, did you?'

'No!' Farrell says. 'We were trying to get out of this fucking dump.'

'Lisa never said she was leaving.' Gertie sounds hurt.

'Yeah, well, she was freaking out. Got spooked. Thinks there's some crazy stuff going on here.'

'I don't blame her. I was telling her just now, it's been blarry mad here—'

'Back in your bed, Mrs February.' It's Lumpy Legs – I'd know that voice anywhere. She'll get the doctor, get someone who can help.

'What's the matter with her?' Gertie asks. 'Why isn't she talking? You given her something?'

'Just a mild sedative. Standard procedure before an op.'

'But she's dead to the world!'

'It's quite normal.'

'She's not talking. How's that normal?'

Good old Gertie.

Lumpy Legs sighs. 'It says on her chart that she's a nervous patient. The nurse who administered it probably upped the dosage.'

That's not true! No! Please, I can't! I've changed my mind, I just want to go home.

There's the squeak of wheels approaching the bed.

No!

'And what are you doing here?' Lumpy Legs's voice again. She must be addressing Farrell. 'This isn't your room. And where's your hospital gown?'

Farrell mumbles something.

'Better do as she says, Frankie,' Gertie says. 'Or they'll get those bed baths I know you like so much.' She cackles.

The mattress shifts again as Farrell stands up.

Don't leave me!

Gertie pats my hand. 'Don't worry,' she says. 'They'll get those sinuses fixed up lekker, you'll see. Although you might regret it when you get a whiff of your boyfriend.'

I feel myself being lifted into the air, I want to struggle, to scream, but my body still isn't listening. I'm shifted onto a harder surface, and cool air brushes my exposed limbs.

Someone throws a blanket over my legs. It feels too heavy.

And then I'm moving.

'See you when you're older, doll!' Gertie's voice floats after me.

This time I manage a strangled 'Mmmfffff'.

Whoever is pushing me doesn't dawdle, and I'm whizzed along the corridor. The ceiling tiles flash by above me, most are stained yellow, a few are cracked. There's a slight bump as I'm wheeled into a lift. My heart throbs in my chest, and my lungs ache. I can't seem to suck in enough air. The lift cranks into action. Are we going up or down? I can't tell, and a surge of nausea joins the panic. I can't throw up, I'll choke.

Oh God, oh God, oh God.

The lift's lights flicker, then hiss. There's the sound of grinding gears as it judders to a stop. The lift doors ping open.

I'm wheeled down another corridor, the ceiling just as grimy as the last. The gurney slaps though a pair of black rubber doors, and jolts to a stop as it bangs against a wall. I can't see where I am. All I know is that the ceiling is slightly cleaner, the light brighter.

'Incoming!' a voice behind me yells. Where have I heard that before?

Oh God.

That's what the porter said in the morgue.

The cold fist tightens again. What if he's taken me to the wrong place? What if they think I'm dead? That I've got that zombie disease when you don't show any vital signs and they bury you or cremate you or—

A head surrounded by a halo of fuzzy white hair appears above me.

'Hello, Ms Cassavetes. I'll be your anaesthetist for today's procedure.' His accent is posh: old-school South African English. He looks to be about a hundred, his hair-filled nose pitted with large pores. He smiles down at me with stained teeth and kind eyes. He pats my arm. 'There, there. There's nothing to worry about.'

Speak!

All I can manage is another strangled 'Mmmfffff'.

'My, my, that sedative really worked on you, didn't it?' he says, chuckling. 'Count yourself lucky.'

There's the sound of Velcro ripping and something grips my upper arm.

'Just taking your blood pressure, my dear.' He whistles a meandering tune through his teeth.

The cuff on my arm tightens. I try to speak again, I need to tell him to stop, that I've changed my mind, that I don't want this to happen.

'Hmmm,' he says. 'You'll do.'

The pressure on my arm eases and then I'm moving again. Another corridor, shorter this time. Another slight bump. I have to shut my eyes against the glare in here.

'Now. There's nothing to worry about. As the bishop said to the actress, one little prick and it will all be over.'

I feel the ache of the needle sliding into my arm.

'Before you know it, you'll be back safe in your ward. Count down with me, dear. Ten, nine, eight…'

There's no point in panicking anymore. This is it. I can't stop it, it's too late.

Seven, six…

*

70

Music. I can hear music. My eyes are closed and white spots dance behind my lids. I open them slightly, but the light above me is still too bright. The music is familiar. Something from the sixties. Dad used to play this in the car on the way to school. Made me cringe in front of my friends when it was our turn to do the car pool. But what's it called? It's on the tip of my tongue.

Then I have it: 'Hang on Sloopy', that's it.

Someone – a man – is trying to sing along with the song, but he's getting the words wrong, just like Dad used to do. 'He-ey Snoopy, Snoopy hold on, mmmhmmm, mmmhmmm.'

Something presses against my face. No pain. Just pressure. Is it warm or cold in here? I can't tell. I have no awareness of my body at all. My mind could just as well be stuck in a jar somewhere.

'Doing anything nice at the weekend, Doctor?' a woman says. She sounds giggly, young.

'Oh, you know… the usual. Golf, golf, golf!' I don't recognise the voice. It's not the Indian doctor I've seen and heard before. This voice is similar to the anaesthetist's – male, posh, clipped, but with an African edge. Nigerian maybe? 'Swab for me please, Nurse.'

'Yes, Doctor.'

'And you, Alisha?'

A giggle. 'Oh, you know, Doctor, just the usual. Party, party, party.'

'You young people. All go.'

The music stops abruptly.

Footsteps approach.

'Doctor, we have a problem.' A different voice – a woman's. It's low and unaccented, familiar.

'What problem?' the doctor says.

'There's a mix-up with patient Cassavetes's medical records.'

'What sort of mix-up?'

'With the payment options, Doctor. It's a matter of the greatest urgency.'

'Well, it will have to wait,' the doctor says. 'Can't you see I'm—'

'Doctor!' the theatre nurse says, the giggles gone from her voice. She sounds nervous, unsure. 'Doctor, quickly!'

The machine next to my head blips and then beeps and then screams. There's a sudden smothering pressure on my face.

'What a *freak*.'

'It's just another brown.' This from a different voice. 'More karking browns at primo sales these days than normal people.'

Laughter. Cruel, cold laughter.

I open my eyes, wincing as they're hit with that too-bright artificial light again. My vision is blurry, but I make out plate glass windows and a shadowy figure scurrying past me. I blink fast several times, trying to shift the fog from my eyes. Hang on. I'm standing up. I can move! But there's something wrong with this picture. The scene is still out of focus, but... am I, *am* I... in a shopping mall?

Because that's what it looks like.

But how did I get here?

Impossible.

I'm dreaming.

I must be dreaming. It doesn't feel like it though. I touch my face. The dressing is gone, and I can't feel any stitches. I pinch the skin on my forearm as hard as I can. Feels sore. Must be an especially vivid dream.

The woolly veil over my sight gradually lifts. It's a mall all right, but I don't recognise it. The shop opposite me is selling what looks like bondage gear. The mannequins in the window are headless, their bodies twisted into impossible shapes – a wrist bent back the wrong way, a knee joint bending inwards. And the place is immense, even larger than the Gateway in Durban. The aisle I'm in seems to extend for miles in both directions, a double bank of brightly lit shops stretching on forever. Distant figures weave back and forth, spectral shoppers criss-crossing the central passage. They're too far away for me to see them clearly, but their bodies don't look right, they look warped somehow.

A man slides out of the bondage shop's door, pauses and heads my way. I shrink back instinctively. One of his eyes is smothered beneath a knot of scar tissue. He leers at me, sticks out a pointed tongue and waggles it. 'Freak,' he hisses. 'Why don't you modify?' before slithering away into the shop next door.

It's just a dream; that's all it is. A stupid nightmare.

But my hollow stomach and clammy palms feel way too real. Dream or no dream, I have to get out of here.

A loudspeaker crackles. 'Attention, shoppers!' a voice croaks out. 'Lockdown will commence in eight, seven, six, five...'

I need to run. I *want* to run, but I can't move. My legs aren't listening.

'... four, three, two, one.' With an ear-splitting screech, some sort of machinery clanks into life; it sounds as if it's coming from below my feet. And something's happening at the far end of the passage. A reedy scream echoes, mournful and distant.

Then I realise that the shop lights are turning off one by one, starting in the far distance and heading my way. The approaching blackness swirls and creeps, alive and ravenous, and I know with a chilling certainty that if it reaches me I'm finished.

The lights of the bondage shop opposite click off. Then the blackness comes. Laps over my feet, runs up my legs, and oh it hurts it burns it hurts it feels like fire...

Freezing. I'm freezing cold. Lying down again, this time on a hard, rough surface. I try to sit up, but something's stopping me. Someone's holding me down by my wrists. I struggle, try to pull them free. But the grip is too strong.

I crane my neck to see who it is but no one's there. It's not a person holding me down. Thick leather straps, like you see in asylums, pin my wrists to the gurney I'm lying on. I attempt to kick my legs up but my ankles are also strapped down, my legs spread wide.

Another nightmare?

Must be.

Has to be. But it's also too vivid.

I let my head flop back down to ease the pain in my neck. I count to three and lift it as high as I can again so that I check out my surroundings. I'm in a long, dark room. The walls are made of polished white stone peppered with spots of mildew. Rivulets of water snake down the walls. The only light source is a single bulb swinging from the ceiling. There are several other hospital beds in here, all arranged in a long line, but I can't tell if they contain other bodies or if the lumpy shapes on top of them are just empty sheets and pillows.

Deep down I know this is not a nightmare: it's too real. The pain in my wrists, the ache in my neck, the freezing cold are all way too visceral to delude myself.

Is the operation over? Am I in a strange recovery room?

'Hello?' I call out. 'Hello? Anyone?' My voice seems to bounce off the walls; it sounds echoey and amplified.

A door slams.

'Hello?' I try again.

I hear the sound of scuffling footsteps, the sound of a dragging limp.

I lift my head again.

A bulbous figure is making its way past the beds, heading in my direction. I can't make out any facial features; there's just a dark nothingness where the face should be, topped with a thatch of dirty orange hair. Simply a trick of the light. Right? It's gloomy in here, but gloom or no gloom I can clearly see that the faceless figure is holding something in its hand. Something that glints in the bulblight.

Oh Christ, oh Jesus.

It's a huge and viciously serrated pair of shears. The shape pauses at one of the beds. I hear the murmur of conversation, and then a schwick as the shears snap shut.

Please don't come near me, please don't! Please don't, please...

The footsteps shuffle nearer. More muffled conversation. Another metallic clip, louder this time.

My bladder lets go, a flow of wet warmth on my thighs.

Please please don't let it get me. Dad, I need you, come and get—

An icy, greasy hand, like the underbelly of a toad, presses down over my eyes.

'Which payment plan would you prefer?' a scratchy, obscene voice hisses. 'Pieces of eight, or just pieces? Shall we take your eyes, or your tongue? A finger? A toe? What's that? Oh yes. Good idea! A part payment. A *lay-by*. Yes. A toe. Perfect. Now hold still, missy miss. This little piggy went to maaaaaarket...'

The slippery hiss of spit being sucked back through teeth. The cold touch of the shears on my skin. The scything sound of them snapping shut.

This isn't happening, isn't happening, isn't happening, please God, I'll never do anything bad ever again just make this stop and I'll—

Blip. Blip-blip. Blip. Bliiiiiiiiiip.

Bluish, comforting light. A smooth white ceiling, warm air, the soft hum of air conditioning.

The memory of that horrible *thing* snaps into my mind and immediately I check that I'm not shackled. Thank God! I can move freely again.

I force myself to calm down and breathe slowly. It was just a stupid dream. Just a nightmare brought on by the anaesthetic.

My legs are still a bit numb, but I can lift them a couple of inches off the mattress.

Now I just have to figure out where the hell I am.

I'm still feeling wobbly and groggy, but I make myself sit up.

This can't be right. Have they moved me to a private room?

The place has the feel of a luxurious hotel suite. There's a watercolour of a whitewashed farmhouse on the wall opposite, a flat-screen television on a stand in the corner and a plump armchair next to my bed. But it's definitely a hospital. There's a machine next to my bed that's blipping continually, and there's a drip stuck into my arm. The solution in the bag hanging from the stand is tinged with brown, as if a tea bag has been dropped into it. It's probably some kind of antibiotic.

So, if I've had the op, then... I run my fingers over my face. My cheeks feel numb, but not unpleasantly so. There's a slight tingle, probably the after-effects of the anaesthetic. My skin feels slippery and... rubbery. I gingerly touch my nose, trying to trace the shape. The slight bump on the bridge doesn't seem to be there anymore, and, while it also feels oddly smooth, the bandage has gone.

It's too quiet here, too comfortable. Did Dad find out where I was and transfer me to another hospital while I was out of it?

I can't think of another rational explanation.

Then I see it.

The imprint of a buckle on my wrist.

Doesn't mean anything.

It doesn't mean anything!

So why am I so reluctant to pull the covers off my legs to check that my toes are all still attached?

Chapter 9

FARRELL

I wake up from a dream, images of the garden separating like mist. Poor Lisa. She's a real space case. But I'm still amazed how easily I fell for her paranoid stories. It just goes to show that, if someone really believes in something, they can convince other people, even if it's just a lie, even if it's just a grotesque fantasy.

I wonder how her surgery went.

I open my eyes and see the supply cupboard, my little isolation ward. After that run through the morgue and the casualty ward, I feel almost as if I'm home again. I feel safe. The lights are dimmed, but I can make out the rows of drawers and shelves and cupboards. They're all pretty neat, just a couple of discarded rubber gloves on the floor, some packaging overflowing the red bin under one of the counters, a dark stain on the mottled lino. The door's open to the main passage. The lights are bright but it's quiet, nobody rushing past. I lie still, watching the doorway, until eventually an old woman with a walker shuffles by. Sick, man. She didn't make it to the toilet in time: the back of her pink gown is wet through.

Hang on. I'm seeing all this. I can fucking see!

I swing myself out of bed and stand up. No dizziness. I'm feeling stronger. And I can see! It's time to go home.

Home. Katya screaming at me. Then blood. Something glinting. Blood on my hands. Blood on her face.

What the fuck? My knees give way and I slump down onto the tacky floor.

Katya's crying. *Josh, let me go!* There's blood on her lips. What did you do?

I don't know. Jesus! What happened?

Take a look, Josh. Look at your hands.

I don't want to look, but on cue the itching pain starts up immediately. The dressing on my right hand hasn't been changed since I got here and is now caked with dirt and the end flaps loosely. The itch is deep inside my hand and I have to get at it. I wind the dressing off and after a number of layers get to a brown-crusted pad of cotton wool. I toss the roll of crepe aside, and, without thinking of the pain, I rip the padding off. The deep gashes glare wetly back at me: slices on my first two fingers, and the biggest one on my palm. There's still a sheen of the russet disinfectant, but the large gash on my palm stings. What could have cut me?

That glint in the light. Remember, Farrell.

I remember. Flashes. It was glass. I was holding a broken shard of glass in my hand. *You only love me for my face*, Katya is screaming. *Well take a good, long look, you bastard. It's the last time you'll see it.* There's glass in my hand and blood on her face.

Holy fuck. What have I done?

I feel like there are insects crawling underneath my skin, biting at me, pissing their acid piss into my wounds.

This is bullshit! I didn't do anything to Katya. I love her.

So where do these cuts come from? What are these memories?

It could be anything. Hallucinations, dreams. I've been out of it for so long. But I can't shake the image of Katya's perfect skin smeared with blood. Her dark eyes smudged black and swollen with tears.

Christ. I have to find out what happened.

I struggle up and move out of the closet. The security guard is nodding off in his plastic chair by the security gate and there's nobody at the nurses' station, just a burly orderly mopping something down at the far end of the corridor.

Double-checking to make sure there are no nurses around, I reach behind the counter and pick up the phone. Shit. There's just a long beep in my ear. I try pressing 0 for an outside line, but the beep doesn't change. I press each of the other numbers in order. Nothing. Who knows if these phones are even connected? Come to think about it, I haven't heard them ringing for ages.

Now what? Lisa said she had a phone – but the battery was flat. But what about the old hag in the bed next to hers? It's worth a shot. Maybe Lisa can help me convince her to let me use it.

I pass the old women's ward next to my closet. A low sobbing. One of the women moans in her dreams. Eight beds with eight permed grey hairstyles, all waiting. Like sheep for the slaughter.

Christ, Farrell, snap out of it. This is a fucking hospital. People come here to lie in bed and get better. And you think Lisa is the fucked-up one?

I hurry to Lisa's room and peer inside. Only two of the eight beds are occupied. There's a sweating mama in the far corner and, snoring in the middle bed on the right, that sour old bitch who can't stop talking. Gertie: that's her name. Lisa's bed is empty, she's clearly not back from surgery yet. I don't want to deal with the old cow on my own, so I turn to leave.

'Back again, Frankie?' Gertie calls after me. She wipes her mouth with the back of her hand and sits up, rheumy eyes groggy with sleep. 'What, can't stay away from me, that it?'

'It's Farrell. Josh Farrell.' I immediately feel like a prat. *The name's Farrell. Josh Farrell.* I don't know what it is about this woman that sets my nerves on edge.

'You seen Lisa?' she asks, pawing in a glass next to her bed for her teeth. My stomach rolls over.

'Not since she went in for surgery.'

'She should've been back by now. Missing her, are you? Sexy chick like that? Don't blame you.'

I know she's trying to get a rise out of me, but I can't help snapping back at her. 'It's not like that. Lisa was... She's... she's got problems.'

'You're talking kak. Nothing wrong with that chick. You're the one with the problem, you ask me. Mind you, you're smelling a lot better now. I mean, seriously, Frankie. Let me give you a tip. If you wax your back and your bottom it's more permanent than Veet, okay?'

What the fuck does she mean by that? Christ, she's a bitch. I'll have to play this carefully. 'Look, I've got a bit of an emergency and I really need a phone.'

She looks at me craftily. 'That so?'

'Yeah. You don't have one by any chance, do you?'

'Might do.'

Jesus. It's like pulling teeth. 'I'd really appreciate it if you'd let me use it. I'll pay for the airtime, of course.'

She looks me up and down. 'What with? Your body? No thanks.'

What I really want to do is tell her to shove her phone up her flabby arse, but I need to get hold of Katya. 'Please, Gertie.'

She points an arthritic finger at me. 'You pay me back, you hear?'

'I will. Soon as I get my stuff back.'

'And extra.'

'Yeah. When I get my wallet I'll give you fifty rand, that cool?'

'Hundred.'

Fuck. 'Fine.'

She takes her time ferreting around in her bedside cabinet, then finally hands me a battered plastic Nokia out of the Stone Age. 'Thanks,' I say, grabbing it before she can change her mind.

'Don't use up all the airtime, Frankie,' she says. 'And I want my hundred.'

I step out into the corridor. Jesus, this phone is a piece of shit. I tap the number in, and wait.

Ring-ring. Ring-ring. I haven't heard that sound for more than a week and it makes me feel part of the world again.

'Hello? Hello? Who is this?'

I recognise June's voice instantly. June always sounds like this: both timid and stoned, but she's always liked me. Which is more than I can say for Glenn. So Katya went home to her parents. But why isn't she answering her phone?

'Hello, June. It's Josh.' Now that I open my mouth the nerves hit me. If these memories I've been having are true, I'm probably the last person Katya wants to speak to.

A long pause, and then an almost whispered 'Josh'.

'Uh, hello, um. I wanted to find out... Is Katya there?'

June sighs. 'She's not, Josh.' Now she sounds angry – fuck, I've never heard June use that tone of voice. I can imagine Katya sitting there behind her, that furious look on her face making her even more gorgeous, folding her arms and shaking her head.

'Do you know where she is? I need to talk to her. Find out if—'

'Where are you calling from, Josh?'

Of course! They don't know. 'I'm in hospital. I've been here since Monday.'

'Oh, Josh. I didn't know. Why didn't you answer your phone? The po— What's the matter?'

'I had measles. But it was quite bad. I couldn't see. Could barely walk. I was completely out of it for a few days. I'm getting better now.'

'We tried to get hold of you. There was no answer.'

'I know. I'm sorry. I got taken to New Hope Hospital, and my phone's dead. Nobody came. I've been desperate to get hold of Katya.'

Another pause. Someone talking in the background. A muffled whisper. 'She's missing, Josh.'

'What?'

'We couldn't get hold of her on Monday so we went round to the flat. She wasn't there.'

'I can't remember what happened, June. I think we had... a fight. I don't know about what. Didn't she go home to you?'

'She didn't,' June says in an eerie, dead tone. More muffled talking. 'When we went to your flat, there were... signs of a struggle. Her phone was lying on the floor. Tell me honestly, Josh. What happened?'

'I can't...' *I can't remember?* How does that sound? I have no fucking idea. Where the fuck is Katya?

'And she was supposed to do the L'Oréal shoot this week,' June says in that same weird voice. 'There's no way she would have just...'

That's it! Maybe she was so upset after we broke up that she went on a coke binge or something. That would be like her. Fucking Noli and the other hangers on are always dragging her back. But June's right. She would never have missed the L'Oréal shoot. Never in a million years.

'Do you have any idea—?'

'If you hurt our girl, you piece of turd' – Glenn has come on the line – 'I will kill you. Do you understand me?'

I don't say anything. Of course I understand him. I know Glenn would do it, is just waiting for an excuse, in fact. He's always hated me; I'm not fit for his favourite daughter. And he could kill me and get away with it. Glenn has a lot of money, a lot of people in his pocket.

'Please stop, Glenn,' I hear June saying in the background. 'We don't know tha—'

'June's had her way and called the police,' Glenn continues. 'And when they fuck it up, I will find you and make an example of you. Do you understand me, Farrell?'

I disconnect the call.

I send a text back to Katya's phone, hoping June will receive it. **<June, I love Katya. I'll help you find her. J>**

My legs are quivering again and there's a sharp pain in my chest. I slump back against the wall. Until I remember exactly what happened that morning, I'm in serious shit. A harried doctor jogs through, pausing when he spots me. 'Are there nurses on duty in this section?' he asks, as if I'm in charge here.

'Sorry, I haven't seen anyone.' I'm amazed at how normal my voice sounds. 'I think they're on skeleton staff. The train. How are things in casualty?'

'They just keep pouring in. Two coaches jammed in the mouth of the tunnel until the middle of last night. So many dead. So many badly injured.' He looks like he's about to cry. His eyes are wild, unfocussed, like someone on a bad drug trip. 'If only we had got to them earlier…' he mumbles as he wanders off.

I think of what we passed through yesterday. I think of that mess getting worse. I can't shake the sound of the kids whimpering quietly. That sound cut through all the running and shouting and screaming. Up here in Green Section, we're safe. That's why the old women are lying so still. The world outside has gone insane.

Shit! I told June I was here in New Hope and now Glenn will come looking for me. Who knows what they found at the flat? I don't even know what happened. I glance at the dozing security guard. Will he be able to stop Glenn from getting in? Or the cops?

Glenn's going to get here sooner or later, and I have to have a plan for when he does.

The ward is silent and still. I can hardly imagine the chaos just three floors down. The air-conditioning hum mutes any sound from outside. The lumbering orderly has mopped his way halfway up to my closet door.

I return to Lisa's room to give the phone back to Gertie but she's asleep, her teeth floating in the glass next to her bed. It's only got one bar of battery life left, so, if I want to use it again, now's my chance. I can't think of anywhere else Katya would be. Or, rather, I can think of a hundred places she could be bingeing with those strung-out bitches she calls her friends but there's no phone access in cocaine heaven. And her cellphone's with June and Glenn.

None of this is getting me any closer to finding Katya. The fact is she's not with her phone and nobody can get hold of her. Who else might know anything?

The phone's time display reads 15.27. I dial work.

'Da Bomb Studios, hello?'

'Yeah, hi, Lizzie. It's Farrell.'

'Farrell. My God. Are you okay? Where are you?'

'I'm fine. But in New Hope Hospital.'

'No Hope? What the fuck are you doing there?'

'Maybe I should ask you. They said there was a medical-aid fuck-up... You're supposed to handle that shit.'

'But Mike said that he'd checked you in at Morningside.'

'Who the fuck's Mike?'

'The new guy in accounts. You know...'

'No. Anyway, thanks for coming to visit.'

'We tried! Christ, Farrell. Eduardo and I have been going out of our minds. We went to Morningside, they said you weren't there. We thought maybe you'd been discharged. We've tried your phone a hundred times. I even went to your flat on Wednesday. Nothing.'

'Jesus. Who's this Mike guy again?'

'That little guy, you know. The one with the limp. He actually hasn't been in for a few days.'

'Christ, Lizzie. Jesus fucking Christ. You should have checked. You should have taken me.'

'I know, Farrell, I'm sorry. We've been so worried. Are you sure you're fine?'

'Ja, I'm feeling better. I'm hoping to get out of here soon. But now all the fucking doctors are busy on this fucking train thing... Tell me, Lizzie. What happened on Monday? I can't really remember anything.'

'You came in about nine, said Katya had left you. You were seriously bummed. Then next thing you're all grey and sweaty and you collapsed. That's all, really. Are things okay? I mean, with Katya?' Lizzie knows as well as anyone that Katya has left me a number of times.

'No... um, that's what I was... She hasn't phoned, has she? At work? My phone's been dead.'

'No. No messages. Sorry. Fuck, Farrell, can I do anything?'

'Nah. Soon as I'm home it'll be okay. See you soon. Tell Eduardo for me?'

'Sure. Take care, boss.'

I disconnect, processing what I've heard. So Katya hasn't tried the studio. Where the hell is she?

'How are you feeling today, Mr Farrell?'

'Nomsa. Jesus.'

'Sorry, Mr Farrell. I should try to walk louder.'

'I just heard... I just got some bad news. My girlfriend's missing.'

'Sorry to hear that, Mr Farrell. How did you find out?'

'I borrowed a phone from Gertie.'

'I didn't know she had a phone.'

What's this fucking interrogation about? 'Is it important?'

'It's not, Mr Farrell. How are your eyes?'

'Oh yes! I'm seeing just fine now. I'd say about eighty per cent normal.'

'Excellent news. But you must keep using the drops twice a day, all right?'

'Yes.'

'I see you're moving around a lot better too. But take it easy; don't overdo it. Small steps. You'll almost be ready.'

'Nomsa?'

'Yes, Mr Farrell.'

'How's Lisa? How did the surgery go?'

'Oh, very well.'

'Is she in ICU?'

'No.'

'Why isn't she back in the ward?'

'We've transferred her, Mr Farrell.'

'Where to?'

'The Wards.'

'Yes, but *which* ward?'

Nomsa hesitates. 'I mean… In the new wing.'

There's a new wing? Lucky Lisa. I hope it's fucking cleaner than this dump. 'Can I go and see her?'

'Not at the moment, Mr Farrell.' Nomsa smiles. 'She'll need more time. Then you can join her. In the meantime, your job is just to get strong.' Nomsa says this often.

I look at her, a thought on the edge of my consciousness. I can't grab it.

'You're doing very well, Mr Farrell. You'll soon be ready. Remember those drops!'

All the stuff I've just heard – about Katya and collapsing at work – is muzzing loudly in my head. I feel like it's going to explode. Nomsa's right. I need to take it easy. I've done more this afternoon than I have for days. I need to lie down. Then I can sort through all this information.

I get back to my room and check in the cubby that my stinking clothes are still there. I check on the top of the makeshift nightstand for the eye drops. Thank God they're still there. But something else catches my eye, something I haven't noticed before.

A stack of Polaroids.

Holy shit. They're pictures of my body, lying on this very bed, marked out in segments. Just like Lisa said. In the pictures the sheet is folded aside and I'm stark naked. In seven of the pictures the drip tube is still shunted into my arm. In the rest it isn't. In the corner of one of the pictures I make out a small hand. A woman's hand.

I ruck my gown up. The fading black lines are clear as a map on my skin.

Chapter 10

LISA

There are no windows in here, so I haven't got a clue of the time. But for now I'm happy just to lie here in this comfortable bed, safe and warm, savouring the fact that there's no one around to look at me, talk to me or judge me.

I wiggle my toes again. All present and accounted for.

For now, a wicked voice whispers in my head. *Snip, snip.*

Stupid. It was just a crazy dream – a warped nightmare. Dr Meka says that I should write down all my dreams, but I won't be telling her about that one in a hurry. She'll only assume that I've started fixating on other parts of my body as well as my face. And the mall nightmare – well of course that makes sense. It's been years since I've felt confident enough to just 'pop to the mall' without hiding behind a hoodie, sunglasses and layers of make-up.

And it's hardly surprising that I freaked out after what Farrell and I saw in the morgue and casualty. But what did I expect? There had just been a major tragedy. Of course there would be blood everywhere and people screaming. And now that I'm in here, in this civilised, clean room, it's mortifying to think about how I overreacted. Like Gertie is always saying, people die in hospitals all the time, and that awful grey-faced guy was just some pervert who tried to spy on me while I was showering. Big deal.

But what about the photographs of Farrell? And the lines on his body?
Some nurse's idea of a sick joke. Has to be.

Farrell must think I'm some kind of neurotic loser. God, it's embarrassing. Cringe-worthy. When I see him again the first thing I'll do is apologise.

If I ever see him again, that is.

But why shouldn't I? I must still be *somewhere* in New Hope. Sure, it doesn't *feel* like the same place, but the idea I cooked up that Dad moved me to another hospital is mental. I was careful. Very careful. I deleted the flight information and all the hospital details off my hard drive, and I even cleared out the computer's recycle bin and browsing history. I paid the first instalment personally with a bank deposit, so there's no way he'd be able to trace it to New Hope's accounts department.

No. The only way he could have tracked me down was if he'd phoned every hospital in South Africa, and I really can't see him doing that. The last thing he'd expect me to do is hop on a plane to Joburg, especially as just before I made the decision to go under the knife again I was going through another one of my 'social isolation' periods, reluctant to leave the house, unable to stand seeing anyone but Dad and Sharon; freaking out when Sharon's school friends came over. The only time I actually ventured outside was when Dad insisted that I keep my cognitive-therapy appointments with Dr Meka, ramping up the emotional blackmail to force me into the car.

And I know how Dad's mind works. He'll probably assume that I took our last argument to heart and that this time I've left for good (one way or the other). Maybe he feels guilty now for leaving the latest batch of hospital bills on the kitchen table for everyone to see. My last trip to Margate Private Hospital's emergency department wasn't covered by the dwindling medical aid. Getting your stomach pumped isn't cheap.

I can hear his voice now: 'It's not just you I have to think about, Lisa. What about Sharon? You're tearing this family apart, bankrupting us! How many therapists and shrinks and God knows what have you been to in the last two years? Seven? Eight? How could you do this to us after your mother suffered like she did?' And the last thing he said to me, a note of finality in his voice: 'You have to get over this, or get the hell out. You're twenty-four, for Christ's sake.' Perhaps he meant it this time.

I try to imagine what he's thinking, what he's feeling. Worry? Relief that he won't have to shell out for any more of Dr Meka's sessions and Luvox prescriptions? I'm not exactly sure how many appointments I've missed since I left the South Coast, but it has to be at least four. Good. Her last therapeutic exercise, designed so that I'd 'get an objective reaction to my appearance' was beyond stupid. How is taking a photograph of my face and showing it to random people in the mall going to help? People are hardly going to tell the truth, are they? If some stranger came up to me and showed me a picture of a freak, I'm hardly going to admit that I think she's a monster, am I?

No one gets it. Dad and Sharon just think I'm self-involved and neurotic to the point of madness, and Dr Meka thinks she knows what I'm going through with her 'change your behaviour patterns and learn to deal with your anxiety issues' spiel, but she actually doesn't have a clue. They should be glad I'm not like the other BDD people I've read about on the forums. The ones who don't have the cash for conventional procedures and who perform their own surgeries, cut into their bodies and make things worse. Like the girl from the States who was hospitalised after hacking away at her thighs with a paring knife – her version of DIY liposuction; the guy from Ireland who filed his teeth down to the nerves because he thought they stuck out too much.

So, if it wasn't Dad who moved me here, who was it?

It has to be someone connected with New Hope. The doctors here know that I lied to them about my previous surgeries. Oh God. What if they've figured out I've got a 'problem' and have moved me to some sort of psychiatric ward?

That's just stupid. I'm just being paranoid.

I trace my fingers over my face again. The material covering my skin is perfectly smooth and reminds me of the silkiness of scar tissue. It's some sort of hi-tech surgical mask. I can feel the slight raised edges of it around my hairline and below my chin, and it's extremely light and flexible. I can move my mouth and blink, but when I press my fingers over my cheek, the skin beneath still feels numb and tingly, almost as if it's gone to sleep. It's not an unpleasant feeling. And I'm almost positive that my nose has changed shape. I've been down this road before, but this time... this time I think it might have worked. Can I allow myself to hope? Why not?

My bladder is aching, but what I really need – even more – is to find a mirror. There must be a bathroom behind the door on the other side of the bed. I suppose I should really see if I can locate a nurse or a doctor, but first things first.

I kick the covers off and slide down off the bed. My legs are still slightly shaky, but I can use the drip stand for support. At least my head is no longer woolly, and after the first couple of steps it gets easier. I'm tempted to look at my reflection in the darkened screen of the television, but I resist. It will only give me a false impression, and I want my first glimpse of my new face to be perfect.

Yuk. My mouth is dry and there's a slight medicinal taste on my tongue. If I can find where they've stashed my stuff I can brush my teeth and hair before I look in the mirror. I try the cupboard next to the bathroom door, but it's empty. Dammit. Where are my clothes? There's no robe to cover the skimpy hospital gown I'm wearing, but at least it's warm in here, and there's no one to see me.

It's pitch black inside the bathroom. I'm hit with the strong scent of cleaning fluid – I can smell again! I slide my fingers over the wall until they touch the light switch. I breathe in deeply, and manoeuvre the drip stand into the bathroom. There's plenty of space in here; it's much larger than most of the hospital en suites I've been in. It's decorated floor to ceiling in pale-pink ceramic tiles, and there's even a sunken bath and a bidet next to the toilet. It's just the kind of bathroom you'd find in a plush hotel, except there's a contraption suspended from the ceiling above the bath. I push the shower curtain aside. Ugh. It doesn't look anything like the orthopaedic hand rails and equipment Dad installed for Mom after she got sick. Six curved and spiky stainless steel arms hang down from some sort of hydraulic mechanism, like a giant metal spider waiting to pounce. I don't like the thought of lying in the bath and staring up at that thing. It must be a hi-tech lifting device, maybe for paraplegics.

The temptation to check out my reflection in the mirror above the sink is so intense it almost hurts, but I make myself wait. I'll pee first. The toilet paper – pink, 3-ply – is folded at the edge, just like in a high-end hotel. And there's a sign tacked up next to the towel rail: 'Be A Good Client. Use Towels More Than Once ☺'.

A good client? Don't they mean 'patient'?

But I've got more important considerations right now. I flush, stand up and shuffle over to the sink. I wash my hands first, and then, holding on to the edge of the sink, I allow myself to look in the mirror.

Breathe, Lisa.

My limp blonde hair frames nothing but a pale-pink blankness. The mask is flawless – it's almost as if they've applied a perfectly smooth cosmetic face mask that covers every inch of skin apart from my lips, my nostrils and around my eyes. I tug gently at the edge that curves under my chin. It moves slightly, but it's probably a bad idea to mess with it until a nurse or doctor says I can. I don't think it's been actually glued onto my skin, but it tingles; it feels like part of me. But why not just protect my nose? Why my whole face?

Hang on. My lips look a shade darker, as if I've applied magenta lipstick, and are they… are they plumper? I run my tongue over them. Like the rest of my face, they're still fairly numb, but that has to be from the last traces of the anaesthetic. I turn my head to the side and check out my profile. Is my chin less prominent? It is! I'm almost sure of it! And my nose. There's no question that it's smaller, maybe even slightly upturned. A *cute* nose.

I practise smiling, watching as the mask seamlessly moves with my facial muscles, almost like a second skin. Are my teeth whiter? They can't be. It must be the light in here.

Amazing.

I lean right over the sink, so close to the mirror that condensation from my breath clouds my reflection. Whatever it is they've done, it's definitely something radical. That Indian doctor said they might have to do some drastic reconstruction… Is this what he meant?

The sound of the door slamming makes me jump. There's someone in my room. I can hear the clatter of a trolley.

'Good morning!' a woman's high-pitched voice calls. 'Where are you, luvvie?'

I wheel the drip out of the bathroom. A middle-aged woman wearing a short pink smock and long white socks is standing next to the television. She smiles and waves at me. Her short brown hair is tied into jaunty schoolgirlish bunches.

'Hello, my dear. Breakfast time! Yummy yum!' Where do hospitals find these relentlessly cheerful women? I find myself smiling back at her.

'Hi,' I say. 'Look, this is going to sound weird, but… where exactly am I?'

She chuckles. 'What a question! You're in the Wards, of course, dear.'

'Which ward, though?'

She rolls her eyes as if we're sharing an in-joke. 'I know what you must be thinking. There was a mix-up at first, but it's all tip-topped now.'

'What do you mean, a mix-up?'

She peers at the door as if she's concerned about being overheard, and whispers, 'About your status, of course.'

'Status?'

'Yes!' She claps her hands. 'Exactly.'

'Which ward am I in, though? You mean, this is another section of New Hope?'

She looks slightly confused. 'I'm sorry, dear?'

'I mean, why was I moved? Why aren't I back in my old ward?'

The woman tuts. 'Because you belong here, dear, you know that.'

I'm getting nowhere. 'But I'm still in New Hope, right?'

She acts as if she hasn't heard me. 'Now, pop yourself back into bed, and I'll serve you your breakfast. Come on, choppity, chop, chop!'

I catch a whiff of something delicious – toast and eggs? My stomach growls. Breakfast time already; I must have been out for longer than I thought. God, I'm starving. I manoeuvre the drip stand past the trolley, and slip back into bed.

'Good girl!' She approaches the bed and plumps the pillows behind my head. I try not to flinch away from her. She reeks of a strange scent, like rotting strawberries. As she pulls the tray table over my legs, I realise that three of her fingers – middle, ring and pinky – are missing on her right hand, and the stumps are painted with nail polish.

My stomach lurches and I shudder before I can stop myself. It's the same reaction I always get when I see any type of injury or deformity. Dr Meka says that it's not actually revulsion I'm feeling, but guilt, because I know in my subconscious that, compared to people who are deformed or badly injured, I look just fine. But that's crap. I know it's crap from the time that Dad dragged me to the Port Shepstone Public Hospital burns unit to shock me out of my 'delusions' as he called them. He made me go into a ward full of kids whose faces and bodies had been horribly scarred in paraffin fires and car and taxi accidents. 'Do you think these kids have a choice, Lisa?' he said, haranguing me right there in the ward, while the kids' parents stared and nurses shook their heads in disapproval. 'There's nothing wrong with you, my girl. You're beautiful, perfect. Just like your mother was. These people have real problems.'

The woman is staring at me. 'Everything okay, luvvie?'

'Yes. Yes, everything's fine.'

'Goody good.'

She scratches idly at the back of her neck, and, as she traipses back to the trolley, I catch sight of a large scab just below the parting where her hair is tied into bunches. God, what could have caused that sort of injury? She picks up a tray containing a covered plate, a pot of what smells deliciously like filter coffee and a glass of orange juice. She slides it onto my table and whips the metal cover off. 'Ta da! Smoked salmon and scrambled free-range eggs. Your favourite.'

'How... how did you know that?'

'It's in your file, dear.'

'What file?'

She chuckles again. 'Your details. We have all your details. The Administration insists on it.'

The food looks delicious, but I don't attempt to pick up the fork. 'When can I take... this mask off my face?'

'When it's ready, dear.'

'And when will that be?'

'That's entirely up to the Administration, dear.'

'You mean the doctors, don't you?'

She laughs as if I've said something funny. Up close her teeth look like plastic Chicklets glued together. Her tongue is tiny and stained black in patches as if she's been drinking too much red wine.

'No, no, dear. The Administration makes all the decisions in the Wards. Now, eat your breakfast! Yummy yum!'

I still make no move to pick up the cutlery. My stomach might be empty, but I need answers first. 'When will I get to see a doctor?'

A look of desperation flicks into her eyes and she glances at the door again. She picks up the fork and spears a sliver of smoked salmon onto the tines. 'Come on, dear. It's very important that you feed your face.'

'Feed my face?'

'Oh yes, dear,' she says, with another one of those wide plastic grins. 'After all this time it must be hungry.'

Chapter 11

FARRELL

Lisa was right after all. Something bad's happening here.

These Polaroids aren't some idea of a nurse's prank. This isn't a fucking joke. Someone left them here for me to find.

As the panic rises, my legs stiffen. I can hardly pull on my puke-caked jeans. Stained T-shirt. Shoes. That's all I have in the world. And that old cow Gertie's dying cellphone. Make that a dead cellphone. And useless without a charger. I hurl it onto the floor, enjoying the sound of cheap plastic shattering in the silent ward.

I gather up the photos of me laid out like a slab of meat. Those night-mares I had on my first night here weren't just dreams after all. Someone must have stripped me naked every time they took a picture. Without me knowing it. Marked me carefully with that pen every time I fell asleep. The markings in each picture are subtly different. As if someone's been adjusting the segments, fine-tuning the measurements.

I flip through the photos again. Who the fuck would choose to use a crappy Polaroid camera, of all the weird, outdated tech? In one of the pictures the bruising on my right arm is clear from the night someone messed with the drip. A flash of the terrifying grey face floods my mind for a moment. A sudden roll of nausea hits me. I retch and just avoid vomiting on the floor; a swill of bile washes my mouth.

I have to get out. If the police don't come for me soon, Glenn and his goons will. If the fucking psychopaths who have been stripping and photographing me every night don't get me first. Frankly, that's my first worry. Glenn and the police are outside. They – whoever the hell they are – are in here.

I shove the photos into my back pocket and run out the closet door. Straight into a solid body. I lose my balance and crumple to my knees at the man's feet and he leers down at me with his sweaty grey moon-face, its unnaturally narrow forehead, his thick glasses, and I remember him hanging over me in the middle of the night. Another wave of bile fills my mouth.

I force myself to stand.

'You!' I say. 'What were you doing in my room?'

His breath stenches so badly it slicks at my face like a wet towel.

'I clean,' he says in a thick slur.

'What do you mean? You were fucking with my drip the other night. Have you been coming into my room and taking photographs of me?'

I know even as I ask it that it can't be him. This man is retarded or deranged.

He shakes his head, backs away. 'Don't call Administration. I clean. You see. I clean.'

'What do you mean?' I press, but the man starts blubbering, his massive frame quivering.

'Is everything all right, Mr Farrell?' Nomsa sneaks up out of nowhere again.

'This man... he was...'

'Isaac? Have you been troubling the patients again? I thought we discussed this.'

'I clean, Nurse. I don't trouble.'

'You remember, Isaac. You don't want me to call Administration. I don't want to call Administration.'

'No, Nurse.' The big man heads straight back to his bucket, twitches his head down and starts mopping the floor.

'We let him stay here, Mr Farrell. And he helps clean when we need extra hands. Poor Isaac has nowhere else to go. I found him sleeping in the mouth of the furnace chute. That wouldn't do. The poor man could have died.'

'Oh.'

'If he's bothering you we can—'

'No, really. It's fine.' I'm sure it was he who was messing with my drip that night, but I don't want to ask Nomsa. She'll just make me feel ridiculous again. Behind Nomsa, an old woman emerges from the dying women's ward, using a plastic chair to prop herself up as she goes. The front of her grey gown is patched with blood. She coughs, and a clot of blood spatters onto the floor. Her face is a study in determination.

Nomsa doesn't look round. 'Why are you dressed, Mr Farrell? Has Doctor discharged you?'

'No. My girlfriend called,' I lie. 'She's in trouble... she needs me. I'm feeling fine... and I have my eye drops.' I smile. 'I really would like to go. I'm fine now.'

'Well, you look a whole lot better to me, Mr Farrell. I'm sure you can go.' Oh, thank God. 'But we'll need a doctor to sign your discharge papers before security will let you out.' She nods towards the guard lazing on his garden chair at the gate and shrugs, as if to say, 'Those are the rules. Nothing to do with me.'

'Is the ward doctor available?'

'The train accident, Mr Farrell. Everyone's on call. It's worse than anyone imagined. I doubt there will be rounds until tomorrow, at the earliest.'

'But isn't there anything you can do? Isn't someone else authorised to sign if there's no doctor? My girlfriend. She's in trouble.' I consider telling the whole story to Nomsa, showing her the photos, even telling her that the police might be looking for me, but then I realise that's just stupid. Patient shows nudie photos of self to nurse then tells her he's wanted by police.

'I'm sorry, no. That's why we're not allowing visitors. There's not enough staff to handle the floor.'

'Can I at least get my phone and wallet?'

'When you're discharged, Mr Farrell. For your own protection, of course.' She looks at me with a brick-wall smile.

I'm clearly not going to get any further with her. 'Okay, thanks,' I say. 'But as soon as a doctor's available you'll ask them to discharge me?'

'Of course, Mr Farrell. You really seem ready to go as far as I can tell.' She smiles. 'But then again, I'm just a nurse.'

'A very good one,' I say. She's still my only ally here; I need to keep her on my side. And to be honest, talking to her has calmed me down. She has a way of making my fears seem irrational.

'Oh, Mr Farrell. I'm just doing my job.' She walks briskly down the corridor.

Once Nomsa's out of sight, I hear the grey-faced man muttering something under his breath as he mops. I start to walk away, ignoring him, but a word in his mumble catches my attention.

'Drngnwrds... drngnwrds... drngnwrds.' He rocks on his heels while he mops, back and forth, back and forth over the same spot. 'Drngn-wrdsss... drngnwrdssssss.' Maybe it's just a song he's singing. I head back to my closet-room.

'*WARDS!*'

I wheel around, my heart cracking my ribs. 'What the fuck, man? You nearly gave me a heart attack.'

Now he looks at me, completely in focus, while everything else around him blurs into nothing, his face a circle of clarity like I remember from that night. It was him, it was him fucking with my drip that night.

'Don't go to the Wards,' he says, clear as a news anchor. Then he puts his head down and resumes his mopping and mumbling.

'The Wards.' That's where Nomsa said Lisa is. Some new wing, she said. I'm surprised they haven't called it the Manto Tshabalala-Msimang Memorial Wing or something. Just 'the Wards'. Anyway, whatever: If I can't get out, it's got to be safer than here. The police or Glenn's goons could be here any minute. I've got to move. I look at the grey man again. An access card hangs on a lanyard around his neck. Does that card let him in and out of Green Section?

'Listen. Listen.' I try to rouse him. 'Do you mind if I borrow your card for a minute?'

He looks back at me, his eyes now as opaque as they were clear a moment ago. He mops and mutters, 'I clean, I clean. See. I clean.' He's gone back into that cage of his.

There's a rattle on Green Section's main security gate. A pregnant woman, her face creased with pain, stands with a small wheeled suitcase on the other side. The security guard slowly stands up from his slouch, gradually removes the earphones from his ears and tries to make out what she's asking. He makes 'No, no. Wrong place. Not us' gestures at her, plugs back in and sits down, staring at his boots in front of him. The woman bucks and sways through a contraction then wanders back down the corridor. The guard looks on officiously. There's no way past him; I have to get that card. And I'll have to be fast. That grey man may be slow, but he's big. Who knows how he'll fight back? Probably like a dumb animal. And even if I manage to get it, I'd better hope that card opens doors. Christ. Do I really want to do this?

I start to get distracted by images of Katya's face, of Glenn's... and I shut them out. It's all converging on me, here. I need to get the hell out.

The time is now.

I dart to the grey man, girding myself for his counter-attack. Ignoring his moistness and his odour, I grab him from behind and try to immobilise him with my left arm, but I can't even get it all the way around his massive torso. He slowly turns to look over his left shoulder, like some kiddie trickster has tapped him. I take the chance to grab the card with my left hand and unclip the lanyard with my right. Got it!

I run, expecting him to chase me, but he stands there like a confused bear, looking down at his chest where the card was. By the time he looks up, I'm around the corner, heading for the nurses' kitchen.

Which is the opposite fucking side of the section from the main gate. Not that I would've just been able to saunter out there anyway. The guard knows I'm a patient. I didn't think it through.

There has to be more than one exit from this section. I swerve into the kitchen. There! There's a door with an access panel. Must be where catering staff come in and out. I swipe the card. Shit. The light's still red.

'Been looking for you, Frankie.'

It's Gertie. She's standing at the door, arms crossed. I pretend not to see or hear her. Try the card again. Still nothing. Am I swiping it the right way?

'Hey! I'm talking to you. Where's my fokken phone? And my hundred bucks?'

Shit. 'I'll get it back to you just now.'

'Ja, right. What are you doing, anyway?'

'Um, something's come up. I need to go.'

She snorts. 'And you're going out the kitchen door?' She's shuffles up close to me and I get a nostrilful of old lady stink. 'Let me tell you something, my boy, you're not going anywhere till I get what's mine.'

I really *really* don't need this right now.

'Look, Gertie—'

'It's Missus February to you.'

'Look. I'm worried about Lisa, okay? That's why I'm trying to get out of here.'

She narrows her eyes. 'You being straight with me?'

'Of course.'

'So why you going out this way?'

'She's in the new wing – wherever the fuck that is – and they won't let me leave Green Section until I'm discharged.'

She looks me up and down, wrinkling her nose as she takes in my filthy jeans and shirt. 'Then I'm coming with you.'

'What? No ways! Look, I'll tell Lisa you said hi or whatever, but—'

'I said I'm coming with.' She pulls a box of menthols out of the pocket of her tatty robe. 'Need a smoke.'

'So have one here!'

'Can't. The fokken waiting room's locked. Besides, wouldn't mind seeing Lisa. She's a lekker chick.'

'It's not going to happen, Gertie.'

She shrugs. 'Have it your way.' She looks meaningfully at the swipe card. 'But not sure I'd be able to keep my mouth shut about your whereabouts. If anyone should come asking.'

'What? What do you know ab—' Then it dawns on me. 'You mean the hospital staff?' If she's willing to tell them, then I'm fucking sure she'll tell all if the cops come asking. They'll probably be able to track my movements with the card. It's probably safer to keep her with me. I can always ditch her. What I really need is some time to figure all of this out. 'There's nothing to tell. A cleaner lent me this card. But if you want to come, why not?'

'Right answer, doll.'

She snatches the card out of my hand, swipes it and the light goes green.

She rolls her eyes and cackles. I follow her into a service stairwell. We take the stairs down carefully; I feel as crocked as she is.

Gertie grabs hold of my arm. She's puffing and panting like a heart case on a cross-trainer. 'You got the hots for Lisa, then?'

'She's just a... friend.'

'Ja. That's what they all say. Next thing you know you're knocked up and on the bones of your arse.'

'Whatever,' I mumble, sounding just like one of the studio's teenage interns.

'You're a dark horse, Frankie, a dark horse. I can see how women would be your biggest problem.'

I hold my tongue this time. She doesn't know anything, she's just making old women's generalisations. She doesn't know anything.

It's going to be a slow and long journey to wherever this stairwell leads. I wonder if I'll be stuck in the back corridors of this godforsaken hospital with this old hag for days, shuffling through, trying to find our way out.

There's a white door at the foot of the stairs. There are no signs or markings on it. I try to calculate how far we've come down. Green Section was on the third level and casualty and the main reception area are on the ground floor. With any luck the access card will work there too. I'll worry about that when we get there. But maybe the best course of action is to ditch the old hag and leave through casualty like Lisa and I did before. Without the detour this time. Straight into a taxi – there'll be cash at the flat – then find out what's happened to Katya.

I grab the card out of Gertie's hand, slide it and the door clicks. I push it open, wondering where best to lose Gertie. I could probably outwalk her among the rows of chairs in reception.

A blur of movement. A jab in my thigh.

What? I turn to look at Gertie, did she just—

'Mr Farrell, Isaac needs his access card.'

Darkness, then lights rolling past. I lift my head and see Nomsa smiling down at me.

Jab.

Chapter 12

LISA

The room dips sharply to the left. My gut clenches and I shut my eyes and wait for the wave of dizziness to pass. When I open them again, the room has stopped lurching, but my head still feels woozy. I remember the aide bringing my breakfast, but I don't recall actually eating any of the food. I burp, and the salty tang of smoked salmon floods into my mouth. So I *must* have eaten it.

I'm alone in here again, but why can't I remember that freaky woman leaving the room? She can't have been gone long though – there's still a lingering trace of that cloying body spray she was wearing. The scent of it makes me want to gag.

The drip bag next to my bed is almost empty. Is there some kind of painkiller in the brownish fluid? Something that's making me feel dizzy and out of it? Maybe there was something in the food?

Stupid. I've just had an operation. It's understandable that I'm still feeling crap.

Water. I need water. I lift my arm to reach for the glass next to the bed, but it's like I'm moving in slow motion. Careful not to drop it, I lift the glass to my lips and take a sip. That's better.

A glimmer of movement catches my eye. The nurses' aide must have left the television on when she left. A fuzzy black-and-white image flickers on the screen – there's no sound, just a random collection of vaguely people-shaped shadows. Gradually, the picture sharpens and I start to make sense of what I'm looking at. It's a man – middle-aged, overweight, with a round jowly face. He's lying flat on his back on what appears to be a metal table. The image wobbles slightly and at first I think I've been hit with another spate of dizziness – but it's not me, it's the actual film. The picture's wobbling around like in that old horror film Sharon loves, the one where the kids go missing in the forest. I couldn't watch all of it. It felt too *real*.

The picture pulls back from the close-up of the man's face so fast that the image blurs for a few seconds. The screen flicks to black and then the camera moves slowly over the rest of the man's body. He's wearing a short hospital gown and his legs are covered in thick whorls of dark hair. Oh God... his right arm ends at the elbow in a scabbed and seeping stump. What on earth is this? Some sort of low-budget horror film?

The remote is lying next to the water glass and I snatch it up and start pressing buttons at random. None of them are labelled and I can't find the off switch. I'm trying not to look at the awful scene, but I can't help it, my eyes keep being drawn back to it. Now there's a close-up of the man's face. He's smiling. Why would he be smiling? A white shape flits into view, the image wobbles again, and then I make out a skinny woman dressed in a baggy overall and thick plastic gloves. Her bulging eyes look way too large for her face, totally out of proportion to her thin nose and almost non-existent lips. She grins wolfishly into the camera, dips down to the floor and re-emerges clutching a long, curved metal tray covered in a stained cloth. Now she's looking straight out of the screen at me. Then she bends down to the man and whispers into his ear. The scene changes and now we're looking *down* at the unsettling scene from the ceiling. With another hungry grin, the woman grabs the corner of the cloth covering the tray, and then, like a proud chef whipping the lid off a plate of gourmet food, removes it with a flourish, revealing a long twisted *something*. I lean forward slightly. What is that? Is it... a tentacle?

No ways. This is sick! The special effects are really good, which makes it even worse. Although it isn't attached to anything, the thing twitches and flicks in its tray and I can make out every detail on its glistening surface – every lump and pulsing vein. I really don't want to know what she's going to do with it. Whoever thought this up is seriously warped.

I jab at the buttons on the remote again. Dammit. The batteries must be dead. I bang it on the top of the locker, hoping to jolt it into life; the vile horror film flicks off and the television bursts into silent static. Thank God. I slap the back of the remote and the screen flickers again, and another image shivers into view, this time in colour. I have to really concentrate to figure out what I'm looking at. Then I get it... Ugh! It's a massive close-up of a huge furry spider. I can see every hair on its body and each one of its bulbous glistening eyes. Is this some sort of nature show?

The screen wavers, showing a slightly grubby bathroom. I haven't touched the remote. It must be jammed; it's changing channels by itself. Hang on... The camera moves towards a dark shadow in the corner of the shower, which gradually comes into focus. It's the spider again. Its body appears to be rippling, its legs twitching. Then scores of baby spiders pour out of its body, spilling around it.

What is this? I press the buttons again, slam the remote on the locker, but nothing happens. I think of climbing out of bed and turning the TV off at the wall but I don't want to go near it. I shudder as if thousands of spidery legs are skittering over my body. I squeeze my eyes shut and repeatedly jam the buttons with my thumb.

I count to twenty.

When I open them, the screen is blank, the television dead. All I can see is the ghost of my reflection. For once it doesn't fill me with disgust. My mask is still comfortably in place.

Did I fall asleep again? Was it just a nightmare?

I'm not sure what I'd rather believe. But I do know that I don't want to be here anymore. It's almost as if those images have dirtied me some- how. I rub my hands over my arms. They're covered in goosebumps.

I want to go home.

I want to be back in my room with the curtains drawn, Dad grumbling in the kitchen, Sharon playing Katy Perry at full volume down the hall. I need to find a nurse, tell her that I'm going to discharge myself. Then I'll phone Dad, explain everything and admit what I've done and make sure he knows how sorry I am.

But what about my face?

I'll go to a clinic in Durban. That's it. I'm not well. I know that now. Dr Meka will know what to do. I need to get help, I just need to go home and—

Beeeeeeeeeeep. Beep. Beeeeeep.

The machine next to the bed is signalling that the drip bag is empty. Will someone come or should I—?

The door flies open and a nurse strides into the room. She doesn't look anything like Lumpy Legs and the other nurses in my old ward. She sparkles with efficiency and is dressed in an old-fashioned starched uniform; she's even wearing a pointed paper cap. She carries a large, curved metal tray covered with a white cloth. My stomach shifts greasily as I remember what was on the tray in that horrible TV programme.

'Hello,' the nurse says with a wide smile. I can't tell how old she is; her face is perfectly smooth and unlined, and she's wearing opaque John Lennon glasses that make her eyes look like flat silver spheres. 'I'm Nurse Jova. My sincere apologies for not arriving here immediately.'

She strides over to the nightstand by my bed, her starched uniform crackling as she moves, and places the tray on it. She touches a button on the machine and it stops beeping.

She turns to face me, head cocked to one side, hands clasped in front of her, radiating professional concern. She tucks a stray strand of red hair under her cap. 'How are you feeling?'

'I'm not sure. A bit groggy, and...' Can I trust her? She's a nurse, she's *paid* to help me, isn't she? Gertie's voice pops into my head: *Yeah right, doll. Like they really give a monkey's arse.* But I don't have a choice right now. 'Actually, I'm having a few problems.'

'Problems?' She sounds genuinely concerned. 'We don't like our Clients to have problems.'

'Don't you mean patients?'

'Please continue.'

'I'm having some strange dreams. Nightmares.'

She pats my leg and coos. 'There, there. What sort of nightmares?'

'This is going to sound weird...'

'Go on.'

'I think I've been seeing things. Horrible things. Imagining stuff.'

'Oh dearie, dearie me. We can't have that now, can we?'

She glides towards the nightstand, slips a hand under the cloth covering the tray and brings out another bag of that brownish fluid. She attaches it to the stand, and flicks the tube attached to my arm to get rid of the air bubbles.

'What's in that drip? It's making me feel a bit spaced out.'

'Don't you worry about that. That's perfectly normal.'

'Can you tell me... where exactly *am* I?'

She laughs lightly. 'You're in the Modification Ward, of course. One of our lucky ones. One of our *special* guests.'

'Modification Ward? Is it like a cosmetic surgery section or something?'

She smiles at me again, the reflection of the overhead light dancing in the lenses of her glasses. 'You are so very, very fortunate. Not everyone gets to come here. Very few browns. You're a very lucky Client. Oh yes.'

'Look, I need to get hold of my family. My dad... he doesn't even know I'm here. He'll be worried.'

She cocks her head again. 'Oh, you don't want any excitement,' she's saying. 'Your only job is to recover.'

'Can't you bring me a phone? Please?'

She smoothes the covers of the bed. 'There, there. Baby steps. It will take some shifts for you to recover. You must be patient.' She chuckles. 'Oh yes! Patient patients are our favourite. And client Clients are...' She frowns. 'No, that doesn't...'

'When is the doctor going to come?'

'Oh, that won't be necessary. You're a Client.'

'But shouldn't he... she... check that everything's fine?'

'No need for that. I'm here to look after you.'

I touch the mask. 'And how long before I can take this off?'

She clicks her tongue. 'That depends on you and your face, of course.'

'And my clothes – my stuff. Where is it?'

'You don't need your clothes, Client Cassavetes. The Administration will supply everything you need on schedule. Would you like some more desensitisers? We have lots. Many kinds.'

'Um. Do you mean painkillers? No. I'm not in any pain.' Almost as I finish the sentence the dull ache in my temples ramps up to a sharp twinge. I shut my eyes and will it to fade.

'Are you feeling poorly, Client?'

'I'm fine.'

'Goody good.' She claps her hands together. 'Now. How about a lovely bed bath, and then I'll consult with your face.' She digs in her pocket and pulls out a pair of white surgical gloves.

The aide's words slip back to me: 'Feed your face, dear. Feed your face. After all, *it must be hungry.*'

Did I imagine that as well?

I'm either drugged to the gills or losing my mind.

I have to try again. 'Nurse, I really need to let my dad know that—'

My words are cut off as an ear-splitting alarm blasts into the room, making me jump. It sounds like a whooping air-raid siren.

'What the hell is that?'

The nurse sighs and mumbles something under her breath. It sounds like 'karking interlopers', but I must have misheard. She seems to pull herself together and her smile is back in place when she looks at me. 'I will be back shortly. I do apologise.'

'Where are you going?'

'It's nothing to concern yourself with, Client Cassavetes.'

The siren whoops again, then dies. She yanks the gloves off her hands and, with another reassuring smile, glides out.

I lean back on my pillows. When she returns I'll insist that she gets me a phone. I'm in a hospital, for God's sake. Not a prison. I have to be more assertive. Sharon's always saying that I'm a pushover, she's always going on at me for letting other people walk over me and—

Oh no.

I haven't touched the remote, but the television has come on again. The picture shudders and focuses into a crisp black-and-white image of a girl lying on a bed. I know her, don't I? She looks familiar: long blonde hair, wide eyes...

The jolt of recognition makes the room tilt with such force I have to grab onto the covers to stop myself from falling sideways.

Oh God. That's me.

That's me!

I lift my right hand and wave it. The girl on screen does the same.

I lift my left hand above my head, and my mirror image copies the gesture.

I scan the walls and the ceiling for any sign of a camera. I can't spot one. But it could be anywhere.

Why are they showing me this?

Is this another hallucination?

I shut my eyes. Open them again. The girl is no longer on the bed. It's empty, the covers ruffled as if they've been shoved off in a hurry.

So it can't be me. I'm still sitting here. I fight to control another lurch of dizziness.

I stay absolutely still and stare into the screen. It can't be me, but it's my room. There's my water glass. And the remote. And the covered tray and the beeping machine and... and... I scream out loud – I can't help it – as her face (*my* face, my blank *masked* face) fills the screen in close-up.

Oh God oh shit oh crap.

What the *hell* is this?

She's mouthing something. Opening her mouth and closing it. Pausing in between every word. She's trying to say something. *She's trying to tell me something.* I copy the movement of her lips.

She's saying...

RUN!

I must be dreaming. I must be. Just another nightmare. I close my eyes again – count to ten, it worked last time...

I open them again.

The television is blank and dark. The shadow Lisa is gone from the screen.

Drained with relief, I reach over and take another sip of water, my shaking fingers inches away from the covered tray the nurse has left behind.

Look. See what's under there.

But I don't want to see. I really don't.

What if it's a tentacle?

Stupid. Absurd. Would be funny if it wasn't so...

Possible?

Holding my breath, I whip the cloth away.

I breathe out with relief. Nothing but a soft white towel and a bar of pink soap.

Yes, but what's under the towel?

I pull it aside. Holy Christ. There's a pair of curved forceps and an outsized scalpel in the metal dish.

I don't stop to think. I pull off the tape that holds the drip tube in place and yank the needle out of my arm. I swing my legs off the bed, grabbing the side of the nightstand to steady myself. My legs are shaky, but I can't let that stop me. I grab a sheet off the bed and wrap it around me like a toga – for once I don't care anyone will think. All I know is that I have to get out of here. I need to find a phone. Tell Dad where I am. Beg him to come fetch me. I shake my head to clear it, and when I take my first few steps I stumble slightly as the floor slants sharply to the side, as if I'm on board a listing ship.

I fumble for the handle – certain that it will be locked, that I won't be able to get out – but it opens smoothly.

I step out into a long, carpeted corridor, letting the door crump shut behind me. If I didn't know I was in a hospital, I'd swear I was in a hotel hallway. The walls are papered in pale-pink silk, and the doors are all made of heavy oak. The words 'Welcome to the Modification Ward' loop across the wall in elaborate gold letters. There's no sign of any hospital equipment or a nurses' station, and there's not a soul to be seen. The place has a hushed, luxurious atmosphere. The thick carpet isn't helping my muzziness. It's wildly patterned with multi-coloured interlocking circles in deep red, infected yellow and pukey green, and the more I stare at it the more it seems to undulate sickeningly.

Don't look at it.

Which way should I go? My room is situated halfway along the corridor, and both directions appear to end at an elevator door. There's no sign of any other exits, connecting corridors or a stairwell.

The elevator door to my right opens, making the decision for me. I turn left and walk as fast as I can. I don't seem to be going in a straight line and the carpet's stomach-churning design keeps trying to rise up and hit me in the face. I realise I've sunk to my knees, and using the wall as support I force myself up.

'Client Cassavetes!' a woman's voice calls from behind me. It sounds like that mirror-eyed nurse but I don't turn round.

I force myself into a shambling run, but the sudden burst of exertion makes my already watery legs give way. I stumble and slam into one of the doors as I pass. Whoever's behind it is laughing at something.

'Client Cassavetes!' Nurse Jova calls. 'You are not authorised!'

The lift suddenly looms within touching distance.

I'm dimly aware that the siren I heard before is wailing in the background. Praying for it not to take too long, I slam my fist onto the single lift button. The doors slide open immediately. I half crawl inside and press all of the buttons on the control panel.

Nurse Jova glides towards me. 'Client Cassavetes!' she calls. 'Please return. If you go to the Terminal Ward you will—'

The doors slide shut.

Ha. I made it! I have the sudden urge to laugh, but I don't have the energy. The lift starts moving, but I can't tell if it's going up or down. I don't care. I swivel round and lean my forehead against the door. It helps. My legs regain some of their strength, but my hands are shaking and cold sweat runs down my sides. The puncture wound in the crook of my elbow is leaking blood, and I use the sheet to wipe off the rivulets trailing down my arm.

The lift pings and the door opens.

This corridor looks reassuringly more like a hospital. The floors are shiny polished pink linoleum, and the portholed doors that line the passage are painted a peppermint hospital green. There's an empty wheelchair a few yards from me, and an abandoned drip stand leans drunkenly against the wall next to it.

At first I think I'm back in another public section of New Hope, but this area is spotlessly clean and uncluttered. The words 'Welcome to Preparation Ward!' are printed in comic-book writing along the wall in front of me. There's a shiny poster of a clown's winking face tacked up next to it. 'A Good Donor is a Happy Donor' is printed in a speech bubble above his orange hair. At the far end of the corridor a hunched figure scuttles around the corner.

My temples are throbbing again and there's a dark spot dancing into the far corner of my right eye. Using the wall for support, I shuffle along and just avoid tripping over the end of the sheet that's unravelling from around my body. God, I'm tired. But there has to be a phone around here somewhere. I have to keep going.

I push against the first door I reach. It doesn't budge. I stand on my tip-toes and peer through the round window. I glimpse a body lying prone on a metal gurney. It's covered with a clean white sheet and partially hidden behind a folding screen. I lean my ear against the glass and I can just about make out the murmur of voices, followed by a pneumatic hissing sound and a quick burst of a mechanical whine. I stagger back as unseen hands pull the gurney further behind the screen.

Am I on a surgical ward?

A third of the way down the corridor, a door bangs open and a plump pink-smocked nurses' aide pulls a catering trolley out of one of the rooms.

A laugh echoes down the corridor, followed by 'How's about another cup of tea, doll? And a biscuit if you've got one!'

I know that voice. I'd know it anywhere! It's Gertie! Thank God. Gertie will know where I can find a phone. She knows everything about this place. Everything seems to shift back into perspective, and I pick up my pace.

The pink-smocked orderly hesitates and stares at me as I approach, her mouth dropping open, revealing stumpy teeth. She's old – ancient in fact, her skin scarred and yellowed with age.

'Excuse me,' I say to her, doing my best to smile. 'I'm looking for a phone. Could you tell me where I could find—'

Her eyes widen and she shakes her head and hustles off. She actually looks frightened.

The door through which she emerged is still swinging slightly, and I push it open.

I can hear the faint sound of television voices and canned laughter like in a sitcom. It's another private room, with a single bed and armchair. It's not as plush as the luxury room I was in, but it's as smart as most of the private clinics I've stayed in. I move closer. Yes! The figure lying on the bed is Gertie.

She's pointing the remote at the screen, her face scrunched up in concentration, and she doesn't look up until I'm almost at the foot of her bed.

'Hi, Gertie.'

She leans forward and shakes her head. 'Who the hell are you?'

I've forgotten about the mask. 'Oh! Sorry. It's me. It's Lisa.'

'Lisa? Seriaas? What's that thing on your face?'

'Some sort of surgical mask. To protect my face, I guess. I don't really know for sure.'

'No offence, doll, but it makes you look like Hannibal Lectern.'

'Lector.'

'Thass what I said.'

The slur in her voice chills me. She's also attached to one of those drips, the same brownish fluid eking its way into her veins.

'When did they move you here, Gertie?'

'Just now. Not bad here, is it, eh, doll? Been treated like a queen since I woke up.'

She plumps the pillows behind her and leans back with a sigh. She takes a sip of tea. The cup rattles in its saucer and I hurry to steady it for her.

'Are you okay, Gertie?'

'I think so, doll.' She scrunches her eyes up as if she's trying to remember something. 'I think I had a relapse.'

'In the other ward?'

'Ja. Funny, me and your boyfriend were coming to look for you.'

My stomach leaps. 'You were? Farrell's here?' And he was *looking* for me?

'Ja. Next thing I know, they've moved me to a private room.' She cackles. 'Buggered if I'm paying for it though, doll. If they've made a mistake, it's their problem.'

She yawns.

'How the uvver half live, hey?' She's really slurring now. 'Nurshes treating me like I was gold. But I don't think much of this D-esh TV. Find me *The Bold and the Beautiful*, hey, doll?' The word comes out as boosifuuul.

'Did they give you something, Gertie?'

'Give me something?'

'You sound... a bit groggy.'

'Do I, doll? Come to think of it, I do feel a bit tired.'

I've deliberately been avoiding looking at the TV screen, but there's no horrible image on here. It's definitely some old eighties sitcom. A couple of women with fake tans and skin-tight Lycra dresses are perched on stools at a garish breakfast nook, talking to a man with a chest wig and a medallion.

'I don't wanna watch this kak, doll.' Gertie waves her hand vaguely at the television.

'Gertie, do you know where I can find a phone?'

She yawns. 'Wass that, doll?'

'A phone. Do you know where I can find one? Is there one on this floor?'

'Your boyfriend hass the phone, doll. I gave it to him. He crooked me though. Blarry stole it and my hunned bucks.'

'There you are, Client Cassavetes!' A nurse bustles into the room. I recognise her instantly, but I can't remember her name.

'You're Farrell's nurse.'

She smiles at me and clucks her tongue. 'That's right. Now, now, what are you doing down here? You don't belong here.' She waggles her finger at me as if I'm a naughty child. 'You were sent to the Modification Ward.'

'What's wrong with my friend? She seems a bit out of it.'

Gertie chuckles. 'I'm fine, doll.' But she isn't. She seems to be having problems focussing and her eyelids are drooping.

'Mrs February is going to have a lovely sleep now. Aren't you, dear?' the nurse says.

Gertie nods. 'Ja, Nursie.'

This isn't like the Gertie I remember.

'Yes,' the nurse continues. 'A lovely, lovely long sleep.'

Gertie's eyes flicker and close. Her head droops to the side and her breathing evens out.

The nurse pulls the covers up to Gertie's chin.

'Will she be okay?' I say.

The nurse turns to face me. I take a step back. The smile is gone from her lips. Her eyes are cold and dead and all I can think is *those are the spider's eyes. The real spider's eyes.* 'Now,' she says, her voice still silky smooth but somehow also dangerous. 'Just what am I going to do with you?'

Chapter 13

FARRELL

God, it feels good to be in my own bed again. I breathe in the fresh-smelling air, taking a delicious lungful, and stretch until my skeleton cracks satisfyingly. I almost feel up to working out again. I can't wait to get back to the gym. I roll onto my side and something snags on my arm.

Wait a second. There's a drip needle taped into my arm.

I open my eyes. They take a moment to clear, but then I can see. I'm not at home. I'm in a hospital room. A big, comfortable room with a proper bed. That fresh smell hits me again. And the perfect temperature. Thank God someone sorted out the medical-aid fuck-up and transferred me to a private clinic.

But I'm better; I should have been discharged, not transferred. Why am I on a drip again?

I spot the eye drops on my bedside table, and I decant a dose into each eye and lie back.

Competing memories batter each other inside my head. I force myself to relax; let them through one at a time. And Katya's always first on my mind. I look at my hands. The big gash on my right hand is now dressed with Micropore tape. It feels much less angry. I see Katya's bloody face. I can't make myself believe that I hurt her. But I can't piece together those jagged images. I see Katya crying, angry, taking her bag and leaving. *Take a good, long look, you bastard*, she said. *There were signs of a struggle*, June said.

What have I done? If she doesn't turn up, Glenn will kill me. *I will find you and make an example of you.*

The last thing I want to think about, the thing that knocks most urgently inside my skull, are those Polaroids. My body, portioned up like meat. My hand makes straight for my back pocket, but I realise I'm not wearing my jeans. I'm in clean and comfortable flannel pyjamas; my body feels like it's had a long, hot bath. I lift up the top and my skin is scrubbed and spotless.

There. On the vanity. My clothes are folded up with military tightness. Jeans and T-shirt. I swing my legs out of the bed and pull the drip stand along with me. It rolls lightly over the tiled floor, as if its castors have been oiled and cleaned. The pole itself looks brand new and is made of a light but strong alloy. 'Mørke Ferli' is discreetly etched in the metal, some Scandinavian manufacturer, no doubt. This, right here, is why we pay for private healthcare. I should have kicked up more of a fuss; I could have been here for a week, instead of in fucking No Hope, that filthy hellhole.

Someone's washed my clothes – they no longer stink of puke. I unfold my jeans and check the pockets for the photos. Nothing. I lift up my T-shirt, and there they are, neatly packed in a transparent ziplock bag. I fumble with the seal of the bag, my cut hand still too stiff and sore for the job, and drop it on the floor. As I squat to pick it up, my bones crackling and my muscles bunching intensely as I go, I notice a manila folder under the vanity table, half wedged under the table's leg. 'Joshua Alphonse Farrell' reads the label on the top left corner. 'Strictly Confidential.' Brilliant! I pick up the file and take it and the photos back to the bed.

It's not often you get the chance to read your own case file. These damn doctors never tell you anything when you ask them. It will be great to get some real answers at last. At this clinic they probably keep proper records and test results. It's likely they'll have ordered copies of all the tests from New Hope already. Finally I can find out exactly what was wrong with me. And what's in this drip. And where I am, for that matter.

'Mr Farrell! So *wonderful* to have you up and about. We *really* should refresh that drip.'

I shove the folder under the sheets before the nurse notices it. She's dressed in a retro-cool nurse's uniform: short skirt, bobby socks. There's nothing sexy about it, mind you – she's too squat and middle-aged to pull it off – but it's comforting.

'I'm Nurse Essigee, Donor Farrell, and I'll be taking care of you until your procedure. Welcome to Preparation Ward.'

Did she just say *Donor*? She does have an odd accent. I thought she was Bulgarian or something at first, but it could be Italian. Maybe she said 'Don'. Don Farrell. I like the ring of that.

'Okay, but I was supposed to be discharged. I had the measles, and I've recovered.'

'You have a wonderful spirit,' she trills. 'Just *perfect*! Now I'll change your drip. It appears that someone gave you the... Let's see...' She checks the label on the drip bag, which is half full of clear liquid and then consults the chart at the foot of my bed. 'Yes, that's right... Soon sort that out.' She bustles out and comes back a few seconds later with a brownish liquid and hangs it up. With incredible efficiency, she switches the drip. I watch her trained hands moving with graceful speed. The needle and loop in my arm are inserted so delicately that there's not a snag of pain. The sticky tape doesn't even pull at my skin. My bruised right arm – where that grey freak did something to me back in New Hope – has been treated and covered with a gossamer dressing.

'But can you tell me why I still need to be on the drip?'

'Administration's orders. The representative will be doing the rounds later, and you can ask him everything you really need to know.'

Her voice reassures me. I do feel at ease. I can remember feeling panicky about something a moment ago, but now I'm not sure what it was all about. I know I was thinking about Katya – my gorgeous Katya, I really hope she's okay. And her dad – of course he's worried. Who wouldn't be? I can worry about it all later. I feel a bit tired. For now, my—

'For now, your job is just to get big and strong. You're almost ready.'

'Yes, Mom.'

An alarm pierces my sleep.

The nurse rushes out, muttering under her breath. The alarm must have disturbed her while she was changing my drip. I roll over, trying to shift the cobwebs from my head, and remember the folder as my body crumples over it. God, I'm tired, all I want to do is drift back into oblivion again, but this might be my only chance to find out why I'm in here. The folder nags me as it presses into my side. Maybe I should just find out why they're giving me this goddamn drip, and when I can go the fuck home.

And find Katya.

It's an effort, but I shove a pillow behind me, shift up to a slumping sitting position and open the folder.

```
Joshua Alphonse Farrell
Ward: Preparation H
Donor
```

Is that what I heard the nurse calling me?

```
Node: Johannesburg, ZA, New Hope Hospital (Node
   2:34:765/f)
Age: 31y 267d
Weight (pre-catalyst): 208.77 lb
Weight (admission): 168.21 lb
Weight (projected post-prep): 192.87 lb
Est. Harvest Mass: 117.63 lb
Height: 6'3"

Viabilities:
All intern. organs viable (ex. liver, right temp. lobe,
cardiac left vent.) - spec. note: special value hair,
teeth. Skin suitable for grafts (ex. upper arms,
thighs, some acne on neck and shoulders). Ocular
```

compromise (keratitis as side-effect of catalyst) but
intervention by transfer agent should result in viable
ophthalmic elements (assess corneas on harvest and
discard if suboptimal).

Close this folder. Now. Put it away. Forget you ever saw it. Nothing good
will come of this.

But I can't pull my eyes from the page. I keep reading, guiltily, hungrily,
like I'm delving into someone else's diary.

Supervisor assessment:
Excellent, high-gain candidate, but special care to be
taken during preparation to maintain levels of organic
stimulants to avoid aggressive withdrawal. Suggest this
be balanced with 70% rather than the normal 80%
solution of sulfamethazine hormone, in a haemoglobulin
base. 1 unit 3-hourly for preparation term to encourage
optimum haemopoiesis and tissue bulking. Monitor heart
stress 2-hourly and escalate donation cycle if the
stress rate reaches 85th centile. This Donor is liable
to have a short viability span on such an intensive
preparatory course, but viable tissue is of high value
and priority harvest is recommended.

    Sedate with opiate-family suspension if necessary.
Mild to medium aggression.

Sales Department (Improvement Division) input:
Client workups have been performed. 9 potential Clients
already shortlisted. (See Workup Figures 1 through 9,
appended hereto, reflecting Client specifications.) Will
have no difficulty with immediate placement.

Scout Department report:
Candidate has been shortlisted for several months.

Scout team was concerned by elevated adenosine triphosphate levels, dissatisfaction at work, and lifestyle of sexual partner, Katya Angela Forrest, who is an habitual reliant on semi-organic stimulants. On-site scouting agent M.R. monitored candidate and noted improved alpha-E tendencies which, if continued as plotted, would lead to optimal induction in 3 to 5 periods. However, a domestic dispute at the candidate's dwelling on 3rd Wet Shift, Deep Discount Cycle 3 (14 November upside), increased risk ratio to viable tissues beyond the Pot-Eichmann scale recommendations and necessitated immediate catalysis.

On upside 14 November, immediately following the departure of Katya Angela Forrest, catalysis was initiated by the scout team. The candidate was intercepted on approach to his vehicle and infected with an accelerated paramyxovirus which presented within 150 upside-equivalent moments as acute measles. The domestic dispute prior to induction was regrettable, as it resulted in raised cortisol and adrenalin levels in the candidate's muscular tissues, which then had to be flushed at the transfer node as effectively as the short timeframe allowed.

In accordance with Ministry frugality procedure, section 14a, candidate was sequestered in upside facility to recover to optimum recyclability. Suboptimally, candidate absconded from the upside facility and early transfer to Preparation Ward was necessitated. Viability of muscular tissue will be compromised at an estimated range on the Walters-King scale of 3.4-5.1%.

Despite these factors, the Supervisor and Administration concurred that the risks were outweighed by the potential harvest and that the unscheduled

```
catalysis was the optimal course of action. (See
Appendices 1a [records of consultation with Senior
Administrator Plate and Supervisor Blow], 1b [record of
advice from same] and 1c [responsibility escalation
addendum], herewith in duplicate. Original and copies
duly captured and forwarded to Procedures Office.) The
candidate is a mild to moderate security risk, and
should be handled with caution, and the Supervisor has
suggested that the donation cycle should be given
priority scheduling status.
    (Transfer agent N.M. reports that the candidate has
reacted well to calm authority and non-invasive
techniques. Preparation staff may try persuasion rather
than invasion at first contact.)

Administration protocol checklist:
Tissue analysis requisition
Contact report templates
```

'What have you got there, Mr Farrell?'

I try to shove the folder under the bedclothes again but the contents spill out onto the floor and slide in a slick arc across the tiles. The ziplock bag containing the Polaroids slides fastest and furthest, all the way to the nurse's blue shoes. She looks at me, her dead, black eyes burning me.

Holy fuck. They're planning to feed me up until my heart explodes. They're planning to... They're planning to... There's only one thing for me to do. I have to go. Right now. But my body won't move, and at the same time my leg muscles seize, and pain screams up them and through my spine. I feel the piss warming the mattress beneath me.

'Now, now, Mr Farrell. I was looking for that. A cooperative Donor would have handed it in without reading it. Did you not see the stamp reading "Confidential" on the cover?'

I can't speak. The pain in my muscles blots out every thought in my head.

'I'm sure you did, Mr Farrell.' She approaches my bedside with another drip bag. 'Anyhow, let's move on. I apologise for not refreshing your treatment immediately. I was called away, you see. We seem to have an intruder on the ward, and nobody's quite sure what... to do... with her.' She hangs the drip and the brown liquid starts siphoning through the tube. I feel my veins desperately sucking it in, as if they know that whatever's in there will make the pain go away.

'So many people want to join our wards,' she coos on. 'It's a real honour to be chosen, you know. You are among the elite, Donor Farrell.' I think I believe her. It is really very comfortable here. 'Your job is simply to rest and to grow big and strong.'

Something inside my mind fights sleep. I'm tormented with a roll of images, of unresolved thoughts, and my mind lurches and tumbles as my body wants it to rest. My heart's going to explode. They're going to draw on me. With knives? They've been watching Katya. Where is Katya? Is she at home?

I remember what happened on Monday morning. Somehow those cryptic notes in my file have made it all come rushing back. *Domestic dispute... intercepted on approach to his vehicle...*

Katya was leaving me. And it wasn't a surprise. She'd done it at least four or five times before. Always after a weekend before a big job: always on a crazy downer after a binge. But this time there was something different, something more intense about her. This time it was as if she meant it.

You only love me for my face! she screamed, then she took a cut-glass tumbler from the counter and smashed it against the worktop. *Well*, she said, *take a good, long look, you bastard. It's the last time you'll see it.* And for a moment I thought she was going to hurt herself. I grabbed the shard of glass from her, cutting both of us in the process. She tucked her hair back with her bleeding hand, that's how the blood got on her face. I tried to touch her, but she left. Her bags were already packed.

Then, later, I was pissed off, nothing else to do but go to work. I headed down to the parking garage and this stinking fucking homeless guy came out of nowhere and rammed into me. I nearly had a fucking heart attack, I thought I was being hijacked, but he just mumbled something and stumbled off. *Look where you're going, you stupid motherfucker!* I yelled, taking deep breaths until I got my pulse back under control.

I was so stupid. Katya would never have hurt herself. She would never have done anything to her face. Christ, the amount of time I'd spend watching her make herself up in the walk-in. I'd pretend to sleep and just watch her, five, six in the morning. She'd make herself perfect for me every day before I had to see her. She knew what I liked.

I'm woken by a massive cramp all the way from my back to my heels. It feels as if my leg muscles are tearing themselves off the bone. The momentary relief at having remembered, at knowing that I didn't hurt Katya, dissolves in the scour of pain. I try not to scream; I don't want that nurse to come, but eventually the pain overwhelms me and I let it go. I bellow like it might bring this building down around me, like somehow I might have some luck and that nurse will be killed and—

'My goodness. Nurse Essigee really should be reported to the Administration. The number of times I've noticed guests on this floor with empty drips and, my goodness, Mr Farrell, has she not even bothered to have your sheets changed?'

It's Nomsa. What the fuck is Nomsa doing here?

'I moonlight as a supply nurse on these wards,' she continues, as if reading my thoughts. 'And when I found out that you were transferred, I made sure to look you up. It's lovely to see you. But I'm sorry to hear about your setback.'

'What do you mean? I was supposed to be discharged.'

'You're in no condition now, are you? I heard you crying out across the ward.' She comes to my bed and lays a soothing hand on my arm. 'Muscle pain, is it?'

'Yes. These massive cramps in my legs. All over actually.'

'That's right. This treatment sometimes has that side effect.'

'But what's wrong with me? Why wasn't I discharged?' I stop. I remember having that discussion with Nomsa, but I can't recall anything else. I was in a hurry to get out... That's right. I got that orderly's access card, and went...

Oh my fuck. I was with Gertie. It was Nomsa. She stopped us.

'Where am I, Nomsa?'

'You're in Preparation Ward.'

'Preparation for what?'

She looks at me for a few moments. I can't read her face. That's been my problem all along. I can't read her. I look at her name badge. RN Nomsa Makgatho. *Transfer agent N.M. reports that the candidate has reacted well to calm authority and non-invasive techniques. Preparation staff may try persuasion rather than invasion at first contact.*

'You've been selected, Mr Farrell. It's a great honour. Your physique is of the finest calibre. The measles took their toll, though, so we're simply getting you back to your optimum... To your optimum health.'

If I try to run now, she'll inject me with something. At least now I'm not tied down. She could strap me down if she wanted. They could try 'invasive techniques'. I should convince her that I am cooperating.

'Oh. Thanks. And then will I be discharged?'

She looks at me again, and, despite myself, despite the fear threatening to loosen my bladder again, I can't help imagining kindness in her eyes.

'Yes. How are your eyes, by the way? I see you've still got your drops.'

'Yes. My eyes are fine now. Thank you.' She couldn't be part of some insane cannibalistic scheme, could she? She's only ever been kind and warm to me. I'm not sure whether to trust her, but she's still my only ally. She may still help me.

'That's good.' She tweaks the tap on the drip and the brown liquid starts flowing faster.

'Nomsa.'

'Yes, Mr Farrell?'

'I read a file.'

'A file?'

'It was my hospital file. It said what treatment I was on. What I'm here for.'

'Was this a paper file? In a folder?'

'Yes.'

She laughs. 'Nurse Essigee told me about that. She said you were raving in your sleep. I *am* sorry. This medication is rather… intensive. It has side effects, but it's very effective. Nurse Essigee says you were shouting at her while you slept. Something about meat, something about donations. Your medical aid's been sorted out now, Mr Farrell. You don't need to worry about donations.'

'Nomsa, I'm trying to tell you that I read this file. It recorded my current treatment, what I was here for. They knew things about… about my home life, things that happened before… before I got sick. They knew *how* I got sick.'

'We don't keep paper records here, Mr Farrell. It's the modern world. Look.' She takes a handheld scanner with a large display screen out of her pocket. 'This is your file. Right here.' In the brief glance, I read my name and personal details. Just age, weight, the usual; no 'harvest mass' or any of that other insane shit.

Could I really have imagined it?

Nomsa gives the bag a squeeze. Could I have imagined it?

Hold on a minute.

'You found me and Gertie trying to leave the Green Section at New Hope. You drugged us.'

'You were a danger to yourself.'

'What happened to Gertie?'

'She got discharged. I'll leave you to rest now. Your body has a lot of work to do.'

Nomsa leaves the room and I slump down, prepared for oblivion, looking forward to dreaming of Katya.

Chapter 14

LISA

I sit down on the end of the bed while Farrell's nurse – Nomsa – fusses with the sheets. This room's identical to the one in which I discovered Gertie. They're probably all the same on this floor, and I've been told to wait here before being taken back to my own ward.

'There are very few vacancies on the Modification Ward, Client Cassavetes,' she says, shaking her head as if I'm an ungrateful child. 'Quite frankly, I'm disappointed that you would ignore such a marvellous opportunity. It was I who recommended your transfer here, and I really hope you'll realise just how fortunate you are. Especially considering your... condition.'

Ice shoots through my veins. 'What do you mean?' How could she know about my body dysmorphia? I haven't told anyone. The doctors at New Hope probably suspected, though. Has she been talking to them?

She sighs. 'Wait here. I'll be back for you shortly. We can't have Clients running willy-nilly around the Preparation Ward. It's not... appropriate.'

She leaves the room.

The headache is still gnawing at my temples – no doubt the after-effects of whatever drugs they gave me – but that's the least of my problems.

There's something seriously wrong here. It's not my imagination, I know it's not.

I glance around the room for something I could possibly use as a weapon, but there's nothing in here except for the bed and a lamp that's fixed permanently to the nightstand. I can feel tears welling up in my eyes. I touch the smooth surface of the mask and my fingers come back wet. The tears are trickling through the mask, but I can't feel them on my skin.

Stop being so pathetic, Dr Meka's no-nonsense voice says in my head. *They can't keep you here against your will.*

But I'm not so sure about that.

Get up and leave.

I don't want to. My body feels heavy and sluggish, and all I want to do is sleep. Yes. Maybe if I have a nap I'll wake up and everything will be...

Yeah, right. Now, go. You might not have another chance.

I force myself to stand up. I creep towards the door, pull it open and poke my head out into the corridor.

It's empty. All clear.

Wait!

The door opposite opens and a white-clad figure emerges. Nomsa again. I freeze, but she doesn't look in my direction, she's turning round to poke her head back into the room.

'I'll be back to check on you shortly, Mr Farrell,' she says.

I ease my door shut as quietly as I can and lean my back on it. Farrell's here! Gertie was right.

So I have a choice to make.

Should I just take my chances and make a run for the lift? Or should I first make sure that Farrell's okay? Would I be able to live with myself if I just leave him here? I can't forget those photographs they took of him. Whatever they're planning to do to me, they've also got something nasty in mind for him.

It's now or never. Before I can change my mind, I haul open the door and fly across the corridor. Heart pounding, I slip inside Farrell's room. He's fast asleep, snoring gently, a drip containing that murky brown fluid attached to his arm.

I creep up to his bed and touch his toe.

He wakes with a jolt. 'Katya?'

Who's Katya? His girlfriend?

'No. It's me. Lisa.'

He stares at me blearily. 'Lisa?' There's no sign of recognition in his eyes. Then he blinks. 'Oh, yeah. Lisa.' He sounds disappointed. I'm glad that I have the mask on; it hides the look of hurt that must be plastered all over my face. 'Shit, Lisa, what the hell is that on your face?'

'A surgical mask, I think.'

He screws his mouth up in distaste. 'What are you doing here, Lisa?'

'I've come to get you. We have to get out of here.'

'Nomsa says I will be discharged soon.' He's slurring his words slightly. He closes his eyes again.

I tap his foot and he shudders and blinks. 'You can't trust her, Farrell.'

He shakes his head as if he's trying to clear it. 'Where are we? Is this the new wing?'

'What?'

'No Hope's new wing. Nomsa said—'

'I don't know where we are. When I woke up from the op, I was in a posh hospital room. At first I thought I'd been moved to a private clinic. But now I'm not so sure. I've been seeing some... odd things.'

The understatement of the year. Tentacles, anyone?

'But where *is* here?' Farrell asks.

'I don't know.'

'So you're saying we're still in New Hope?'

'I don't know where we are, Farrell. Gertie's here as well.'

He struggles to sit up in bed, reaches for his water glass. He looks like crap. His eyes are bloodshot, his cheekbones stand out starkly and a vein flutters in his temple.

'Don't drink that. I think they're drugging us. And you're going to have to pull out that drip.'

'You don't think you're being a bit hysterical?'

I'm hit with an unfamiliar bolt of anger. 'No I'm not! Remember the photographs? And the lines they drew on your body? How can you say I'm being hysterical?'

'Okay, okay, calm down.'

I take a deep breath. 'Look, I think I know what they're doing here.'

'What?'

A Good Donor is a Happy Donor...

'I think they're harvesting... bits from people. Organs and things.'

'You mean like some sort of organ-smuggling racket?'

'Yes.'

'That's insane. That sort of thing doesn't happen to people like me, Lisa.' He sounds like he's trying to convince himself. 'I'm not some illegal immigrant who won't be missed. I'm a well-known photographer, for fuck's sake.'

'I don't have all the answers, Farrell.'

'But what you're saying, it's—'

I grab the chart from the end of his bed and thrust it into his hands. 'Look!'

The words 'Joshua Alphonse Farrell. Status: Donor' are scrawled on it in black marker pen.

He doesn't speak for several seconds. 'Lisa, if there is some kind of racket going on, they're hardly going to advertise it like this, are they? I mean, think about it. "Donor" is probably just some kind of politically correct term for a patient or whatever.'

'"*Donor*" is a politically correct word?'

He's still looking at me as if I'm some sort of madwoman. If he doesn't want my help he's on his own. At least I tried. I start heading for the door. 'If you don't want to come with me, I'm going by myself.'

'Wait.'

I turn around. His eyes stray to my legs. I left the sheet in the room and the hospital gown barely covers the tops of my thighs.

'You can't go anywhere like that,' he says.

'I don't have any choice. They took my clothes.'

He pushes the covers from his legs and swings them down onto the floor. His face contorts in pain. 'Christ!'

'What? Did they do something to you?'

'Ouch! Cramp! Fuck!'

'Do you need help?'

He waves his hand dismissively. 'I'll be fine.' He grimaces again, but manages to stand.

He looks at my bare legs again. He points to a pile of clothes on the top of the side table. 'Why don't you take my jeans?'

I grab them gratefully. They're those skinny jeans that only really thin people can wear, and I pray that they'll fit. I snug them over my hips. They're tight on my thighs, but they're better than nothing. They're way too long and I roll up the bottoms.

Farrell unbuttons his pyjama top. His stomach is lean and muscled and I look away before he can spot me staring. He pulls on a fitted T-shirt with the words 'I hate fucking hipsters' and a drawing of a pair of horn-rimmed spectacles printed on it.

'Let's go,' he says.

Then I remember. It's not just us. 'Wait! We have to get Gertie.'

'What? What for?'

'We can't just leave her here, Farrell. You wait here. I won't be long.'

He sighs. 'Okay, but hurry up.'

I nudge open the door. All clear. God, I hope Gertie isn't as out of it as she was earlier.

I tiptoe down the passageway towards her room, and slip inside. The bed is empty, the sheets piled on the floor. Dammit. Where have they taken her? The chart at the end of her bed reads: 'Gertrude February. Status: Undetermined'. Nothing about where she's been taken. Damn, we can't waste too much time looking. If Farrell and I get out, at least we'll be able to tell the police. If we hang around here...

In my hurry to get back to Farrell, I almost bang straight into a pink-smocked male orderly who's pushing a gurney slowly towards the lifts. His matted brown hair drapes over his face and the back of his neck. The body on the gurney is slight, the sheet pulled so far over its head that there's nothing but a fluff of black curls peeking over the top.

'Sorry,' I say automatically.

He raises his head.

I beg my body to freeze, but I can feel my mouth opening in a silent shriek, and for a second I'm sure that my bladder is going to let go.

Oh God. His eyes are sewn shut. Thick black thread loops through his eyelids, pulling them down right over his sockets. He turns towards my voice. The strength leaves my legs and I back up against the door.

If he touches me I'll scream.

But he turns away and continues down the corridor, wheeling the body towards the room next to Farrell's. As he pushes through and into it, there's a high-pitched mechanical whine.

I stagger back towards Farrell's room, starting as the door opens and he emerges.

'Shit, Lisa, you're shaking.'

'There was this guy... He...' I can't finish the sentence. I gulp in a lungful of air, every inch of me yelling: *Run!* 'We have to go.'

'Which way?' he says. A snake of blood is inching along his forearm from where he must have pulled out the drip, but he doesn't seem to notice it.

We've got two choices: the lift or a dash down towards the end of the corridor. The lift is far closer, and Farrell isn't in great shape. His forehead is beaded with sweat. 'Come on.'

Farrell stumbles. 'You're going to have to help me.'

He leans against me. He's heavy, but I manage to support him. Together we hobble towards the lift. I push the button. The doors don't open. I press my ear against them to listen for any sign that it's on its way, every muscle tense, waiting to hear the screech of an alarm, for someone to spot us, for the sound of running footsteps as nurses race towards us ready to pierce us with needles, to poison us with more drugs, to—

The lift opens.

Oh thank you, Jesus. I help Farrell step inside.

'Okay, now where?' he says.

'I don't know.' I jab the buttons at random. The door closes and my stomach lurches as it starts moving. We're going down. Within seconds, the lift shudders to a stop.

The doors open, and I help Farrell to walk out.

We're in a long, straight corridor, tiled wall to ceiling in spotless white porcelain. The walls are bare except for another one of those clown posters. This time the clown sits in a toy train, the words 'Last Stop, Terminal Ward! Choo Choo!' written in a cloud of steam above its head.

'I don't think this is the right way, Lisa,' Farrell says.

The lift doors close behind us.

'We have to try, Farrell. We can always go back if we can't find an exit.' I realise as I'm talking that I don't believe a word.

'Easy for you to say,' he grumbles, but he starts moving all the same.

The corridor leads towards a distant pair of black rubber doors, like the kind we saw in the morgue. Apart from the lift, there are no other doors or exits or adjoining corridors. I'm not completely sure how far underground we are, but the air is thick and warm, like in a mine. And as we get nearer to the doors, I totter and almost lose my balance, as if something behind the door is magnetising me. As if it all leads to this. The building draws its breath.

I push against the doors. They're as heavy as they look, and Farrell has to help me shove them open enough for us to sneak through.

'Fuck,' Farrell says. 'What's that smell?'

I breathe in. One minute it smells like artificial flowers – like those strong air fresheners you plug into the wall – the next I'm hit with a whiff of something rotten, like spoiled meat, only somehow sweeter. We're in another corridor, similarly tiled and spotless, only this one is lined with stainless steel doors. They're all perfectly blank; no handles or keyholes or windows.

There's a sign tacked to one of them, and wordlessly we step towards it. It reads: 'Pre-recycling'.

'Christ,' Farrell says. 'What the hell does that mean?'

'I don't kn—'

The ground beneath our feet suddenly starts vibrating and there's a clanking, hissing noise as if huge bellows are heaving in and out. I get the sense again that the building itself is breathing – through blocked lungs.

'I don't like this,' Farrell says. 'Let's go back.'

'Wait. Remember that delivery entrance in the morgue in New Hope? The one with the truck and all the—'

'Yeah, yeah. How could I forget?'

'Well, maybe there's something like that down here. Another exit.'

'Jesus, Lisa. You mean that this could be another route to the morgue?'

'Maybe.' I breathe in. The stench seems to have lessened, but maybe I'm just getting used to it.

'Fuck it,' Farrell says. 'Let's go back. Try another floor. There has to be another way out somewhere.'

I peer towards the end of the corridor. It ends in a T-junction. The underground machinery clanks and howls again. Farrell has a point. This place just feels... wrong.

'Okay.'

I turn back to the black doors, but they start shifting. Someone is pushing against them. A hand appears in the gap between them: it's filthy, the nails long, sharp and yellow.

We look at each other.

'Come on!' I grab Farrell's hand. He stumbles and swears under his breath, but gets moving. Farrell can only manage a lurching jog and it's all I can do not to sprint away and leave him behind.

I can't hear if anyone's following us – the mechanical clanking is too loud – but over the noise I swear there's a squeaking sound behind us, like rubbery wheels on slick tiles.

Don't turn around. Don't look back!

But I can't help it.

Oh God.

A huge bulbous mass of metal, limbs and rags is shuffling through the door. It emerges and starts weaving slowly along the corridor towards us.

'What the fuck is that?' Farrell says.

I can't make sense of it at first. Then gradually I realise what I'm looking at. It's a man. A hunched, oddly shaped man dressed in layers of ragged hospital sheeting. Is it that grey man? The one who was spying on me? I can't tell. He's pushing a creaking rusty wheelchair piled with what looks to be old artificial limbs and other prosthetics. He jerks to a stop as if he's only just noticed us. I can't make out any facial features. His face is either covered in filth or wrapped in rags.

Or maybe he doesn't have a face?

My limbs are numb. I have to move, but I can't. After seeing that orderly and his sewn-shut eyes... It's too much.

Farrell squeezes my hand.

'Lisa,' he shouts. 'Come on.'

I still can't move.

Without warning, the background noise shuts off and I feel like I'm in a vacuum. The buzz in my ears is replaced by a low mewling sound.

It's coming from the rag-man.

Move!

I make myself step forward, and then manage a shambling run.

We hobble towards the end of the corridor.

'Shit,' Farrell says. 'Which way?'

Both directions look identical. Clinical corridors lined with those same featureless metal doors.

Then I see it.

'Oh thank God!'

There's a sign on the wall reading 'Exit' with an arrow pointing to the right.

We're moving faster now, and Farrell half-runs ahead of me. I can't tell if the raggedy figure is still following us, but this time I resist the urge to turn and check. I don't want to know. All I can hear is the slap of our bare feet on the tiles, Farrell swearing under his breath and groaning.

A door creaks open behind me and someone yells, 'Oi! Kark off or I'll call patrol!'

I run blindly on. The corridor ends in another T-junction, and without hesitating Farrell takes a right. The ground seems to be sloping downwards.

'Look!'

The passageway ends in a pair of arched stainless-steel doors, a huge exit sign shining in red neon above them.

Farrell smiles at me. 'You were right, Lisa.'

The mechanical throb starts up again, humming up into the soles of my feet.

Together, we push against the doors and step through.

Chapter 15

FARRELL

This is not the way out. It's a goddamn waiting room. It's decorated like a Vegas chapel, dim red downlighting and plastic somethings, not flowers, arranged in a vase on the coffee table in the middle of the plush carpet. A pile of magazines and a couple of stacks of brochures sit on the table alongside the vase. An organ rendition of Barry Manilow's 'Mandy' pipes through the room.

A motley assortment of oddly shaped chairs lines the walls, their seats upholstered in lurid pink crushed velveteen, and there's a brushed-steel reception desk against the far wall. It's hard to make out any details in the red light.

The acid cramps course through me again and I have to sit down. I choose a chair close to the door. It's like the worst cramp I've ever had, only multiplied by fifty and attacking every single muscle in my body. I can't fucking think.

It's only when I hear the echo of my voice that I realise I've been moaning in pain.

'Farrell! Farrell!' Lisa says, touching my arm. 'Are you okay?'

No, for Christ's sake, I'm not fucking okay. You should have just left me in that bed. At least I was fucking comfortable. Now I'm fucking running around this godforsaken place with you. Again. Why is this shit happening to me?

'I'll be fine,' I say and grit my teeth so hard my cheeks hurt.

'You won't karking believe it if I tell you, that's why.'

Huh? 'What? Talk louder, Lisa. I can't hear what you're saying.'

'I didn't say anything,' she whispers. 'It came from over there.' She points her chin in the direction of the reception desk. After the white glare in that corridor, my eyes are starting to adjust to the dim lighting and I make out a person's head – a young woman by the tone of the voice – tucked behind the counter. There's a red neon sign behind her head in that wanky Avatar font: 'Welcome to Terminal Ward'.

'Browns, I said *browns*, Styrene,' she's saying. There's some undulating rainbow light which looks like it's coming out of her right ear. Must be some sort of kids' hands-free. Her hair is done in a reverse Mohican. A strip shaved out of the middle and big curly puffs on either side. It's a fucking disaster. Her mom probably copied a style out of a fashion magazine; she looks like a clown. She peers over the counter top at us as she talks, like a shrunken granny in a Datsun, that semi-opaque cellphone glaze over her face.

At least she's no immediate threat. I stretch out my legs and delicately point my toes to try to ease the cramp. It is subsiding.

Lisa sits next to me, also taking the opportunity to breathe. 'What should we do now?' she whispers.

I don't answer. I'm fucking tired. I listen to the receptionist's conversation instead, trying to work out what she's saying. I can't understand the teen slang she's using. God, I feel old.

'No, cereal. Just came in. They're just reposing there in abnormals... They don't seem to have, but who knows?... No... no. They can't understand me... Browns don't speak — Bellowscum, how the kark would you know? Have you ever even seen a brown?... Shoppers don't count. You know they've been assimilated.... Bixit told me that Shoppers go to school for cycles before... Scum! How the kark would you know?'

The rhythm of the girl's conversation is beginning to soothe me, and the pain in my muscles ebbs.

'What do you think, Farrell?' Lisa asks again.

'About what?'

'About asking that... girl.'

'Asking her what?'

'If there's a way out through here, of course! Haven't you been listening to me?' Lisa sounds irritated.

'I don't think that chick speaks our language, Lisa.'

She pauses. 'Okay, well, what about one of those doors, then?' She indicates the two doors on either side of the reception desk. 'One of them could lead outside, couldn't it?'

The door on the left has stylised pictures of clothes painted on it, but badly, like a kid's rendition of a suit and dress. But it's the other door that's more concerning. 'Lisa, take a look at that sign.' The door on the right has a round face with a mask and a reflector strapped around its head. Classic old-style surgeon. Only this one appears to be holding a chainsaw.

'Let's just go back to the lift, okay?' I say.

'Farrell. I'm not going back up there. There has to be—'

The door slams open and two freaks walk in. Lisa gasps. She looks down at her hands and bites her lip. Jesus. They're sprayed head to toe with cheap orange fake tan. The man is dressed in an expensive three-piece suit; he's tall and has a massive square head, as if he's suffered some sort of disease as a child. The woman is leathery and scrawny. She's wearing stripper heels and a microdress that would possibly suit someone half her age. She's plastered with make-up so thick it's peeled in waxy wads onto her dress. Her legs are all sinew and overstretched skin.

They glance at us as they pass and a shadow clouds their faces before they smile broadly. Their veneered teeth glitter with tiny inset diamonds that catch a white light from somewhere. The effect is incredible, so over the top that it actually could work. You know, in the pages of *Itch* or something.

Despite myself, I draft a MindRead update: **freekalert, meeps. &KatyaModel did you see *that* O-o lol**

The orange couple walk up to the reception desk. They mutter something to the receptionist, hand something over to her.

'I have to go, Styrene. Got some voluntaries in.' She hands them each a small parcel. 'Have a wonderful termination, Shoppers. The Ministry of Modifications is delighted that you've chosen to exit with us. The butcher will be with you soonest.'

I must have misheard. But I don't have time to consider the receptionist's words. The orange couple smile at me and Lisa and they walk over to us.

'Browns!' the man says heartily as he pulls up a lopsided chair from under a sign reading 'Custom'. I turn and check out the wall behind where Lisa and I are sitting. The sign above our heads reads 'Abnormal'. He tweaks at its limbs until it fits his shape perfectly. He grabs another chair and contorts it into a slimmer, higher shape for the woman. 'I met some browns just the other day. A primo Shopper and... and a Customer Care Officer. Can't say why she was spending time with him but there you have it. I'm Burt,' he says, extending his hand. He only has a thumb, a forefinger and half his ring finger. The stumps are lacquered and the half-finger has three bulky gold rings on it.

I can't bring myself to shake it. His skin is slick with some sort of perfumed oil. Burt's smile remains unwavering but his eyes fall. 'Did I do it wrong? I read about this shake-hand in the *Manual of Upside Relations*. Published, of course, before the regime change. So it may reflect outdated customs. I must have done it wrong. Forgive me. It's not often we get to meet real browns to practise with.' The man seems genuinely upset.

'No. You did it right. I, er... I'm...'

Lisa jumps in. 'He's not well. His hand – he cut it. It's... um... infected.'

'Yeah,' I say. 'That's right. It's infected.'

The woman instinctively takes two steps back.

'Oh, Leletia,' Burt says. 'An infection isn't going to make much difference now, is it? Brown or not. It's quite exciting, actually. I'm delighted at this last chance to meet more visitors. We're being terminated, you see.'

'What... what does that mean?' asks Lisa.

Leletia takes a brochure off the pile on the table. 'Voluntary termination,' she says. 'That's what we've chosen.' Beaming proudly, she links her arm through Burt's.

'Leletia was dead set on voluntary termination,' Burt says. 'She's an idol, she really is. I said to her, "Leletia, we've got a good ten, twelve shifts before we depreciate. We could shop, we could drink and eat. We could even buy a new apartment." But she said, "Darling, the Ministry encourages scheduled termination to improve systems control. It's the least we can do to repay them. Just think how viable our parts will be." I couldn't argue with that, now could I?'

He pats her on the arm. 'My Leletia is a *primo* idol.'

The woman giggles shrilly. 'Oh, Burt. You are gassy sometimes. It was as much his decision as mine. Every time we went to the sales, it was Burt who said, "Paper bags, please" and "Please recycle those bottles". The Ministries agree that conservation is of the highest priority. We're just doing our little bit.'

'Butcher's ready for you, Shoppers,' the receptionist calls.

'Oh, well. Time to divest, Leletia.' He nods at me. 'Lovely to intercourse with you.'

They carry their parcels through the door to the receptionist's left – the one with the crappily rendered suit-and-dress signage on it. Some kind of changing room? I stare at the brochure the woman handed me.

'Voluntary Termination: The Best Way To Go' it says. 'Make your last stop in luxury.' There's a picture of a grotesque purple-faced man with a blonde wig and wearing a chunky medallion over a suit and tie. Obviously a politician. He looks a bit like the Minister of Health. There's a sort of deformed bump on his nose. It looks just like an extra nostril, complete with hair.

'I don't think you can repose there all shift,' says the receptionist from behind her desk, and it takes me a couple of seconds to realise she's talking to us. 'There's no protocol for handling browns in the Voluntary Termination Salon, but I think I'm going to call the patrol. There must be somewhere else in the Wards you belong.'

This doesn't sound good. What the fuck is the patrol?

Lisa and I share a glance. 'No,' I say. 'There was a mix-up. We were meant to be discharged—'

'Discharged?' she says. 'Pardon me?'

'We were meant to leave,' Lisa tries, 'but we got lost.'

'Leave? You're a Donor, aren't you?' She looks at Lisa. Is it my imagination or is her expression more respectful? 'And you are a Client, I guess?'

Lisa glances at me again. We're both thinking the same thing: say anything that'll get us out of here. 'We've had our procedures.' Lisa touches her mask. 'We need to go home now.'

The girl looks confused, rubs her hand through the left side of her hairstyle. 'There's no protocol. Tell you what, I'll call patrol, they'll check your files and replace you where you belong. There's nowhere for you to go here unless you're scheduled for voluntary termination – which you're obviously not, being bro— visitors. If you were being terminated or recycled the... normal... way' – her eyes skitter over me with a look of repressed distaste, and I remember that sign on the wall: 'Abnormal' – 'you wouldn't come through here. You'd be taken through Pre-recycling.'

The orange man and woman emerge from the changing room wearing sepia pyjamas and carrying their possessions in their arms. They cross to a bin on the far side of the desk and dump their clothes in it. Burt takes Leletia's hand as she sprinkles a handful of gold jewellery into the bin like ashes over the sea. They look down and Leletia puts her arm around Burt's waist. They press their heads and sides against each other like two penitent lovers at a shrine.

Then they straighten. Burt glances over his shoulder and I can't make out his expression. 'Can't take it with you,' he says.

'Happy termination,' the receptionist says, 'and thank you for recycling with us.'

She stands up and waves them towards the door to her right. They walk through without a word. As they go in, I catch a glimpse of harsh, bright light, and a high mechanical whine blots out the muzak. A waft of the sick odour I've pushed into the background hits me straight in the face.

It can't be what I think it is. It must be something else. Maybe all that termination, recycling, divesting nonsense is cult-speak. That's it. It's just a cult. That makes much more sense. Has to be why this place is designed like a chapel. All hospitals have chapels, right?

It's just a cult.

Lisa turns to look at me, wide-eyed. 'Farrell, we can't… We have to go!'

My legs are starting to seize up again and the receptionist appears to be making a phone call on a piece of jelly with lights in it.

'Hang on, hang on,' I say. 'It's a good idea to call the, uh… patrol, but do you mind if we freshen up first?' I indicate the changing-room door.

The girl narrows her eyes at me. 'No. I think that will be catalogue. Please refresh yourselves.'

We push through the door and it clicks shut behind us. Everything's green.

'What the fuck's with the lighting in here?' I mutter.

'What do you mean?' asks Lisa.

'You didn't notice? It's green, Lisa.'

'It's just your eyes. After the red light out there.'

Sure enough, the green cast gradually dissolves away. My legs cramp up again and I stumble back on a sagging couch. In front of us are three mirrored doors, angled just so that I can see four Lisas standing in front of me. She fills my jeans pretty nicely. I can see the curve of her thighs and arse in the mirrors; more flesh than I'm used to, but she's got a nice shape. Katya would look stupid in my jeans.

Lisa starts awkwardly when she realises that there are mirrors behind her and that I'm looking at her. She scurries to sit by my side, a hot blush blotching the skin on her neck and ears. The mask remains calm.

'What do we do, Farrell?'

'Maybe it's best if they just call security and—'

'No! I'm not go—'

'Listen to me! They'll just get us out of here safely and we'll give them the slip on another level. The last thing we want to do is go in there.' I point in the general direction of the other door.

As if to illustrate my point, the thin plywood walls reverberate with the whine of some electrical machine.

I stretch my legs and arch my back, closing my eyes to the pain as another spasm rips through my knotted body.

It's just a cult, it's just a cult. They're talking in cult language. There's no fucking way I'm following those orange freaks to some fucking Jonestown suicide cult.

'Listen,' says Lisa, cutting into my thoughts again. I've been zoning in and out ever since she got me out of that bed. Ever since I pulled out that drip. Fragments of that report come back to me: *sulfasomethingsomething hormone to encourage optimum haemosomething and tissue bulking*. They've been fattening me like a factory pig. That has to be why my body's rebelling.

Christ. I don't want to think about what they do here. My desperate delusions are starting to wear thin. We need to get the fuck out of here.

'What do you think it is?' she's saying again, at the edge of my pain and my panic.

'Huh? What what is?'

'That sound. Listen. It's like a...'

It's a whoosh of water. Then a smell wafts from somewhere again. This time not that sickly sweet smell, but a more common odour. It's the smell of shit.

'... a toilet,' we say together, and we're up and into the first cubicle, checking the walls. Nothing.

The smell is strong enough and the flush loud enough that there has to be some vent or opening here; it's not just coming through the walls.

Then we find it. In the second cubicle. Right at the back. A grated panel. Ignoring the cries of my glutes, I slam down to the carpet and peer through it. I see a tiled floor, a steel bowl fixed into the middle of the floor, and a huge, bare, hairy arse sitting on it.

Chapter 16

LISA

We're lying so close together on the changing room's carpet I swear I can feel the thud of Farrell's heart. The man in the toilet stall mumbles to himself and grunts, another wave of that gross smell wafts through the grid, and I clamp my hand over my nose to block it out. There's a bulky leather bag next to the man's white plastic boots, something metallic poking out of the top of it. I shift my position a few inches to try to make out what it is.

Oh *crap*.

It's a pair of what look to be serrated, razor-sharp shears.

Snip, snip.

The man mumbles again and whistles under his breath. I keep as still as I can. I can't see his face, or even the shape of his body from this angle, thank God. I don't want to see him, just in case he's that...

That what?

That... freak I saw when I was coming round from the anaesthetic.

That wasn't real.

But he looks real enough. Even worse, he smells real enough.

The guy stands up abruptly, pulls up his trousers and, using his foot, presses a black rubber button on the floor. The toilet roars and whooshes. I catch a glimpse of long, red-lacquered fingernails as he bends to pick up his bag, and then he leaves the stall, letting the door bang shut behind him. We listen to the thump of receding footsteps. He's gone, and I can breathe again.

'What now?' I whisper to Farrell.

'Isn't it obvious?' he says. He places his palms on the metal air vent and pushes. It doesn't budge. There are no screws attaching it to the wall; it must be cemented in.

'Shit,' he says. He grimaces as another pain spasm shoots through his legs. 'Fuck, that hurts.'

'Hang on,' I say.

I shift my body all the way around until my bare feet are pressing against the grate. Tensing my thigh muscles, I kick forward as hard as I can. I can feel it budge slightly, and then, suddenly, it falls forward and lands with a crump onto the toilet floor.

'You go first,' Farrell says.

'What if that... that man's outside the door?'

'We've got no choice,' Farrell hisses. 'You want to go back and find out what "Pre-recycling" is all about?'

Snip, snip. A thatch of tangled hair, the feel of a cold blade on my skin. *Paranoia, that's all it is.*

I shake the image away. Farrell's right. This is our only way out.

'You think you'll fit through it?' I say to him. He's slender, but his shoulders are broad, and I'm not convinced he'll be able to squash through the space.

'I'm going to give it my best shot. Now, go!'

I shift my body around again and wiggle through on my belly, ignoring the scrape of concrete from the aperture's edge on my stomach. I scramble to my feet and press my back against the door so that Farrell has enough room to manoeuvre.

For a second I'm convinced he's going to get stuck, but then he twists his shoulders and edges through. He drags himself forward and I help him get to his feet.

Together we press our ears to the door, listening for any sign of movement. There's just the steady drip of water, the gurgle of the cistern refilling, and a low mechanical throb in the background.

Farrell nods at me, and I move back so he can pull open the door. We step out into a large public bathroom. There's a row of stalls, most of which have their doors closed, several sinks – but, oddly, no taps. The place hums with that fake flowery stench. It's spotlessly clean, clad wall to ceiling in large pale-green tiles.

'Jesus,' Farrell says under his breath, nudging me.

No ways. In the far corner there's some sort of novelty urinal in the shape of a huge clown's head. Its mouth gapes open in a horrible leer and there's a sign above it, reading: 'Harvesting is no laughing matter! Now wash your hands.'

'Do you think there's anyone else in here?' I whisper.

'I bloody well hope not.' He pads straight over to the main door, pulls it open and peers out. I catch the murmur of voices. He slams it shut immediately and leans his back against it.

'Shit!'

My heart thumps in my chest. 'What?'

'We can't go out there.'

'Why not?'

'There's someone out there.'

'Who? That guy who was in here?'

Snip, snip.

'Don't know.'

'So what are we going to do?'

'First, check the stalls. Make absolutely sure we're alone in here.' He nods to me. 'Can you do that?'

'Me?'

'Yeah. I don't want to leave the door.'

My heart has now squashed itself into my throat, but I nod and get moving.

I nudge open the first. Empty. The next cubicle doesn't contain a cistern – there's nothing in it at all – just smooth, blank, tiled walls. Then I look down. God. There's a tiny, eye-shaped hole in the floor. I step back instinctively.

The other stalls are all vacant, but a lurch in my gut makes me hesitate at the last door. In Sharon's horror movies this would be where the axe man or the bogeyman would be waiting. Gingerly, I push it open. It's empty, but the interior is different from the others – there's a tightly knotted black-and-grey pattern covering the green tiles. Then it hits me that it's not a pattern at all – it's graffiti, every inch of tile covered with layer upon layer of spidery writing. A skinny felt-tip pen hangs on a string behind the door, inviting people to add their mark. The messages run into each other, and most of the handwriting is bad, but I manage to decipher a few behind the door: 'My handle's Globe, recycle my probe'; 'For a karking good time, call LastCall fc234.78'; 'Next stop, mascot! Wheee!'; 'Are you Pure enough? Read *Gravitology* to find out'.

The messages are even scrawled around the base of the toilet: 'Adios and thanks for all the fish' reads one. 'Don't miss the sale at Fork Off – I will!' says another. 'Karking browns' is scrawled in angry letters.

Browns. That's what that receptionist girl called us.

I also make out a fist-shaped blob with the words 'D loves R 4eva' inside it, and a long message that ends with the line: 'My only regret is that I never saw the upside.'

'Lisa!' Farrell calls. 'What are you doing?'

I step out. I decide not to tell him about the graffiti. Those walls are full of people's goodbyes. Even the smutty-sounding ones. I don't think I could stand it if Farrell said something nasty about them. Somehow those messages are… sacred. I want to protect them. 'They're all empty,' I say.

His face relaxes. I carefully close the last cubicle and join him at the bathroom door.

'Christ, Lisa. What is this place? It's not some sort of back-alley organ scam. How come no one knows about this?'

I shrug.

'Maybe it's funded by rich people who are sick. Euthanasia or… or illegal organ transplants. If you had a lot of money you could set up something like this. Hey? You think?'

'I don't know, Farrell.'

'But that girl – the way she was talking. She's not from here. And she's not Eastern European either. I *know* about these things, Lisa.'

He's saying something else, but I tune him out. There were hundreds, maybe thousands, of messages on the walls of that stall. Did all those people *want* to die? Choose to die? Like the weird orange couple back in that waiting room?

Farrell nudges me. 'Are you listening?'

'Yes. Sorry.'

'Who the fuck *are* these people? How can they get away with this?' He rubs at his face as if he's trying to scour off the skin. 'Christ, this can't be happening. Not to me. I know people.' He thumps his fists on his thighs. '*Fuck.*'

I touch his shoulder. 'It will be okay.' I don't know what else to say. I know it's inadequate and stupid but I'm too shell-shocked to think up a more intelligent response.

'Yeah right,' Farrell snorts. 'We're about as far from okay as we can bloody well get. Why do you think they picked us?'

'What do you mean?'

'Why us? Why pick us specifically? Not… I dunno, some anonymous refugee who won't be missed. There has to be a reason.'

'I… I don't know.'

He sighs. 'Look, Lisa. There's something I didn't tell you. I found my file, doctor's notes, that kind of thing. Nomsa said I was just hallucinating, but now… You were right about those photos.'

'God, Farrell. Did the file say what the photos meant? What they're for?'

He pauses. 'It doesn't matter.' He looks at me, narrowing his eyes slightly. I don't like the way he's looking at my face. As if he suddenly doesn't trust me or something. 'But what I want to know is – are we in here for the same thing?'

'What do you mean?'

He touches my face. 'Take that thing off.'

I flinch away. 'No!'

'Don't you want to know what's under there?'

I shake my head. I don't want to know. Not after what I've seen so far.

'Come on,' he says, his voice turning soft, cajoling. 'If we're going to have any chance to talk our way out of this, we need to know what we're dealing with. We need as much info as we can get. That receptionist called you a "client". Don't you want to know what that means? What's under that mask could give us some answers.'

I back away from him and cover my cheeks with my palms. 'But what if it hasn't healed yet? What if it gets infected or something?'

He shrugs. 'Okay. Up to you. It's your face.' He's disappointed in me.

Farrell might be right, the Dr Meka voice whispers. *If you've just had another nose-job, why cover up your whole face? You have to find out sometime.*

There's a knock on the door and both Farrell and I jump.

'Shit!' Farrell hisses. The handle twists and the door shifts slightly. Our weight is the only thing stopping it from opening. There's another polite knock.

'Hello?' a woman's voice calls. 'Is there anyone in there?'

I try not to breathe or move. There's a muffled mumble of voices, another shove at the door and then – eventually – the clack of footsteps walking away. The handle doesn't move again.

'We can't stay in here forever,' Farrell says, breaking the silence. 'We'll have to face them sometime. It could really help if we knew what they wanted from us...'

He leaves the sentence hanging. I look up at him but he avoids my gaze as if he's pissed off with me.

Come on, Lisa. What have you got to lose?

Everything.

Just do it.

I make my decision.

'Okay,' I say. 'Okay. I'll do it. I'll take it off.'

He smiles at me, wraps an arm around my shoulder and squeezes. 'Good girl.'

'But I want to do it properly.'

I walk over to the mirror above the sinks. It's similar to the one in the crappy bathroom in my old ward – Gertie's ward. It's made of polished steel and distorts my reflection slightly; my face looks narrower than I know it is. The surface is blurry, but it will do. I stare into it for several seconds, preparing myself.

In psychiatric wards, the mirrors aren't made of glass, in case patients smash them and use the shards on themselves. The blurred reflection is deliberate. The last thing you want to see just before you die is what you loathe most of all: yourself.

You'd know all about that, Lisa.

I take a deep breath and hook my nails under the edge beneath my chin.

I feel the sticky tug of the delicate material as it peels away. I lean close to the mirror and examine the section of bare skin before I go any further. Thank *God*. It looks... normal. Smooth. No redness or rawness. But something's different... The small crescent-shaped scar on my chin isn't there any more. Slowly, carefully, I pull more of it away, revealing my cheeks – also smooth and unblemished. This gives me the courage to rip the mask off in one quick yank, like a wax strip. I gasp at the shock of cold sensation on my now naked skin.

Look at it.

Not yet. I close my eyes and trace my fingers all over my face. The numbness is gone and, although my skin is sticky, I can't feel any wounds or incisions. I trace my fingertips delicately over the beautifully soft skin. It's like being touched for the first time.

I breathe steadily through my nose. Cool, pure. It doesn't hurt at all.

'Well?' Farrell says.

'Wait.'

Come on, you can do this. You have to see it sometime.

I drag a deep breath into my lungs, open my eyes and look straight into the mirror.

Oh my God.

'Lisa?'

Jesus.

I'm dimly aware that Farrell's saying something else.

Who is that? This is not me. I recognise my eyes, but everything else...

No amount of surgery could do that.

I touch my cheekbones. They are prominent, sculpted. I run my fingertips over my new, voluptuous lips, and stroke the tiny upturned shape of my new nose.

I'm...

Say it.

I'm *beautiful.*

It's perfect. It really is!

'Lisa!'

'Wait!' I snap. I don't want to stop looking at myself. I never want to stop.

'*Lisa!* For fuck's sake! Let me see.'

Put him out of his misery.

Slowly, I turn around, my stomach dancing with anticipation.

Farrell stares at me, his jaw slack in shock.

I burst out laughing, I can't help it. 'I know! Isn't it amazing?'

Farrell doesn't respond. He clears his throat as if he's about to speak. Nothing comes out of his mouth except for a hiss of air. That isn't shock on his face. That's...

Horror. Disgust.

And fear.

Oh God. What if I'm fooling myself? What if they've made me into a monster and I'm so deluded that I...

'I know it's different, Farrell... but it's not that bad, is it?'

I move towards him.

'Don't touch me!' He backs away.

'Farrell! What is it?'

'Katya,' he says, choking on the word. 'Katya.'

Chapter 17

FARRELL

The first time I shot Katya was the second time we met. It was the morning after the Fashion Week wrap party and I was lying on someone's floor, battling a monster hangover. I'd noticed her the night before of course, shared a couple of glances, assumed she'd left with a posse of coke-fuelled agency girls. But when I woke up, there she was, picking her way over the other party casualties in her stiletto boots and her short skirt, the crochet flounce tilted just right over her shoulder; perfectly polished, ready for the catwalk, ready for me.

I hoisted myself up, leaned on my elbow, retrieved my camera from under the couch and pointed it at her. She looked down at me and smiled with that Jane Birkin freshness, not a hint of coy, none of that 'Oh, I'm not ready' bullshit that so many models or wannabe actors pass off. I was hooked. Katya was always ready, and she knew exactly what her strengths were.

At that time she was getting by on catalogue shoots, the odd advert. She knew she didn't have the current look – she wasn't gamine, tattooed, half-starved – and she didn't care. She knew she'd make it eventually, because she had what the other girls lacked: pure confidence. And not just the confidence that comes from drugs or alcohol or cash. Even before she fell in with Noli and those other coke-snuffling bitches, she had it.

She knew she was beautiful, knew she was capable of projecting every man's fantasies, and all the while making him feel – even though he was looking at her in a magazine – that she was smiling only at him.

Katya was a photographer's dream, and she let me in, let me get close to the real thing, the real smile, the real touch, the real mornings after... She was my dream.

The blunt push of a baton in my back snaps me back into the present. My knuckles are aching from punching that bathroom wall. My muscles are cramping all over and my entire body is a knot of fire.

'Farrell, come on, you've got to...' *She* puts her hand on my shoulder.

'Don't you fucking *touch* me, you freak!' I bellow at her.

She cowers like a dog expecting to be kicked, and hangs back, shuffling along behind me. The security man – the patrol – herds us along the corridor back to the lifts. I can't turn to look at her. My mind is seared with that hideous image, and I'll never be able to delete it.

If she's wearing Katya's face, what the fuck have they done to Katya?

It was the right decision to go back to the waiting room and let that girl call the patrol. At that moment it was either that, or I'd have fucking killed Lisa. She took off that mask, and... I can't say it. I can't make the words happen in my head. Those lips I'd kissed a thousand times, the flawless cheeks I'd run my fingers over, that trademark nose. Thank fuck Lisa still had her own eyes. I would have... I don't know what I would have done, just to make it go away.

Katya's here. Now at least I know. Katya's here.

She must be here. Maybe it's a sick joke, a threat. Maybe these people are enemies of Glenn's, using me and Katya to get to him. Maybe they made a cast or something and put it on Lisa's face. Some sort of grotesque underworld message. Maybe Katya's all right.

I need to hang on to this because the alternative... Katya without a face, blood and bone where her perfect lips, her flawless skin, that textbook nose used to be.

If she's here, I need to find her. Bring her home.

But I can't take her home... damaged. Glenn will kill me. He'll take one look at the ravaged girl he spent so much time and money on raising to be perfect... He's going to look at her, and he's going to blame me, and he's going to kill me. He'll make me suffer and he'll make me disappear. He'll have nothing more to lose. Holy Christ.

My body is wracked by a multiple spasm and I crumple to the ground. The patrolman hoists me up and the rank odour of his sweat and cheap cologne envelops me.

'Farrell! Are you all right?' says Lisa next to me. She doesn't try to touch me.

'Get away from me,' I manage to groan as I start shuffling again.

'You have to let me help you.'

I say nothing. I know it's not really her fault. Whatever's happening to us is in someone else's control. But the way she looked at me after she'd seen her new face. The way she smiled with Katya's lips.

The spasm passes and I start to shiver. She's right. We can't stay here forever.

'If you want to help me, put on the mask.'

'What?'

'You heard me. Put it back on.'

'But, Farrell, it's—'

'I said *put it on!* I can't look at you.'

'Okay. Okay.' She shuffles with something.

'Is it on?'

'Yes,' she sniffles.

I turn to look. She's pressed the mask back into place, but it's stretched and drooping now. It looks like her skin is melting off, but it's better than what's beneath it. I can't help flinching at the sight of it.

'Listen, Farrell. I'm sorry about your girlfriend, but do you think I wanted this?' she says. 'You think I asked for this?'

I just shake my head, but I'm surprised at her confidence. This isn't the timid woman who was cowering like a dog just minutes ago.

'Get moving, browns,' the patrolman grunts. 'Enough karking intercourse. Get back to your wards before I get you unassigned.' The guard's dressed like a sailor in a bad First World War movie, but he's huge, and I'm in no condition to fight him. Besides, he's got waxy, sallow skin that's scattered with inflamed pustules; I seriously don't want to touch him. He'll get us back up to the other wards and hopefully, this time, we'll be closer to the exit. That's as far as my plan extends at this stage.

He shoves us into the lift and presses the topmost button on the row of five. That's good: it's the furthest floor away from the basement we've been in. The lift moves swiftly and silently and pings open.

Another tide of cramp swirls through me and I brace against the lift door. Lisa tries to help me, and the pain's so intense I have no choice but to let her. She puts an arm around my waist and steadies me as I stumble out. We're in the lobby of another ward. This one's far less plush than the others we've seen. Pocked green lino on the floor, cheap, damp-spotted ceiling boards and a scuffed counter that looks like it could be another nurses' station. There's a vague smell of rot and soup. For a second I assume we're back in New Hope, but on the wall ahead of us there's a sign with that stupid clown on it again. This time it's floating in the sky holding a bunch of balloons. 'Welcome to Recovery Ward,' he says, in a jagged, day-glo orange speech bubble.

Don't go to Recovery. That's what that grey cleaning man in the Green Section – Isaac – said to me in his one lucid moment. *Don't go to Recovery.*

Christ. How could it be any worse than where we've just been? I don't want to find out. 'Sorry,' I say to the guard. 'I'm supposed to be in the Preparation Ward.'

'Kark,' he mutters. 'The officer at Voluntary Termination said... Just wait here. I'll ask a drone for your files.'

He walks off, ducks under the counter and disappears into an alcove behind it.

Lisa's whispering something. 'Do you think maybe we should—'

But I stop listening. There's a whiteboard stuck onto the wall behind the nurses' station listing Recovery Ward room numbers and patient names.

The third one down reads: 'K. A. Forrest / Unassigned Donor / Post-Proc. Recovery / Room 7'.

The guard emerges from the alcove. He touches his cap and nods deferentially at Lisa. 'I didn't realise you were a Client, Client. I apologise. Let me call an orderly to help you find your way back.'

He stares at me. 'And you, you are—'

But I'm running.

'Farrell!' Lisa calls behind me.

I follow the signs to Room 7, barge through the open door. Grubby plastic curtains are drawn around the only bed in the room. It's small, sparsely furnished, a door in the corner leading to a tiny bathroom. It's quiet but for the mismatched hush of ventilators and air con and the seethe of oxygen. There's the thump of feet behind me.

'Farrell.' It's Lisa. But that patrolman can't be far behind.

'Lock the fucking door,' I hiss at her.

She nods and does as she's told. I grab a metal foldaway chair and lodge it under the door handle.

Lisa stares at me with wide eyes.

Shit. What was I thinking? I should have made Lisa stay outside.

If Katya sees what's behind that mask... Christ.

'Stay by the door,' I say to her.

'But—'

'*Please* just do what I say.'

She nods. I slip behind the curtain. It's dim in here, but I can make out a body shrouded in a sheet lying absolutely still on a bare mattress. I step forward. I'm hit with a waft of sweat and another perfumed odour I can't place.

Is it her?

I don't know if I want it to be Katya or not. Knotted dark hair that could be hers, pallid skin – and then I see it: the birthmark shaped like a small hourglass on her left bicep.

Her face is completely bandaged, not masked with the hi-tech appliance Lisa was fitted with. Even her eyes are covered and there's only a rough hole where her nose should be. The dressing is fairly clean, but a dark seepage of old blood shows through the upper layers in patches. There's hardly a bump under the bandage but I can hear shallow breath sucking through the hole. She's sleeping or drugged, a greenish mixture flowing from the drip bag into her arm. But it's her. It's unmistakably her. I draw the sheet off her body. She's wearing a short hospital gown. Apart from the face, she's unblemished. Her tight stomach, the hip bones. Her long legs, despite the stubble, are definitely hers. There's the nightingale tattoo on her ankle. Her toenails are still painted alternating green and yellow. If I don't look at her bandaged face, it's almost as if we're back home again, and I'm watching her, taking pictures of her while she sleeps.

'That's Katya, isn't it?' Lisa has come up behind me. 'Is she... is she okay?'

'Jesus! Get away! She'll fucking freak if she sees you.'

'But I'm wearing the... She won't...'

'Fuck it, Lisa. Please? Can't you wait in the bathroom?' I'm trying my hardest to keep it together, but Jesus fucking Christ. After another long glance at Katya's body, Lisa moves back around the curtain.

'Wake up. Wake up, Kay,' I say, shaking her, gently at first but with increasing vigour when she doesn't stir.

'Kay. Kay. Wake up.'

There's a quiet knock on the door. 'Client? Donor?' A woman's voice. 'We realise you've misplaced yourselves and an orderly will be on his way shortly to relocate you. There is no need to panic.'

I'm running out of time. As gently as I can, I remove the drip tube from Katya's arm. I need her awake and I'm betting that she's being pumped full of some kind of sedative, like the kind they gave me.

Fresh air might help. I open the blinds on the wall, but instead of windows there are stylised posters of tropical beaches hastily tacked up in the recesses.

'Uhng.' Katya stirs in the bed.

I rush back to her side.

'Kay, it's me. I've come to take you home.'

'Mm, gnn, hmn.'

Ignoring my terror at what I'll find underneath, I feel around her bandages for her mouth, press against a space bounded by hard nubs of teeth. I finger the layers of dressing apart, and pull out a blood-stained plug of cotton wool. Her breath rattles through her mouth in a mucussy wheeze.

At first I think she's having some sort of respiratory attack, but then I realise she's trying to talk. It looks like she can't swallow or move her tongue properly.

'Lisa! Bring me some water!'

I prop Katya up against the head of the bed.

Lisa pushes through the curtain and hands me a plastic cup. I nod my thanks and wave her away.

I hold the cup to the hole in the bandages; Katya rinses and drools bloody spit into the bandages and down her gown. It seems to help.

'Jjjgh,' she says. 'Jgsh.' She's trying to say my name, and now she starts to scrabble at her face, trying to remove the bandages.

I stop her hands in mine. 'No, Kay, wait. You don't know... You should let it heal.' But it's really because I'm not ready to see what's under there. Katya's hands are weak and they don't put up a fight. There's a small dressing on her left hand. That's where she cut herself with the glass. I look at my scarred hand. For the first time in however long I've been here, something feels real.

'Ah wht... ah wht thee you.' She twines her fingers between mine. Her throat makes a phlegmy wheeze.

'Sweetie, I'm not sure if... if that's a good idea. We'll ask a doctor, okay?' I lie.

She struggles to sit up and I prop her pillows behind her, then give her another sip of water.

'I sh sho cared, Josh.' She clears her throat and I can hear a hard wad of mucus detaching. 'I was so scared.' She grips my hand harder. She's talking! Maybe this was all just a misunderstanding, maybe I was wrong. Maybe Lisa doesn't have her face after all.

But still that image is burned in my mind. The right face, on the wrong head. I trace the bandages with my fingertips, trying to feel the bone structure, trying to draw a picture in my mind of what is really under there. All I feel is gauze, soft to the touch, and the hard patches of dried blood beneath.

Something thumps against the door. I ignore it.

'Kay. That morning. The morning you left. Do you remember what happened?'

'I'm always... I'm always... so...'

I have to concentrate to make out the words, and I can hear from the sounds in her throat that she's crying. Do you need your eyes to cry? But then I remember: Lisa doesn't have her eyes. I consider opening up the bandages over them, but I don't.

'Don't, Kay. So you'll come home. That's all I want to know.'

'Yes.' She squeezes my fingers again, then gasps and chokes. I feed her another sip of water.

Another thump at the door, louder this time.

'Kay?'

'Mm?'

'How did you get here?'

She says nothing. Then, 'I don't know.' I can imagine the frown on her forehead. The way her nose wrinkles when she's confused.

'What's the last thing you remember? Before... here?'

'Fight,' she says.

'After that.'

'Supposed to meet Noli, and then... then... phone call.'

'What phone call?'

'Woman. A stranger.'

'Was it work? What?'

She tries to shake her head. 'She said I should come to—'

The curtain rustles behind me. 'They're trying to get in, Farrell.'

'Please open the door, Mr Farrell.' A different voice – more insistent.

'Farrell,' Lisa says. 'What should we do? They're going to break the door down.'

'Who's that?' asks Katya. 'Who's here?'

'Kay... it's...'

'Who, Josh? Who is she?'

'I'm Lisa. I came with him to find you. Farrell, tell her.'

'Tell me what, Josh?'

I don't know where to start.

A heavy pounding, a screech as the barricade shifts.

Lisa pulls the curtain aside, grabs the bedside cabinet, and wheels it towards the door. She slams it against the chair that's braced against the handle, but the furniture is flimsy and cheap.

'You haven't got long, Farrell,' she says.

'Long before what?' asks Katya.

I could have only seconds here. And I need to know.

'Stay as still as you can, Kay.'

I start unwinding the bandage from her face, finding the first edge, peeling the layers carefully and gently so that I don't hurt her.

The door bangs and there's the crack of splintering wood.

'Donor Farrell? Client Cassavetes? Open the door.' I know that voice.

'What else do you remember?' I ask Katya as I unwrap her face.

'Nothing.'

I'm on the last layer of crepe and the bandage is stuck together, I peel it apart, trying not to see, trying not to feel anything.

'I got so fucked up, Josh,' she says.

One of the chairs falls with a slam. I turn around. Lisa has shoved her body against the pile of furniture to add to the fortification.

The last strand of the bandage falls from Katya's face. A blood-clotted cotton pad covers most of it, apart from the nose and mouth holes. Her hair is stuck to her neck with dried blood. I can see the edge of the incision finely etched around the pad.

Another massive crash on the door and the latch lock comes skating across the floor. The chairs crash away and the cabinet smashes over. Lisa sprawls across the floor.

I remove the cotton from Katya's face.

We'll work this out. We'll work this out. We'll sort this out. We have to work this out. What can be done can be undone. We'll work this out. We'll sort this out.

Bile floods into my mouth. Katya stares at me with massive, unblinking eyes. My God. She's got nothing to blink with.

'Mr Farrell,' Nomsa says in the background. 'We made such an effort to accommodate you. What more could you want? It was I who stuck my neck out and recommended gentle persuasion, and all I get from you is this disregard and your ridiculous attempts to flee.'

All I can see is Katya, dissected like a medical project, angry strands of muscle webbed between bones, the last hitches of cotton wool stuck to her flesh like maggots, those bulbous eyes staring. Hot bile soaks the bed between me and Katya.

Lisa struggles to pick herself up off the floor, hauls herself up against Katya's bed, looks at Katya's pillaged and seeping face and screams.

Chapter 18

LISA

A skull slathered with raw hamburger. That's what she looks like.

I don't want to look again, I really don't, but I can't stop myself.

It's worse the second time.

Her lipless mouth is fixed in a permanent grin, the teeth standing out huge and white in the mass of raw, red tissue. Her nose is nothing but a couple of crusted holes, but it's the eyes that are the most disturbing. They pop unblinkingly out of her skull, oversized orbs that look fixed in horrified surprise.

I want to help her. I have to help her. Farrell's in no state to handle this by himself. She's struggling to rip her hands out of his grasp and he's doing his best to keep her from touching her face, but tears are streaming down his cheeks and he's shaking.

'Mr Farrell,' Nomsa says from behind me. 'Let's be reasonable—'

'Stay back!' Farrell yells, twisting his body to face her. 'Don't you come any closer!'

Katya manages to yank her hands free and her fingers fly to her cheeks. She scrabbles them over her non-existent nose, bats them against the skullish leer where her lips once were. 'Joss, Joss?' she's saying, over and over again. It's difficult to make out the words through her breathy, lipless lisp, but I get the gist of it.

'Joss? Ish ere… ish ere somefink wrong wiv my face?'

Farrell shoots me an agonised glance. 'It's… it's nothing we can't fix, Kay,' he stammers.

Then it really hits me. The sheer absurdity of it, the ridiculous horror of it, the whole twisted *(go on, say it) fucked-upness* of what's happening to me, to Farrell, to Katya.

'Josh, Josh?' she says again.

I hate myself for the thought, but she sounds absurd, like a bad ventriloquist. 'Is there something wrong with my face?' That has to be the understatement of the year.

The beginnings of hysteria burble in the pit of my stomach.

And how does Farrell think *that* can be fixed? A facial? A bar of Dove soap and some Body Shop moisturiser?

Before I can stop them, high-pitched gales of laughter rip out of me in jagged bursts, the force of them sucking away my breath, making my chest ache.

'Lisa?' Farrell's staring at me, eyes wide and mouth half-open.

'Client Cassavetes,' Nomsa says. 'Would you like me to fetch you a calmative?'

Another wave of humourless, uncontrollable laughter jags out of my throat.

'Shut up!' Farrell roars at me.

'Josh? Josh?' Katya says in that same eerily reasonable tone. 'Why's she laughing? Josh?'

Puke rushes into my mouth. I make it to the stainless steel bucket in the corner just in time; the force of my retching so violent that it feels like my stomach is rupturing. Nothing much comes up, but as my body spasms the mask is dislodged and slithers onto the carpet. For several seconds I can't do anything but keep absolutely still, clutching my aching stomach and trying to catch my breath.

'Josh? Please, Josh. I'm scared. What's happened to me?' Katya's voice is becoming fainter, as if she's giving up.

'Shhh, Kay,' he says, his voice wobbling. 'Shhh. It will be okay. I'll make it right.'

'You promise?'

Whatever happens I can't let her see me.

She won't be able to face it.

Another bubble of laughter threatens to surface, but this time I keep it inside. I scrabble on the carpet for the mask and, keeping my head down, push my way into the bathroom. I shut the door, and then lock it.

I run the tap, guzzle gulp after gulp of cool water, washing away the taste of vomit. I know I should reapply the mask. Go back into the room and help Farrell with Katya, but I need to get my act together first.

I need to calm down.

I press my forehead against the cool glass of the mirror.

Now put the mask back on and leave.

But first I just need to see. Just for a second. I raise my head and gaze at my reflection.

In this sharp, bright mirror, it's unbelievable. A thousand times more perfect than I remember from that first look.

The skin is a shade or two darker than mine – olive skin – so flawless that it almost looks airbrushed. The only imperfection is a tiny scar just above the perfectly plucked left eyebrow. They're my eyes for sure, that muddy brown I've always hated, but the lips, the nose, the cheekbones are far more polished and refined than I ever dreamed of.

I pull my hair back. There's a faint line along my jaw and around my hairline, like the tidemark left after applying a too-dark shade of foundation. There's no sign of stitching or even faint scarring. I press my fingers over my cheekbones, chin and forehead. The bone structure beneath has definitely changed, but I'm still not feeling any pain.

How did they do this? I've seen a couple of documentaries on face transplants and they looked swollen and fake and awful. But this... this is something else. How could they do this without any scarring or swelling or blood or pain?

It's impossible. It's *too* perfect. There's not a surgeon in the world who could perform such a flawless transplant.

I turn my head to the side to check out my new profile. What would it be like to look like this all the time?

You can't think like that. It's not your face.

I tilt my head to the side and pout my lips. What would it be like to walk into a room of strangers looking like this? Their glances admiring instead of disgusted, their eyes gleaming with envy or—

'You fucking *bitch*!' Farrell shouts.

Something thumps against the bathroom door.

I fumble for the lock and pull it open. Nomsa is slumped on the floor next to the door, holding the side of her face, and Farrell is standing over her, his breath escaping in ragged bursts.

He doesn't even glance at me. 'What the fuck is going on here?' Farrell screams at her. 'What the fuck are you people up to?'

Nomsa raises a hand. 'Mr Farrell—'

Farrell draws his fist back and I leap over Nomsa's body and grab hold of his arm. He's trembling, and his skin is slick with sweat. I'm expecting him to turn on me, push me back, maybe hit me, but he doesn't. He stands frozen, as if he can't believe what's he done, staring down at the nurse on the floor.

Nomsa gets to her feet, adjusting her skirt as if nothing has happened. Her expression is blank, and she shows no sign of pain or even a flicker of anger or fear. She absent-mindedly wipes the dribble of blood that's dribbling out of her nose with the back of her hand and rubs it onto the front of her crisp white skirt.

She cocks her head to one side and clucks her tongue. 'Now, Mr Farrell, I understand that this must come as a shock.'

'A shock?' he says. 'A *shock*? Are you fucking mad?'

Nomsa smiles calmly and for a second I'm sure that Farrell has hit the nail on the head. She is mad. She must be.

'What are you people doing in this place?' he says. 'What the fuck are you doing? What do you want with us?'

Nomsa sighs. 'You were scouted, Mr Farrell. Chosen.'

'Chosen by who? Chosen by what?'

'By the Ward Administration, of course.'

'You're not making any sense. Is this some sort of sick experiment you people are doing here?' He taps the side of his head. 'Fucking with our brains? Seeing how far you can push us?'

'I assure you that that is not the case,' Nomsa says. 'It really is best if you just accept this situation at face value, Mr Farrell.'

'You can't do this to us! To me! I'm *somebody*, I've shot Sophie fucking Ellis-Bextor, for fuck sakes! And Kay... Katya is... She's...'

'Mr Farrell—'

'I'll go to the police!'

'Oh, Mr Farrell, you don't understand. The police can't help you here.'

'Why not? Are they in on it?'

Nomsa actually laughs. 'In on what?'

'Whatever you're doing here.'

The door bursts open and a male orderly enters the room. He holds a large metal syringe in his hand. He's huge and square-jawed and his eyes have a vacuum of cold blankness behind them.

'It's under control,' Nomsa says, waving at him dismissively. He steps back, but doesn't leave the room.

'Put her face back on,' Farrell hisses to Nomsa. 'Put Katya's face back. Make it right.'

Oh God. The room is beginning to flip in and out of focus, and I have to bite my tongue hard to stop from laughing out loud again.

'I don't have the authority to make those decisions, Mr Farrell.'

I'm still holding his forearm, and I feel his muscles tighten. 'Who does have the authority?' I say, amazed at how calm my voice sounds. Nomsa looks at me properly for the first time since she entered the room.

'The Ward Administration,' she says.

'We need to see them. Can you make that happen?'

Farrell shrugs out of my grasp. 'Lisa, let's just—'

'Shhh,' I say to him. 'Well?' I say to Nomsa.

Nomsa clucks her tongue again. 'Clients are, naturally, permitted to petition the Administration for reversal, but it's most irregular.'

'But it can be done?'

'Of course.'

'You're saying they can fix this?' The fight has gone out of Farrell's voice.

Nomsa ignores him and looks right into my eyes. Her black irises are as dead as those of the orderly standing to attention behind her. 'Are you sure you want to do this, Client Cassavetes?' For a second it's as if she can see right into my soul. That she can read my thoughts. That she knows what I was thinking in the bathroom.

I nod. I'm not sure at all.

'Very well.' She looks at Farrell. 'And I suppose you want him to join you?'

'Of course I'm bloody coming!' Farrell roars. 'That's my fucking girl—'

'Eeeeeeeee!' Katya screeches. 'Eeeeeeeeee!'

She's pointing at me, her mouth opening and closing like a slack-jawed carp. Oh God. The mask! I left it in the bathroom.

'Oh shit,' Farrell says, rushing to her side. 'Katya, Kay, baby, it's going to be okay.'

Katya gawps at me through her death mask; just staring and making that inhuman keening noise.

'Don't you worry, Mr Farrell,' Nomsa says. 'We'll take good care of her.' She nods to the orderly, who slips behind me and approaches the bed.

'No!' Farrell yells. 'Don't you touch her!'

'Now, Mr Farrell,' Nomsa says. 'She needs to keep calm. Who knows what complications will arise if she excites herself too much?'

Farrell opens his mouth to retort, and the orderly takes the opportunity to jab the syringe into Katya's arm. Her eyeballs flip up into her skull like barrels in a slot machine, but she carries on wailing.

Tears are streaming down Farrell's cheeks. He strokes her hair, careful to avoid touching the raw flesh of her face. 'I'll be back, baby. I'm going to make them fix this, you'll see.'

Her screams start losing their power, dissolving into a short-breathed whimper.

'Mr Farrell?' Nomsa says. 'Shall we?'

He glares at Nomsa and stalks away from the bed, pushing past us roughly. I don't look back at Katya as I follow Nomsa out of the room.

Farrell is leaning against the corridor wall, his eyes shut, his fists clamped in his hair.

'This way, Mr Farrell,' Nomsa says, moving past him.

He snaps into life, catches up with her and grabs the back of her uniform. 'You'd better make this right, bitch,' he hisses. 'You'd better make this right. Or I swear to fucking God almighty that I will fucking hunt you down and kill you. Do you hear me? Do you?'

She wriggles out of his grasp and readjusts her clothes. My eyes are drawn to the brown smear of dried blood on her skirt. 'Mr Farrell, let me be clear. I am assisting you. If Client Cassavetes wants you to accompany her to see the Administration, then that is what we will do. She has the right according to the Ward Users' Rights Charter.' She smiles her cold, professional smile again. 'I could always take you back to Preparation?'

'Come on, Farrell,' I say. 'We don't have any choice.'

We follow Nomsa into the lift. She plucks a key out of her pocket and inserts it into a slot below the control panel. None of us speaks as the lift grinds into life and starts moving. Downwards. My head is beginning to hurt again, a dull, throbbing ache. I don't know whether it's a lingering effect of the drugs or simply my battle to stay sane.

The doors slide open and we step out into what looks like the lobby of an extremely plush office. Everything – the walls, the floors, the chairs, and the large S-shaped desk in front of us – is carved out of pale-pink marble. It's cold under my feet and the air con blasting out of the ceiling makes me shiver. A woman suddenly pops up from behind the desk. Her hair is bright yellow and lacquered into a beehive and she's dressed in a smart blue suit with huge shoulder pads. There's some sort of device stuck to the side of her face, some kind of hi-tech earpiece. As we approach I realise that it's actually sewn onto the side of her face with thick black thread. After what I've seen the last few hours, I can't bring myself to feel even a flicker of disgust.

'Yes?' she says to Nomsa.

'Request for fast-track Administrative Intercedence. Client Lisa Cassavetes.'

The woman looks at me and twitches her lips upwards. She points to Farrell. 'And this is?'

'Donor Joshua Farrell. He's...' – Nomsa waves a hand around her head – 'enmeshed.'

'This is most irregular. Have you completed a mid-level station-elevation document and put in a request for a pre-interference form?'

'No. This is a special case, code purple, and I cannot be responsible for any delay in its administration. I will file the requisite documentation post hoc.'

The woman purses her lips. 'It is most irregular.' She mumbles something into the earpiece sewn to her face, then looks down and skitters her fingers on what sounds like a keyboard. She sighs and shakes her head.

Nomsa turns round and rolls her eyes at me, as if we're just two ordinary people dealing with a bureaucratic mess together. Next to me, Farrell is standing absolutely still, his head drooping, his eyes fixed to the floor. He looks like I feel — exhausted, bewildered and utterly shell-shocked. I reach over and squeeze his hand. It's cold, and he doesn't respond.

'Farrell? Are you okay?'

'What do you think, Lisa?' he hisses. He raises his head and looks at me, but his eyes slide away from my face almost immediately. I wish I'd thought to reapply the mask.

The woman behind the desk bends down behind the counter and something beeps a few times. She stands and stretches her back as if she hasn't moved for hours.

'Ensue, please,' she says.

Nomsa gives us a small ironic salute.

'What about Katya?' Farrell says to her. 'What will you do to her while we're here?'

'She will be seen to.' Nomsa smiles her professional, cold smile again. 'And anyway, her welfare should be the least of your concerns right now, Mr Farrell.' Then she turns her back on us and strides into the lift.

We follow the yellow-haired woman down a marble-floored corridor. She scratches at the back of her neck and I catch a glimpse of a large seeping scab beneath her hair. Again, I feel nothing. Just a distanced, numb acceptance.

The woman pauses in front of an arched doorway, pulls open the door and stands back to let us enter first. The room is small and warm, its walls, floors and ceiling covered in flesh-coloured padding. Apart from a pair of square, low benches, upholstered in the same material, there's no other furniture in here.

'Please repose,' the woman says. 'You will be assumed shortly.' She pauses and stares at Farrell in distaste. 'Are you sure you want this donor with you, Client Cassavetes? Shall I relocate it to another salon?'

'No. No... He's part of this. It's fine.'

The door closes, and there's a click as if she's locked it behind her. I'm too exhausted to check, and Farrell looks one notch above comatose. He hasn't bothered to wipe the drying tears from his cheeks. We both flump down on the padded benches, and I lean my head back against the wall.

We sit in silence for a while. Then, abruptly, Farrell stands up and stalks to the door. He pushes against it. There's no handle and it doesn't budge.

'*Fuck*,' he says. 'We can't just let them play with us like this.'

For a second our eyes meet and again he looks away.

'We don't have any choice.'

He kicks the door again. '*Fuck*. And look at this place. We don't even know where the fuck we are.'

I glide my fingers along my jawline.

There's not a surgeon in the world who could perform such a perfect transplant. Not in this world, anyway.

'Farrell, I've been thinking and... and I don't think we're even in Johannesburg anymore.'

'What?'

'I don't actually think we're... Look, I just think we're somewhere else.'

'You mean like a different city?'

No. A different reality.

But Farrell's in no shape to deal with that concept.

And neither are you.

'Yes,' I say instead.

He waves his hand dismissively. 'I'm sure they've just moved us to some... facility. Probably right next to New Hope.'

Or underneath it.

'But it's obvious what they're doing now, isn't it?' Farrell continues. 'You heard what that bitch Nomsa said. They *chose* me. They must've picked Katya, too. Because she's beautiful. Because she's perfect.'

I drop my head so that he can't see the hurt expression on my face. *Her* face.

'Maybe they're... doing this for rich criminals who need new identities or something,' he says.

'But why give *me* a new face, Farrell? I can't pay them. I've got nothing to offer them.'

'Yes. Why *did* they give it to you?' I don't like the sound of his voice, it's cold and hard, and this time he stares into my eyes without flinching. Something in his face frightens me and I lean back as far away from him as I can get.

'I didn't ask for this, Farrell!'

He relaxes slightly. After a long pause he says, 'I know you didn't.'

Yes you did. You did ask for it. You've got what you've always wanted. A new face, Lisa.

I need to change the subject. 'What do you think they've done with Gertie? She was in that... Preparation Ward, too.'

Farrell shrugs. 'Who knows?'

'Do you think they've made her... disappear?'

'How would I know? I just want to sort Katya out and get her home.'

'Do you think they'll really just... reverse what they've done to us? I mean, why would they? And are they just going to let us go?'

'They have to. They must have realised that people are going to come looking for us, asking questions. We're not the kind of people who can just disappear without consequences.'

'Really?'

'Sure.' He nods frantically as if he's trying to convince himself of this. 'Someone's going to come looking for you, aren't they?'

'No one knows where I am, Farrell. I left without telling my father where I was going. If I disappear, no one will know where to look.'

'Yeah. But me and Katya... we're connected.' He strides over to the door. 'You hear me?' he shouts. 'You're not going to get away with this shit!' He kicks it again.

'And what about me?' I say.

'What about you?' Farrell says. The sneer in his voice makes me feel like I've been hit in the gut.

'What about *my* face?'

He blanches as if this is the first time he's thought of that. 'Well, they'll have to sort that out as well, won't they?'

I swallow the lump in my throat. I can't resist running my fingers over the smooth skin again. Farrell doesn't seem to notice, he's mumbling to himself.

What if I... What if I kept it?

You can't think like that.

'Katya's dad, he's probably got half the Metro cops looking for her right now,' Farrell says. 'Not to mention his own people.' He nods. 'That's why they've brought us here. That's why they haven't just... made us disappear. They've realised they've made a mistake, that me and Katya, we're not nobodies.'

Unlike me.

'That must be it,' I say. He needs to cling to something to get out of this intact. We both do. He smiles at me gratefully. Maybe he does care what happens to me after all. 'It's going to work out just fine, Farrell. If they removed Katya's face, they can put it back on.'

'Lisa?'

'Yes?'

He kneels down in front of me and takes my hand. 'Can you do something for me?'

'What?'

'When we see these Administration fuckers, let me do the talking, okay?'

I try to pull my fingers out of his grasp. He's squeezing them so hard it's beginning to hurt and I'm pretty sure he's not aware of what he's doing.

'I can promise you something, Lisa,' he says, finally loosening his grip and standing up. 'They'll be sorry they ever fucked with me.'

Before I can reply, the door clicks open.

Chapter 19

FARRELL

I'm expecting that yellow-haired freak, but a different, dark-haired woman is standing expectantly at the door. She's tall, almost skeletally skinny, dressed in an efficient tailored suit. She's overdone the perfume; I smother a sneeze as her cloying scent wafts up my nose. I can't tell how old she is – she's got that waxy, stretched Joan Rivers skin. Plastic surgery overkill.

'Client Cassavetes?' she says with a rigid smile. 'And Donor Farrell? Please pursue me.'

At least she hasn't looked at me as if I'm dog shit, which makes a change around here.

Lisa looks at me anxiously, but I ignore her. I'm going to need all my energy to convince these fuckers to sort this out, and I'm tired of babysitting. She can look after herself for once.

The skinny woman unlocks the door next to our waiting room and leads us down a long, marble-floored corridor, which ends at a heavy wooden door. The cramps in my legs have eased up, and I don't have any trouble keeping up with her – her knee-length skirt is so tight that she can barely move her thighs as she traipses along. She heaves open the door and ushers us into another large waiting room. There's a red suede couch against one wall and two matching orange armchairs opposite it, flanking a pair of solid-wood double doors. The thick carpet is royal blue with that same nauseating piss-yellow pattern they've used everywhere. Jesus, whoever designed this place must be on some seriously bad acid.

'Please be comfortable here,' the woman says. She indicates an antique table against a wall hung with closed drapes. 'There are beverages and refreshments here. Do help yourselves. You may ablute in here,' she says, pointing at a heavy bevelled darkwood door.

Unlike the limbo room we were just in, it's like a bad-taste five-star hotel in here. The materials are all thick and opulent, the cups and glasses on the beverage table whorled and cut. And here I am in the pyjama pants I woke up in, T-shirt and bare feet, and Lisa, with her dirt-strung hair, gown and my jeans.

This receptionist or whatever she is seems approachable enough. I should try to get some answers out of her, but I don't know what to ask her first. *Why are you doing insane medical experiments on my girl-friend? Who are these people who want to chop me up? Where are we exactly? How the fuck do I get out?* I settle on 'Um, do you know when we are going to get discharged?'

'Oh.' She smiles, her mauve lipstick perfectly applied, her teeth like something out of a buyers' guide. 'You must discuss that with the deliberation panel.'

'This hearing is about correcting the... error... concerning my... Ms Forrest, isn't it? And discharging us?' I say, doing my best to talk in their official jargon. If there's one thing I've learned in life, it's that bureaucrats are big on respect.

'I am unable to illuminate that, Donor Farrell,' she says with that same fixed smile. She's got something painted on her two front teeth but I'm not close enough to make it out clearly. 'Please repose,' she says, gesturing to the chairs. 'The panel will be ready for you in a few moments.' She opens one of the double doors only as far as she needs to and slips inside. As she closes the door behind her, I read the golden plaque mounted on it: 'The Moreau and Verwoerd Memorial Deliberation Chamber'.

I can't help looking at Lisa's arse in my jeans as she turns to sit. I prefer that view of her. That way I don't have to look at her... face. Katya's features with her eyes. I sit on one of the orange chairs so that she won't sit next to me, and immediately realise it's the wrong decision. Now Lisa looks lonely and small as she perches on the couch, her legs clasped together at the knees, the lank golden hair hanging limply over her... the face. It's not her fault, I suppose. I'd see less of her face if I were sitting next to her.

I go for some water. I can't remember the last time I drank anything, and now, without the drip in me, I'm parched. I pour water out of a cut-glass carafe with ice and unidentifiable fruit floating in it. I'm not sure whether to trust it, but it looks and smells appetising. I knock back three glasses.

'Water?' I ask Lisa.

'Please,' she says.

I take a glassful to her, and, as I do, my bladder tells me it needs to 'ablute'. Can't remember when last I did that either.

I push into the bathroom. It's also like something in a five-star hotel. Green-veined black marble tops, designer brass fittings, spotless grey travertine on the floor and black-and-opalescent mosaic urinals on the walls. I enter the furthest of the two stainless-steel cubicles and the new-fangled toilet bowl standing in the middle of the space flushes itself. I take a long and satisfying piss, gazing up at the framed sign on the back wall of the cubicle – 'Ministry of Modifications: Carving for You', it reads, with a corporate blue-and-green ideogram of cupped hands – and notice how dark my urine is. I've been seriously dehydrated. 'Carving for You.' I can't believe this illegal scheme has the balls to advertise. Jesus, it just goes to show: money makes its own rules. Whoever's behind this racket, they need to employ a fucking proofreader. Bastards.

I'm heading for the bathroom door when it opens and I hear two male voices. Shit. I duck back inside the cubicle.

'I don't know why they're allowing it a hearing now. It should be on intensive preparation. Now it's karking around, without its meds. We'll have to move the donation schedule back again. And it's a high-risk Donor...'

My left leg cramps and I have to squat over the lidless bowl, gripping onto the rim, trying not to breathe.

'The Auditor says it was inducted early. Some... domestic situation,' says a second voice. This man sounds like he's got a blocked nose; he snuffles heavily like a bulldog between sentences. 'Did you know it's a glamour photographer? Works upside with fayson mowdels.'

'Aah, mascots.' The first man chuckles knowingly. 'That explains the Auditor's interest. He's so transported by shopping, you'd swear he was a player. It wouldn't surprise me if he auditioned for General Manager at the Ministry of Consumption next term.'

'Ssh! Kark, Mutual. The Auditor's in the chamber. Do you want to be recycled?'

'These walls are thick, Federal. Auditor's orders. Anyway, we shouldn't be karking around with irregular hearings, Client-requested or not. The Donor's high risk.'

'There have been higher-risk cases. Remember when we harvested Donor Lewis?'

'I don't get these browns. You give them a chance to be a Client, give them a primo face interplant, offer to modify them to anything they want, and still they choose to kark around with Donors, making irregular petitions. It's asking for reversal, for contract's sake! The interplant was primo work. I saw the mimeographs.'

The cramp shifts up my leg, my grip slips and my arse bumps onto the bowl. I hold my breath, praying they haven't heard me.

'Lewis would have been a better Donor if she was—'

Fuck. My foot slips off the seat and the toilet flushes. I hoist myself up before my arse gets too wet, trying to shake off the cramp, preparing to run.

'Kark. I hope it's not the Auditor in there.'

'The Auditor uses the golden restroom, Federal.' I hear them zip up.

'Anyone there?' snuffles bulldog.

Another moment passes. 'Just backflush,' the first man says, and at last they leave.

I struggle to understand what I've just heard. They were talking about me, I'm sure of it, but what the fuck did it mean?

The only way I'm going to get to the bottom of this is to be direct and demand answers face to face. They're going to tell me what sort of game they're playing, they're going to apologise and reverse what they've done to Katya, and after that they can talk to my lawyer. Someone's going to correct this. And somebody's going to pay.

I wash my hands, spurting a snot of green hand soap over my T-shirt. I look at myself in the mirror. Christ, I look like shit. The first thing I need to do when I get home is get a shave and a haircut and a serious facial. Thank God no one at the studio can see me like this.

But I have to try to keep positive. I glance around the well-appointed bathroom again, with its smart finish and shining fittings. You'd think that any organisation that kept its toilets this clean would have nothing to hide. So, what can I learn from this? The opulence here, the sheer organisation, means that this is not just random insanity, surely. They're open to reason, to negotiation. There's a system, there's accountability. They're not behaving like this is some banana republic. I should be thankful that this isn't a back-alley operation. If it were, I'd probably be rotting in a shallow grave by now.

I head back into the waiting room. Lisa's paging through a magazine, so absorbed in it that she doesn't look up as I approach. I catch a glimpse of a double-page ad: 'Cut it off on Credit!' the copy screams in cheesy pink letters. The model in the spread is too thin, and I'm sure she has a stump instead of a hand. Jesus.

I sit down next to Lisa and she guiltily slaps the magazine face down on the glass-topped table in front of us. She blushes as if I've just caught her looking at porn. Ugh. I never saw Katya blushing and mottled colouration looks disgusting on her skin.

'There were some horrible photos in there,' she ventures, although she doesn't sound too badly affected. 'Weird stuff.'

'I'm not surprised. Did you see the two men who came out of the bathroom just now?'

'Kind of.' She waves at the magazine. 'I wasn't really paying attention.'

'What did they look like?'

'One was a bit on the big side, I suppose.'

'Did you see where they went?'

She points to the double doors. 'Through there.'

The receptionist pokes her head out of one of the doors, keeping it closed behind her. 'Just a few more moments, valued Client and, uh, Donor,' she chirrups. 'The committee has almost finished rehearsing the case, and they'll be hearing your submission in just a few moments. Please continue to repose.' She ducks back inside.

Feeling self-conscious, I sit as far from Lisa as I can get. I grind the thick pile of the carpet with my bare toes. Lisa presses her hand against her face and the space between us is heavy with the horror behind it. I can't look at her, and I can tell she would prefer to be anywhere but here. I pick up a pamphlet from the perspex holder on the coffee table. It's designed in the same inoffensive colours as the sign in the toilet, and has the same wording: 'Ministry of Modifications: Carving for You'. I notice that the hands in the ideogram aren't the same size. The one on the left is shorter than the one on the right and between the hands, where you might expect a symbol of the earth or maybe a classic heart shape, there's a shapeless, unidentifiable blob.

I open it up. 'MoM, Severing You, Severing Your Community.' These people seriously need some new blood in marketing. I put it back in its holder.

The burn of a cramp starts up in my glute and I stand up immediately to try to tease it out. The spasms are far less intense now than they were when I came off that drip. How long has it been? A few hours? It seems like weeks. I don't even know what date it is, never mind what time it is. I walk across to the drapes behind the drinks table and push one aside to check out the view. Only there's no window, just another bricked-in alcove.

Lisa comes up behind me. 'What's there?'

I draw the curtain wider and show off the wall. 'We went quite far down in that lift getting here. We're probably underground.'

'It's like we're in a casino or something,' she says. 'Like they're deliberately trying to deprive our senses. Why do they bother with the curtain?'

'It must be something to do with these... experiments they're doing.'

The receptionist appears again. 'Please proceed into the chamber.'

'Sorry,' I say to her. 'Do you know what time it is?'

'Meeting time.'

'No, I mean, what *time*?' I tap my wrist where my watch used to be before that fucking Nomsa bitch stole it.

She looks at me blankly then cocks her head like I'm telling a joke she's not getting. 'It's meeting time, Donor,' she repeats, the smile not wavering.

'Come on,' Lisa says, and touches my hand. 'Let's do this. But keep calm, okay, Josh? Losing your temper won't help anything.'

'Call me Farrell,' I snap. 'Only Katya calls me Josh. And don't worry, I know how to win an argument. I didn't grow up in some Natal backwater.' Since when has Ms Inferiority Complex started dishing out advice?

We enter the meeting room, followed by the receptionist, who closes the door behind her.

Four people in business suits are seated at the end of an expensive minimalist thirty-seater table, and the receptionist ushers us into chairs a few places down from them. At the head of the table sits a gaunt man with a hypertensive purple cast to his skin. The skin sags as if it's too large for his bones, and at first glance the folds make him look ancient, but then I realise the skin itself is smooth and soft, barely marked apart from that even bruise colour. He has a full head of silver hair. To his left sits a woman with a blonde bob and a power suit, just as sharp and tight as the receptionist's. A flight of goosebumps ripples down my neck and spine. The whole left side of her face is scarified and tattooed, while the right is a little slack and looks too young for her eyes. Opposite us are two men in white-collared blue shirts and gold-buckled braces, their jackets slung over the backs of their chairs. One of them is fat and ashen, and judging by his constricted breathing I'm guessing he has to be 'Federal' from the bathroom. That means the other, dark-haired one must be 'Mutual'. And, Jesus, what I took to be a full head of greased-back hair is actually an expertly rendered tattoo drawn onto his pale bald pate. 'Federal' wears a pink tie and 'Mutual' green.

The receptionist takes her seat across from us and poises her fingers over a thin electronic tablet.

It's the blonde woman who talks first, reading from a file in front of her. 'Thank you for attending, Client Cassavetes. For the record, this is an expedited reassignment and procedure reversal application hearing under Ministry of Modifications ward procedure grievance protocol 34a, section 93, for Class I or Class II temporary residents authorised by transfer agent codename Nomsa Makgatho on behalf of Node 2:34:765/citizen Client Lisa Francina Cassavetes. All correct?'

The blonde looks up at Lisa and smiles. The buttoned panel on her constrictive blouse flattens her chest, smothering any hint of breasts. 'I'm Senior Grievance Secretary Ada Gass, and we have in attendance Auditor Abacus' – she indicates the purple man, who grunts softly – 'and medical-aid representatives Federal and Mutual.' They nod.

'We have Assistant Foundation monitoring, Client Cassavetes submitting and' – she looks down at her notes – 'Donor Joshua Alphonse Farrell in attendance. Why exactly is the Donor present, Client Cassavetes?'

'Um... he... he...' Lisa stammers. She blushes again, and I have to look away.

'What I mean to ask, more specifically, is have we in any way disappointed your expectations or failed to live up to our mandate? Have we failed you in any way, Client Cassavetes?'

'No, I...'

'Are you dissatisfied with your surgery or post-operative care?'

Lisa touches her face.

I look across to her, pleading silently. Come on, Lisa, we discussed this. You've got to help me. You've got to help Katya.

She smoothes her hand over her cheeks again.

'She wants the surgery reversed, don't you, Lisa?' I say.

'Donor, please. You have no status in this chamber. Your opinion as to the client's wishes has really no legal import. Client Cassavetes?'

Lisa looks at Ada Gass, and then the medical-aid men. She looks at the receptionist and at the purple man. Finally she looks at me. Still she says nothing.

'You're simply representing the Donor's grievance. Is that it, Client?' says Mutual, and he grins at Federal as if they're about to high-five.

That seems to snap Lisa out of her trance. 'That's right,' she says. 'I didn't ask for this... for her face. And she didn't ask for it either.'

'That's right, we're also appealing on behalf of Katya Forrest,' I say.

'Donor, please!' Gass snaps without looking at me. 'It's highly irregular, Client Cassavetes.'

'What is?'

'This whole case. The early induction of the Donor is irregular; its preparatory treatment is irregular. An expensive and unwarranted facial interplant on a Client is unprecedented, your submission on behalf of a Donor while you yourself are satisfied with your procedure is irregular, your appeal for reassignment and reversal at a single hearing is irregular. Honestly, this is what we in the Ministry thought we had stamped out after the previous regime—'

'Ada,' the purple man interrupts in a hoarse but urbane voice, 'we must not discuss politics. Especially in front of br—, uh, temporary residents.'

'Yes, Auditor. I forgot myself.'

'Your loyalty to the Scrupulists is in no doubt, Secretary Gass.'

'Thank you, Auditor. As I was saying, this is an irregular case, Client Cassavetes, in fact unprecedented, and I don't see any justification for authorising your reassignment or for reversing a procedure that was unnecessary and irregular in the first—'

'Wait a minute! You listen to me,' I cut in. 'You'll be lucky if I don't call the police as well as my lawyers. As far as I'm concerned, I'm being held here against my will. You need to reverse that surgery immediately and let me... us' – I remember Lisa as she nudges my ankle with her foot – 'out of here.'

Gass frowns as if irritated by a fly and finally looks at me. 'Against your will? Assistant Foundation, please issue the Donor with a copy of admission form 12TG signed in its own hand and witnessed.' The receptionist stamps and signs a copy of a document before sliding it across to me. 'Is this not your hand?'

'It looks like it, but...' I don't remember signing any forms, but this is definitely my signature.

'This, as you can see, Donor, is your admission and transfer authorisation docket, and your legal representative is very welcome to examine it. I'm sure it will only confirm the accuracy of our records. The Ministry prides itself on its business units' record-keeping. In fact, this Ward has been commended with a five-pound certificate in Administrative Procedure in all but one of the last seventy-three periods. You will find, Donor Farrell, that we stick to the very letter of the law.'

'I want you to tell me where we are and when we can get the *fuck* out of here.'

The receptionist looks up from her machine. The Auditor and Gass stare at Lisa and the medical-aid reps look at me with that mixture of disgust and pity I've seen elsewhere in this place. It's underlaid with a palpable feeling of threat. Bad move. I shouldn't have lost my temper.

'Ms Gass,' says Lisa, 'can we fix this? What must we do to have the surgery reversed and go home? You can't just deny the request because it's unprecedented. Surely you must consider each submission according to its merits?'

I glance across at her. Where the hell did that come from?

'As I was saying, Client Cassavetes,' Gass resumes, 'the facial interplant between you and Donor Forrest was entirely unnecessary, and the agent and surgeons responsible have been reprimanded for their disregard and for squandering valuable Ministry time and resources on what amounted to nothing more than a game. This Ministry does not play, Client Cassavetes, unlike other—' The Auditor grunts, and Gass gets back to the point. 'For this reason, the Auditor is prepared to grant the reversal request.'

'Oh, thank God,' I sigh.

'Clients have their rights, according to the Charter, and we have no reason not to proceed with the reversal. Only to note, of course, its unprecedented irregularity.' She looks at Lisa again, confused or disappointed. 'If you are entirely certain...'

The last thing I need is another moment for Lisa to think. Lisa says nothing and at length Gass continues. 'The interplant appears to be primo work, although the plasma dressing does seem to have, uh, mislocated itself somewhere.'

She turns to me. 'Despite your... misgivings... about our scrupulousness, Donor, you too have your rights. Client Cassavetes has successfully submitted on your behalf and all that remains is for us to invoke your upside legal standing – such that it is – to guarantee commensurate payment. This is why we have the medical-aid representatives with us today. They can help you understand your options. We'll leave you to it, then, and Assistant Foundation will have your reassignment paperwork ready for you when you're done.'

Gass waits for the Auditor to haul himself out of his chair, and they leave the room, followed by the receptionist.

Federal and Mutual each slide a thick folder across the table to me. Mutual turns on a million-dollar grin. 'The reassignment product available to upside citizens is the Donor Swap payment method. This is our brochure describing the policies available under this product and the repayments required. I'd suggest you spend some time reading through the literature, familiarising yourself with the structures of each, and your liabilities.'

Each brochure must be two hundred pages long. There's no way I'm going to wade through this rubbish. 'Whatever,' I say. 'Where do I sign?'

'Hang on, hang on, Farrell,' Lisa says, like she's suddenly my business manager. She turns to the reps. 'We're running out of time here, Representatives. Do you think you can give us the executive summary?'

'What would you like to know, Client?'

'Firstly, what's the difference between your two schemes?'

'Should I answer that or will you, Federal?'

'You go ahead.'

'Nothing, Client. We're owned by the same agglomeration and our benefits, payment and usury schemes are precisely the same.'

'It really comes down to whether you like pink or green.'

'Green, I take it, Farrell?' Lisa nudges me.

'Okay, whatever.' I just want to sign and get Katya's face back and go the fuck home.

'Representative Mutual,' says Lisa, 'could you give me the CEO overview of your scheme?'

'Right, Client,' Mutual says, clearly invigorated by Lisa's businesslike tone and interest. 'The Mutual Medical Shortfall Insurance Donor Swap Programme involves a commitment to payment of an industry-standard 150 per cent viable donation mass within thirty-three shifts – that's 134 upside hours – from signature. The viability criteria are listed in Appendix C and Schedule 23. The Donor's viable mass for contract purposes is measured and notarised on discharge. Do note that, in the event of default or breach of contract, the contracted 150 per cent viable mass will be payable within three shifts after registration of breach.'

'I'm not sure if I understand,' Lisa says. 'What mass are we talking about? Does that mean—'

'*Enough*, Lisa!' I snap. 'Where do I sign?'

'Right here, Mr Farrell,' says Mutual, fingering his green tie like it's a wad of banknotes. 'Personals here, triplicate on the back page, initial every page of the contract, and you're covered.'

'Wait, Farrell, please. You shouldn't sign anything you don't understand.'

'This is all a fucking sick joke, Lisa. All I care about is reversing the surgery. Let's just fucking get to the operating theatre.'

Mutual's expectant expression hasn't changed. He wants to clinch the deal as much as I do. I take the heavy pen from him and spend a few minutes signing in every appropriate spot, not bothering to look at the text. Lisa just sits next to me, shaking her head.

When I'm done, I slide the folder back to Mutual. He removes the signed contract and slides the folder back to me.

'Congratulations, Mr Farrell. You are now officially enrolled in the Mutual Medical Shortfall Insurance Donor Swap Programme. Please keep this copy of the contract and the product brochure. It details all the product features, as well as contact details of upside Client Care Centres, node quality controllers and collection centres. A pleasure, sir.' He offers his hand, which I have no choice but to take. It's cold and dry, like a snake's skin.

Chapter 20

LISA

We're lying side by side in the same room and, if I really wanted to, I could reach over and touch her. She's totally out of it, her breathing is shallow and erratic, and she hasn't moved once since I arrived. I'm selfishly relieved that her face is once again swathed in tightly wrapped bandages, a small jagged hole ripped in the dressing so that she can breathe through her mouth. There's no way I could have dealt with another glimpse of that seeping skull face with its bulging, lidless eyes.

Still, the rest of her is beautiful: her wrists fine-boned and delicate, her body under the covers long and slender. Lucky Farrell. Soon he'll have the complete package back together again.

Now, now, the Dr Meka voice says.

'Katya?' I whisper. For some reason I feel like I should be apologising to her. It's crazy, none of this is my fault, but I have to fight the urge all the same.

That's your inferiority complex speaking.

'Katya?' I try again.

Still no response. They've probably doped her up to the eyeballs. She's surrounded by several softly humming machines, and a drip line containing that brownish fluid snakes out of the back of her hand. A fine tube attached to a blipping screen seems to have been inserted right into a vein in her chest. The pink-tinged liquid inside it pulses and bubbles every time she breathes.

It's ominously quiet, just the sound of Katya's breathing, the thump of my heart and the occasional beep of the machine next to her bed. The door's open, but there's no sign of life in the corridor beyond. No sign of Farrell.

When that brisk nurse crackling with starch and efficiency led us in here – a double room on the Preparation Ward level – after our meeting in the boardroom, she made it very clear that Farrell wasn't welcome.

'Tush, tush. No spare parts allowed in here,' she snapped at him. 'There's a comfort room at the end of the ward. You can wait there.'

I expected him to kick up a fuss and insist that he had to stay by his girlfriend's side, but he didn't argue. His eyes skated over Katya's bandaged face, and without a word he slunk out of the room. No 'Good luck, Lisa' or 'It will work out fine', or any other words of comfort.

Don't be too hard on him, that's his girlfriend lying there. He's struggling to deal with this.

He's not the only one.

The nurse treated me like I was an invalid, carefully helping me wash myself down and change into a clean hospital gown. I didn't bother to question her, exhaustion and spent adrenaline leaving me limp and voiceless, but I'm regretting that now. I've lost track of how long I've been in here, waiting for whatever they're going to do to me.

Still, I'm tempted to slip into the bathroom and have one last look at my Katya reflection.

Don't go there, Lisa. For the thousandth time, it's not your face.

Dr Meka's right. After this is all over, I'll just be me again. I try to picture my old reflection, the face that's been staring back at me in the mirror for the last twenty-four years, but all I can call up is a blurry image, superimposed with Katya's high cheekbones and full lips. What will I look like when I next face the mirror?

It hits me with a jolt. Oh God. What if I wake up with someone else's face? What if I wake up with Gertie's face?

Don't be ridiculous.

It's not ridiculous. Maybe they brought her down here for a reason. Just like Katya, just like me. Where is Gertie? What have they done with her?

Not your problem. Sort your own troubles out first.

God. How much longer will we have to wait? I just want this over and done with.

And then what will you do?

Go home. Promise Dad that I'll go back into therapy, take the Luvox, finish my correspondence degree, get a job and—

Heard it all before, Lisa. You're not fooling anyone.

This time it's different. This time I really think I can—

'Greetulations, Client Cassavetes!' A nurse I've never seen before bustles in. She gives me a professional smile, but, even though she looks to be my age, her face appears to have been Botoxed to death, and none of the muscles around her eyes or cheeks actually moves. She rustles over to my bed and needlessly starts fussing with the sheets.

My stomach flips. Is it time?

'How are you feeling, Client Cassavetes?'

'Scared.'

She tries to smile sympathetically, but the end result is as soulless as a fixed mannequin grin. 'Don't be headless, you're in the Wards. You shouldn't be scared. You should be wonderful.'

'Wonderful?'

'Oh yes of course. And just think, Crane will be butchering you today. Aren't you the lucky one!'

'Butchering? You mean operating?'

She chuckles. 'Yes, yes.'

'What will happen to me?' I touch my face. *Katya's face.* 'Will I get my old face back?'

'That's not my department, Client Cassavetes, but I can assure you that you will be a happy maggot when all's done.'

'When do we get to see... Crane? The one who will be doing the operation?'

The nurse laughs as if I've said something genuinely funny. 'Butchers don't deal with Clients in person!' She plumps my pillows. 'They're far too important for verbals.'

'But there are things the surgeon needs to know about me.'

'Shhh. You're getting your intestines imbricated over nothing. We're well aware of your Client history. Why else would you be here with us?'

'How long, before…?' I can't finish the question.

She tucks the blanket covering my legs firmly under the mattress. 'There, there. Try to repose. It won't be long now. Shall I bring you some remedies to make you happy?'

'No, thank you.'

She tries to move her cheek muscles again. 'Goody good.' She turns as if to leave.

'Aren't you going to check on Katya?' I say.

'Who?' she says brightly.

I point to Katya. 'The other patient.'

The nurse sniffs and glances at Katya, her face pursed with disgust. 'Oh, that Donor is fine. We'd know if there were any kark-ups. Now, are you absolutely sure I can't get you anything?'

Some answers would be nice.

'No. Thanks. I'm fine.'

'Goody good.'

She smoothes her skirt, shoots me a last stiff grimace, and crackles out.

My stomach is a cold, hard ball. My mouth tastes like rusty iron.

Pre-op nerves. You have to relax. After all, you're an old hand at this.

Am I really going to go through with it? After the meeting with the suits, it was crystal clear that Farrell's only interested in Katya's welfare. He's willing to go along with anything, deluding himself that all we're dealing with is some warped medical screw-up.

The fear twists into a tight fist of anger. But what about me? He's not the one who's going under the knife, is he?

I kick the sheet off my legs. Dammit. What can I do, though? It's not as if I have a choice.

Not true, the Dr Meka voice says. *You do have a choice, Lisa. You can get up out of this bed, and leave.*

And go where? What if they don't let me leave?

Even Dr Meka hasn't got an answer for that.

A gurgling sound suddenly erupts out of Katya's throat. I nearly jump out of my skin. 'Guuhhh,' she says.

'Katya? Katya? Are you awake?'

'Finkso.' Her voice is faint and blurry and I have to strain to make out what she's saying. 'Firsy.'

'Firstly?'

'Firsy. Die.'

Then I get it. She's thirsty, dry. There's a plastic cup and straw on the cabinet between our beds. I slither off my gurney and hold it to the slit in her bandages, trying not to look too closely at the dark hole rimmed with raw flesh, her white teeth revealed all the way up to the top of her gums. My tongue instinctively darts out and touches my lips. *Her* lips.

My hand is shaking, but she manages to suck some of the water onto her tongue. The rest dribbles out, soaking the bandages. I dab at the sodden dressing with the edge of the sheet.

'Fanks. Wah ah I?'

'Um... you're in hospital.'

How can she not remember? Has she blocked everything out? Thank God her eyes are covered. The last thing she needs is another glimpse of her own face staring back at her.

'Wis hossital?'

Good question.

'Joburg.' What else can I say? But Katya seems to accept this vague answer.

'I cahn see. I bee in a accident?' It's getting easier to make out what she's saying.

'Um. In a manner of speaking.'

She really can't remember what happened in that Recovery room. Or, it seems, anything that came before it.

A perfectly normal reaction to shock.

She lifts a shaking hand and touches her face. 'Bandages.'

'Yes.'

'Wha happened? I had this horrible dream.'

'Did you? That's quite normal,' I say, my voice straining with false cheer and sounding horribly like the nurse's.

'I feel funny. Woozy.'

'You're likely to feel a bit disoriented. Just try to relax.'

You've missed your calling, Lisa. Maybe they'll give you a job here after it's over.

'My boyfriend... Josh. I think he was with me. The accident. Is he okay?'

'Josh is fine.'

'Are you a nurse?'

'No. I'm a... patient. Just like you.'

She touches the dressing on her face again. 'Oh God. Am I burned? My face, it's...'

'Yes. This is a burns unit. That's right.'

Christ. I wish that nurse would return. I press the call button next to Katya's bed.

Katya coughs. 'Is it bad?'

'Um... it's not too bad, no.'

'Because my face... I'm a model. I need to look... perfect.'

'A model?' I chirp. 'That must be exciting.' I'm making myself feel ill.

Why? You're well versed in the pleasures of self-delusion.

Katya groans again. 'God. My head hurts so bad. Is my dad here?'

'You'll see him soon.'

'I need my dad. He'll fix everything.'

'I'm sure they'll let you see him soon.'

'And Josh. Need to tell him...' Her voice wavers.

'Katya? Can you hear me?'

'Sowwy.'

'What?'

I can hear her struggling to stay conscious. 'Tell Josh... sowwy.'

'Sowwy? I don't understand.'

Yes you do. She's saying sorry.

She emits a long sigh and her body seems to lose tension. Her breathing is irregular and laboured, and there's a rattling edge to it.

I touch the back of her hand. 'Katya?'

She's out of it.

I can't stay here listening to her struggling for each breath. She needs help. I press the call button next to her bed again, and head to the door to find a nurse. The corridor outside is deserted. I pace back and forth, but no one comes.

Hang on, the nurse who brought us here said there was a waiting room at the end of the corridor.

'Farrell?' I call.

Tinny voices are floating out of an open doorway at the end of the passageway. I pad towards it and slip inside. Farrell is sitting slumped in an armchair, his head lolling to one side. He's fast asleep, his mouth hanging open. I'm about to reach out and shake him awake when my eye is drawn towards the television perched on a stand in the corner. That's the source of the voices.

Oh God. A jowly man dressed in a baggy crumpled suit fills the screen. I know that man. I've seen him before. He's standing in the aisle of a shopping mall, hands on his hips, his mouth down-turned in an over-the-top expression of sadness. A cheesy voice-over is saying: 'Feeling down and brown? Tired of being a karking grey-boy freak?'

The man nods mime-style. A woman with three breasts barely covered by a fishnet vest stalks past him. She shoots him a look of exaggerated disgust and he drops his head.

'Why look like an abnormal brown when you can modify?' the voice-over woman says. 'At the Wards we can make your modification dreams come true.'

There's a shot of a gleaming hospital corridor and the camera pans past a group of smiling and waving nurses, and then, oh God, I instantly recognise the next scene. The smiling man with an amputated arm is lying on the metal operating table. So it wasn't a nightmare after all. It wasn't just in my imagination. I've seen this exact scene before on the TV in that room I was in – just before Farrell and I tried to escape.

But this time I know exactly what it is.

A sick giggle burbles out of my throat. I'm watching a twisted home-shopping ad.

The woman with the bulging eyes appears on screen. Oh God, I really don't want to see this again. The sound was muted when I saw it first and somehow the cheery voice-over makes it even more disturbing: 'From simple starving-and-amputation techniques to original custom-designed re-enhancements, we can do it all.' I know what's coming next, but I can't tear my eyes away. She pulls back the cloth covering the tray, revealing that tentacle thing. 'There's a modification to suit everyone!'

Now the man is strolling through the mall's aisle, a fixed grin on his face. 'Be the envy of your friends, frenemies and Shoppers.' The woman with the three breasts stalks past him, but this time she hesitates, licks her lips and gazes at his tentacled arm with exaggerated admiration.

The man winks at the camera. 'Book into the Modification Ward now,' he says. 'I did. It's catalogue!'

Then he and the triple-breasted freak stroll away into the distance, the woman's skinny arm locked around his tentacled limb.

'All modifications subject to extensive credit checks and or Donor-deals. Terms and conditions apply,' the voice-over says, in the familiar fine-print rush. 'Modifications are brought to you by the Ministry of Modifications and are subject to unannounced amendments by Ward Administration.'

The screen goes black. But next up is a flurry of applause. Synthesiser music blares and the caption 'I Married a Brown!' is superimposed over a shot of a wildly screaming studio audience. Most of them appear staggeringly obese, their faces blotchy and distorted.

Jerry Springer meets Dawn of the Dead.

I can't watch any more of this. I snatch the remote from the side of Farrell's chair and jab the off button. Farrell snaps awake, wiping drool from his chin. He gazes around in confusion, flinching slightly when he sees me.

'Lisa? What are you doing in here? The nurse said—'

'It's Katya.'

'She's awake?'

'She was.'

He twitches slightly. 'Did she say anything?'

'She thinks she's been in an accident. She doesn't remember anything about...' My hand strays to my face again.

'That's a good thing, isn't it? I mean, it will make things easier when we get home.'

He stands up.

Something shifts inside me. I'm not sure if it's the mention of the word 'home' or the aftertaste of seeing those sickening images again, but I suddenly feel as if I'm going to burst, that I'll start screaming, and, if I start, I won't be able to stop.

'Lisa?' Farrell's voice says. It sounds like it's coming from far away. 'Lisa? Are you okay?'

I'm shaking, and I'm not sure my legs will hold me up anymore. Farrell steps towards me and I collapse against him.

He holds me up stiffly, and slowly his arms loosen into a hug. The sobs rocket out of my chest, taking my breath away.

'Shhh. It's going to be fine.'

Listen to him, Lisa.

But how can it be fine? Nothing's ever going to be fine again. I know this with a cold certainty.

But it wasn't exactly fine when you started, now was it?

'Shhh,' he says. 'We're in this together.'

'Are we?' I say, my voice muffled against his chest.

'Of course we are.'

I don't know how long I stay leaning against him, breathing in the scent of his skin, listening to the steady thump of his heart.

There's the sound of a high-pitched siren. *Beeeeeeep. Beeeeeeep. Beeeeeeep.* Feet thud past the waiting-room door. The squeak of a trolley. Loud voices.

Something's wrong. Something's happening.

I lean back and look up into Farrell's face, his eyes closed. He looks so... natural. Like he belongs here. I should tell him what Katya said, that she was sorry, but he probably won't want to hear that right now.

Maybe he's right. Maybe everything's going to work out. Five more minutes won't hurt. I rest my head back on his chest and shut out the world.

Beeeeeeep. Beeeeeeep. Beeeeeeep.

PART 2 >>

Chapter 21

FARRELL

Someone's fucked with the settings on my iPhone. I'm trying to fix its internet profile, but I give up halfway. Actually, after what we've been through, going online and talking inane shit on MindRead is the last thing I feel like doing. What the fuck would I say, anyway? **hola MRers back from the dead – found a gr8 new recycling place**

I hear a car door thump in the street below our apartment. I peer out of the window. Oh fuck, they're early. Glenn and June slamming out of the Jaguar. Now Glenn's saying something offensive to the car guard and I can just imagine June's face shutting down in embarrassment. What am I talking about? It's permanently shut down.

I drop the phone on the couch. 'They're here,' I call.

Fuck. *Fuck.* June said they'd be here at eleven, and it's barely half past ten. I straighten the cushions on the couch, collect the dirty dishes and pile them into the sink. I check my face in the mirror in the hall, run to the guest bathroom and pat some serum onto my cheeks. Better.

Bang, bang, bang. Glenn's unsubtle pounding on the door. That bastard seriously thinks he owns everything and everyone, including me and my fucking apartment.

I instinctively check again to make sure that everything's in place.

Bang, bang, bang!

'A bit of respect would be nice, arsehole,' I mutter to myself, then open the door.

'Where is she?' barks Glenn from inside the marquee-like three-piece Italian suit he thinks makes him look sophisticated. The expensive cologne and the sweat, last night's cognac and this morning's mouthwash waft off him in waves as he barges past me. My stomach's still not a hundred per cent.

June hovers behind him. 'Hello, Josh,' she says, giving me a weak smile. 'My, you've lost so much weight. How're you feeling?'

'Where is she?' Glenn says again.

'She's sleeping, Glenn. The medication makes her very tired, but the doctor says that's the best thing for her. I'm sure she'll wake up soon. Can I get you some coffee?'

'Let me see her,' says Glenn, his voice softer. According to Katya, the quieter his voice becomes, the closer he is to hitting someone. I'm not going to be able to delay him much longer.

'Come on, Glenn, five minutes isn't going to make a difference,' June says.

I shoot her a grateful smile. For some lucky reason, she's always believed I'm good for Katya. Probably because Katya's other boyfriends were bullying oafs, carbon copies of Glenn. June's my one ally in that family, and Christ knows I need her on my side now.

One step at a time. It will be fine. One step at a time. We'll get through this.

'Coffee would be lovely, Josh,' June says. 'Thank you.'

I fill the kettle, keeping an eye on them from behind the kitchen counter. The scar on my right hand stings. It must have worked itself open when I was fucking around with that phone. I think of Katya smashing that glass against the counter, and how much has happened since then.

Glenn slumps back on the couch, his massive frame sagging under the weight of all those overpriced dinners and the booze he knocks back 24/7. June sits primly perched on the edge of the couch, knees together in her narrow linen Jackie O dress, on high alert in case Glenn instructs her to scurry for more milk or sugar. He checks his watch, his bracelet jangling. He always wears that fucking thing, a heavy gold chain with an ID tag reading 'LOVER' in a big slab serif. Meanwhile, June stares at the portrait Dennis Rossouw did after Katya came third in the New Face of the Year, Catwalk Category.

'It's a nice one, isn't it, June?' I call over. It's taken with a Sinar P2. Large-format camera, I think of adding for her benefit, even though she won't have a clue what the fuck I'm talking about. 'The quality is amazing, don't you think?'

Glenn snorts in derision. I know exactly what he's thinking: Fucking moffie photographer, why doesn't he get a fucking proper job, a man's job?

June finally glances over at me. 'What, Josh? Oh, the picture. Yes,' she says vaguely. I wonder just how medicated she is on any given day. 'I can hardly recognise her.'

'What you talking about, Juney? Can tell a mile away it's her,' Glenn huffs. It always annoys him when June acts concerned about Katya, when she suggests she might be working too hard or eating too little. All Glenn wants for his daughter is success, no matter the personal cost. But of course he's never there to clean up when Kay goes off the rails. That's left to June and me.

Hard as it is to admit it, though, he does love Katya, in some twisted way.

We spent the whole of Saturday night and Sunday just recovering, trying to feel normal: bathing for hours, eating decent food – God, I realised just how much I missed fresh fruit – and watching crap on TV. I could only bring myself to phone June this morning, and, despite the fact that it's a Monday, Glenn blew off an early meeting to come straight here.

I pour boiling water into the plunger. I'm making organic, free-trade Ethiopian. Glenn's one of those blustering nouveau riche bastards: 'Only Colombian is good enough for me, and I have to taste the kids' tears in it.' God, if he knew his coffee was African, he'd probably spit it out.

'What hospital did you say you were at?' Glenn asks.

We've been through all this on the phone already. Another thing I did yesterday was get our story straight. 'I wound up at New Hope. Some mix-up. But then I was transferred to Morningside, where I found Katya.'

'And explain again why I couldn't find you or Kat there? My people called all the clinics, every day.'

As if asking me repeatedly is going to make a difference. I will my heart to stop thumping and pray that my face isn't beginning to sweat. Christ, as obvious as his tactics are, I can see why he uses them – they work.

Not for the first time, I consider dumping rat poison into his coffee and getting him out of my life once and for all. I wouldn't blink, I swear. But if it went wrong, if he lived, I'd be finished. I still don't know what I'm going to do after this. I keep on saying it's going to be all right, that it will work out, but I still don't have a fucking plan.

I force myself to smile benignly at him. 'They had my name wrong. They had me down as Joshua Alphonse. They thought Alphonse was my surname.' I laugh, looking at June, and she smiles back in timid support. She trusts me, I think. 'And Katya, well, you know…'

Katya always books in under an assumed name: when she went to rehab for a week; when her nose wouldn't stop bleeding. Standard practice. They know this as well as I do. I don't have to say any more, and Glenn won't want to pursue this line of questioning. He checks his watch again and huffs, and June pats his hand, gets up and wanders over to the Moroccan mosaic on the mantle. She stands there, her back to us, staring into the inlaid shards of mirror, stretching her cheeks with her fingers. The way her shoulders slope from her neck, that intense, unforgiving scrutiny of herself in that neurotic mirror, that's hereditary; Katya got those genes in spades.

I froth the microwaved milk and bring a tray through to the coffee table.

June returns to the couch and pours two cups. 'How has she been, Josh? You said there was nothing broken?'

'No, thank God. She was lucky. They did a scan and after a few days the swelling on her brain – the haematoma – disappeared. Apart from a few contusions on her face, she's—'

'You didn't say anything about her face!' Glenn roars.

'It's not serious, it's just… Look, she's quite sensitive about it, though, so when you see her—'

'Have they found the kaffir who drove into her?' Glenn interrupts. 'It was a taxi, right?'

That's what I told him. Unroadworthy minibus taxis smash into lots of people and then just drive away, don't they? And they're not registered and you never find the culprit.

'No. The police are still looking.'

'My fucking arse, they are. I'm going to get some of my people onto it and we'll find the motherfucker. Where's her car?'

Shit, I didn't think about that. It's parked downstairs in the tenants' parking lot, completely unscathed. 'Uh, I think it was scrapped. I don't know. I can find out.'

'Hmpf,' Glenn scoffs, slopping his coffee on the carpet as he reaches for more sugar. 'We'll get onto the licensing department.'

'Lovely coffee, Josh,' June says. She hasn't even tasted hers.

'And what about this fight you two had?' Glenn says.

'What fight?' I say innocently.

'Don't fucking play coy with me, arsehole. When you phoned from the hospital, you told June you and Katya'd had a fight. What was it about?'

'It was nothing. Just something stupid.'

'That right?' Glenn says. 'Then tell me this, when we came here the next day, how come there was broken glass and drops of blood on the floor?'

I'm still seething about the fact that they came in here. But now's not the time to make an issue of it. 'You know how Katya gets, Glenn. She was upset, she smashed a glass and we both cut our fingers clearing it up. But it blew over. It was nothing.'

Glenn glares at me, but then his phone beeps and he pulls it out of his pocket, momentarily distracted.

'I hope you don't mind us coming into your apartment uninvited, Josh,' June flutters. 'We were so worried when we couldn't get hold of Katya, and Glenn explained the situation to the building supervisor and he let us in.' Explained the situation in Glenn's inimitable style. I'll bet he fucking did.

Glenn pockets his phone. 'Bit of a coincidence, isn't it?'

'What?'

'Both you and Kat ending up in hospital at the same time? You with the...' He waves his arm vaguely.

'Measles,' I say, swallowing a surge of panic. Fuck, where's he going with this?

'And Katya being hit by a fucking taxi.'

'I don't know what you're trying to—'

'You know exactly what I'm saying,' Glenn says, his toad eyes fixed on mine, his voice dangerously soft. 'If I find out you've hurt my girl, I will fucking kill you.'

'Glenn,' June tuts. 'She had an accident. Josh explained what happened.'

Glenn points a pudgy finger at me, and the LOVER bracelet rattles. 'If I find out different then you know what I'll do to you. Count yourself lucky that she's okay this time. But I tell you one thing, she should be around her family at a time like this, not stuck in this shithole.' He sneers at me as if I'm a bit of crap on his shoe. 'In fact' – he stands up and walks towards the bedroom – 'enough already with the fucking tea party. I'm going to see my daughter, and I'm taking her home.'

'Glenn!' June raises her voice, and I brace for an explosion of rage, but instead he just stops and turns to face us. June cowers, wringing her fingers in her lap. 'Katya doesn't need any upset right now. I'm sure Josh is taking very good care of her. He loves her, which is...'

'What?' he says.

'He loves her,' she almost whispers. 'That's all.'

Glenn tenses and June's hand flies to her mouth as if she wishes she could take the words back. But he thinks better of transporting their usual domestic drama to my flat.

'Joshua,' he says, using my name for sarcastic effect. 'When will my daughter be able to see me?'

'I'm sure she'll be awake soon. Let me just go and check on her, okay?'

'Hurry up.'

I go into the room, pushing the door closed behind me. 'You ready?' I whisper.

She nods and smiles but she's nervous. I should have given her a couple of painkillers, just to take the edge off. It would have been better if she was woozy. Too late now.

'It'll be okay,' I say again, and she settles herself back under the duvet.

I head back to the lounge. 'She's just waking now,' I whisper. 'But be prepared, she's really out of it.' I follow close behind them. 'Katya,' I call softy. 'Your parents are here.'

Glenn's first to the bedside, June close behind. Thank God there's nothing personal on display. The reality of Glenn being in my bedroom never struck me before. June looks up at me and gestures to ask whether she can sit on the edge of the bed. I can't help wondering whether Glenn snooped around here last time he was here, and what he found.

'Kat?' Glenn says, peering down at her. 'It's Daddy. Everything's going to be fine now.'

She's lying in the bed, as if asleep, face pressed between the pillows, her back to us.

'It's Daddy, Pumpkin.'

Glenn steps back and impatiently waves June forward. 'You try.'

June reaches out a hand and gently smoothes the dark hair spread over the pillow. She rouses and turns slowly to face June. My heart stops. Oh, Jesus Christ, I can't watch.

'Oh.' June turns her face away. Without this, there's no next step. Without this, it will never work. 'This is... this is not...'

'What is it?' Glenn leans over June's shoulder. 'Jesus.' He turns away, looking for someone to blame. Finds only me.

'Mom?' she whispers. 'Daddy?'

'I'm here, Kitty-Kat,' Glenn says. But he keeps his distance. Who knew he was squeamish? Not that there's much to see. Not with the dressing covering most of her face.

'Oh, Katya. My God.' Then June is down and hugging her, crying snot into the duvet cover. Overreacting as usual. 'I'm so sorry,' June says.

'Sleepy. Need to sleep.'

'Leave the girl alone, June,' Glenn says. 'The last thing she needs is you crying all over her.'

'It's not as bad as it looks,' I explain. 'I know the dressing looks quite frightening, but really, they say that the scarring will be very limited.'

'Will she be able to work again?'

'Glenn,' June snaps. She turns back to the figure on the bed. 'You just rest, my love, and we'll see you soon, all right?'

But she's already snoring softly.

'Like I said, the painkillers knock her out,' I say. 'She should be fine in a day or so.'

'I just have to... to go and freshen up,' says June, wiping her eyes and disappearing into the bathroom.

Glenn opens his mouth to start laying into me, but then his phone trills and he heads out into the hallway.

When June comes out, she turns to face me with a vacant stare, motionless on the surface but jittering inside like a hive of wasps, synapses spattering and failing all through her mind. I bet she's downed another handful of pills in there.

She turns to Glenn, and without a word to either of us she wanders like a ghost through the hall, unlatches the front door and drifts down the front stairs to the Jag without a backwards glance, like she was never here.

Phone stuck to his ear, Glenn jabs me in the chest. 'You take care of her, you hear? It's Juney's birthday on Wednesday. We'll see you at the house then. Or if she's not up to it we'll all come here.'

'No, no,' I say, trying to kill that idea before it lodges. 'She'll be fine by Wednesday.'

Then he follows his wife out of the apartment, letting the door slam behind him.

I race into the hallway and peer out of the window to watch them driving away. It's only then that I allow myself to relax.

It's over.

A hand on my shoulder. I turn around.

She pulls the dressing from her face, revealing the flawless skin beneath. 'What do you think?' she says. 'Did it go okay?'

'You did great, Lisa. I think we did it.'

Chapter 22

LISA

Thank God that's over.

The nervous sweat that's been dribbling down my sides is drying, and my stomach is starting to unknot itself. I head back to the bedroom and sit down on the bed. Farrell follows me in.

'So what do you think, Lisa? You think we pulled it off? It went okay, right?'

I try to smile reassuringly at him. But the truth is, I'm not sure we did pull it off. Even though half of my face was hidden by the dressing, as Farrell suggested, there was something in Katya's mother's eyes – a flicker of confusion, a flash of horrified disbelief – that makes me think she knew. Still, I liked her; she seemed compassionate. But Farrell was right about the father. He reeked of aftershave and had 'bully' written all over him. The kind of alpha male my father looks up to. The kind of man my father has always wanted to be.

'Fuck it,' Farrell says. 'I need another drink.' He stalks out of the bedroom, slamming the door behind him.

I stand up, take a deep breath and gaze into the bank of full-length mirrors that camouflage the huge, wall-length closet space. The Katya face, framed by the long black wig, stares back at me. I place my hand on my hip, turn around and look at myself over my shoulder.

208

Mirror mirror on the wall, who's the most deluded of them all?

I block out the Dr Meka voice, and concentrate on my reflection, trying to avoid looking too closely at the rest of my body; it spoils the illusion. But my eye keeps being drawn to my thick thighs, heavy shoulders and non-existent ankles.

The face is perfect. It's the rest of me that's hideous.

That all-too-familiar wave of despair threatens to swamp me. How could I ever have thought I could do this?

My point exactly. It's insane.

But I'm not going to give up. I can't – I *won't* – let Farrell down.

I tiptoe to the door and place my ear against it to double-check that he's not coming back in here. There's the faint thump of bass; he must have put a CD on.

I pull open the doors that lead to Katya's walk-in closet and let my fingers trail through the loaded racks of designer clothes. Katya clearly favoured delicate fabrics in jewel colours: short summer dresses, skinny jeans and tiny Barbie-sized tops. I've sneaked in here several times, but I haven't dared try anything on. I riffle through the hangers. The garments – most with labels I've never heard of – still hold a trace of her perfume, Midnight Poison. There's a huge bottle of it in the bathroom, and I sprayed a dab on my wrist yesterday. But on me it smells cloying and slightly sour, as if it clashes with my skin.

I pull out a plain black short-sleeved dress. It's loose and summery, not as skimpy and fitted as the other clothes. There's no label inside it, but I can tell by the fabric's impossible lightness that it must have cost the earth.

I shrug off the T-shirt and sweatpants, and pull it on over my head, praying that it won't rip; praying that it will fit. It does! It's tight around the back and shoulders, but it will do. I turn to the shoe racks, and pick out a pair of soft black wedge heels – the others are all high strappy things I'll never be able to walk in. They're slightly too big, but only by half a size or so.

Now for the moment of truth. I close my eyes, and turn to face the mirror.

Oh God. It's terrible. The dress exaggerates the size of my mottled thighs, and the wedge shoes make my ankles look even thicker.

What did you expect? Those are a dead woman's clothes. And then that old Dr Meka refrain: *You must learn to be happy in your own skin, Lisa.*

Too late for that. And besides, I like this skin better. Especially the face. The beautiful face. I'll concentrate on that. I turn around, smile at myself over my shoulder.

'Hi,' I whisper. 'I'm Katya. Call me Kat. No, call me Kay.'

'Katya hated that dress,' Farrell says from behind me, making me jump. Red heat floods to my cheeks. I've been so absorbed I haven't heard him come in. 'She got it for free after a shoot,' he says. 'Never wore it.'

'God, Farrell, I'm so sorry.'

'What for?'

'I was snooping. I shouldn't have gone through her stuff. Not without your permission.'

'It's fine. You look... You're...' He doesn't finish the sentence. 'I've made lunch. It's getting cold.' He dips his head and leaves the room. Face still burning, I rip the dress off too roughly and it splits under the arms. I kick it away, yank the wig off my head and pull the sweatpants and T-shirt back on.

I tie my hair into a bun at the nape of my neck and hurry through to the living space.

He doesn't look up as I sit down at the breakfast counter. He's made some sort of spicy omelette. It's not the sort of food I'm used to, but my stomach grumbles anyway. I don't dare eat more than two or three bites.

Farrell finally looks up at me. 'Not hungry?'

'I need to lose weight. Katya was way thinner than me.' I remember the slender shape of her body lying in that hospital bed.

'She wasn't. It's just that her bone structure is... was different. Finer.' He glances at my arms. 'You'll have to keep your hands and arms covered, wear long sleeves, that kind of thing.'

I look down before he can see my burning face, pretend to brush crumbs from my T-shirt.

'But on the plus side, at least you're the same height, give or take an inch. That would be a fucking disaster. We can't fake that.'

'You're right,' I say, struggling to smile.

'We can't get too complacent. I think we fooled Glenn, but next time you'll have to watch your voice. You spoke to Katya, didn't you? You know what she sounds like.'

'Yes. But at the time she was...'

What, Lisa? About to die?

For a second the silence is so heavy I'm scared to breathe.

Then he nods. 'You can say it. She died. Those bastards killed her.'

It's the first time he's mentioned anything to do with the Wards since we left, but he must think about it all the time. I know I do. I still haven't figured out why I haven't told him what Katya said to me just before she died. That she was sorry. Something must have happened between them. If he knew that she was sorry, he'd... he'd feel differently about her. Miss her more.

And of course you don't want that, do you, Lisa? You can't compete with a dead woman.

Would it have made a difference if we'd been in the room when that alarm first sounded? When she had her heart attack or whatever it was that killed her?

But what could we have done?

It must have happened quickly. She couldn't have suffered for long. When Farrell and I finally raced in there, minutes after we first heard the alarm, Nomsa was already pulling a curtain around the bed.

'What's happening?' Farrell said. 'What's going on?'

At that stage he seemed calm, in control. And strangely, even though it must have hit me straight away that something awful had happened, I felt oddly distanced from the scene, as if I was watching it on television.

'She's gone,' Nomsa said.

'Gone where?' Farrell said.

Nomsa smiled. 'To the great catwalk in the sky.'

'But... but why? How?'

'Something in her system didn't agree with our medication.'

'What's that supposed to mean?'

Nomsa rolled her eyes. 'She was taking methamphetamine. And cocaine.'

'Not in here, she wasn't!'

'It was still in her system.'

'She was on drugs?' I said.

'Sometimes. They all do it,' Farrell said, something heavy and blank in his voice.

'I'm sorry for your loss,' Nomsa said to him. She didn't sound sorry; she sounded bored.

'She's gone,' Farrell said. And then his face crumpled, his body sagged. For a second I was certain he was going to collapse. 'Oh Katya. Oh God.' He took a step towards her bed, but then seemed to change his mind. He suddenly pushed past me and Nomsa and charged out of the room.

I raced after him.

He weaved down the corridor, punching the wall as he went. 'Fuck it!'

He stumbled into the waiting room and slumped onto the couch, head in his hands.

Someone had switched the TV back on again, and that horrible image of a spider giving birth in the shower cubicle was showing on screen. It looked like part of an advert for some kind of birth control, and I felt relieved that I hadn't realised that the first time I saw it. I snatched up the remote and switched the TV off.

'I'm fucked,' Farrell said. 'I'm fucking fucked.'

I grabbed his arm and squeezed it reassuringly. 'No you're not. It's not your fault.'

He looked up at me, eyes blazing with anger or fear or both. 'You don't get it, Lisa. If I don't bring Katya back home, Glenn will kill me. I mean, *literally* fucking kill me.'

'But why? You just have to explain to him that—'

'*What?* What will I explain? Well, see, Glenn, we were trying to put her *fucking* face back onto her *fucking* head when she *fucking* died because she's a *fucking* drug addict? You don't *explain* things to Glenn, Lisa.'

212

Tears were now streaming down his face. 'God, Katya. No. God. *Fuck!* I loved her, Lisa, I fucking loved her!'

'I'm so sorry, Farrell.'

'I'm dead. What the hell am I going to do?'

'There is another way,' I said. The words popped out. I didn't plan them; it was as if, just for a moment, someone else had actually spoken.

'What?'

'Look at me, Farrell.' We stared at each other for several seconds. Maybe for as long as a minute. 'I can help you.'

We shared another long silence.

'You'd do that for me?' he finally said.

'Yes.' Something shifted in my chest. I was hit with the overwhelming feeling that, if I committed to this, there would be no going back.

'Sorry to intrude,' Nomsa said from the doorway. 'But you have both been discharged. Effective immediately.'

'You mean we can go?' I asked. 'After all we've been through, it's that easy?'

'Of course.' She chuckled. 'This isn't a prison, Client Cassavetes. I've called a taxi for you.'

She held out a plastic bag to Farrell. 'These are yours, Mr Farrell. I said I'd keep them safe for you.' I peeped inside the bag and quickly turned away again. It stank of week-old vomit, but his shoes and belt, his iPhone and wallet were all there.

He ignored her, his arms hanging limply at his sides. I grabbed the bag from her instead. 'What about my things?'

Nomsa laughed. 'Oh I think we both know you won't need them anymore, don't we?'

Still numb with shock, we followed Nomsa silently to the lifts. She waved us inside and stepped back.

'Goodbye. Oh, and don't be a stranger, Mr Farrell.'

Farrell opened his mouth to retort, but then the lift's doors slid shut. In a few seconds they opened straight out into New Hope's casualty ward. We were right back where we started. The plastic waiting-room chairs were full of bar-brawl casualties, homeless people clutching swollen eyes and bloody noses. For a fleeting second I thought I caught a glimpse of a shadowy grey figure sitting among them, but I didn't have time to be sure. Farrell snapped back to life, locked his arm through mine and propelled me towards the exit doors.

I don't know why, but I expected it to be night when we finally got outside. Down there, in the Wards, I'd lost track of time. I stood for a moment, feeling the sun on my skin, and listening to the normal sounds of everyday life: the distant roar of traffic, the mumbled conversation of people heading for casualty. No one tried to stop us. And, true to Nomsa's word, a taxi was waiting for us outside the exit. The driver acknowledged us with a grunt and didn't show any surprise that I was barefoot and dressed only in a short hospital gown. Then we were free and speeding away.

I don't remember Farrell giving the driver directions, but he seemed to know exactly where we were going. We wove through posh residential streets, and pulled up outside one of those chic converted warehouse blocks, freshly painted in dark grey, with bright-red doors and window frames.

'Come on,' Farrell said. He fumbled in his bag for his keys, and it took several attempts for him to find the right one to unlock the security gate.

The apartment was large, open plan. I peered into the darkened kitchen and something on the tiles glinted in the light falling through from the hallway – glass?

'Don't go in there,' Farrell said, steering me away.

'Why?'

'I've just got to… clean up,' he said vaguely.

Face still shut down, Farrell ushered me into a bedroom decked out in turquoise and black. I didn't argue. I was hit with a wave of exhaustion so acute it felt as if someone had whacked me over the head. He pulled back the silky covers, and I slipped between them.

The next thing I knew, Farrell was shaking me awake. 'Lisa!'

'Wha?' I sat up, disorientated. 'What time is it?'

'One.'

'In the morning?'

'Afternoon.'

'How long have I been sleeping?'

'Twenty hours or so.'

'Seriously?'

'Don't worry, you needed it. We both did.'

He looked fresh, his cheeks free of stubble and his clean hair flopping over his forehead. 'We've got work to do today,' he said, 'so rise and shine.'

He dug in the drawers next to the bed, pulling out a pair of baggy grey sweatpants and a black T-shirt. He hesitated and then strode to the chest of drawers on the far side of the room. It was full of diaphanous lingerie. *Her* lingerie. He picked through it and pulled out a pair of simple black lace panties. Without looking at me, he said, 'You can wear these for now. Hurry up and shower. I'll meet you in the kitchen.'

Avoiding my reflection, I stumbled through to the bathroom. The shelves were cluttered with jars and tubs of Clarins and Clinique moisturisers, M.A.C body foundation and skin cleanser and the kinds of shampoos, conditioners and serums you can only buy from top-end hairdressers. Two electric toothbrushes, one blue, one pink, sat side by side in a crystal tumbler above the sink. I pulled off the hospital gown, ran the shower as hot as I could stand, and scrubbed my skin until it was pink.

Then, for the first time since I left the hospital, I gazed at my reflection. Katya stared back at me. I smiled, she smiled. I frowned, she frowned. She was me. I was her. I leaned forward so that my nose was nearly touching the glass, drinking in every inch of the smooth, olive skin. My new lips, eyelids, eyelashes, that gloriously tiny nose, the new bone structure.

Trying not to think too deeply about what I was doing, I slipped on the panties, which were slightly too small, and put on the baggy pants and T. I found a brush on the nightstand next to the bed – straight black hair still twirled in its tines – and brushed my fringe back from my face. I was ready.

Farrell was waiting for me in the kitchen-cum-lounge, a clutter-free sun-filled room with spotless stainless steel worktops and black-and-white floor tiles. He was sitting at the breakfast bar, his MacBook open on the counter in front of him.

'Better?' he said. He pushed a mug of coffee towards me. 'Now. First things first. You need to get hold of your family. Let them know you're okay.'

'Why?'

'Just in case they start searching for you. We don't need that shit right now.'

'Isn't that a bit paranoid?'

'We have to be paranoid. It's the only way to get through this.'

He stood behind me while I clicked onto my Gmail account. I shifted uncomfortably on the stool. There was only a single unopened message in my inbox. Even the spambots didn't think I was worth it. The message was from Dad, the subject line: 'Where are you?'.

There was no message.

'What shall I put?' I asked.

'Say you've met someone. That he's not to worry, that kind of thing. It's not much of a lie, after all.' Farrell tried to smile convincingly, but didn't quite succeed. At least he tried.

I typed in: 'Hi Dad. I'm well and happy. I've met someone and moved in with him, so don't worry about me. Please send my love to Sharon. Love, Lisa'.

Without hesitating, I pressed 'Send'. A lump formed in my throat and I had to blink furiously to hold back the tears.

'Sorry,' I said to Farrell, wiping my eyes.

'What for? You're doing great.' He put his hand on my shoulder, and my heart doubled its pace.

'Now. Here's the way I see it. We have to convince Glenn that Katya's alive and well. We can't say she's been in rehab again: that's the first place Glenn would have checked. I'm thinking maybe she – you, I mean – was in an accident. Knocked over by one of those gung-ho taxis or something. That would explain where she's been. You'll only have to see Glenn a couple of times, and then I'm thinking we can tell him you're going off to South America for a shoot – Katya's scheduled to go to Rio next month anyway – and then you can just disappear.'

'But where will I go?'

'Up to you. Think about it. A whole new start. I've got some cash. Not much, but enough to get you started.'

It was on the tip of my tongue to say that I didn't want a new start. I wanted to stay with him.

'With luck we can make this work. We've got a few things going for us. It's good that you're about the same height. And the hair's not an issue, Katya's got a whole bunch of made-to-order wigs.'

'She has?'

'Sure. Tricks of the trade. In case she gets a bad haircut or has a bad-hair day.'

He leaned down and gazed into my eyes. 'Your eyes are a bit lighter, but we'll get away with it for now. Katya often wears dark glasses, even indoors.' He made me bare my teeth. 'That's okay. Don't smile too often.'

It went on and on. Katya doesn't bite her nails. Katya doesn't do that with her hair. Katya never wears lipstick, only lip gloss. Katya wouldn't dare leave the house without mascara.

It was exhausting. But the worst was to come.

'This will help,' he said. He pushed the computer towards me.

There she was, filling the screen. She was dressed in a tiny red bikini, her tanned skin glowing in the sunlight, her lean flesh on display. She was dancing across a white beach, laughing and mugging for the camera, a million miles from the bandaged sobbing wreck I'd met in the hospital.

He cleared his throat. 'I filmed this when we were in Bali last year.'

I could hear Farrell's voice saying, 'You look gorgeous, baby.'

Then Katya's laugh, filling the kitchen as if she was actually back from the dead.

'Watch it again.'

Fighting back the tears, I did as he said.

After that he made me practise certain words over and over again. She used the words 'darling' and 'fuck' liberally, often ended a sentence with 'don't you agree?'. Her laugh was deep and sexy. Farrell suggested that I speak in a whisper whenever possible, to mask the differences in our voices. He also made me practise her straight-backed, slightly splay-

217

footed walk, coaxing me out of my habit of hunching my back and curling into myself.

'Katya expects everyone to look at her when she enters a room,' he said. 'And they do.'

I didn't tell him that, until recently, that was my worst nightmare.

'Lisa?'

I've been pushing a sliver of red pepper around my plate, lost in thought. 'Sorry, Farrell. Were you saying something?'

'You okay?'

'Yes. I'm fine.'

He stands up. 'I'll have to go to the studio, show my face. I'll bring back some fake tan to sort out those pale areas. And try not to bite your nails, okay?'

There's another subject we've been avoiding. But we can't ignore it forever. 'Farrell, aren't you worried about... I mean, about what they want you to do?'

'They?'

'The people... whoever they were, back in that... place.'

I wait for him to speak. He doesn't.

'I know we can't go to the police or anything, not now...' I don't need to finish the sentence. 'But shouldn't you at least—'

'We can talk about this later. I've got to go. And don't open the door, whatever you do.' He grabs his keys and leaves.

I take a sip of coffee. It's cold and tastes like bile. It's the first time I've been alone in the house. Katya's ghost is everywhere: in the photographs that line the walls, the piles of fashion magazines slotted into custom-made racks, the clothes, the beauty products, the lingering trace of perfume. *She* must have sat here where I'm sitting now. Eaten breakfast. Made coffee.

Made love to Farrell in that bed you're sleeping in, Lisa.

A chill dances across my skin at the thought.

The intercom buzzer blares, making me jump.

Oh God. What now?

What if it's Glenn?

Maybe June's convinced him that the woman in the bed isn't actually his little girl after all.

It buzzes again, this time in a long, continuous blast. Whoever's there is holding their finger down on the button.

I can't listen to that for much longer. Not without going mad.

Too late.

Unsure that I'm doing the right thing, I press the answer button, take a deep breath and say, 'Yes?'

A woman's voice barks, 'Who's that?'

'It's... Katya.'

'Kat? Kat, it's me!'

'Who?'

'Noli, for fuck's sake. Let me in, girl. I saw him leave, it's totally cool.'

Christ. This Noli must be one of Katya's friends. What the hell should I do? If I don't let her in, it could look suspicious.

I'm about to press the gate-release button when, with a jolt, I remember that I'm not wearing the wig.

'One second,' I whisper into the intercom.

Heart thudding, I race into the bedroom. I grab the wig and pull it over my hair, making sure there are no blonde strands visible, then root in Farrell's ordered closet for a hoodie or cardigan, something with sleeves long enough to hide my arms and hands. I unearth a sweatshirt and carefully put it over my head without dislodging the wig.

The buzzer goes again. God!

I check my reflection. It will have to do.

Hands shaking, I open the door to an astoundingly tall and beautiful black woman, her hair shorn to her scalp. She's dressed in heels and a tiny shift dress that barely covers her thighs.

She looks me up and down, eyes brimming with horror. '*Fuck*, Kat. You look like shit.'

She grips my shoulders, air-kisses both sides of my face, and sweeps past me in a cloud of nicotine and perfume, heading straight for the lounge.

'What in the hell happened, Kat? I've been calling and texting you like a motherfucker.'

'I was in an accident,' I whisper.

'Yeah. That's what Glenn said. God. What's wrong with your voice? Why you whispering?'

'Damaged my vocal cords.'

'In the accident?'

I nod.

She looks at me dubiously, then shrugs. She flounces down on the couch and crosses her legs. 'Now, I want to know everything.'

'Not much to tell.'

'Fuck, Kat. Glenn said a taxi hit you or something? When you didn't show up I was seriously worried.'

'Show up?'

'Yeah. You were supposed to meet me. Don't you remember?'

I shake my head.

'That night. We were supposed to hook up at Harley's. This is getting weird. You hurt your head or something?'

'Something like that.'

'Hang on. Have you got that... whatdoyoucallit? Amnesia? Where you can't remember stuff?'

'Um...' Why not? 'Slightly. It's as if my memories are all jumbled up.'

'Ja. I got you.' She laughs again. 'Like after a late night, right? She sighs. 'Fucking taxi drivers. But apart from that, you're okay now, right?'

I nod again. She uncrosses her legs and leans towards me, peering at my face. 'You wearing contacts?'

Oh God. 'No.'

She shakes her head. 'Must be the light. And who did your make-up this morning, girl? A blind man?'

She laughs, digs in her bag and pulls out a box of cigarettes. She pops one in her mouth and passes the box to me.

'No thanks.'

'Fuuuuuck. You quit?'

I hesitate. What would Katya do? Farrell hadn't mentioned that she smoked. Trying to keep my hands hidden beneath the sleeves, I tentatively pull out a cigarette. Noli chucks her slender gold lighter to me. It takes me several attempts before I figure out I have to inhale before it will catch.

'God, girl,' she says, shaking her head in disgust. 'You really are in a mess, aren't you?'

I take an experimental puff, trying not to inhale too deeply. It tastes revolting. Noli is flicking her ash straight into my coffee cup; there's no sign of an ashtray anywhere.

I take a deeper drag, fighting not to gag.

'That's my girl,' Noli says. 'Now listen. What the fuck are you still doing here?'

'I don't... I don't know what you mean.'

'Whoa. Okay, listen, Kat. Seriously. I can see you're not yourself, but come on.'

I don't trust myself to speak.

Noli sighs. 'Christ. Look, when you called me, just before the accident, you said you were going to leave Josh.'

'I was?'

'Ja. Like, *finally*. You'd had a big fight, said that this was it. Finished and klaar.'

'Really?'

'Okay, now I know you're seriously fucked in the head.'

'Just humour me, Noli,' I say, trying to sound like the woman in the video image – confident, sure of herself, used to being obeyed.

Noli lights another cigarette, drops the butt of the last in my coffee cup. 'Well, you said his controlling behaviour was getting worse. That he would hardly let you take a shit without his approval.'

'I did?'

'Ja. And when he started picking out your clothes and telling you which jobs you could or couldn't take, and when he started freaking out every time you had an itty bitty hit, you decided enough was enough.'

'That doesn't sound that bad.'

'Girl? You crazy? He was ruling your life. You had to sneak off to even see me. He'd phone you, like, twenty times a day, to check where you were. So, what I'm saying is, the offer still stands. You need a place to stay, you can come stay with me.'

'Thanks.' I drop the vile cigarette stub into the cup where it dies with a hiss. 'Did he ever... you know. Hit me?'

'Nah. Well, you never said. And he insisted you looked perfect all the time. You seriously don't remember? Okay. In the beginning you used to get up early, put on your make-up, get back into bed. So that when he woke up you'd be all, like, perfect. You were honestly buying into fucked-up shit like that. God, I can't believe you can't remember any of this.'

'But, since the accident, he's been so... nice.'

'Yeah? Well I'm just saying, girl. Watch your back.' She stands up, adjusts her dress with a wiggle. 'It'll all come back to you in time.'

I walk her to the door and she steps forward and enfolds me in her arms. 'Sheesh, girl, your tits get bigger or something?' She stands back. 'You're not pregnant, are you?'

'No!'

'Anyway, must fly. Hey, I got the Miss Sixty gig, how cool is that?'

'That's great, Noli.'

For a second she really looks at me, her eyes narrowing suspiciously. 'Call me, yeah?' she says.

I let her out of the townhouse, and lean my forehead against the door.

That was way too close.

Now will you see sense, Lisa?

Chapter 23

FARRELL

I'm trying hard to pretend everything's normal, but it feels like a lifetime since I last sat at this desk. A different life, in fact. Out of habit, I log on to my MindRead dashboard, but it all seems trivial to me now. I don't give a shit what these chattering people are talking about, or understand how I ever did.

Lizzie brings me my coffee.

'Thanks,' I say, and she smiles and turns away, just as she always has. 'Wait,' I say. 'Lizzie. Sit. You mind?'

'No,' she says, 'of course not.'

'Everyone's looking at me, like, I don't know, like I'm contagious or something.'

She smiles. 'It was scary, when you collapsed.'

'It was just measles.'

'You still look a bit rough though, Farrell. Are you okay?' She hesitates. 'I mean with Katya as well. Is everything all right?'

'Yeah. Sorted out. She's... you know.'

'Farrell?'

'Ja?'

'I'm so sorry that you were taken to No Hope. I swear, I should have taken you to Morningside myself.'

'It's fine. It's all sorted out now.'

Eduardo strolls into the studio wearing sandals and plus-fours, carrying lunch in a pretentious brown bag. He spots me at my desk. 'Farrell! Amico! You're back,' he yells in his faux continental accent. He's a fucking Portuguese boy from Edenvale, not a catwalk fixer from Milan or whatever he passes himself off as. But that's our little secret. Over the years he's kept some of mine. 'I would have fired that Mike bastardo, but he did the job himself. Never came back to work. But listen, listen, we're going to help you deal with what happened.' Knowing his management style, this means he'll probably arrange a group therapy session or a seance or something.

'Thanks, but I was just sick. A virus, that's all. I'm fine. Really. I just want to get back to work.' Lizzie notices me minimising my MindRead screen as he passes me en route to his office.

I don't even know where to start to 'deal with what happened'. But here at the office, away from hospitals and bandages and masks – and away from her – at least I have a bit of space to myself.

This afternoon I should really be getting back to annotating the Camps Bay Slick shoot, and I try to lose myself in the images on the screen.

'Phone!' Lizzie calls from her cubicle.

'Who is it?'

'Doctor somebody, sorry, didn't catch the name. From the Media Park medical centre.'

Finally. The first thing I did on Saturday afternoon while Lisa slept was head to the clinic to get a full check-up and blood tests. I didn't care that I had to pay weekend rates; I needed to know that whatever they'd done to me hadn't caused any permanent damage.

I snatch the receiver up.

'Mr Farrell, Dr Traverso here. How are you feeling today?'

'Fine. Better, anyway. Are the blood test results in?'

He harrumphs. 'I'll get to that in a minute. How is your vision?'

'Great.' Thank God for that, at least. The images on screen are sharp and crisply defined; I'm still able to doctor a single pixel on the fly. Whatever else that fucked-up Nurse Nomsa might have done, she at least gave me the right drugs. Dr Traverso confirmed that Maxitrol was the appropriate medication. If it wasn't for her, maybe my eyes wouldn't have healed at all.

'And the test results?' I prompt him.

He hesitates. 'Well, your white-cell count is normal, which indicates that the infection is no longer in your system; liver count's good, protein's fine, mm-hmm, mm-hmm. So you're looking fine. But I must tell you, the bloodwork findings did reveal some other... oddities.'

'Like what?'

'It's probably nothing you should worry about, Mr Farrell, there don't seem to be any serious side effects. But it would help if you could tell me the name of the doctor or doctors who treated you at New Hope.'

I almost laugh out loud. *Doctors, Dr Traverso? In No Hope? I don't think so. Maybe you should speak to my butcher.* 'Um... Can I get back to you on that? I don't remember... I'll have to look them up.'

'No problem. And we'd like to schedule some follow-up tests at your convenience.'

Christ. The last thing I want to do is go back to a fucking doctor's room. I'll make an appointment as soon as things have settled down here. For now, as long as my eyes are fine, I'll get by.

'I don't know *what* they were giving you in there,' he's saying. 'But I'd really like to know what they had in mind.'

No you wouldn't, Doctor. If I tell him, he'll think I'm insane. I mumble something about calling him back and hang up.

What the fuck was that place? I'm still not sure. Could an illegal organ-harvesting ring be so slick and organised? That's a fucking scary prospect. It's probably the black ops of the medical-aid or pharmaceutical companies. And what's scary is that there must be experimentation like that going on all the time. It's a massive industry. Drug trials are just the tip of the iceberg. I must have signed whatever authorisation they needed when I was out of it. Jesus, what a nightmare. But at least there's some explanation.

But an experimental face transplant? On a perfectly healthy woman? The idea of Katya's perfection being so needlessly destroyed... that I cannot fucking understand. And what the hell happened to her before the corrective surgery? How could she have crashed so badly? Could it really have just been the coke? That's what Nomsa seemed to blame it on, but I wasn't really listening. I *knew* she was still using, but I refuse to feel guilty. We've been over it a hundred times; she has to make her own decisions. She's a fucking adult.

Was.

Was a fucking adult.

I'm still struggling to accept that she's dead. That this time she won't come back.

'Josh? You okay?' I look up at Lizzie, my vision blurred.

I wipe my eyes with the back of my arm. 'Yes. Sorry.'

'More coffee?'

'Thanks.'

And what about this Mike guy? The one who apparently delivered me to New Hope and then disappeared? He must have been working for them. Should I get on to HR and track down his CV? Fuck, what would be the point now? Eduardo said he's long gone.

I turn back to the photos on my screen. Blue sea and palm trees. The interns will airbrush out the litter and the hobos.

It doesn't make it any easier to accept that Katya's dead when her face is still living in my apartment. That Lisa's a strange woman. She's so unconfident; it's irritating how she curls into herself. If she just stood up straight and pushed her chest out, wore some decent clothes, she wouldn't have any reason to feel ugly. This morning, in Katya's summer dress and trying on some black wedges, her legs didn't look too bad. Not toned, of course, but long and a decent shape. When I walked in and she was wearing one of Kay's wigs, I remembered a photo June showed me of Kay as a kid, twelve, maybe thirteen years old. All long legs and puppy fat. Seeing Lisa like that, it made me wonder what Kay would have looked like if she hadn't wanted to model – if Glenn hadn't wanted her to model. Probably a lot like Lisa. In body shape, at least.

Now, I don't know, it would almost be like taking that young Katya and giving her a second chance. If it wasn't for that fucking pig, Glenn. And

June, his pathetic little enabler. Just because she's nice to me doesn't mean she's not as much to blame for what happened to Katya.

That's right. If they weren't the crap parents they are, Katya wouldn't have started taking drugs in the first place. She wouldn't be dead. The fucking miserable bastards make me sick.

I realise I'm about to snap my stylus and get up before I break anything. I climb the stairs to the mezzanine deck and grab a sparkling water out of the fridge. A group from design is sitting on two of the couches looking at a set of pozzies. A couple of them smile across at me.

And what exactly *am* I going to do with Lisa? Katya's Sedal shoot in Brazil is not until next month – three weeks away. Christ. Can we fake it for that long? Maybe I could tell Glenn and June that a designer's booked her for Rio Fashion Week as an in-house model, and they need her in a week or so for preliminary fittings. That way they'd believe that she'd be away for two, maybe even three months. That would give me some time to make a proper plan.

Say we have a big farewell at the airport, make sure that Glenn's convinced that she's off on a long trip. Then Lisa emails Glenn and says she's staying in South America, she's dumped me and is living with Enrique fucking Iglesias. But that would never work; Glenn will just jump on an aeroplane to see her.

Fuck. It has to be a permanent plan. Glenn's *always* going to be up my nose. He's always going to want to see her. Lisa can't be Katya forever. And something about the way June looked at Lisa this morning makes me nervous. I don't know if she bought it. If she says anything to Glenn, he'll be straight round, probably with a couple of his heavies. If he finds out what's really happened, he's going to kill me and Lisa. Twice.

I hear myself giggle, but it's panicked hysteria. *Jesus*, I'm still in so much shit. I shouldn't have listened to Lisa when she suggested the plan in the first place; it's insane. But what else could I have done?

One step at a time. I invoke my calming mantra as I walk back to my desk. If I can get Lisa to South America for a couple of months, at least I'll buy myself some time. It's the best I can do for now. And in the meantime, before she goes, I'll have to work harder at turning Lisa into Katya, because we're going to have to see Glenn and June again – there's that fucking birthday dinner on Wednesday. We'll have to go. If we start making excuses, June will just get more suspicious.

Lizzie approaches with my coffee, a man in a suit following closely behind her. 'Mr Farrell, you have a visitor.' *Mr Farrell?* She obviously thinks this is someone important, and is bringing her A-game: the attentive and professional personal assistant. Who the fuck is he, anyway? He's wearing a fedora for God's sake, even though they went out in the nineties. The suit he's wearing isn't cheap, but it's badly cut. Unremarkable face, no product. Seiko watch. Barker shoes, polished but not glistening. Too out of touch for a designer or creative. Too badly tailored to be a fashion rep. Too smart to be a cop or a taxman. He might be an advertising sales rep.

'Thanks, Ms Gebhart,' I say. 'Please, sit,' I say to the man and shove some papers aside so that he has some desk space in front of him.

'Mr Joshua Alphonse Farrell?'

Lizzie snickers on her way back to her station, but I'm suddenly skewered by a stave of ice. Nobody, except for those bastards in that experimental fucking clinic, ever uses my middle name.

'That's me. How can I help?'

'I'm Node Agent Rosen, associated with Mutual Medical Shortfall Insurance.' He extends his hand and only his thumb and ring finger are intact. His index finger and middle finger are lopped at the first joint. His little finger is missing altogether.

I feel like I've just woken up again, as if I just dreamed coming home. My face is instantly sheened with cold sweat. I glance around me; I'm still in the studio. Lizzie looks across at me and I smile weakly at her. She watches me with concern for a few seconds then turns back to her screen.

He's still holding his hand out. I can't bring myself to touch him. I pretend to reach out my hand and hammishly knock a pile of prints off the desk. I bend to pick them up, taking my time. I look up briefly, then drop down again. That folder he's just placed on the desk. That's the fucking contract I signed in the clinic. Jesus. This can't be happening. I pray for a hole to open up in the floor, but nothing happens, and eventually I have to surface.

He's smiling at me expectantly, apparently unfazed by my rudeness.

'Why I'm here, Mr Farrell, is because you haven't yet met with a node agent, so I have come for a courtesy consultation. I hope this is a convenient time for you. I would have called, but it appears the numbers you left are out of operation.' Of course they are. I just made up any fucking number when I was filling in the form. He smiles across at me, mutilated hand lying like a claw on the folder. 'Just as well we know where you work and live,' he says. The smile snaps off. 'You have your copy of the contract?' he continues.

'Uh. It's at home.' One of the first things I did when I got home was chuck it in the wheelie bin outside the apartment. It was just a scam. I just signed it to play their game and get out of there. It was just a fucking *scam*.

The fact that this mutilated man – so clearly one of *them* – is sitting across from me in *my* office, in *my* life, makes me want to vomit. I feel like I'm going to have a heart attack.

'Everything okay, Mr Farrell?' Lizzie says, walking over to us.

'Uh, um. Maybe just... maybe... Can you bring some water please?'

'Anything to drink, Mr Rosen?' she asks, flashing me a look of concern as she does so.

'Oh, no thanks, miss. I won't retard you.'

'Excuse me?' she says.

He smiles blandly at her, and with a shrug she heads up the stairs to the fridge. 'I can tell it's not an optimal juncture to meet, Mr Farrell. You're busy. I just wanted to introduce myself. I am here to help you understand your contract and your obligations to the Mutual Medical Shortfall Insurance Donor Swap Programme.' He pauses and smiles in a way that's probably intended to be reassuring. Despite my panic, it is. 'We understand that the rehabilitation period is a difficult one and this is why we offer a lengthy interest-free settlement period. Your contract specifies... Let me recall...' He pages through the folder. 'Here. You have until Thursday, your calendar, to deliver. Ample time. I am here to serve and aid you, Mr Farrell. I will help you understand anything you need to know.'

Rosen stands up, removes his hat and smoothes his hair with his claw before pushing the green folder across to me. 'All my contact details are in the pack, as is a copy of your signed contract. All the terms are listed in detail there. Please peruse them and don't waver to contact me. Once you are ready to arrange payment, I personally will facilitate your deliverance. Have a nice day, and please, recover well.'

He turns to leave as Lizzie arrives with the water.

'Remember, Mr Farrell,' he says, 'Mutual Medical Shortfall Insurance is everywhere you are.'

It's close to seven when I finally make it home. The hallway and lounge are shadowed and gloomy. I turn on the lights.

'Hello?' I call. 'Lisa?'

Nothing.

'Lisa? You here?'

She's probably just taking a shower, but an uneasy feeling gnaws at me. Not panic, exactly, but the sense that something is wrong. It's too quiet.

'Lisa?' I call as I walk towards the bedroom. She might be sleeping. That's it. Why not? I turn on the passage sconce and peer into the bedroom. The bed's neatly made.

I hear a muffled sob.

'Lisa?' I whisper. I turn into the room.

Katya's crumpled in the doorway of the walk-in closet. She's sitting with her legs folded under her, her back turned to me. All I see is her black hair cascading down over her back, the pale points of her elbows, the soles of her feet.

'Katya?'

She's crying, her head bowed into her hands in front of her, a discreet shuddering you wouldn't even notice if you weren't looking closely.

'Kay? Is that—'

'Uh-mm.' A big snort, and she turns to face me. And, although I'm shunted back into the present, and while I know this is Lisa sitting in front of me, she looks so much like Katya. The way she's crying. The way Katya would collapse into a little ball when it got too much, the way she'd shed everything she'd learned and become a little girl again. I will Lisa to stay sitting just like that in one of Katya's wigs, crying, making Katya's sounds, tears smearing Katya's eyeliner over Katya's face. I kneel down next to her and hold her, smelling her familiar perfume, feeling her warm breath against my chest, the snot smearing from Katya's nose onto my shirt.

'What's the matter, sweetheart?'

'I can't do it, Farrell.'

'Call me Josh.' I close my eyes, and I've time travelled. I never want to come back.

She raises her arms and wraps them tight around me. 'I can't do it,' she repeats, hiding her face deeper in my shirt.

'Can't do what?'

'I can never be her.' She pulls away from me now.

'What do you mean?'

'She was beautiful.' I say nothing. 'I... I can't even look at myself. It's... it's like painting a... bloody pig with lipstick. It's filthy. It's disgusting. It's not even making a monster. It's just a stupid joke.'

'What is?' I know what she's talking about, but what am I supposed to say? 'What do you mean?'

She looks up at me. 'Oh, come on, Farrell! Josh. Whatever. Nobody's ever going to believe I'm a model. I'm bloody ugly.' She plants her face back into my shirt.

Christ, this is all I need now. Lisa's got to go with the fucking plan. There's no way she can opt out now. If she loses focus, I'm dead.

I've done this countless times before in the studio, preening the egos of unconfident girls. If only Lisa knew that even the swimsuit models have doubts. The biggest doubts. And the deepest habits to block them out.

'You want to know what I see?' I say, using the speech I've used a thousand times before. 'I see a beautiful, sad woman. A woman who needs to look at herself and see what the world sees.' I gently detach her arms and try to swivel her round to face the mirror set into the far side of the closet behind her. Lisa's found the light switch that illuminates it. Katya used to spend hours there, polishing away every blemish, smoothing herself to perfection. 'Take a look, Lisa. Really look.'

She resists, I try to push harder, and she fights like a cat being forced into water. I let her go and she jumps up out of my grip with a feral squeal. She stands over me, her long legs planted into the floor, her back resolutely towards the mirror. She's wearing a green T-shirt of mine and a pair of Katya's baggy pink satin pyjama shorts. It's a fucking awful ensemble.

'That's all I've been doing since I got here. I've been standing here, looking at myself in the mirror' – she pulls a bundle of silk from a shelf and throws it at me – 'tearing your beautiful girlfriend's beautiful clothes.'

'Hang on—'

'Don't you get it, Farrell? I'm a *Fat. Ugly. Pig.* What the... *fuck...* are you doing with me?'

I've never seen Lisa this worked up, but anger really suits her. It makes her taller, tauter, sexier somehow. I was right all along. There's something to work with here.

I stand up. 'It's your turn to listen to me, Lisa.' I grab her shoulders, spin her to face the mirror, then clamp her around the chest with my arm. She's writhing and thrashing her head around as if I'm trying to force poison down her throat.

'What do you see?' I demand. '*What do you see?*'

She realises that I'm not going to release her and stops struggling. In the mirror, I see her open her eyes. She looks at us for a moment, expressionless. Then she closes her eyes again and goes limp and cold. I let her go. Without a word, she turns and leaves the closet. She pulls some tracksuit pants and a sweater out of my chest of drawers, runs into the bathroom and slams the door behind her. I hear the shower spurting.

Fuck. She's insane; she's never going to believe the truth.

But the fact remains, I *can't* have her drifting around in baggies. She's *got* to be Katya, until Katya leaves for South America. If she doesn't get her shit together, I'm finished. We're supposed to be having dinner with Glenn in two days. If she acts like this, it's over.

I stand there for a moment and look at myself in the mirror. I look okay, better than most, I'd say. I'm toned, I keep my skin healthy. I trim my nails and cut my hair. I know my failings too. But I have a realistic picture of myself.

And no matter how messed up the girls at work are, whatever the reasons, they *always come back to work*. Lisa has *got* to come back to work.

I follow her into the bathroom. She can't see me through the cubicle glass but I let her know I'm there. 'Lisa,' I say.

Nothing.

'Lisa.'

'Farrell? Please get out.' Her voice is tense.

'No.' A moment more, then the water goes off. Her dark-blonde hair trails down heat-pink skin. She plucks the towel from the top of the shower door and wraps herself in it. Finally she steps out of the shower. Her face is rigid as she grabs another towel from the rail, turns her back and winds her hair into it.

'Will you let me get dressed?' she asks in a horrible, toneless voice.

I do the only thing I can. I pull her towards me and kiss her on the mouth. I expect her to flinch away, but I'm surprised at how her body relaxes. Her tongue tentatively slips inside my mouth. Then she stops herself, goes rigid, and I draw her closer and move my hands over her back and sides. A brief hesitation, but soon her hands follow as if she's learning from me.

I open my eyes for a second and see Lisa gazing into the mirror over my shoulder with a look of surprise in her eyes. She doesn't look away.

The towel drops to the floor and she wraps one of her legs around my back and sinks back against the shower stall.

That's the spirit, Lisa.

Chapter 24

LISA

An endless line of rush-hour traffic stretches in front of us, and we're
forced to crawl along bumper to bumper. I relax my grip on the present
on my lap. My sweaty palms have left blotch marks on the wrapping
paper, and it's beginning to look tatty and crumpled.

I just want this evening to be over. The dread is making me feel physically sick, and Farrell's not doing much better. He's clutching the
steering wheel so tightly that his knuckles shine white, and dark circles
bruise the skin around his eyes. Neither of us got much sleep last night.
After we'd made love, we both lay staring at the ceiling, lost in our own
thoughts, and instead of spooning his body against mine like he did the
night before, he turned away from me and curled into himself.

'Now remember,' he says, as a minibus taxi that's been haring along the
hard shoulder cuts in front of us, 'the sister, Marina, is the smartest of the
lot of them and she's always been jealous of you – of Katya – so just
watch yourself around her. I'll try to keep the conversation neutral. Katya
wasn't one for small talk anyway.'

'What does she look like? Marina, I mean.'

'God. She's a dog. Nothing like Kay. Kay got all the looks. And Clive,
her husband, is a complete prick.'

'What does Marina do for a living?'

Farrell shrugs. 'They're both in investment banking or some shit. And June's mother will probably also be there. They all call her Gran-Gran. You don't have to worry about her. She's senile. They wheel her out of hospital every now and then on special occasions.'

For the thousandth time I wish we could have come up with an excuse. But Farrell's adamant that it would look weird if we didn't show up.

My stomach cramps. 'God, Farrell. I don't think I can do this.'

He slaps the steering wheel. 'How many more times? Call me Josh.'

'Sorry.'

He glances at me, smiles apologetically, leans over and squeezes my knee. 'No, *I'm* sorry, Lisa.' I smile back at him. I'm always expecting him to slip up and call me Katya. But apart from that one time when he caught me crying he hasn't, and little by little I've started to convince myself that it's me he sees when he's touching me late at night, and not her. He's been patient with me. Caring and gentle. Nothing like the controlling man Noli described when she came to the apartment. She was probably just jealous. Probably wants Farrell for herself.

'You'll be fine,' Farrell says. 'I told Glenn you're still feeling weak. Not yourself. We'll show our faces and get out of there asap. And just think, after this is over, we can...'

'We can what?'

'We'll be fine. It's almost over.'

He hasn't mentioned his plan of shipping me – Katya – off to a shoot in South America again. I can't squash the hope that he'll let me stay. That he wants me to stay.

I pull down the sun visor and check my make-up and the dressing over my right cheek. It's smaller than the one Farrell applied when Katya's parents came to see me – her – on Monday. 'Do I look okay?'

'You look fine.'

Farrell insisted I wear one of Katya's long, floaty summer dresses and a pair of strappy high heels. The dress is slightly too tight around the chest, which doesn't help my nervous nausea, but with a long-sleeved cardigan covering my fake-tanned arms it should be good enough.

Farrell indicates, turns and draws to a stop at an intersection. A guy in a cabriolet next to us ogles me. Colour floods into my cheeks, I still can't get used to being stared at. Yesterday's trip to the Highgate Mall was an absolute nightmare. It was the first time I'd been out of the house and I didn't realise just how much attention my new face would attract. It was like being under a microscope; strangers' eyes tracking my every move. Eventually I couldn't take it anymore. The relentless assessing looks – some pervy and greedy, but most jealous and bitter – sapped my strength and I had to slip into the ladies and lock myself into a stall to stifle a panic attack. I don't know how I'm ever going to get used to it.

You made your bed, Lisa. You made your choice.

I'm getting better at smothering the Dr Meka voice and I push it out of my head. I don't need that right now.

'You think the present is okay?' It had taken me ages to find something suitable, before I finally settled on a blue silk Christian Dior scarf that I thought would match June's eyes.

'I'm sure it's perfect,' Farrell says. We cruise into a wide, sloping road, leaving the clogged traffic behind. We pass a townhouse estate flanked by towering columns, a massive building that resembles the Parthenon and, next to a bright-orange hacienda house, the shell of a half-built townhouse, weeds forcing their fingers into the crumbling brickwork.

Farrell draws up to a colossal pair of copper gates embedded in a massive wall topped by a nine-strand electric fence. A security guard with angry eyes emerges from his wooden booth and finally acknowledges us. The gates slide open, revealing a curving driveway leading up to an enormous Tuscan-style mansion surrounded by a manicured, emerald-green lawn. As we glide towards the house I catch the wink of blue from a swimming pool partially hidden behind the silhouettes of statues and towering palm trees. I picture Katya lounging by that pool; I imagine her perfect body sliding through that water.

I'm totally out of my depth, and I fight to hold back the tears. How would it look if I arrived with mascara dribbling down my cheeks?

Farrell parks behind a silver Jaguar and pats my knee. 'Deep breath, Lisa. You can do this. You know you can.'

'But what if...?'

'Come on. Let's get it over with. Don't worry. Glenn will be half pissed by now anyway.'

The museum-size front door slams opens and Glenn appears on the front step, clutching a half-full glass of whisky. He's wearing a loose white shirt, the open neck showing off several gold chains, and he has a thatch of grey chest hair.

'Kitty-Kat!' he calls.

Farrell steadies me as I totter up the steps on the too-high heels. Ignoring him completely, Glenn pulls me forward and wraps his arms around me. He stinks of whisky. I don't like the way he squeezes my side. It's too intimate and it's all I can do not to squirm out of his grasp.

'How's my best girl?' he breathes into my ear.

Meaty arm still wrapped around my waist, he leads me inside. Oh my God. It's an act of will to keep my mouth from dropping open. We're in a double-volume hallway, the floor a gleaming expanse of white marble shot through with veins of shocking pink, the walls painted to look like crumbling plaster. A chandelier the size of a small car hangs from the ceiling, and a statue of Venus peeks from behind a plant pot spewing silk orchids. An enormous oil painting of a white stag gazing over fields of bright-green countryside dominates one entire wall.

It's beautiful.

Glenn finally loosens his grip around my waist and steps back to assess me. 'You're looking better, Kitty-Kat. Knew you'd bounce back. It's in the genes, my girl.'

'Thanks,' I whisper. I really *really* don't want to say the word 'Dad'. My father may not win any prizes for Dad of the Year, but it still feels like a betrayal.

Glenn narrows his piggy eyes. 'Why you still talking like that? You still sick?'

Farrell nods. 'I told you she wasn't a hundred per cent, Glenn. She's still got a touch of laryngitis.'

'You taken her to a doctor?'

'Of course.'

'Well, what sort of fucking quack is he?' He points a ringed finger in Farrell's face and his heavy gold bracelet jangles. 'You'd better take her to June's doctor, he'll sort it out. I pay the fucker enough. June!' he roars.

There's the skittering of heels on tiles, and June bustles through, looking flushed and exhausted. She's wearing an apron over a sensible dress. 'Oh, hello, Katya. Hello, Josh.'

I make a move to approach her, but she keeps her distance.

'What's the name of your doctor?' Glenn says to her.

Before June can answer, a small black shape suddenly hurtles out of a doorway and rushes towards me, barking hysterically. I take a step back, almost twisting my ankle in the high heels.

'Selebi!' Glenn yells, grabbing the dog's collar and yanking it back so hard that it yelps. 'What the fuck's got into you?'

The dog wriggles and wheezes, its flat button eyes fixed on me.

'Happy birthday, June,' Farrell says, doing his best to divert attention from the dog.

'Yes. Happy birthday,' I echo.

'Thank you—'

'Lock your fucking dog up, June, for Christ sake,' Glenn snaps.

June immediately starts pulling the dog away. It whines and scrapes its claws over the marble, leaving a dribble of pee as it goes.

'Let's get you a drink, my girl,' Glenn says, draping an arm over my shoulder.

The lounge is even more opulent than the hallway. It's packed with huge puffy white leather couches, a glass-and-gold coffee table, and countless ivory statues, mostly of naked nymphs holding jugs of water aloft.

'What do you want, Kitty-Kat?' Glenn says. 'Some bubbly for my girl?'

I nod. I'll have to be careful not to drink too much. I'm not used to alcohol and I need to keep myself in check. Farrell catches my eye and smiles at me. He's looking way more relaxed. I'm still worried about June's frosty reception but for all I know she's always like that. The knot in my stomach loosens slightly. Maybe it will be okay after all.

Careful not to overbalance on the heels, I approach the mantelpiece.

It's covered with framed photographs of Katya, ranging in age from a fresh-faced and naturally beautiful teen to a series of recent bikini pics. There's a single photograph of a small dark woman with Glenn's piggy eyes, wearing a mortar board and triumphantly holding a degree certificate, who I assume must be the sister, Marina. Half hidden behind a blown-up shot of Katya posing on a ski slope, there's a glossy seventies wedding photograph. A younger, thinner Glenn, wearing sideburns and a purple tux, grins into the shot, his arm wrapped around a slender dark-haired woman. I barely recognise June. She was beautiful once, and happy.

'Josh. Help yourself to whisky,' Glenn says tersely, popping a champagne cork.

Glenn hands me a glass of champagne and I smile the Katya smile I've been practising. He clinks his glass against mine. 'Here's to you, Kitty-Kat,' he says.

June enters the lounge, wiping her hands on her apron.

'Can I get you a drink, June?' Farrell says.

'She's fine,' Glenn says, draining his own glass and refilling it.

The Katya smile still glued to my face, I hand her the parcel. 'I hope you like it.'

'Oh. Thank you.'

'Well, open it, Juney,' Glenn says.

She unwraps it carefully, folding the paper as if she's planning to use it again. She runs the scarf through her fingers and glances at me in confusion.

'I thought it would suit your colouring,' I whisper. Dammit. Why hasn't she said anything? Did I make a mistake? What if she never wears scarves?

Then she finally fixes a smile onto her face. 'How thoughtful. It's beautiful. Thank you.'

'And how's Gran-Gran?' Farrell asks June.

'See for yourself,' Glenn grumbles, waving his whisky glass at the corner of the room. I've been so preoccupied I haven't noticed the elderly woman hidden behind a white leather recliner. June scuttles over to her

239

and wheels her towards us. She's curled in her wheelchair, her hands clawed in her lap, her head drooping to the side like a dying flower. Farrell nods meaningfully at me, and I step towards her.

'Look who's here, Mother,' June says, adjusting the blanket and smoothing the sparse strands of the old woman's hair.

A chime rings out.

'That'll be Marina. Get the door, Josh,' Glenn says. Farrell hesitates, clearly uncomfortable at the thought of leaving me alone. 'Go on, man,' Glenn snaps.

Farrell shoots me a supportive glance, then hurries out.

'Hello... Gran-Gran,' I whisper, bending down to kiss a papery cheek. She smells of lavender and baby powder. She doesn't react and I'm about to step back when she suddenly grips my wrist. She looks up at me, watery eyes fixed on my face. 'Who are you?' she croaks.

Glenn sighs loudly. 'It's Katya, Gran-Gran,' he says. 'Your granddaughter.'

'I'm not your gran, you cunt,' she says in a clear, lucid voice, and then the life seems to blink out of her eyes again.

June winces, but Glenn merely snorts and takes another slug of whisky. 'Dementia's getting worse,' he says. 'If that happens to me, shoot me in the fucking head.' He roars with laughter.

'Can we have that in writing?' a gruff woman's voice says behind me.

I turn around. I recognise the dumpy, short-haired woman immediately from the photograph on the mantelpiece. She's pregnant – probably six or seven months – and her belly protrudes in a plain white blouse from under her navy suit jacket. She's followed by a small, round man who reminds me of a mole. He's dressed in a dark suit, his short black hair is slicked to his scalp and he peers myopically through rimless glasses.

Marina kisses Glenn on the cheek – I notice he doesn't squeeze her waist – does the same to June and with a wince of distaste bends forward to kiss the air next to my cheeks. I can't see any trace of Katya in her features whatsoever. The husband scuttles forward. With a lurch I realise I've forgotten his name. Calvin? Charles? Then I have it. Clive. Thank God.

'Lovely to see you, Kat,' he says to my chest. He moistens his lips with a small pink tongue.

'That from the accident?' Marina says, indicating the dressing on my cheek.

'Yes,' Farrell says. 'It's healing nicely.'

'You done something to your hair, Kat?' Marina says.

'Why do you say that?' Farrell says.

Marina shrugs. 'There's something different about her.'

If you only knew! Dr Meka pipes in.

'Well?' Marina says to me.

'Not really…'

'Why are you whispering?'

'Laryngitis,' Farrell says. 'She's had it since the accident.'

'Oh well, it's not as if they expect you to talk in your line of work, is it?' She gestures impatiently to her husband, whose eyes haven't left my chest. 'Clive, give Mom the present.'

He hands a wrapped box-shape to June. I notice that she's dropped the scarf onto the coffee table.

'It's an external hard drive,' Marina says. 'So you can back up your computer.'

'Oh. What a thoughtful present,' June says.

'How long before we bloody eat?' Glenn says.

'You can come through to the dining room now. Marina, will you help me in the kitchen?'

Marina sighs. 'Where's Primrose?'

'I gave her the day off. Family funeral.'

'Fucking darkies. Everyone in the township's their fucking mother or brother.' Glenn turns to me and grins as if he expects me to agree. I look down and blush.

I make a move to follow June and Marina, but Farrell grips my arm and shakes his head. There's a loud insistent beeping sound. Farrell fumbles in his pocket and pulls out his phone.

Glenn glares at him. 'Turn that bloody thing off.'

Farrell stares at it in confusion. 'I thought I had turned it off.'

June hesitates at the door; for a second our eyes lock. That same look of confusion flashes over her face. 'Clive?' she says, her eyes still on me. 'Would you mind wheeling Gran-Gran into the dining room?'

Farrell pockets his phone and pats my bum. 'You're doing great,' he murmurs in my ear.

Like the rest of the house, the dining room is stunning. The table could easily seat twenty and is laid with crystal glasses, piled with wine bottles and strewn with more silk-flower arrangements. There's a hotel-style buffet set out on an enormous sideboard; serving platters are laden with vegetables, a slab of beef Wellington and the largest pork roast I've ever seen.

Glenn pours me a glass of red wine, fills his own glass and passes the bottle to Farrell. 'Make yourself useful, Josh.'

Farrell's phone trills again.

'I told you to turn that bloody thing off,' Glenn snaps. 'Where are your fucking manners?'

Farrell kills the call, but it rings again immediately. I don't like the way he's staring at the screen. 'I'll just be a second,' he says, leaving the room.

'Go on, Kat. You go first,' Glenn says, earning me a spiteful glance from Marina.

I pick up my plate and head to the buffet. I don't know where to start, and I don't know how I'll even manage to swallow a single bite. I take a couple of potatoes, a slice of pork and a portion of beef Wellington and wobble back to the table.

Everyone is staring at me.

'When did you start eating meat again?' Marina snipes.

Oh God. Oh shit. 'Um...'

Farrell returns just in time. He stares at my plate. The blood runs out of the pastry casing and pools around the potatoes. 'Doctor's orders,' he says. 'Low blood pressure. Kay has to up her iron intake.'

'But I thought you were going to do that PETA shoot?' Marina says. She's like a dog with a bone. 'They're not going to like that, are they?'

'Katya's health must come before any of that animal-rights shit,' Glenn says.

I sit down, hoping to God that I don't look as flustered as I feel.

'June! Get my girl here some of that crackling,' Glenn slurs.

'No, it's fine,' I say.

'You used to love crackling when you were a girl,' Glenn says.

I do my best to smile at him. The smell of the beef is starting to make me feel sick again. I take a sip of wine, wipe my sodden palms on the dress.

'Who was that on the phone, Josh?' Glenn says.

Farrell shrugs. 'Persistent editor. Needs some mock-ups for next week's layout.'

Glenn grunts, instantly disinterested. 'June? I'll have some of the beef and make sure you pile on the potatoes.'

June hands him a plate and he takes it from her without a word of thanks. No one seems to think that it's strange that, although it's her birthday, she's the one who's waiting on him.

'Where's the gravy? You know I like gravy.'

'Sorry.'

She heads back to the sideboard. Glenn glances at me and rolls his eyes. I don't know how to react to this. It's clearly a father–daughter moment. I drop my gaze and start cutting into the beef.

'Mom, why didn't you make any cauliflower cheese?' Marina grumbles.

Clive tops up his wine glass and leers at me. I'm trying to avoid looking at him.

'So tell us what happened, Kat,' Marina says. 'The accident.'

'She'd rather not,' Farrell says.

'Can't she speak for herself anymore?'

'I can't really remember much, to be honest,' I mumble, almost forgetting to whisper.

'We don't want to go over that again,' Glenn says. 'Clive. How are my stocks doing?'

Clive almost chokes on a mouthful of food in his eagerness to answer. 'Great. Great, Glenn.'

'That's what I like to hear.'

Talking with his mouth full, Glenn launches into a monologue about some poor senior manager he's fired for what sounds to me like absolutely no reason. June hasn't sat down to eat yet; she's now cutting Gran-Gran's food into tiny pieces. The old lady picks up her fork and stares at it. Then she chucks it onto the floor. I bend down to pick it up.

'Can I help?' I whisper to June.

She looks at me as if I've sprouted another head.

'Your mother's fine,' Glenn slurs. 'She knows how to deal with that senile old relic.'

'Dad,' Marina says. 'Don't say that about Gran-Gran.'

'Why not? That's what she is. Not as if she can understand, is it?'

Clive smiles sycophantically at Glenn. Glenn ignores him.

'It's disrespectful.'

'Don't you talk to me like that, my girl,' Glenn says, pointing his knife at her. 'I know more about respect than you'll ever learn.'

I manage to swallow a mouthful of meat, and try to catch Farrell's eye. He's staring down at his phone, the food on his plate forgotten.

June finally sits down to eat just as everyone else is finishing. I push the rest of my pork behind the potatoes.

Glenn pats his stomach. 'June, what's on the menu for dessert?'

Silently, and without eating a mouthful from her plate, June starts stacking the dishes. Again, no one offers to help.

There's another series of beeps. Farrell jumps, almost sending his glass flying.

Glenn slams his fist on the table. 'I told you to switch that fucking thing off!' he roars.

'Dad, calm down,' Marina says.

Farrell excuses himself and leaves the room again.

'What the fuck is the matter with him, Kat?' Glenn says. 'Fucking rude.'

I can't just sit at the table. I can't stand it any longer. I stand up and start gathering plates together.

'What the hell are you doing?' Glenn says.

'It's fine,' I whisper. 'I want to.'

Marina rolls her eyes. 'Jesus. Suddenly she's turned into the Good

244

Samaritan.' I grab the plates and head in what I hope is the direction of the kitchen. I can hear muffled whines and scratches from behind a door as the dog scrabbles to be let out of its prison, and then the sound of running water at the end of the corridor.

The large kitchen is plainly decorated with simple white tiles and melamine cupboards. June is leaning over the sink, her back to me. She doesn't turn around as I enter. 'Thank you for the food,' I whisper. 'It was—'

She whirls around. 'Who are you?'

Time freezes for a second. 'I'm your daughter.'

'No you're not,' she says, almost matter-of-factly. 'You can fool that monster out there, but you can't fool me.'

My hands start shaking and I have to put the plates down on the marble counter before I drop them.

'What are you going to do?' I whisper.

She turns back to the sink. 'Do?' she says bitterly. '*Do?* Nothing of course. Who'd believe me? They'd only think I was cracking up again.'

'Again?'

'Oh dear. Josh has forgotten to fill you in on the sordid family history, hasn't he?'

'He—'

'I don't know what's going on,' June says. 'And you know what?' She slowly turns to face me. 'I don't really care.'

'Everything all right in here?' Farrell walks in carrying the pork platter. 'Christ, Kay. You look sick as a dog.' His eyes flick from me to June and back again.

'I'm not feeling well, Josh,' I say.

'Let's get you home.'

'I think that's best,' June says with a cold smile. She staggers slightly and clings to the edge of the sink to steady herself. Is she drunk? I didn't see her drinking any alcohol at the dining table.

'Goodbye,' I say.

'Don't be a stranger,' she says, and lets out a noise that could be a laugh or a hiccough.

Farrell leads me back into the dining room. 'What did she say to you?' he hisses. 'Why the fuck did you go in there?'

His grip on my arm tightens. 'Nothing. She didn't say anything. I just couldn't sit there doing nothing. I had to help.'

He relaxes. 'Right. Yeah. Sorry. What a fucking family.' He brushes a strand of hair away from my forehead. 'Look, just say a quick goodbye and we're done.'

I stand at the doorway and let Farrell do the talking.

'We have to go,' he says to Glenn, who's pouring the dregs of a bottle of wine into his glass. Gran-Gran has fallen asleep, her toothless mouth gaping open, and Clive looks as if he's about to pass out.

'What the hell are you talking about?'

'Katya's not feeling well.'

'Then she should stay here. I know how to take care of my own fucking daughter. Kat, Pumpkin, you can have your old room.'

'No, it's fine,' I whisper, looking at my feet. It takes all my strength not to run to the front door.

'You doing the *Sports Illustrated* this year, Kat?' Clive slurs, managing to smirk and resemble a *Wind in the Willows* character at the same time.

'Shut the fuck up, Clive,' Glenn says, then to me, 'Come and give Daddy a kiss, Kitty-Kat.'

Marina rolls her eyes and mutters something under her breath. I do my best impression of a Katya smile and hobble over to his chair. I lean my face to the side, but he manages to kiss me on the lips.

'Bye,' I say.

I wave at Marina but she's too busy glaring at Clive to acknowledge me. Then Farrell ushers me towards the front door and escape.

Farrell flops backwards onto the bed. He's wearing nothing but a pair of bright-blue boxer shorts.

'Don't be long,' he says, patting the sheets next to him. 'I know just what you need.'

Extensive therapy and a serious reality check.

'What?' I say, ignoring the Dr Meka voice.

'A foot massage.'

I wonder if this is something he used to do for Katya, but for once I don't feel the stirrings of jealousy. I've got other things on my mind.

'Farrell? Who was trying to call you?'

'What?'

'At Glenn's house. Who was it?'

He doesn't answer straight away. 'Wrong number.'

'Really? Because you were acting... strange. Worried.'

He sighs. 'It's all under control, Lisa. Chill out.'

'You really think we did okay?' I ask again. I haven't told him about June, just like I didn't tell him what Noli said to me.

Coward.

'How many more times? You were brilliant. Stop obsessing.'

'But the vegetarian thing—'

'It's cool. We did okay. We're almost done.'

A stone drops in my gut. So this must mean it's time for the second part of the plan. For Katya to disappear. For *me* to disappear out of Farrell's life.

'Now hurry up and come to bed.'

'I'll just be a minute.' I slip into the bathroom and drag the dress over my head, breathing with relief to be free of the constricting fabric. Using Katya's Clarins lotions, I carefully wipe off the make-up.

Oh God.

I lean closer to the mirror. My left eyelid seems to be drooping slightly. I turn my face to the side. Has it always been like this? I would have noticed it before, wouldn't I? It's just my imagination playing tricks. I'm just tired. That's it. Exhausted.

'Lisa?' Farrell calls. 'What are you *doing*?'

'I'll be out in a second.'

I pull the wig off and kick it away, shaking my own hair over my face. It's greasy and flattened from hiding under the mop of fake hair all evening.

'I'm just going to shower.'

'Jesus. Get a move on.'

It's only the thought of Farrell waiting for me that allows me to wrench myself away from my reflection.

I turn the water on full power, scrub my body and wash my hair twice. Dammit. I'll have to reapply the fake tan. It's starting to streak over my belly, my pale white skin shining through in jagged strips. I rub myself dry and smear the foul-smelling stuff over my stomach and along the tops of my thighs. A quick last glance in the mirror while it dries.

Oh God. My left eyelid is *definitely* hanging lower than the other. I blink rapidly. It doesn't help.

Dr Meka sighs in my head.

Five more minutes, and then I'll stop. I swear it.

Chapter 25

FARRELL

Christ, Lisa's not bad in bed. She's got something Katya didn't have. Along with that extra bit of flesh to grab, there's something else. I don't know. Need. Urgency. Lisa fucks as if she wants it just that little bit more.

But she's seriously nuts. Last night, after June's birthday dinner, she locked herself in the bathroom for two and a half hours. And I'm pretty sure she was at it all day today as well. At least this evening I've managed to keep her occupied. What the fuck does she do in there? I know she's got some serious self-esteem issues, but come on.

Still, Glenn believes Katya's fine, and that's the most important thing. Lisa's neuroses I can deal with.

I felt better than I have for weeks today, so I came home early this afternoon, bringing takeout from Carlito's and a bottle of Veuve. Lisa started to relax after a couple of glasses, and we took the rest of the champagne to bed.

I slump back panting and my phone vibrates again. I pick it off the nightstand and check it. It's Rosen again.

I've been ignoring the messages all day. Told Lizzie that I was unavailable; that some guy was hounding me to buy life insurance and that she should field his calls.

'Who is it?' Lisa asks, shaking her hair over her face.

I wonder for the hundredth time whether to tell her the truth. Fuck knows how Rosen got those messages through to my phone yesterday while it was off. There must be some way to push a message through with the charge from the SIM card or something, because the phone was definitely off. I took the battery out after the second message. The third message came through regardless.

And the messages today are getting increasingly... urgent. And strange. I still haven't dug that fucking medical-aid contract out of the bin to read it; it's like I've got some mental block or something. I fucking hate small print at the best of times. That's why we have a fucking PA and accounts department, for fuck's sake. But from what Rosen said at the office on Monday, I need to pay something. I scroll down through the messages I received during dinner while Glenn was bursting an artery. They all say much the same thing, if you can get past the piss-poor English:

<Mr Farrell. Remindering you that moments are running away. I am here to assist your deliverance.>

<Mr Farrell. Meeting necessitated for deliverance. Time is running away. Alacritous contact essential. Yours in service of the Ministry of Modifications, Agent Rosen>

And more of the same bullshit today:

<Contracted Donor Farrell. You will be in disregard of the contract after midnight. URGENT exchange to arrange deliverance. Second notice.>

All from the same number. Something with a foreign prefix.

'Josh? Who is it?'

'Sorry. It's...'

We were both in that clinic; we were in it together. I decide to tell her the truth.

'This guy visited me at the studio on Monday. Remember that medical-aid contract I signed? Apparently I owe them something. Urgently.'

'God. I told you. I said you shouldn't just sign it without reading it.'

'I know. I know. I was going to read it, I promise. But, you know, I got busy.'

'But you've signed it now, and those people... you know they're going to want you to pay. When must you pay?'

'By midnight tonight, apparently.'

She glances at the clock. It reads 20.02. 'And how much?'

'I don't know.'

'Don't you think you should speak to them and find out?'

'It's all bullshit, Lisa,' I say. 'They'll go away eventually.'

She doesn't say anything, just peers at me through Katya's fringe.

The phone beeps again, and Lisa flinches.

This time it reads: <Final notice.>

Fuck.

She's right. I'm going to have to speak to this guy – Rosen – and sort it out. Stall him or something.

I dial the number, looking at Lisa's legs on my sheets as the call connects. One ring.

'Rosen intercoursing.'

'It's Josh Farrell calling.'

'Mr Farrell! I'm thrilled to parts that you have chosen to contact me. You must deliver on your Donor Swap contract by midnight tonight and I am here to assist you. The Ministry does its utmost to assist contractees to find their stumps in the complex.'

'How much do I owe? Can I make an electronic transfer?'

'Excuse me, Mr Farrell?'

'A transfer. Can I make a payment into your account?'

'Oh! Apologies, Mr Farrell. I did not understand. I believe you are referring to brown currency.' He laughs as if I've told an unfunny joke. 'The Ministry does not deal in figurative currency. I shall come to your abode in fifteen moments to introduce you to the deliverance kit and to offer any physical assistance you may require in your collection.'

'No, hang on. Not here.' I don't want him in my apartment. 'Let's meet at the studio.'

I hang up. Lisa is watching me wide-eyed, unconsciously pinching the skin on the left side of her face. I stop myself from reaching out and slapping her hand away.

'Don't worry,' I say. 'I won't be long.'

She nods, swings her legs off the bed, scuttles into the bathroom and slams the door behind her.

Rosen is already waiting at the studio door when I arrive. We swap greetings and I hastily unlock and lead him to my desk before he offers to shake my hand. He's dressed the same as when I met him on Monday, and still has the fedora lodged on his head. Along with his briefcase, he carries a small steel make-up case.

'Time is running away, Mr Farrell,' he says as he sits. 'It was a good idea to meet here, because it is likely we can collect some viable right here at the workplace. Shall we proceed?'

'Hang on. Hang on, please. I don't understand what you need from me. Just explain it slowly.'

'You have read the contract, Mr Farrell?' he says, and there's a cold edge to his voice that puts me on guard.

'No, I, uh... I meant to. But contracts and finance aren't my strong point.' I hear an ingratiating tone in my voice, a scared tone. I scan the corners of the ceiling for the comforting red wink of the security cameras. 'Can you talk me through it?'

'Really, Mr Farrell, time *is* running away.' He sighs and scratches at the back of his head with his mutilated hand, digging under the rim of the hat. 'You should have been aware of the terms by now. If you are in breach, as your case agent, I will be in disregard. We *must* act.' He pulls his finger away. It's discoloured with something dark but I don't get a close look before he wipes his hand on his trousers. 'We have until midnight.'

'You keep saying that! What must I do?'

Rosen lays his briefcase and the silver case on the desk and brings out his copy of the contract. When he looks up at me, he's regained his professional composure and smiles thinly. 'Bullet tips, as you upsiders say. Your viable harvest mass was notarised as 117.63 pounds on release from the Modification Ward. Your Donor Swap policy stipulates delivery of 150 per cent viable mass within thirty-three shifts. By midnight tonight, upside time, you may deliver' – he takes what must be a novelty soft-gel calculator out of his pocket and taps out a sum – '176.445 pounds of viable tissue to a collection node conveniently located near you. Remember that the final tally will only be made after termination and recycling of the viable. The assessors will let you know if there is any further shortfall. In this unlikely circumstance, you will have ample time to make up the shortfall once the assessment is lodged. Failing this, you will be in breach and subject to an out-of-contract termination.'

As the reality of what he's talking about starts to sink in, I'm astounded that he's talking about it so openly. 'What are we talking about here? Is it organs? You're organ traffickers, is that it?'

'Organs, muscle, tissue, bones. Anything viable,' he says, and in that moment I've caught him on camera admitting to organ harvesting. I *have* this fucker.

I clear my throat, speak loudly and clearly. 'So if I... deliver... people weighing 176 pounds, I'm out of debt with you. Is that right?' I've *got* them. Motherfuckers.

'176.445 pounds viable, not total.'

'What does viable mean?'

'The viability criteria are appended to your contract here, Mr Farrell.' He runs his mutilated fingers down the list. 'High-quality, intact facial tissue is rated five; slightly compromised but still high quality could be four; uncompromised eyes, hearts and brains could be rated up to five; bulk muscle tissue rated anything from one to three; skin from one to three and a half. Raw blood is rated on a sliding scale. If you have a look at your in-ward assessment schedule here' – he passes me a list of numbers from the file – 'you will see that your viable total was super-estimated because of the high quality of the skin and muscle tissue, but was rated down because of stimulant content. The hormone therapy you received in Preparation Ward unfortunately compromised various of your components. Your eyes, lamentably, were listed as unrated and of marginal viability.'

'And who makes these assessments?'

He looks at me oddly. 'The Ministry's assessors. We submit a mimeograph and they return an estimate, but the final assessment is only notarised once the poundage is delivered and recycled.'

'And then what happens to the—'

There's a click and a creak over my left shoulder. I whirl around. Eduardo is standing in his office doorway.

'I thought I heard someone,' he says. 'Working late, Farrell?'

'Uh, yes. This is my, er, broker.'

'Jesus, that's service. Can I get your card?'

'He's primo,' Rosen says.

'What?'

Instead of answering, Rosen clicks open the little steel case and removes a gadget that resembles a stubby remote control. He walks over to Eduardo, presses the thing against his neck and Eduardo folds quietly into an unconscious heap. Rosen crouches over him, unlaces Eduardo's shoes then starts undressing him.

'Please assist me, Mr Farrell.'

But I can't move.

'Mr Farrell!' he snaps, and something vicious in his eyes tells me to listen. I move across to the doorway. 'Remove his trousers, and please help me lay him out flat.' I follow Rosen's orders. There's a sheen of sweat on his face as he struggles to pull Eduardo's tight Hello Kitty top over his head. As Rosen bends and turns, I notice a stain behind his ear under his hat. It looks like old blood.

When Eduardo is naked, Rosen goes back to the case on the desk and removes a marker pen and a Polaroid camera, those sick bastards' technology of choice. My mind claws at the inside of my skull and my stomach heaves; I know exactly what he's going to do. Sure enough, he draws lines on Eduardo's body, portioning him up into segments, and takes a photograph of him, the flash popping my mind blank.

'Nothing better than a stumps-on tutorial, Mr Farrell.' Rosen smiles at me as he wafts the photo in the air, waiting for it to develop. 'Especially when the moments are running away. We signal this mimeograph to the assessors, and they'll signal back an estimate and then we can take this to collection. Easy as that.'

'Take him? But why?'

Rosen looks at me as if I'm an idiot. 'To deliver on your contract, of course. This brown is primo. At least a hundred pounds viable, I'd estimate. More than half your debt right here.'

'What would happen to him... after I deliver?'

'He'll be terminated and recycled.'

'You're serious, aren't you?' This is the first time that I accept it, deep down.

'The Ministry of Modifications doesn't play, Mr Farrell. And neither do its agents.' He hands me the Polaroid. A greenish-beige body with lines drawn on it. Just like the photos they took of me in the hospital.

'I can't. I can't... use... him. He's done nothing to me.' But now I know exactly what to do. The answer to all my problems. It *is* as easy as that, after all.

Rosen shakes his head. 'It's your decision.'

The cold shock of what I've just seen, and of what I know is about to come is perfectly balanced by the liberating euphoria a different part of me is feeling.

So I feel nothing as we dress Eduardo again, and lay him on his couch. I consider leaving the surveillance files intact, recorded proof of what this racket is doing, but I know I can't. I'm complicit now. I log into the surveillance server, stop the cameras, deindex the night's files, pick up the steel case and escort Rosen out of the building.

Rosen chats companionably as he drives. His car is a cross between a Renault Scenic and a hearse with tinted windows. 'The Ministry of Paraphernalia is still working on a prototype of an invisible pen that only shows up in the mimeograph flash,' he says. 'But you know how these things go. They table a research tender, then the results must be scrutinised and the research budget extended to the practical experimentation phase, then those dockets need to be cycled up to the Minister's office, then through to Senate ratification. It takes a while. But mostly, it takes lemons.'

'Lemons?'

'Yes. Not so easy for us to grow.'

Lemons.

'You have a primo workplace for scouting. What your mascots lack in weight, they more than make up for in quality ratings. The mascots you work with – provided they don't toxify – have up to a ninety-three per cent viability ratio. It's like picking viable from the meat tree.'

'What do you mean "mascots"?'

'Oh, sorry. What you call "mowdels", I think. Sorry, I haven't been upside for some periods.' He drifts off into a reverie, and scratches at the wound behind his ear. It's definitely blood, and still wet. Every time he fiddles with the wound, his fingers pull off it with a sticky lisp.

'I was hoping to see some mowdels tonight, like I did the other day. All that primo Donor material.'

'Most people leave the studio at six or so.'

'Pity.' He drives on in silence. All I can think about is what's to come. I fidget with the stunner, tapping it on the steel case, eager to zap that fat bastard to the floor.

Easy as that.

It's close to nine thirty when we reach Glenn's street. We stop three blocks down and, as planned, Rosen gets in the back and lies down. I drive the rest of the way. When we get to Glenn's gate, there's a new security guard on shift and she asks me my business.

'Tell Mr Forrest that I'm bringing Katya back. She wants to come home.'

The guard doesn't bother to look into the car and phones up to the house. She presses the button to open the gate and watches me in.

I pull up at the front of the house. Glenn is already standing on the entrance terrace, eyeing me suspiciously. I check that the stunner in my hand is on, pull up the handbrake, open the door.

'Where is she?'

'In the car.'

'What the fuck are you driving?'

Oh shit. 'It's from work. The Alfa had a flat.'

He jogs down the stairs, peers into the tinted passenger window. 'Kat?' He taps on the glass. 'Kitty-Kat?'

His body flies back from the window, flopping onto the gravel like a ragdoll. Damn. *I* wanted to do that.

Rosen opens the door. 'This is suboptimal. He's quite hefty, you're right.' He pokes the prone body with his shoe tip. 'Low ratio, though. The assessors will decide. Assist me, Mr Farrell, we must carry him up the stairs.'

Rosen hauls Glenn by the shoulders and I take his ankles. I can barely get a grip around their bulbous girth and we struggle and jostle to get him to the first step, then take a rest. I check down the drive to the front gate. Just paranoia. There's no way that guard can see us from here.

'One, two, *three*,' says Rosen, and we heft him up a few steps; just a few more to go.

'Josh! What are you...?' June appears in the doorway and lets out a shrill scream.

Before Rosen can react, I rush up the stairs. 'It's okay, June, it's...' *Yes, a strange man in a suit and your would-be son-in-law are hauling your husband's body up the stairs. I can explain.* I put the stunner to her neck and press the button. She collapses, easy as that. That felt good. This zappy thing is fucking awesome.

I look to Rosen, but he's gone. Shit. Has he left me to deal with this by myself?

Then I hear the crunch of jogging footsteps on gravel, and Rosen returns, pocketing his stunner. Security guard. I skate June's bird-like body into the lounge and go back to help with Glenn.

I feel motivated. I feel strong. I look at Glenn's angry face, his slabby hands – those hands that are way too free with Katya, way too free with June – and I feel nothing. I know exactly what's going to happen to this grotesque chunk of meat, and I feel nothing. He's lucky. This end is too good for him, too clean, too painless.

I hear myself thinking these words, and still I feel nothing. Glenn's a blight. We're putting him down more humanely than he deserves.

Once he's in the lounge, I start stripping him without even being asked. Rosen gets the pen and the camera from the car, marks Glenn up like a dummy printout for correction and takes the picture. I look around the house, knowing I will never come here again.

When the photo is developed, Rosen scans it through his phone. 'What about her?' he says, indicating June. 'No more than forty, fifty viable, but every bit helps. There are all types of Clients with all types of needs.'

'No. Just him,' I say. June never did anything overtly to hurt me or Katya. That's enough to save her.

'Frankly, if the Ministry wanted you to settle your debt with high-ratio parts, Representative Mutual should have stipulated that in the contract. But stipulated it is not. So this' – he indicates Glenn's blubbery form on the carpet in front of him – 'is contractually acceptable. The representatives missed a finger there, I'd say.'

Rosen's phone beeps; he stops muttering and reads the message. He raises his eyebrows. 'Hmm. One hundred and forty, the assessors report. I'm sixed it's that much. But the Ministry has recently endorsed assisted fattening and they've added lipids to the new draft viability schedule. Could be that.'

'One hundred and forty. But that means...'

'You're still 36.445 short.' He nods at June's body and smiles.

I look at June. Remember her feeble performance at dinner last night. What did she ever actually do for Katya? Did she ever protect her from Glenn? Or did she just stand by and let him paw her and contort her all those years? Change her from that happy girl to a driven and self-obsessed woman. Katya always called her pathetic, never forgave her for being so weak.

She doesn't even know that her daughter is dead. A mother's supposed to feel that in her bones. She thought Lisa was Katya, for fuck's sake.

'Yeah. Throw her in.'

I look away as Rosen strips and marks June. The Polaroid flashes. I drink a tumblerful of Glenn's single malt.

I'm gazing up at the oil painting of the miserable stag – Glenn's appalling taste in art another reason why he won't be missed – when the assessment comes in.

'Forty-seven,' says Rosen. 'Congratulations. We're clear to deliver.'

Rosen backs the car right up to the stairs and we haul the bodies into the back and cover them with a blanket. We stop at the gate, lift the security guard from where she's lying prone on the driveway and place her back on her chair in the hut. I eject the disc from the security monitor.

'You don't need to worry about that, Mr Farrell. Your society has so many little holes where evidence can disappear. You simply don't have the systems.'

The way he says it makes me believe him. Besides, there are recorders and cameras all over the house. I check my watch. 10.26. We haven't got time. I'll worry about the repercussions when they come. I have a feeling nobody's going to miss Glenn Forrest too much.

'Where do we deliver?' I ask.

Rosen checks his list. 'Closest node is Highgate Mall. Delivery entrance 7B.'

Half an hour and we'll be done.

Late on a Thursday night, the mall is eerie. The neon lights blast out for nobody, and disoriented birds swoop around sleepily. All the shops and restaurants are long closed and I wonder whose cars these are, dotted about the parking lot.

Trucks are parked outside the Woolworths delivery entrance, drivers snoozing, waiting for their turn to unload, but Rosen drives onto the rooftop. It's deserted, except for a dusty red VW Fox.

We park in front of the massive steel door to a truck-loading bay and Rosen gets out of the car. He sends a message on his phone and waits, stretching and arching his back as if he's taking a rest stop on a long journey, keen to get home. As I watch out the car window, I think I notice the shadow of someone skittering between the rooftop bulwarks, but I can't be sure. I look back and everything's still again. Rosen and I said little to each other on the drive here, but our silence has been comfortable; just two workmates getting on with the job in hand. I'm feeling calm, almost relaxed. I should be feeling guilty, paranoid, terrified... But I'm not.

There's a metallic thump from behind the loading-bay gate and it rises. Rosen gets back in and drives inside. The gate closes with a crash behind us. The space we're parked in is a huge concrete vault, empty apart from a few large steel trolleys like luggage floats at an airport.

Rosen guides one of the trolleys to the back of the car. 'In here,' he says. We heft Glenn's and June's naked and marked bodies over the edge of the trolley and they slam in like the simple flesh they are. They're just meat.

Rosen takes a small ledger out of his briefcase and fills in a page in carbonised quadruplicate then passes the book to me. 'Here you go, Mr Farrell. I've entered your policy number here, assessment numbers here, date and time here, and all I need is your signature here. Congratulations, Mr Farrell. You have settled your debt with the Ministry of Modifications.'

He extends his half-hand and this time I have no objection to shaking it. He gets back into the car and before I join him I peer over the lip of the trolley for one last look at Glenn's and June's bodies, their shallow breathing reorganising their flesh against each other. June lets out an unconscious whimper.

I turn away. My problems are solved.

Chapter 26

LISA

Something flutters on my cheek.

'Rise and shine!'

I groggily register the feel of Farrell's lips on my forehead and breathe in the smell of freshly brewed coffee.

I open my eyes and struggle to sit up. Farrell's standing in front of me, dressed in a fashionably rumpled black suit and white T-shirt. He smiles down at me.

'What time is it?'

'Nine.'

'What time did you come to bed?' It wasn't before 4 a.m., I know that for sure.

He grins and rolls his eyes boyishly. 'Stayed up all night. Me and Eduardo had a couple of drinks in Melville. Turned into an all-nighter. I would have called only... I lost track of time.'

He doesn't look like he's been up all night. He looks fresh. Hair flopping over his forehead in that Robert Pattinson way, eyes sparkling. I've never seen him this happy and relaxed before.

'Did you see that guy? The guy from... that place?'

'Yeah.' He leans down and kisses me again. 'All sorted.'

'Really?'

'Absolutely. Nothing to worry about.' He places a mug on the nightstand. 'Here. Made you coffee,' he says.

'Thanks.'

He touches the top of my head, wraps a strand of black hair around his finger. 'You forget to take this off last night?' I twist my head so that the hair flops over the disgusting side. 'Don't look so worried, Lisa.'

'I'm not worried.' I try to smile at him but fail miserably.

'Yes, you are.' He tries to brush the hair away from my face and I flinch away. 'What's wrong?'

'Nothing. It's just that I must look awful this morning. Didn't get much sleep.'

'Well, you look gorgeous to me.'

'Really?'

'Of course.'

I watch him carefully, but he doesn't seem to be lying. I know I should tell him about what's happening to my face – to *her* face. But how can I expect him to understand? No one does. No one ever has. Not Dad, not Sharon, not even Dr Meka.

'Lisa? You listening?'

'Sorry. Were you saying something?'

'I was saying, I think this is going to work out just fine.'

'What is?'

'You know. You and me. Our arrangement.'

I know what he's going to say and I don't want to hear it. I take a sip of scalding coffee.

'Look, I've been thinking,' he says. 'Maybe... now that things are sorted out with Glenn, you could stay here a bit longer.'

It takes a second for what he's just said to register. 'Really? You mean with you? Here?'

'Yeah. I like having you around.' He runs his fingers along the inside of my arm, and I shiver. 'Me and Katya... we had some problems. But... Look, we'll talk when I get back. I'd better get out of here, got a lot of stuff to catch up on at the studio.'

'Wait.' I grab his wrist and pull him back towards me.

He smiles. 'Later, okay? Much as I'd like to, I've got to go.'

Blood rushes to my cheeks. 'I didn't mean that. That man you met with last night... It's really going to be fine?'

He glances at his watch. 'Absolutely. Tell you what, I'll stop at Woolies on the way home, grab us a bottle of bubbly, cook us a Thai curry. We can talk then.'

'Okay.'

He pauses as if he's about to say something else. Then he smiles, shrugs and leaves the room. I can hear him whistling as he strolls down the passageway.

I lie back and think about what he's just said. Could I really stay here? Live with him? Be a permanent part of his life? *Could* I? My limbs feel tingly and a strange, pleasant warmth swirls in my belly.

How cosy. You, Farrell and Katya's face. The perfect love triangle.

It could work. I could make it work. And now that Glenn thinks that Katya's fine...

But you're forgetting something, Lisa. You haven't fooled everyone, have you?

June. How could I forget about June? If Farrell finds out that she doesn't believe I'm Katya, will he change his mind?

Of course he will. He's not stupid.

I kick the covers off, grab one of Katya's kimonos and wrap it around my body. I stare down at my feet to avoid catching a glimpse of myself in the mirror. The thought of seeing my reflection makes me feel physically sick. I pull the wig off my head, dump it on the floor and head towards the lounge area.

Her lounge. Her shrine with its walls of framed photographs. I've been avoiding them, but I have to look at them closely sometime. And I have to stop seeing her as a threat. The last thing she said to me was that she was sorry. She must've done something to hurt Farrell. Betrayed his trust, maybe. And I would never do that. Maybe it's me – the *real* me – Farrell wants, and not her.

I step towards a large black-and-white studio portrait of her gazing moodily at the camera, eyes glistening, her head thrown back, and try to ignore my shadowy reflection in the glass, my flat blonde hair weakly superimposed over her long black tresses. She's perfect, flawless. A dream woman.

How can I compete with that?

The phone in the hallway shrills. It dies and then rings again. I've always ignored it before, but what if it's Farrell? And if it's not him, I can always hang up, can't I? Hesitating for a second, I pick up the receiver.

'Hello?'

A pause. 'It's June.' I almost drop the receiver. 'Hello?' she says. 'Hello? Is anyone there?'

I fumble for something to say, wondering if there's any point in disguising my voice now. 'Hello. How... um... are you?'

'I'm...' There's a gasp as if she's been crying. 'I'm not... I'm...' She clears her throat. 'Is Glenn there?'

'No.'

'Are you sure?'

'No. I mean yes, I'm sure.'

'He didn't come and see you?'

'No.'

'I'm outside in the car. I'm coming in.'

Oh God! 'No!'

But I'm talking to a dial tone.

Oh God, oh God. *Shit*. What should I do? I need to talk to Farrell. But my mind has gone blank and I can't for the life of me remember his number.

Think!

I'm sure I've seen one of his business cards in one of the drawers next to the bed. I stumble blindly into the bedroom. I'm not looking where I'm going and I skid on the wig and crash onto my hands and knees. I crawl to the chest of drawers, yank it open and root through it, finally locating the card underneath a pile of flavoured condoms.

The doorbell buzzes.

I scramble down the hallway and press the intercom button. 'I'll be with you in a second.'

I tap the number into the phone with numb fingers. It seems to ring forever and then goes to voicemail. I babble out a message: 'Farrell. It's me. Please. You have to come home. June's here. What should I do?'

The door buzzer goes again.

It's completely pointless for me to pretend I'm not here. I'll have to let her in. I take my time unlocking the security gate and she bursts in the second the door opens, heading straight for the kitchen. She sits down at the breakfast bar and slaps her handbag onto the counter in front of her.

'Something happened last night,' she says. 'To me. To Glenn.'

I slowly sit down opposite her. She looks terrible. She's dressed in a baggy velour tracksuit, and her hair is standing up in sweaty clumps. 'What do you mean?'

'He's missing. He's gone.'

'Gone? Gone where? '

'Why don't *you* tell *me*?'

'How would I know?'

Then she seems to really see me for the first time. Her eyes widen and her face contorts into a mixture of disgust and loathing.

'What?' My hand automatically flies to my face, but that isn't the problem. She's staring at my hair. Oh *shit*. The wig is still on the bedroom floor. *I've forgotten to put it on.*

'Katya always wanted to know what she'd look like as a blonde,' she says matter-of-factly. 'Now we know.' Seconds pass while we just stare at each other. 'How much did it cost?' she says finally.

'How much did what cost?'

'The hours you spent under the surgeon's knife so that you could make your face like hers. That's it, isn't it?' She screws up her face as if she's thinking hard about something. 'That has to be it. But I can't figure out *why* you'd do that.'

I don't know what to say. She's closer to the truth than she realises, but I can't openly admit that I'm not her daughter. I just can't. I wrack my brain for something to say. 'Would you like some tea?' God. Where did that come from?

She jerks back in surprise. 'Yes, please,' she says, touching her lips after she's spoken as if, like me, she can't believe we're actually going to be doing something as mundane as drinking tea.

I flick the kettle on and fuss about with mugs and the sugar pot and teaspoons so that I won't have to look at her. The panic has evaporated, leaving a strange, airy mood in the space.

'You know what I've been thinking ever since Wednesday night?' she says. 'Maybe I *am* going mad. Maybe I've got some rare disorder that's making me believe that my relatives are actually imposters.'

I keep quiet and stare into the kettle's curved metal side. I can see her distorted reflection without having to turn around.

'There is a condition like that, you know. I googled it. Just before...' There's a long pause and then she clears her throat. 'But now I know better.'

I dump the teabag in the sink; fetch the milk from the fridge.

'You know, there's no rule that says you have to love your children,' she says as if we're just two old friends catching up on gossip. 'There's not a law that says you have to get on with them. Does that shock you?'

Still keeping my back to her, I shake my head.

'What's your mother like?' she asks.

'You're my mother,' I whisper.

She snorts in disgust and mumbles something I can't catch.

The phone rings in the background.

'I should probably—' I make a move to head into the hallway, but she grabs my wrist as I pass.

'Leave it,' she says. Now I'm up close to her I can smell the stale sweat and vomit wafting out of her pores. Her eyes dart and dance over my face, but they don't seem to be focussing properly. We both listen in silence until it stops ringing. She loosens her grip and, not knowing what else to do, I head back to the sink and carry on making the tea.

'Katya was always more Glenn's child than mine. Even when she was a tiny girl. "Daddy" this and "Daddy" that. I was just the person who made the food and told the maids what to do. I knew even then that she didn't think much of me.'

Still floating on the tide of unreality, I hand her a mug and pass her the sugar and milk. She starts spooning sugar into the mug, spilling granules all over the counter. She stirs it as if in a trance. Without looking at me, she says, 'Is she dead?'

Oh God. It's as if all my insides have been vacuumed out, leaving a cold empty space. But June doesn't seem to expect an answer. She digs in her bag and pulls out a bottle of prescription pills, shakes three of them into her palm and knocks them back, dry-swallowing.

What the hell am I supposed to do now?

There's a beeping sound and she starts rooting in her bag for her phone. She finds it, frowns down at the screen and then answers. 'Hello? Yes, this is she.'

There's the rattle of the key in the door. 'Li— Katya?'

It's Farrell. Thank God! I race past June and cannon straight into his arms.

'Is she here?' he says.

'She's in the kitchen. She knows, Farrell,' I hiss into his ear.

'Knows what? What does she know?'

'That I'm not Katya.' I'm expecting him to flip out, or snap at me for forgetting to wear the wig, but he doesn't. His breathing hitches momentarily, but that's all. 'And she says Glenn is gone or missing or something.'

He steps back and grips my upper arms tightly. 'Is that all she knows?'

'What do you mean?'

'She hasn't said anything else?'

Then it dawns. 'Did you have something to do with Glenn's disappearance?'

'No!' But he doesn't look at me as he says this.

'Farrell, *please…*'

He gazes past me. 'Oh, hello, June.'

I turn around. She's standing in the kitchen doorway, clutching her phone and staring at us, eyes glassy. 'What's going on, Josh?'

'Nothing, June. Everything's fine.'

She looks from me to Farrell and back again. I'm expecting her to start accusing us of murdering Katya, to scream and threaten us with the police, but she merely waves the phone at us. 'They found his car,' she says. 'The tracking company. They just called me back.'

'Glenn's car?' Farrell says.

She nods.

'Where?'

'The airport. Lanseria.'

I watch Farrell carefully. He almost looks relieved. 'He must have gone on a business trip.'

'No!' she says. 'He wouldn't do that. Not without telling me. We were supposed to meet Marina for breakfast. And his wallet is still next to the bed.' She scrubs her hand over her face. The pills must be kicking in because she's sounding increasingly groggy. 'And it's not just that. Last night—'

'What about last night?'

'Something happened.'

'What?'

She shakes her head as if she's trying to clear it. 'I'm... It's so strange. I don't remember going to bed. And Glenn's side of the bed... it was untouched. And then I woke up and I couldn't find him and his car was gone and...'

'And that's all you remember?'

She nods.

Farrell smiles reassuringly at her. 'Like I said, he probably had to go to Cape Town on business and forgot to tell you.'

'You really think that could be it?' She's beginning to look defeated, and I feel a perverse desire to stick up for her.

'Why are you so worried about him anyway?' I say. 'He treats you like crap.' Farrell stares at me. 'Sorry,' I say. 'I didn't mean to—'

'I know how he treats me,' she says. 'It's not right. I know that. But... something's happened to him. I just know it.'

'I'm sure it's just a misunderstanding,' Farrell says in that same comforting voice. 'What does Marina say?'

'She thinks I'm just being paranoid. I do get confused sometimes and...'

We're not that dissimilar, she and I. I reach for her hand. She smiles at me gratefully and then something clicks in her eyes and she snatches it back.

'I'm going to go now,' she says, speaking stiltedly.

'Will you be all right to drive?' Farrell says.

'Yes. You'll let me know if you hear from him, won't you?'

'Of course, June.'

Farrell walks her out.

There's the murmur of voices, followed by the sound of the security gate slamming shut. Farrell strides back into the kitchen and thumps his fist on the counter. 'Fuck! Fuck. *Fuck!*'

'Farrell, calm down! I don't think she's going to—'

'It's not that, Lisa. No one's going to believe *her* anyway. It's... It's... *Fuck*. I am so screwed. *Fuck*.'

The security-gate buzzer trills making both of us jump. 'Don't answer that,' Farrell says.

'But what if it's June again?'

'It's not June.'

'How do you know?'

'I just do.'

The buzzer blares again, and Farrell's phone beeps at the same time. He reads the message, chucks the phone on the hall table and runs his hands through his hair.

'You think it might be Glenn?' I ask.

'I fucking hope not.' He presses the intercom button and shouts into it. 'Fuck off and leave me alone! I did what you said.'

A smooth male voice I don't recognise says, 'There is an issue with your quota, Mr Farrell. Please allow me access so that we can discuss.'

'Fuck off.'

A chuckle. 'Upside disregard! That's so karking funny!'

'Just go away.'

'That is not an option for either of us, Mr Farrell.' The cold humour is gone from the voice. 'Allow me access immediately.'

'Fuck off or I'll call the police!'

This time there's no response.

Farrell turns to look at me.

'Who is that?' I whisper. 'Is it the man you met last night?'

'You don't want to know, Lisa.'

'Do you think he's gone?'

Farrell opens his mouth to answer. The front door swings open with such force that the mirror in the hallway shatters shards of glass all over the floor.

Chapter 27

FARRELL

'Go into the bedroom,' I snarl at Lisa. The bevelled and hand-ground Deknudt mirror Katya had shipped in from Milan is scattered in slivers across the parquet. I look down, catching a montage of myself staring back up. I look like shit; I'm fucking pale. I can't avoid thinking it: seven years' bad luck.

Rosen's crouching in the doorway, adjusting the cuffs of his trousers. 'Jesus! Did you have to break the fucking door down?'

He looks up, his fedora and tie calmly in place, crisp white shirt, same middle-management suit. 'There's no time to kark around, Mr Farrell. You're in breach, and, if I don't conclude your contract, I'm in danger of being cited for disregard.'

Lisa is still milling around in the hallway.

'I said, go to the fucking bedroom!'

There's a momentary flash of fear on her face, but almost immediately her expression hardens.

'Please, Lisa?' I say, far more gently.

Lisa stares at me a while longer, then does as she's told, slamming the bedroom door behind her. She's grown some guts; it suits her.

I usher Rosen into the lounge. He looks at the giant print of Katya's face covering the wall. 'Primo,' he says. 'That's a fine Donor you had there.

They did a good job, didn't they?'

'What?'

'The butchers. The transplant was catalogue.'

It's true. They did. The surgery was impeccable. But I'm fucked if I'm going to give Rosen the satisfaction. I say nothing. Rosen nods appreciatively at the picture again then sits on the couch and places his briefcase on his lap. That stupid hat, perched at the back of his head, makes him look like someone from an old boy band. Rosen and the Debt Collectors. Ha ha.

'Tell me, Rosen. What the hell's going on? You said I'd delivered enough. And what the fuck is June doing back?' She's probably right now weaving through the traffic, high on tranks.

'June?'

'The woman we took last night to make up the… uh… shortfall.'

Rosen chuckles. 'Oh that. Rejected. Too old, too toxified. The assessors couldn't judge that from the mimeograph. There was no viable tissue. Well, something like three pounds. Not worth the butchery. So we brought her back, dressed her, left her in her bed. She wouldn't have remembered anything. But you're still short by thirty-six pounds and your time is up. You're in breach.'

My mind replays a garbled version of the contractual gobbledygook he was spurting last night. 'But you said if the assessment was cleared I'd have ample time to make up the difference in the event of a shortfall.' Christ, I'm beginning to sound like them.

'You did. You had three shifts – approximately twelve upside hours. Now they're up.'

'But what about the shortfall insurance I signed up for with Mutual?'

Rosen shrugs. 'Those are the terms.'

Thirty-six pounds. How the hell will I get thirty-six pounds of viable now? Eduardo? Can't do it now; it's the middle of the day, there are too many people around. Noli? She's definitely near the top of my shit-list, but I don't have her number, and she's probably sleeping off a coke binge in some Bulgarian gangster's penthouse at this hour. I can't believe I'm thinking like this, but there's no way I'm getting so close and not finishing this. Thirty-six fucking pounds.

'So, what now? What do I have to do?'

He beams at me with a slick insurance-salesman smile. 'We're not unreasonable, Mr Farrell. We collect the shortfall now and I'll put late-payment procedures in place.' The smile falls like a brick. 'But it has to be now. Concluding this contract in your favour becomes less likely every moment we kark around intercoursing.'

The way he talks, in that bureaucratic singsong, gives me an idea. Clive. Marina's idiot husband. Nobody will miss that smarmy little prick, always fucking perving at Katya. And that way we can keep it in the family. Nice and neat. 'Okay, you're right. Let's stop messing around. I know someone we can deliver.'

'Primo. I'll give you ten moments to get ready. I have some paperwork to complete.' He clicks open the pale leather briefcase and removes a sheaf of forms and a fountain pen.

On my way out of the room, I stop and turn back. 'Rosen?'

He looks up, raises his eyebrows enquiringly.

'Are you sure she won't remember what happened last night? June, I mean.' She didn't appear to know what the fuck happened to her, but memories can come back, can't they?

'Remember?' he says, as if talking to a child. 'Mr Farrell. Do you think we'd kark around with potential detection? Make ourselves vulnerable to the *memories* of browns?'

He says it derisively, and something inside me knows that by 'browns' he means us. Normal people. Not people from there... where he comes from. Where that hospital is. It's the first time I admit it to myself: he's not from here; he's from somewhere else. That hospital... Lisa and I were somewhere else, and we managed to get home.

'Are you sure? That's all I'm asking.' A lot depends on his answer. I sincerely hope he's sure.

'I'm sure, Mr Farrell. Browns are hardwired to forget.'

'Okay.' I walk to the bedroom.

Lisa's sitting on the edge of the bed looking tragic. 'What have you done, Farrell?' she asks.

'What?'

'I know you've done something. And I know it's got to do with the Wards, with the contract you signed there. I'm not stupid, you know. In that meeting, they were talking about weight and tissue. They want their payment... They want it... in body parts. Is that right? This man. He's from there, isn't he?'

Lisa's the only person in the world who knows what I've been through; she's the only person in the world who can make sense of what's happening. She's the only person I don't have to lie to, and the compulsion to tell her the whole truth is overwhelming. She'll understand.

I watch her face as I tell her about meeting Rosen at the office, about stunning Eduardo and drawing those lines on him. She keeps fidgeting with her left eye, rubbing at it as if it's irritating her. She looks so preoccupied I can't even tell if she's listening.

'The lines we drew on him were the same as the ones in those Polaroids of me. So I had to make a decision. I thought if I gave them Glenn it would be enough, but it wasn't. June made up the weight. Rosen and I delivered them last night.'

'Where?'

'At the Highgate Mall.' I can't read Lisa's expression. I couldn't ever read Katya's face. 'Rosen took the car. He said nothing would come back to me.' Still she doesn't respond. 'Do you think I'm an animal? Do you think I'm... evil?'

'Farrell. We know what they do in there. They were going to cut you up.' She puts her hand on my thigh. 'I'm glad they didn't.' An electric feeling jolts through me. I've been expecting her to break down or something, but she's so calm about it all. I should be relieved, but her blank acceptance scares me. 'But how come June came back?' she asks.

'That's the problem. They didn't want her. So Rosen and I are going to Clive's office to take him. I wish last night had been the end, but I've gone this far...'

'What if you get caught?'

I consider that. Something about Rosen, the way he never has a doubt, gives me confidence. 'We won't.'

'But poor Clive. He doesn't deserve that.'

Poor Clive? 'Fuck's sake, Lisa. You just said yourself, they're going to cut me up. It's me or him. I wish I didn't have to, but...'

'What about Marina? What about the baby? You can't.'

She stands up, walks to the vanity table and stares at herself in the mirror. Christ, not this again.

'Lisa?'

She doesn't answer, just runs her fingers over her face.

'Lisa? Jesus. We haven't got time for this.'

Now she's scrubbing her palms over her cheeks, harder and harder. I'm about to shout at her, shake her out of it, when she says something.

'Excuse me?'

'Take me.'

'What?'

'Take me.'

'What the fuck are you talking about?'

'They can take me instead of June or Clive or whoever. I can make up the difference.'

'Don't be stupid, Lisa. I'm not going to—'

Now she's opening the bedroom door. 'Hey, Mister,' she's calling down the hall. 'You can take me.'

I chase after her. 'No. No, no. Just ignore her, Rosen.'

Lisa stops, looks at me and at Rosen with his papers in neat rectangles on his briefcase. 'No. Do *not* ignore me. I know what I'm doing, Farrell. I'm not going to last here.' She raises her hands to her face and runs her fingers down it, like a blind woman committing a face to memory. 'This face is melting.'

'What are you talking about? It's perfect. *You're* perfect. Jesus, Lisa, just stop.'

But she's got this weird look in her eyes. I turn to Rosen for help. 'Tell her, Rosen. Tell her what you said about the transplant. It was perfect, wasn't it?'

'Primo,' he says.

Lisa sits down next to him. 'I want you to take me to pay off Farrell's debt. Okay?'

'It's irregular, but not unprecedented.' He gathers the papers, clicks open the briefcase and rifles inside it. 'You'll just need a brown, uh, upsider's voluntary consent form and a transfer of indebtedness addendum... Ah, here we go.' He closes the briefcase, lays the forms out on it and hovers the pen above them. 'If you're confident?'

'Lisa!'

Lisa takes the pen. 'What do I need to...'

'Oh, just name here, sign in the green boxes, initial at the bottom of each page. I'll fill out the rest.'

I try to grab the pen from her hand but Rosen restrains me with his clawed fingers, crushing my hand. 'Mr Farrell. The Client is a willing signatory of sound mind, and I cannot notarise the contract if there has been coercion or interference in any form.' He grinds my bones together until I let go.

I yank my hand back. 'Jesus, Lisa. Don't do it. I thought we had a future together. We were making plans.'

'You're sweet, Farrell,' she says. 'A really nice guy.'

She signs the forms.

'Congratulations, Mr Farrell. I believe that will release you from your contract. In late-payment situations like these, we perform viability assessments on site. Would you like to accompany me' – he consults the form – 'Ms Cassavetes?'

'Why not?' Lisa says. She glances around the flat as if she's double-checking for any personal items she might have left behind. As if it's a hotel room and she's just been here on holiday. She faces me, and she looks happy, lighter, less worried than I've ever seen her. 'I don't belong here,' she says to me as she walks out with Rosen.

I stand in the hallway and watch them leave. I close the door and turn. I'm confronted by hundreds of little shards, a mosaic of my pallid face staring back at me.

Chapter 28

LISA

'Client Cassavetes!' Nomsa is waiting right outside the lift, a clipboard slotted under her arm. 'How *wonderful* to see you again.'

'You too,' I find myself saying. That unreal feeling I had while talking to June is back; I'm so numb, in fact, that I honestly don't care what happens to me now.

It must be the shock, I suppose, but I remember hardly anything about the drive to New Hope. I dimly recall Rosen pulling up outside the casualty entrance, helping me out of the car like an old-fashioned suitor and leading me past a blur of faces in the waiting area. He deposited me in the lift, tipped his hat to me and then the doors shut me in.

And here I am. Back in the Wards.

Nomsa places a hand on my back and gently propels me along the passageway, my feet moving robotically. I recognise the sickly red, yellow and green pattern on the carpet, the gold lettering of the Modification Ward sign and the soft, hotel-style lighting. The last time I was here I was running through this corridor, fuelled by panic, desperate to get out.

But I'm not panicking now.

Nomsa stops outside one of the doors lining the corridor, opens it and steps back to allow me to enter first. 'We thought you would prefer to be in here,' she says. 'So that you feel perfectly at home.'

Either the rooms are identically furnished or I'm back in the same place I woke up in after the face-swap operation. It's all familiar: the watercolour of the homely farmhouse on the wall, the floral bedspread, the pale-pink carpeting. The television lurks in the corner, but even the sight of that doesn't faze me.

But I don't understand what I'm doing here. Why haven't they just taken me straight to the Terminal Ward? For... recycling, or whatever. And how did Nomsa know I was coming back here? I don't remember Rosen calling anyone on the drive to the hospital.

I turn to face her. 'When are you going to do it?'

'Don't let that concern you,' she says soothingly. 'Now, why don't you settle into bed and rest? I'll get a drone to bring you some refreshments.' She checks her clipboard. 'We've updated the list of your dietary requirements and preferences.'

'Please. I need to know. How long?'

'It won't be much longer now.'

'Will it hurt?'

'Of course not, Client Cassavetes. You won't feel a thing.' She laughs. 'We're not monsters!' With a flash of her professional smile she leaves the room.

I numbly strip off Katya's kimono. There's a hospital gown draped on the edge of the bed and I slip it on. I drift over to the bed, pull back the covers and climb in.

So this is it.

Do people on death row feel like this? Numb, empty, almost accepting of their fate? I stare into the watercolour painting, at the pointless curtains and windowless wall. This room could be the last thing I ever see. In a way, it's a relief.

The first time I tried to 'check out' (as Sharon calls it), I was in my bedroom, staring at a poster of Agyness Deyn, popping the saved-up Diazepam into my mouth, trying to pretend they were Jelly Tots. Part of me knew that I'd be found before the pills could do their work, but I swallowed them anyway. The second time, I locked myself in the bathroom with an old-fashioned disposable razor, the kind they only sell in corner shops with bars on the windows, and sat on the edge of the bath staring down at my wrists. I didn't get far. I stopped the second the blade drew the first pearl of blood.

This time there won't be any Diazepam or razor blades or fathers to rush me to Margate Private Hospital. Will they score black marks all over my body like in those Polaroids before they do it? Or will they just get on with it? I hope they anaesthetise me in here before taking me to the Terminal Ward. I don't want those bland functional corridors with their stainless steel doors to be the last thing I see. I don't want the stink of cleaning fluid and death to be the last thing I smell.

But better me than Farrell. He has a life to live. I don't. I run my hand over the left side of my face, fingers automatically searching for flaws.

And this time, I can't find one. Even my left eye feels perfect.

Maybe you're cured. How ironic would that be?

I wonder what Farrell's doing now, if he's missing me. If he's grateful, regretful, depressed, or if he's simply overwhelmed with relief. But the numbness is still there and when I try to call up his face all I get is a blurry image, a bland melding of Bradley Cooper's and Robert Pattinson's features.

It's pointless to think about Dad and Sharon. They're better off without me. No more hospital and psychiatrist bills, no more embarrassment, no more worrying and endless, wearying 'It's all in your head' lectures.

For a while I stare into the flat black eye of the television. My distorted reflection doesn't bother me now.

The door bangs open, and a dumpy orderly pushes a trolley into the room. She's bent right over the trolley and I can't see her face, but there's something familiar about her wiry halo of grey hair.

'Hello, doll,' she says.

Oh God. The voice is muffled but I recognise it immediately. 'Gertie?' She looks up at me.

What have they done to her? The skin on her face is as shiny and featureless as that of a mannequin, the lips are pink and pouting and the eyes are slotted into almond-shaped lids. It's a varnished doll's face. If I hadn't heard her voice I would never have recognised her. But it *is* her – I *know* it's her – and something flickers into life inside me.

'Gertie! It's me!'

'Do I know you, doll?'

'Of course! It's Lisa, remember?'

She frowns, tilts her head to the side and places her chin in her hand like a parody of someone thinking hard about something. 'Lisa? Sorry, doll. Don't know any Lisas.'

'But you must! We were both in the same ward in New Hope. Our beds were next to each other.'

'New Hope? I don't need any hope, doll. All hoped up here!'

'Yes! I even met your daughter...' I scrabble for her name. 'Kyra.'

A brief spark flares in her eyes, but then she blinks and it dies. She shrugs. 'I've probably just got one of those faces,' she says.

It's no good. She really doesn't remember me.

Well you do have a new look, Lisa.

It's more than that. They've done something to her.

Of course they've done something to her. That's what they do here, isn't it?

'Gertie? What did they do to you?'

'Do to me, doll?'

'Your face...'

'Oh, this!' She fumbles under her chin, pinches the skin and pulls. The shiny covering lifts, revealing grey sagging skin beneath. It's a mask! And not one of those hi-tech surgical masks either, just a slightly more sophisticated kids' mask like the kind you can buy in novelty stores. 'They let me choose any face I wanted.' She pats it back into place, but one side of it doesn't stick properly and curls up like old paper. 'Induction gift.'

'What are you doing here, Gertie?'

'I'm working of course,' she says proudly.

'And...' God, I don't know what else to say. 'Um... are you well? Are you... happy?'

'Happy, doll? Of course I'm happy. Happy as a clam in a tummy.'

'But what are you...? Are you a prisoner here? I mean, are they keeping you here against your will?'

She laughs a deep, chesty Gertie laugh. 'Course not, doll. Why would

I want to be anywhere else? You're a funny one with all your questions.'

'What about your family?'

'My family's here, of course. We're all a big family. Working together to make the world go round.'

'What do you mean?'

Gertie places the tray table over my legs and whips off the stainless steel lid to reveal a bowl of mushroom risotto. My favourite. The room fills with the scent of herbs, white wine and chicken stock, and my stomach grumbles. But how can I possibly eat anything now?

'Don't let it go cold, doll,' she says. 'Scoff up every karking scrap.'

'There's no point.'

She sighs and rolls her eyes. 'Why does there always have to be a point with you browns?'

'They're going to recycle me, Gertie.'

She looks at me blankly and scratches the back of her neck. Then she brightens again. 'But it's your favourite!'

'I can't...'

'Please, doll,' she says in a wheedling manner the old Gertie would never have used in a million years. 'You don't want to get me into scum, do you?'

She stares at me pleadingly and I pick up the fork and take a mouthful. It's delicious and creamy – restaurant quality – and I find myself clearing the bowl.

Gertie nods approvingly. 'That's what I like to see. You'll need your strength.'

'What for? I'm only going to die, aren't I?'

Gertie scratches her neck again and the blank look reappears, like a robot who's suddenly lost power. She takes my empty bowl away, and now she has her back to me I can see the bloody, viscous hole in the back of her neck. I wait for the nausea and shock to hit. It doesn't. She starts wheeling the trolley towards the door.

'Gertie, wait!' She might not remember me, but I suddenly don't want her to leave me alone.

She pauses. 'Still hungry, doll?'

'No! I... I just...' I just *what*? 'Thanks,' I finish lamely.

She smiles a doll's empty smile. 'That's all right. You have a nice nap. See you when you're older.'

And she's gone.

I lie back on the pillows again and stare at the ceiling. I shut my eyes, breathe deeply and try to call up an image of Farrell's face.

Bang. A door slams. I jerk awake, open my eyes and stare into blackness.

Oh God. Is this it?

Is it time?

I sit up, senses straining. I blink several times and my eyes gradually adjust to the darkness. I can make out the familiar shape of the television and the folded shadows of the curtains. Thank God. I'm still in my room. Someone's turned off the lights, that's all.

But that's not all. Something's different. Something's wrong. There's a smell, a sour smell. A mixture of unwashed bodies, shit and vomit.

I keep absolutely still, listening to the burr of the air conditioning, the thump of my pulse. Then I catch something else: a shuffling sound, followed by wet, laboured breathing.

I'm wide awake now, clammy fear rolling in my belly. Someone's in here. Someone's in my room! An image of that hunched thing snipping away with a pair of rusty scissors pops immediately into my mind.

'Who's there?'

Another snuffling breath.

A shadow shifts darkly in the corner of the room.

'I said, who's there?'

The dark shape uncoils and edges closer to the bed. My guts turn to water and suddenly I know that I don't want to die, not like this. I need to get out of the bed, run out of the room, but my limbs won't work, terror pinning my body to the sheets as effectively as if it were nailed down. I open my mouth to scream for help but nothing comes out. I will my hand to reach for the call button, and my fingers fumble to press it.

There's a sudden blur of movement and a face looms out of the darkness towards me – a gaping toothless mouth, wild rolling eyes.

'Run, run, run, why you no listen?' a nasty grating voice screams in my ear and my cheeks are flecked with stinking spittle.

I try to roll away from the face, but it's too close and the stench of stale sweat and filth makes me gag. It tugs at my gown, clammy hands grab me under my armpits and I feel myself sliding sideways, my head hanging into empty space. Oh God, it's trying to drag me off the bed.

I kick out, connecting with something soft. There's a grunting sound and then a weight falls onto my chest, crushing the breath out of my lungs. I grope to find its eyes with my nails, then the room is flooded with light and suddenly the weight is gone and I can breathe again. I draw in jagged sobs of air and catch sight of a jumbled mass of grey rags skittering towards the corner of the room.

'Not again!' a woman's exasperated voice says. It's Nomsa. She strides in, hands on her hips. 'I'm so sorry, Client Cassavetes.'

She's followed by two burly orderlies who head straight for the thing in the corner. I pull my knees into my chest, eyes drawn to the twitching mass of grey dusty rags. Then I start to make sense of what I'm seeing. It's a man. *That* man. He's curled himself into a ball, and he's shaking and sobbing and mumbling 'Run, run, run, run, run,' over and over again.

The two men wrestle him up and start manhandling him towards the door. The man's face is as grey as his clothes and his head is lumpy and misshapen. He looks back at me once with jaundiced idiot eyes, and then he's dragged from the room.

Nomsa sits down on the bed next to me and wipes my face with a cool flannel. The panic ebbs away, spent adrenaline leaving an iron taste in my mouth.

'I apologise, Client Cassavetes. That should never have happened.'

'What – who – *is* that?'

Nomsa smiles ruefully. 'Just an interloping brown. We try to keep them upside but they *will* keep wandering down here. They're like rats drawn to a rotten limb.'

I shudder. 'I've seen him before. He was telling me to run.'

Nomsa taps the side of her head and rolls her eyes. 'Brain malfunction. We'd recycle them but they jam the system.'

'So he isn't a patient – a client, I mean?'

'No, no. He was once, of course. Very occasionally there's a glitch in the system, and the modifications and spine shunts don't take. Interlopers, we call them.' She smiles reassuringly at me. 'But don't worry. That hasn't happened for weeks.'

She smoothes the sheets and plumps the pillow behind my head. 'Now. Otherwise, how was your nap?'

'When are they going to do it?' I blurt. 'I just want it to be over.'

Liar!

'It won't be long now.'

'And it really won't hurt? When they... recycle me, I mean?'

She lets out a brief laugh that sounds genuine. 'You're a client. Why would you be recycled?'

A brief flare of hope. 'But that's why I came back here! I'm paying off Farrell's debt.'

Nomsa clucks her tongue. 'You're back so that we can make you happy. We prefer it when our Clients come back to us by their own free will. It makes things less... tangled.'

'I don't understand.' The numbness is completely gone, replaced by overwhelming relief and a lesser feeling of anxiety. Because if I'm not going to be recycled, what does that mean for Farrell? 'But... I signed the form.'

'What form, Client Cassavetes?'

Dammit. What was it called? 'Um... the donor consent thingy.'

Nomsa tuts. 'Don't you worry about that, Client Cassavetes. That situation is all under control. Just a minor administrative kark-up, if you'll excuse my language.'

'But what about Farrell? If I'm not... What will happen to him?'

What do you care? He was happy to send you to your death, wasn't he?

But I do care.

'He'll be just fine,' Nomsa says smoothly.

I can't tell if she's lying or not. 'Really? You promise?'

'Of course.'

'And me? What's going to happen to me now?'

'Your current interplant was only partially successful. Quite frankly, it wasn't intended for the rigours of upside life. The Administration has granted you an upgrade.'

'What does that mean?'

'Would you like to see the proposed modification?'

I nod, still dazed with relief. I'm not going to die. *I'm not going to die.*

She digs in her pocket and pulls out an electronic screen. 'This is what we propose. We have re-scanned your vitals and psychological statistics and have come up with a super-optimal interplant option that we just know will make you happy.'

'And then... you'll let me go?'

Nomsa rolls her eyes. 'Client Cassavetes! You and I both know that you don't want to go anywhere. There are countless options for you here with us.'

I think about what's happened to Gertie – her bitterness and cynicism smoothed away; the horrible tentacled man on the advert and his blithe almost childish happiness; the nurses I've encountered here, all of whom seem content and at ease with themselves.

But at what price?

'Here,' Nomsa says, handing me the screen. 'Take a look.'

I stare into the screen, which displays a 3D revolving image of a woman's naked body. It takes me a few seconds to figure out that it's *my* naked body. I recognise my breasts, my hair, my neck... But the face... Oh *God*.

'Do you approve?' Nomsa says.

I wait for the Dr Meka voice to comment. She doesn't. She's gone. And anyway, there's not much she *could* say.

I look up at Nomsa and smile. 'It's perfect.' It is.

Nomsa smiles back at me. 'In fact, I think you'll find it's better than perfect, it's karking *primo*.'

I find myself laughing along with her and it's then that the realisation hits me. The grey man was wrong. I'm *meant* to be here. I was always meant to be here.

There was never any reason for me to run, after all.

Chapter 29

FARRELL

I wake up with her body warm against mine. My arm's flung over her side and I cup her small breast with my palm. Always a perfect handful. Light glares through the curtains and it sets the deep pain of a hangover groping inside my head. I squeeze my eyes shut and nuzzle my face into her hair. I run my fingers over her ribs. Dink dink dink.

'This is great. It feels like we haven't done this forever.'

She mumbles something, stretches her long, thin, smooth legs.

'It's nice to have you back, Kay.'

'It's Roxy, sweetie,' she says in a bored tone.

I open my eyes again and the auburn of her hair resolves itself, my bedroom around it. Crumpled sheets, discarded clothes, a condom on the lampshade. The reek of stale whisky hits me as soon as I see the empty glasses and the overturned bottle on the nightstand.

'You want to get us some coffee?' I say. 'Everything's in the kitchen.'

She makes a show of yawning and stretching but gets up without complaining. I jam the pillow over my head and peek at her as she walks naked out of the room. I can see her ribs through the skin on her back; her scapulas jut out like stunted wings. There's a small tattoo of a thorny rose right at the crack of her arse. Her hipbones swivel as she walks.

I gird myself and get up. Rinse the glasses in the basin and throw the bottle in the bathroom bin. There's another half-bottle of Ardbeg on the dresser and I down a glassful. My capillaries rush open and let in some air. That's the way.

I sit on the edge of the bed and look down at my naked body. My pecs look a bit saggy and I flex them to convince myself I can still make them tight. There's a hint of a tyre around my stomach. I pump my abs a bit and it goes away. No permanent damage. If I just get back into my stride I can get back to normal, put it all behind me. I lift up my limp cock, pluck out a grey pube and the pain clarifies something. I'm not sure what. That I'm alive? The back of my head tingles, and I rub at it.

So what's the sum total of this experience? My girlfriend's dead. That's the worst of it. Her father too, I suppose, but I couldn't give a fuck about that. The world's a better place without Glenn. And Lisa? A girl I met in the hospital while I was sick. She has her own issues. There was nothing I could have done to stop her going back, was there? It's what she wanted. I didn't know her. Who was I to stop her? Who was I to tell her what to do?

Rosen hasn't called again. I guess it's over. It feels over. Tomorrow's Monday again. I'll get into a decent working week, I'll go to the gym every day, have some consensual adult time with good-looking girls like Roxy. I'll up my game, try to bag a High Talent award. Bring beauty to the world. That's meaningful work.

But my words sound unconvincing in my head. I suppose it's just the shock of everything that happened. I've been unwell, not as resilient as I might have been. It's understandable. Tomorrow, back to normal.

Roxy comes through with two mugs of coffee. 'Here you go.' Her little landing strip makes me want to do nothing more than tell her to put some clothes on. She looks far better in jeans and a push-up than naked. She needs some fucking accessories. A thin chain necklace that creates the illusion of cleavage. Long earrings. Hair up. Belly ring or fake tat to break that monotonous flat plain of her stomach. Despite myself, I think of Lisa.

Roxy goes round to Katya's side of the bed and lounges back.

'I think you'd better... I've got things to do now,' I say, without looking at her. I try to make my voice sound nice. 'I'll see you at the shoot tomorrow, okay?'

'Yeah,' she says. She gets up, picks her clothes off the floor and pads into the bathroom. She comes out, smiling at me like from a billboard, all hello-stranger-you-don't-know-me-but-I-want-to-come-home-with-you. 'See ya tamorrow, Farrell,' she says, as if she's an American.

I get up, fill my coffee with whisky and slouch back down on the bed, staring at my toes for a while. I'm not used to feeling so listless. I pick up my phone to check MindRead, but as it's loading I press cancel. It just seems too much effort. If Katya was here, I'd have some of her blow. The thought crosses my mind that she may have left some in the dresser drawer, but I can't be bothered to dig through her underwear. I can't be bothered to be energetic, even if it's from coke. I just want to be... nothing for a while.

So I drink some more, run a bath, pass out in the tub, then get up feeling cold and waterlogged.

At lunchtime I get into Katya's Mini and go for a drive. I take the top down and the hot sun warms me up. I pretend I don't know where I'm going, but I end up on the kerb outside Glenn's house. Katya's house. June's house now, I suppose. There was a story in the paper yesterday: 'Joburg Businessman Missing: R37m owing in taxes, says SARS'. The security guard – that grumpy woman Rosen tasered all those aeons ago – glares at me from her post. She jumps to attention as the gate starts sliding open. I put the Mini in gear and ready myself to pull away. The nose of Marina's BMW emerges, engine gunning as it pulls into the traffic. I catch a glimpse of two figures in the front seats: Marina and June? June will be okay with Marina. The only normal person in that whole family.

I need another drink so I drive straight to the Highgate Mall. I head to JB's – the only restaurant in the centre with a decent selection of Scotch – and sit at the bar, staring at myself in the mirror behind the row of elegantly downlit bottles. Katya used to love shopping in this mall. The shop assistants would struggle to keep their tongues in their mouths as we came in, laden with bags. I could almost hear the cartoon ka-ching as cash-register signs went up in their eyes. Here's a real shopper who's not going to try on everything and stretch it and fuck us around. Thing is, Katya was built like a mannequin. The size fours slipped over her and gathered around her collarbones and nipples and hipbones just as the designers intended. God, she was a pleasure to watch.

A barman materialises and takes away an empty glass. Oops, not sure when that happened. He pours me another double and I notice he's missing half of his ring finger. Probably robbed for his wedding ring or something.

So now, back to normal.

I still can't help thinking of Lisa, though. Could they seriously have harvested parts from her? No, I'm sure she's fine. But thirty-six pounds is a lot to take.

She wanted to go. She wouldn't let me stop her. I tried. What was I supposed to do?

If I just forget about her, I can get my life back.

There's nothing I could have done about Lisa.

I really want to concentrate on my work, really raise the bar. You know, get creative. Be the next Peter Lindbergh. Or even better, Steven Meisel. Leave something behind when I die.

The barman with the half-finger has given me a triple now. I'm struggling to read the labels on the bottles across from me, and the memory of being blind for those few days in the hospital shocks me out of my fugue. I'd better go home. Sober up, get ready for work. Get ready for my new start.

I leave some bills on the bar and walk out. Did the bar stool fall over behind me? I don't look back. It takes all my concentration to walk forward, find the correct exit, pay the parking ticket, find the car, fumble the key in the ignition and gun out of the garage. When the machine accepts my ticket and the boom comes up, and when I drive out from the covered parking and into the hot sunlight, I feel a strange flush of relief and I realise it's all going to be okay.

I kept on telling Lisa it would be okay, but the only destiny I can control is my own.

I get into the lane to turn right into Main Road, grab my sunglasses from the cubby, and put them on as the car hums me to my new life, edging into the intersection. I am free. I am in charge of my own destiny. I take a deep breath, feeling the freshness, feeling the sunlight detoxing my body. The light changes and I turn left and the Mini is smashed side-on by a four-ton delivery van. My seatbelt keeps me in my seat as I am rolled and then wedged under the front of the truck. The Mini is scraped along the tarmac under the hood of the truck, and, as the car is crushed further under the van, I get closer and closer to the road. I feel the heat of the sparks. I smell petrol and oil and shit. I taste copper in my mouth.

The truck and the Mini come to a stop and I can hear just the quietest sounds. The ticking of cooling metal, two or three fluids dripping, making contrapuntal patterns. I can't feel anything, except a buzzing at the back of my head. I can't move my legs or my arms. I can't move my neck. I open my eyes to orient myself. I'm half suspended from my seat and half lying on my side. I see a big front tyre, and beyond it the logo on the truck's side. A fat and complacent-looking clown points a gun at a street kid in a mask and striped and tattered jersey.

'McColon's,' the logo reads in yellow and red, 'Meals for a Steal'.

That can't be right, I think, and close my eyes.

When I open them again, I'm lying in a hospital bed in a private ward. Oh God, no, not again. I'm tired of hospitals.

A nurse enters the room and jiggles the drip bag by my side. She's tall – six foot at least – bottle-blonde and her eyes are hidden behind round mirrored sunglasses. My eyes can't focus further than the nurse and my body is numb. I would speak, but speech is beyond me.

'Salutations, Donor Farrell. We've been waiting for you.'

My heart races to escape. It's thudding like a terrified animal against my chest but the rest of me can't follow. I'm numb and I know the drip is blocking me from a world of pain. Just lie here for a while longer. It will be all right.

'It's been an exciting shift, Donor. The new mission statement is being ratified by the Administration after boost shift, so it's an alacritous day for your termination. We'll all be watching the telestration in the common room. They've even supplied finger victuals for the announcement. The Administration is super-munificent. Last time we had a mission change, they terminated a primo Donor for us all to enjoy. Fingers this time, because there are constraints this period, but that's just primo...'

I fade into an opiate doze, but when I wake she's still talking. Did I even pass out? I'm not sure.

'... we're getting a new plaque in the drones' station. It will be made of gold. "Here to Sever Clients" it will say. The Administration's mission statements certainly assist us to discharge our duties to the best of our potential. They help each and every drone know precisely what our job is. None of that gratuitous redeployment they get away with in other Ministries—'

The door rattles open and someone comes in, pushing a gurney.

'Time to go, Mr Farrell. I'll be your terminating agent today.' It's Nomsa's voice. She rips the tape from my arm and pulls out the IV needle with efficient precision. 'You certainly have given us your fair share of... excitement... this last period. But I'm delighted that things have settled into their rightful arrangement.' Two orderlies follow her in and hoist me onto the gurney. Nomsa carries on talking. 'You and Miss Forrest made excellent Donors, Mr Farrell. Despite the challenges. We didn't choose you for nothing, and I'm pleased that you've validated our selection processes.'

I'm so limp I can barely stiffen my muscles, never mind fight. My mind feels the same; completely flaccid. I can think clearly, but I can't muster up fear or panic as they strap my legs and torso to the rails of the gurney and cover me with a sheet. My mind's as passive as my body.

As I'm pushed along, I see the tube lighting passing like a repetitive pattern in the ceiling above me, and I see Nomsa's face bobbing in and out of my sight. I notice a gold chain dangling from her wrist, jangling as she pushes. 'LOVER'.

'You like it? Me too. Benefit of being the primary transfer agent on a case. Sometimes we get Donors' invaluables. Rosen didn't want it. Didn't suit his image, he said.'

I'm wheeled into an elevator and it jerks as it starts moving. I can't really tell, but it seems like we're going down.

My mouth is dry, tastes like blood. I make myself speak to her; it's a gargantuan effort. 'Why am I here, Nomsa? I paid off my debt.'

'Not according to your file, Mr Farrell. You were in breach. You were repossessed.'

'But... Lisa... came in my place.'

'Ms Cassavetes is a Client, Mr Farrell,' she explains slowly as if to an idiot. 'Clients cannot be reassigned as Donors in a Donor Swap contract. Those are the terms.'

'But I had insurance from that guy, Mutual. I was covered.'

The lift opens and Nomsa handles the gurney down another corridor. This one is lit with smaller, brighter lights and has a pungent chemical odour. Red emergency lights are positioned between every white light. 'Your cover lapsed after your second default. You didn't read the fine print, did you? That's how we get ourselves into these situations.'

'What time is it?' At first I don't know why I ask.

'I can't see how that makes any difference.'

'Please, just humour me.'

Call it a last wish. I want to know what time I died.

She shows me a pocket watch. There are four hands on it, all of the same length. No numbers are inscribed on the dial.

'Oh, apologies. That's 6.37 p.m. upside.'

People are watching TV and cooking dinner right now. At home. I'm wheeled through a pair of doors and into an operating theatre. Katya would have been watching FTV or the Reality channel with a big glass of red.

I'm parked under a set of glaring operating lights and Nomsa removes the sheet and sticks ECG electrodes to my chest. 'You're very privileged today, Mr Farrell. Look who's going to be your butcher!'

A man with a full black beard and a bald head, a piggish nose and dark, angry eyes comes into my field of vision and straps a mask over his expressionless mouth.

'Why is it still conscious, Nurse?' he grunts.

'It's been a tricky case, Doctor. We had to let him go free range. We were unable to complete the hormone course. We had to balance the contingency collection with the tissue's long-term viability. The full dose of the sedative would be—'

'Should we do this hot, then? I haven't got time to kark around.'

'I suppose so. There's no difference. Eyes are viable—'

The butcher swings an appliance like a claw-ended vacuum tube from the ceiling rig.

There's a light tap at the door.

'What?' the butcher barks.

I turn my head towards the door and see the tall orderly peeking nervously through it. 'So sorry, Butcher, Nurse. But the Donor has a visitor. A Client.'

'Oh, kark. Make it quick,' says the pig-faced man.

The nurse glides over to me, takes my wrist in her dry hand and stage-whispers, 'You must be polite, please. Client Cassavetes is being assigned to the mall as soon as she's recovered.'

The mall?

'She's going to be a Shopper, Mr Farrell! Can you imagine! You are a very fortunate Donor. Please come in, Client,' she calls.

Something in my numbed brain is screaming out: Lisa! Oh, thank God. Lisa!

The door opens gradually and I see her shape come through it. I recognise her blonde hair and her form, but my eyes can't make out the details. She stands in the doorway, saying nothing. I'm desperately trying to find my voice, squeeze out a drop of saliva to lubricate my throat. The nurse finally excuses herself and Lisa moves towards me. She stops again, halfway across the floor. Her face is a pink blur and I wonder if they've done something to it. I need her to come closer so that I can focus.

'Lisa,' I manage to croak out. 'You're... you're fine.'

She nods, the pink blur bobbing up and down. Seriously, my eyes are fucked again. I can't seem to make out...

'Come closer,' I say.

She takes another couple of steps. And then I see it. There's nothing on her face to make out. It's like I'm looking at a giant pink egg with blonde hair on the top. The surface is smooth and glossy, like plastic. Utterly even, utterly featureless, just a neat oval hole for a mouth, little punch marks for her nose, clear lenses over the eyes. I crane my neck up as far as I can and stare closer into the mask.

I can't help it. I reach my hand out and touch her face. It's not a mask; it's skin. It's like a baby's skin. It's warm and it's living and it is beautifully smooth. A flood of bile fills my mouth and I have to swallow it down or else choke.

'What... have they done to you?' I croak, my throat burning.

She shakes her head and points to her chest, and speaks out of the little hole, softly, differently, but it's quiet enough in the theatre to hear her. 'It's what I wanted.' She puts her hand on mine. Her nails are still buffed and clean like Katya's, not the chewed nubs she had when I first met her. 'Thank you,' she says.

'For what? I didn't help you... I didn't save you.' I try to bite back another wave of nausea.

'I could never have done it without you, Farrell.'

'Done what?'

'Got this far. Nomsa says that with my looks I could become a mascot.'

'A mascot?' Where have I heard that before?

'Sorry. That's what they call models down here, Farrell. Me! A model!' She pauses. 'Just like Katya.' Dear Christ, it sounds like she's smiling. 'Who would have thought I could ever—'

'Lisa. Listen to me. Go and talk to the.... the... Administration board or whoever the fuck they are. You have to tell them to let me go.'

The blank face hovers over me for a minute. 'Why?'

Christ, Lisa. 'Because I... because I—'

She shakes her head and strokes my fingers. 'You belong here, Josh. Just like me.' She walks towards the door. Halfway she stops, without turning back. 'You make a primo Donor.'

The butcher's eyes fill my field of vision as he swings the claw-vacuum back over me. Something starts whining below me. My eyes water and my sight blurs as the tube reaches my face. It goes dark.

'Shall we commence?'